PAT'S VERY SPECIAL PLACE

It was so beautiful in the garden, in the late twilight, with a silvery hint of moonrise over the Hill of the Mist. The trees around it...old maples that Grandmother Gardiner had planted when she came as a bride to Silver Bush...were talking to each other as they always did at night.

The big crimson peonies were blots of darkness in the shadows. The blue-bells along the path trembled with fairy laughter. Some late June lilies starred the grass; the columbines danced; the white lilac flung passing breaths of fragrance on the dewy air.

Pat ran from plot to plot and kissed everything, and when she had kissed all her flowers good-night she stood for a little while looking at the house. How beautiful it was, nestled against its wooden hill, as if it had grown out of it...a house all white and green, just like its own silver birches, and now patterned over charmingly with tree shadows cast by a moon that was floating over the Hill of the Mist.

"Oh, I've got such a *lovely* home," breathed Pat, clasping her hands. "It's such a nice *friendly* house. Nobody...*nobody*...has such a lovely home!"

Lucy Maud Montgomery fans will also enjoy
these other Bantam Books by the author

CHRONICLES OF AVONLEA
THE STORY GIRL
THE GOLDEN ROAD
THE BLUE CASTLE
MAGIC FOR MARIGOLD
JANE OF LANTERN HILL

The Anne of Green Gables Series
ANNE OF GREEN GABLES
ANNE OF AVONLEA
ANNE OF THE ISLAND
ANNE OF WINDY POPLARS
ANNE'S HOUSE OF DREAMS
ANNE OF INGLESIDE
RAINBOW VALLEY
RILLA OF INGLESIDE

The Emily Books
EMILY OF NEW MOON
EMILY CLIMBS
EMILY'S QUEST

PAT OF
SILVER BUSH

L.M. Montgomery

ACB 0533

BANTAM BOOKS
NEW YORK · TORONTO · LONDON · SYDNEY · AUCKLAND

RL 6, IL age 10 and up

PAT OF SILVER BUSH

*A Bantam Book / published by arrangement with
the author's estate*

PRINTING HISTORY
Copyright 1933 by McClelland and Stewart Limited.
Canadian Favourites edition 1974

Bantam edition / July 1989

ISBN 0-553-28047-3

PRINTED IN CANADA

COVER PRINTED IN U.S.A.

U   0 9 8 7 6 5 4 3 2 1

To
Alec and May
and
The Secret Field

Contents

CHAPTER I
Introduces Pat

1

"Oh, oh, and I think I'll soon have to be doing some rooting in the parsley bed," said Judy Plum, as she began to cut Winnie's red crepe dress into strips suitable for "hooking." She was very much pleased with herself because she had succeeded in brow-beating Mrs. Gardiner into letting her have it. Mrs. Gardiner thought Winnie might have got another summer's wear out of it. Red crepe dresses were not picked up in parsley beds, whatever else might be.

But Judy had set her heart on that dress. It was exactly the shade she wanted for the inner petals of the fat, "raised" roses in the fine new rug she was hooking for Aunt Hazel... a rug with golden-brown "scrolls" around its edges and, in the centre, clusters of red and purple roses such as never grew on any earthly rose-bush.

Judy Plum "had her name up," as she expressed it, for hooked rugs, and she meant that this should be a masterpiece. It was to be a wedding gift for Aunt Hazel, if that young lady really got married this summer, as, in Judy's opinion, it was high time she should, after all her picking and choosing.

Pat, who was greatly interested in the rug's progress, knew nothing except that it was for Aunt Hazel. Also, there was another event impending at Silver Bush of which she was ignorant and Judy thought it was high time she was warned. When one has been the "baby" of a family for almost seven years just how is one going to take a supplanter? Judy, who loved everybody at Silver Bush in reason, loved Pat out of reason and was worried over this beyond all measure. Pat was always taking things a bit too seriously. As Judy put it, she

1

"loved too hard." What a scene she had been after making that very morning because Judy wanted her old purple sweater for the roses. It was far too tight for her and more holy than righteous, if ye plaze, but Pat wouldn't hear of giving it up. She loved that old sweater and she meant to wear it another year. She fought so tigerishly about it that Judy...of course...gave in. Pat was always like that about her clothes. She wore them until they simply wouldn't look at her because they were so dear to her she couldn't bear to give them up. She hated her new duds until she had worn them for a few weeks. Then she turned around and loved them fiercely, too.

"A quare child, if ye'll belave me," Judy used to say, shaking her grizzled head. But she would have put the black sign on any one else who called Pat a queer child.

"What makes her queer?" Sidney had asked once, a little belligerently. Sidney loved Pat and didn't like to hear her called queer.

"Sure, a leprachaun touched her the day she was born wid a liddle green rose-thorn," answered Judy mysteriously.

Judy knew all about leprachauns and banshees and waterkelpies and fascinating beings like that.

"So she can't ever be just like other folks. But it isn't all to the bad. She'll be after having things other folks can't have."

"What things?" Sidney was curious.

"She'll love folks...and things...better than most...and that'll give her the great delight. But they'll hurt her more, too. 'Tis the way of the fairy gift and ye have to take the bad wid the good."

"If that's all the leppern did for her I don't think he amounts to much," said young Sidney scornfully.

"S...sh!" Judy was scandalised. "Liddle ye know what may be listening to ye. And I'm not after saying it was all. She'll *see* things. Hundreds av witches flying be night over the woods and steeples on broomsticks, wid their black cats perched behind them. How wud ye like that?"

"Aunt Hazel says there aren't any such things as witches, 'specially in Prince Edward Island," said Sidney.

"If ye don't be belaving innything what fun are ye going to get out av life?" asked Judy unanswerably. "There may

niver be a witch in P. E. Island but there's minny a one in
ould Ireland even yet. The grandmother ave me was one."

"Are *you* a witch?" demanded Sidney daringly. He had
always wanted to ask Judy that.

"I might be having a liddle av it in me, though I'm not
be way av being a full witch," said Judy significantly.

"And are you sure the leppern pricked Pat?"

"Sure? Who cud be sure av what a fairy might be doing?
Maybe it's only the mixed blood in her makes her quare.
Frinch and English and Irish and Scotch and Quaker... 'tis a
tarrible mixture, I'm telling ye."

"But that's all so long ago," argued Sidney. "Uncle Tom
says it's just Canadian now."

"Oh, oh," said Judy, highly offended, "if yer Uncle Tom
do be knowing more about it than meself whativer are ye
here plaguing me to death wid yer questions for? Scoot, scat,
and scamper, or I'll warm yer liddle behind for ye."

"I don't believe there's either witches or fairies," cried
Sid, just to make her madder. It was always fun to make Judy
Plum mad.

"Oh, oh, indade! Well, I knew a man in ould Ireland said
the same thing. Said it as bould as brass, he did. And he met
some one night, whin he was walking home from where he'd
no business to be. Oh, oh, what they did to him!"

"What... what?" demanded Sid eagerly.

"Niver ye be minding what it was. 'Tis better for ye
niver to know. He was niver the same again and he held his
tongue about the Good Folk after that, belave me. Only I'm
advising ye to be a bit careful what ye say out loud whin ye
think ye're all alone, me bould young lad."

2

Judy was hooking her rug in her own bedroom, just over
the kitchen... a fascinating room, so the Silver Bush children
thought. It was not plastered. The walls and ceiling were
finished with smooth bare boards which Judy kept beautifully
whitewashed. The bed was an enormous one with a fat chaff
tick. Judy scorned feathers and mattresses were, she believed, a modern invention of the Bad Man Below. It had
pillowslips trimmed with crocheted "pincapple" lace, and was

covered with a huge "autograph quilt" which some local society had made years before and which Judy had bought.

"Sure and I likes to lie there a bit when I wakes and look at all the names av people that are snug underground and me still hearty and kicking," she would say.

The Silver Bush children all liked to sleep a night now and then with Judy, until they grew too big for it, and listen to her tales of the folks whose names were on the quilt. Old forgotten fables... ancient romances... Judy knew them all, or made them up if she didn't. She had a marvellous memory and a knack of dramatic word-painting. Judy's tales were not always so harmless as that. She had an endless store of weird yarns of ghosts and "rale nice murders," and it was a wonder she did not scare the children out of a year's growth. But they were only deliciously goosefleshed. They knew Judy's stories were "lies," but no matter. They were absorbing and interesting lies. Judy had a delightful habit of carrying a tale on night after night, with a trick of stopping at just the right breathless place which any writer of serial stories would have envied her. Pat's favourite one was a horrible tale of a murdered man who was found in pieces about the house... an arm in the garret... a head in the cellar... a hambone in a pot in the pantry. "It gives me such a lovely shudder, Judy."

Beside the bed was a small table covered with a crocheted tidy, whereon lay a beaded, heart-shaped pin-cushion and a shell-covered box in which Judy kept the first tooth of all the children and a lock of their hair. Also a razor-fish shell from Australia and a bit of beeswax that she used to make her thread smooth and which was seamed with innumerable fine, criss-cross wrinkles like old Great-great-aunt Hannah's face at the Bay Shore. Judy's Bible lay there, too, and a fat little brown book of "Useful Knowledge" out of which Judy constantly fished amazing information. It was the only book Judy ever read. Folks, she said, did be more interesting than books.

Bunches of dried tansy and yarrow and garden herbs hung from the ceiling everywhere and looked gloriously spooky on moonlight nights. Judy's big blue chest which she had brought out with her from the Old Country thirty years ago stood against the wall and when Judy was in especial good humour she would show the children the things in it... an odd and interesting *mélange*, for Judy had been about the world a bit in her time. Born in Ireland she had "worked out" in her teens... in a "castle" no less, as the Silver Bush children heard with amazed eyes. Then she had gone to England and worked there until a roving brother took a notion to go to Australia and Judy went with him. Australia not being to his liking he next tried Canada and settled down on a P. E. Island farm for a few years. Judy went to work at Silver Bush in the days of Pat's grandparents, and, when her brother announced his determination to pull up stakes and go to the Klondike, Judy coolly told him he could go alone. She liked "the Island." It was more like the Ould Country than any place she'd struck. She liked Silver Bush and she loved the Gardiners.

Judy had been at Silver Bush ever since. She had been there when "Long Alec" Gardiner brought his young bride home. She had been there when each of the children was born. She belonged there. It was impossible to think of Silver Bush without her. With her flair for picking up tales and legends she knew more of the family history than any of the Gardiners themselves did.

She never had had any notion of marrying.

"I niver had but the one beau," she told Pat once. "He seranaded me under me windy one night and I poured a jug av suds over him. Maybe it discouraged him. Innyway, he niver got any forrarder."

"Were you sorry?" asked Pat.

"Niver a bit, me jewel. He hadn't the sinse God gave geese innyhow."

"Do you think you'll ever marry now, Judy?" asked Pat anxiously. It would be so terrible if Judy married and went away.

"Oh, oh, at me age! And me as grey as a cat!"

"How old are you, Judy Plum?"

"'Tis hardly a civil question that, but ye're too young to know it. I do be as old as me tongue and a liddle older than me teeth. Don't be fretting yer liddle gizzard about me marrying. Marrying's a trouble and not marrying's a trouble and I sticks to the trouble I knows."

"I'm never going to marry either, Judy," said Pat. "Because if I got married I'd have to go away from Silver Bush, and I couldn't bear that. We're going to stay here always... Sid and me... and you'll stay with us, won't you, Judy? And teach me how to make cheeses."

"Oh, oh, cheeses, is it? Thim cheese factories do be making all the cheeses now. There isn't a farm on the Island but Silver Bush that does be making thim. And this is the last summer I'll be doing thim I'm thinking."

"Oh, Judy Plum, you *mustn't* give up making cheeses. You must make them forever. *Please*, Judy Plum?"

"Well, maybe I'll be making two or three for the family," conceded Judy. "Yer dad do be always saying the factory ones haven't the taste av the home-made ones. How could they, I'm asking ye? Run be the min! What do min be knowing about making cheeses? Oh, oh, the changes since I first come to the Island!"

"I *hate* changes," cried Pat, almost in tears.

It had been so terrible to think of Judy never making any more cheeses. The mysterious mixing in of something she called "rennet" . . . the beautiful white curds next morning . . . the packing of it in the hoops . . . the stowing it away under the old "press" by the church barn with the round grey stone for a weight. Then the long drying and mellowing of the big golden moons in the attic . . . all big save one dear tiny one made in a special hoop for Pat. Pat knew everybody in North Glen thought the Gardiners terribly old-fashioned because they still made their own cheeses, but who cared for that? Hooked rugs were old-fashioned, too, but summer visitors and tourists raved over them and would have bought all Judy Plum made. But Judy would never sell one. They were for the house at Silver Bush and no other.

3

Judy was hooking furiously, trying to finish her rose before the "dim," as she always called the twilights of morning and evening. Pat liked that. It sounded so lovely and strange. She was sitting on a little stool on the landing of the kitchen stairs, just outside Judy's open door, her elbows on her thin knees, her square chin cupped in her hands. Her little laughing face, that always seemed to be laughing even when she was sad or mad or bad, was ivory white in winter but was already beginning to pick up its summer tan. Her hair was ginger-brown and straight . . . and long. Nobody at Silver Bush, except Aunt Hazel, had yet dared to wear bobbed hair. Judy raised such a riot about it that mother hadn't ventured to cut Winnie's or Pat's. The funny thing was that Judy had bobbed hair herself and so was in the very height of the fashion she disdained. Judy had always worn her grizzled hair short. Hadn't time to be fussing with hairpins she declared.

Gentleman Tom sat beside Pat, on the one step from the landing into Judy's room, blinking at her with insolent green eyes, whose very expression would have sent Judy to the stake a few hundred years ago. A big, lanky cat who always looked as if he had a great many secret troubles; continually thin in spite of Judy's partial coddling; a black cat ... "the blackest black cat I iver did be seeing." For a time he had been nameless. Judy held it wasn't lucky to name a baste that had just "come." Who knew what might be offended? So the black grimalkin was called Judy's Cat, with a capital, until one day Sid referred to it as "Gentleman Tom," and Gentleman Tom he was from that time forth, even Judy surrendering. Pat was fond of all cats, but her fondness for Gentleman Tom was tempered with awe. He had come from nowhere apparently, not even having been born like other kittens, and attached himself to Judy. He slept on the foot of her bed, walked beside her, with his ramrod of a tail straight up in the air, wherever she went and had never been heard to purr. It couldn't be said that he was a sociable cat. Even Judy, who would allow no faults in him, admitted he was "a bit particular who he spoke to."

"Sure and he isn't what ye might call a talkative cat but he do be grand company in his way."

CHAPTER II

Introduces Silver Bush

1

PAT's brook-brown eyes had been staring through the little round window in the wall above the landing until Judy had made her mysterious remark about the parsley bed. It was her favourite window, opening outward like the porthole of a ship. She never went up to Judy's room without stopping to look from it. Dear little fitful breezes came to that window that never came anywhere else and you saw such lovely things out of it. The big grove of white birch on the hill behind it which gave Silver Bush its name and which was full of dear little screech owls that hardly ever screeched but purred and laughed. Beyond it all the dells and slopes and fields of the old farm, some of them fenced in with the barbed wire Pat hated, others still surrounded by the snake fences of silver-grey "longers," with golden-rod and aster thick in their angles.

Pat loved every field on the farm. She and Sidney had explored every one of them together. To her they were not just fields . . . they were persons. The big hill field that was in wheat this spring and was now like a huge green carpet; the field of the Pool which had in its very centre a dimple of water, as if some giantess when earth was young had pressed the tip of her finger down into the soft ground: it was framed all summer in daisies and blue flags and she and Sid bathed their hot tired little feet there on sultry days. The Mince Pie field, which was a triangle of land running up into the spruce bush: the swampy Buttercup field where all the buttercups in the world bloomed; the field of Farewell Summers which in September would be dotted all over with clumps of purple asters; the Secret Field away at the back, which you couldn't see at all and would never suspect was there until you had gone through the woods, as she and Sid had daringly done one day, and come upon it suddenly, completely surrounded by maple and fir woods, basking in a pool of sunshine, scented by the breath of the spice ferns that grew in golden clumps around it. Its feathery bent grasses were starred with the red of wild strawberry leaves; and there were some piles of large stones here and there, with bracken growing in their crevices and clusters of long-stemmed strawberries all around their bases. That was the first time Pat had ever picked a "bouquet" of strawberries.

In the corner by which they entered were two dear little spruces, one just a hand's-breadth taller than the other. . . brother and sister, just like Sidney and her. Wood Queen and Fern Princess, they had named them instantly. Or rather Pat did. She loved to name things. It made them just like people... people you loved.

They loved the Secret Field better than all the other fields. It seemed somehow to belong to them as if they had been the first to discover it; it was so different from the poor, bleak, little stony field behind the barn that nobody loved... nobody except Pat. She loved it because it was a Silver Bush field. That was enough for Pat.

But the fields were not all that could be seen from that charming window on this delightful spring evening when the sky in the west was all golden and soft pink, and Judy's "dim" was creeping down out of the silver bush. There was the Hill of the Mist to the east, a little higher than the hill of the silver bush, with three lombardies on its very top, like grim, black, faithful watchmen. Pat loved that hill dreadfully hard, although it wasn't on Silver Bush land... quite a mile away in fact, and she didn't know to whom it belonged; in one sense, that is: in another she knew it was hers because she loved it so much. Every morning she waved a hand of greeting to it from her window. Once, when she was only five, she remembered going to spend the day with the Great-aunts at the Bay Shore farm and how frightened she had been lest the Hill of the Mist might be moved while she was away. What a joy it had been to come home and find it still in its place, with its three poplars untouched, reaching up to a great full moon above them. She was now, at nearly seven, so old and wise that she knew the Hill of the Mist would never be moved. It would always be there, go where she would, return when she might. This was comforting in a world which Pat was already beginning to suspect was full of a terrible thing called change... and another terrible thing which she was not yet old enough to know was disillusionment. She only knew that whereas a year ago she had firmly believed that if she could climb to the top of the Hill of the Mist she might be able to touch that beautiful shining sky, perhaps... oh, rapture!... pick a trembling star from it, she knew now that nothing of the sort was possible. Sidney had told her this and she had to believe Sid who, being a year older than herself, knew so much more than she did. Pat thought nobody knew as much as Sidney... except, of course, Judy Plum who knew everything. It was Judy who knew that the wind spirits lived on the Hill of the Mist. It was the highest hill for miles around and the wind spirits did always be liking high points. Pat knew what they looked like, though nobody had ever told her... not even Judy who thought it safer not to be after describing the craturs. Pat knew the north wind was a cold, glittering spirit and the east wind a grey shadowy one; but the spirit of the west wind was a thing of laughter and the sound wind was a thing of song.

The kitchen garden was just below the window, with Judy's mysterious parsley bed in one corner, and beautiful orderly rows of onions and beans and peas. The well was beside the gate... the old-fashioned open well with a handle and roller and a long rope with a bucket at its end, which the Gardiners kept to please Judy who simply wouldn't hear of any new-fangled pump being put in. Sure and the water would never be the same again. Pat was glad Judy wouldn't let them change the old well. It was beautiful, with great ferns growing out all the way down its sides from the crevices of the stones that lined it, almost hiding from sight the deep clear water fifty feet below, which always mirrored a bit of blue sky and her own little face looking up at her from those always untroubled depths. Even in winter the ferns were there, long and green, and always the mirrored Patricia looked up at her from a world where tempests never blew. A big maple grew over the well... a maple that reached with green arms to the house, every year a little nearer.

Pat could see the orchard, too... a most extraordinary orchard with spruce trees and apple trees delightfully mixed up together... in the Old Part, at least. The New Part was trim and cultivated and not half so interesting. In the Old Part were trees that Great-grandfather Gardiner had planted and trees that had never been planted at all but just *grew*, with delightful little paths criss-crossing all over it. At the far end was a corner full of young spruces with a tiny sunny glade in the midst of them, where several beloved cats lay buried and where Pat went when she wanted to "think things out." Things sometimes have to be thought out even at nearly seven.

2

At one side of the orchard was the grave-yard. Yes, truly, a grave-yard. Where Great-great-grandfather, Nehemiah

Gardiner, who had come out to P. E. Island in 1780, was buried, and likewise his wife, Marie Bonnet, a French Huguenot lady. Great-grandfather, Thomas Gardiner, was there, too, with his Quaker bride, Jane Wilson. They had been buried there when the nearest grave-yard was across the Island at Charlottetown, only to be reached by a bridle path through the woods. Jane Wilson was a demure little lady who always wore Quaker grey and a prim, plain cap. One of her caps was still in a box in the Silver Bush attic. She it was who had fought off the big black bear trying to get in at the window of their log cabin by pouring scalding hot mush on its face. Pat loved to hear Judy tell that story and describe how the bear had torn away through the stumps back of the cabin, pausing every once in so long for a frantic attempt to scrape the mush off its face. Those must have been exciting days in P. E. Island, when the woods were alive with bears and they would come and put their paws on the banking of the houses and look in at the windows. What a pity that could never happen now because there were no bears left! Pat always felt sorry for the last bear. How lonesome he must have been!

Great-uncle Richard was there... "Wild Dick Gardiner" who had been a sailor and had fought with sharks, and was reputed to have once eaten human flesh. He had sworn he would never rest on land. When he lay dying of measles... of all things for a dare-devil sailor to die of... he had wanted his brother Thomas to promise to take him out in a boat and bury him under the waters of the Gulf. But scandalised Thomas would do nothing of the sort and buried Dick in the family plot. As a result, whenever any kind of misfortune was going to fall on the Gardiners, Wild Dick used to rise and sit on the fence and sing his rake-helly songs until his sober, God-fearing kinsfolk had to come out of their graves and join him in the chorus. At least, this was one of Judy Plum's most thrilling yarns. Pat never believed it but she wished she could. Weeping Willy's grave was there, too... Nehemiah's brother who, when he first came to P. E. Island and saw all the huge trees that had to be cleared away, had sat down and cried. It was never forgotten. Weeping Willy he was to his death and after, and no girl could be found willing to be Mrs. Weeping Willy. So he lived his eighty years out in sour old bachelorhood and... so Judy said... when good fortune was to befall his race Weeping Willy sat on his flat tombstone and wept. And Pat couldn't believe that either. But she wished Weeping Willy *could* come back and see what was in the place of the lonely forest that had frightened him. If he could see Silver Bush *now*!

Then there was the "mystery grave." On the tombstone the inscription, "*To my own dear Emily and our little Lilian.*" Nothing more, not even a date. Who was Emily? Not one of the Gardiners, that was known. Perhaps some neighbour had asked the privilege of burying his dear dead near him in the Gardiner plot where she might have company in the lone new land. And how old was the little Lilian? Pat thought if any of the Silver Bush ghosts did "walk" she wished it might be Lilian. She wouldn't be the least afraid of *her*.

There were many children buried there... nobody knew how many because there was no stone for any of them. The Great-greats had horizontal slabs of red sandstone from the shore propped on four legs, over them, with all their names and virtues inscribed thereon. The grass grew about them thick and long and was never disturbed. On summer afternoons the sandstone slabs were always hot and Gentleman Tom loved to lie there, beautifully folded up in slumber. A paling fence, which Judy Plum whitewashed scrupulously every spring, surrounded the plot. And the apples that fell into the grave-yard from overhanging boughs were never eaten. "It wudn't be rispictful," explained Judy. They were gathered up and given to the pigs. Pat could never understand why, if it wasn't "rispictful" to eat those apples, it was any more "rispictful" to feed them to the pigs.

She was very proud of the grave-yard and very sorry the Gardiners had given up being buried there. It would be so nice, Pat thought, to be buried right at home, so to speak, where you could hear the voices of your own folks every day and all the nice sounds of home... nice sounds such as Pat could hear now through the little round window. The whir of the grindstone as father sharpened an axe under the sweet-apple-tree... a dog barking his head off somewhere over at Uncle Tom's... the west wind rustling in the trembling poplar leaves... the saw-wheats calling in the silver bush—Judy said they were calling for rain... Judy's big white gobbler lording it about the yard... Uncle Tom's geese talking back and forth to the Silver Bush geese... the pigs squealing in their pens... even that was pleasant because they were

Silver Bush pigs: the Thursday kitten mewing to be let into the granary... somebody laughing... Winnie, of course. What a pretty laugh Winnie had; and Joe whistling around the barns... Joe did whistle so beautifully and half the time didn't know he was whistling. Hadn't he once started to whistle in church? But that was a story for Judy Plum to tell. Judy, take her own word for it, had never been the same again.

The barns where Joe was whistling were near the orchard, with only the Whispering Lane that led to Uncle Tom's between them. The little barn stood close to the big barn like a child... such an odd little barn with gables and a tower and oriel windows like a church. Which was exactly what it was. When the new Presbyterian church had been built in South Glen Grandfather Gardiner had bought the old one and hauled it home for a barn. It was the only thing he had ever done of which Judy Plum hadn't approved. It was only what she expected when he had a stroke five years later at the age of seventy-five, and was never the same again though he lived to be eighty. And say what you might there hadn't been the same luck among the Silver Bush pigs after the sty was shifted to the old church. They became subject to rheumatism.

3

The sun had set. Pat always liked to watch its western glory reflected in the windows of Uncle Tom's house beyond the Whispering Lane. It was the hour she liked best of all the hours on the farm. The poplar leaves were rustling silkily in the afterlight; the yard below was suddenly full of dear, round, fat, furry pussy-cats, bent on making the most of the cat's light. Silver Bush always overflowed with kittens. Nobody ever had the heart to drown them. Pat especially was fond of them. It was a story Judy loved to tell... how the minister had told Pat, aged four, that she could ask him any question she liked. Pat had said sadly, "Why don't Gentleman Tom have kittens?" The poor man did be resigning at the next Presbytery. He had a tendency to laughing and he said he couldn't preach wid liddle Pat Gardiner looking at him from her pew, so solemn-like and reproachful.

In the yard were black Sunday, spotted Monday, Maltese

Tuesday, yellow Wednesday, calico Friday, Saturday who was just the color of the twilight. Only striped Thursday continued to wail heart-brokenly at the granary door. Thursday had always been an unsociable kitten, walking by himself like Kipling's cat in Joe's story book. The old gobbler, with his coral-red wattles, had gone to roost on the orchard fence. Bats were swooping about . . . fairies rode on bats, Judy said. Lights were springing up suddenly to east and west . . . at Ned Baker's and Kenneth Robinson's and Duncan Gardiner's and James Adams'. Pat loved to watch them and wonder what was going on in the rooms where they bloomed. But there was one house in which there was never any light . . . an old white house among thick firs on the top of a hill to the south-west, two farms away from Silver Bush. It was a long, rather low house . . . Pat called it the Long Lonely House. It hadn't been lived in for years. Pat always felt so sorry for it, especially in the "dim" when the lights sprang up in all the other houses over the country side. It must feel lonely and neglected. Somehow she resented the fact that it didn't have all that other houses had.

"It wants to be lived in, Judy," she would say wistfully.

There was the evening star in a pale silvery field of sky just over the tall fir tree that shot up in the very centre of the silver bush. The first star always gave her a thrill. Wouldn't it be lovely if she could fly up to that dark swaying fir-top between the evening star and the darkness?

CHAPTER III

Concerning Parsley Beds

1

THE red rose was nearly finished and Pat suddenly remembered that Judy had said something about rooting in the parsley bed.

"Judy Plum," she said, "what do you think you'll find in the parsley bed?"

"What wud ye be after thinking if I told ye I'd find a tiny wee new baby there?" asked Judy, watching her sharply.

Pat looked for a moment as if she had rather had the wind knocked out of her. Then...

"Do you think, Judy, that we really need another baby here?"

"Oh, oh, as to that, a body might have her own opinion. But wudn't it be nice now? A house widout a baby do be a lonesome sort av place I'm thinking."

"Would you... would you like a baby better than me, Judy Plum?"

There was a tremble in Pat's voice.

"That I wudn't, me jewel. Yo're Judy's girl and Judy's girl ye'll be forever if I was finding a dozen babies in the parsley bed. It do be yer mother I'm thinking av. The fact is, she's got an unaccountable notion for another baby, Patsy, and I'm thinking we must be humouring her a bit, seeing as she isn't extry strong. So there's the truth av the matter for ye."

"Of course, if mother wants a baby I don't mind," conceded Pat. "Only," she added wistfully, "we're such a nice little family now, Judy... just mother and daddy and Aunt Hazel and you and Winnie and Joe and Sid and me. I wish we could just stay like that forever."

"I'm not saying it wudn't be best. These afterthoughts do be a bit upsetting whin ye've been thinking a family's finished. But there it is... nothing'll do yer mother but a baby. So it's poor Judy Plum must get down on her stiff ould marrow-bones and see what's to be found in the parsley bed."

"Are babies really found in parsley beds, Judy? Jen Foster says the doctor brings them in a black bag. And Ellen Price says a stork brings them. And Polly Gardiner says old Granny Garland from the bridge brings them in her basket."

"The things youngsters do be talking av nowadays," ejaculated Judy. "Ye've seen Dr. Bentley whin he was here be times. Did ye iver see him wid inny black bag?"

"No...o...o."

"And do there be inny storks on P. E. Island?"

Pat had never heard of any.

"As for Granny Garland, I'm not saying she hasn't a baby or two stowed away in her basket now and again. But if she has ye may rist contint she found it in her own parsley bed. What av that? She doesn't pick the babies for the quality. Ye wudn't want a baby av Granny Garland's choosing, wud ye, now?"

"Oh, no, no. But couldn't I help you look for it, Judy?"

"Listen at her. It's liddle ye know what ye do be talking about, child dear. It's only some one wid a drop av witch blood in her like meself can see the liddle craturs at all. And it's all alone I must go at the rise av the moon, in company wid me cat. 'Tis a solemn performance, I'm telling ye, this finding av babies, and not to be lightly undertaken."

Pat yielded with a sigh of disappointment.

"You'll pick a pretty baby, won't you, Judy? A Silver Bush baby *must* be pretty."

"Oh, oh, I'll do me best. Ye must remember that none av thim are much to look at in the beginning. All crinkled and wrinkled just like the parsley leaves. And I'm telling ye another thing... it's mostly the pretty babies that grow up to be the ugly girls. Whin *I* was a baby..."

"Were *you* ever a baby, Judy?" Pat found it hard to believe. It was preposterous to think of Judy Plum ever having been a baby. And could there ever have been a time when there was *no* Judy Plum?

"I was that. And I was so handsome that the neighbours borryed me to pass off as their own whin company come. And look at me now! Just remimber that if you don't think the baby I'll be finding is as good-looking as ye'd want. Of course I had the jandies whin I was a slip av a girleen. It turned me as yellow as a brass cint. Me complexion was niver the same agin."

"But, Judy, you're not ugly."

"Maybe it's not so bad as that," said Judy cautiously, "but I wudn't have picked *this* face if I cud have had the picking. There now, I've finished me rose and a beauty it is and I must be off to me milking. Ye'd better go and let that Thursday cratur into the granary afore it breaks its heart. And don't be saying a word to inny one about this business av the parsley bed."

"I won't. But, Judy... I've a kind of awful feeling in my stomach,..."

Judy laughed.

"The cliverness av the cratur! I know what ye do be hinting at. Well, after I'm finished wid me cows ye might slip into the kitchen and I'll be frying ye an egg."

"In butter, Judy?"

"Sure in butter. Lashings av it ... enough to sop yer bits av bread in it the way ye like. And I'm not saying but what there might be a cinnymon bun left over from supper."

Judy, who never wore an apron, turned up her drugget skirt around her waist, showing her striped petticoat, and stalked downstairs, talking to herself as was her habit. Gentleman Tom followed her like a dark familiar. Pat uncoiled herself and went down to let Thursday into the granary. She still had a queer feeling though she could not decide whether it was really in her stomach or not. The world all at once seemed a bit too big. This new baby was an upsetting sort of an idea. The parsley bed had suddenly become a sinister sort of place. For a moment Pat was tempted to go to it and deliberately tear it all up by the roots. Judy wouldn't be able to find a baby in it then. But mother... mother wanted a baby. It would never do to disappoint mother.

"But I'll hate it," thought Pat passionately. "An *outsider* like that!"

If she could only talk it over with Sid it would be a comfort. But she had promised Judy not to say a word to anybody about it. It was the first time she had ever had a secret from Sid and it made her feel uncomfortable. Everything seemed to have changed a little in some strange fashion... and Pat hated change.

2

Half an hour later she had put the thought of it out of her mind and was in the garden, bidding the flowers goodnight. Pat never omitted this ceremony. She was sure they would miss her if she forgot it. It was so beautiful in the garden, in the late twilight, with a silvery hint of moonrise over the Hill of the Mist. The trees around it... old maples that Grandmother Gardiner had planted when she came as a bride to Silver Bush... were talking to each other as they always did at night. Three little birch trees that lived together in one corner were whispering secrets. The big crimson peonies were blots of darkness in the shadows. The blue-bells along the path trembled with fairy laughter. Some late June lilies starred the grass at the foot of the garden: the columbines danced: the white lilac at the gate flung passing breaths of fragrance on the dewy air: the southernwood ... Judy called it "lad's love" ... which the little Quaker Great-grand had brought with her from the old land a hundred years ago, was still slyly aromatic.

Pat ran about from plot to plot and kissed everything. Tuesday ran with her and writhed in furry ecstasy on the walks before her ... walks that Judy had picked off with big stones from the shore, dazzlingly whitewashed.

When Pat had kissed all her flowers good-night she stood for a little while looking at the house. How beautiful it was, nestled against its wooded hill, as if it had grown out of it ... a house all white and green, just like its own silver birches, and now patterned over charmingly with three shadows cast by a moon that was floating over the Hill of the Mist. She always loved to stand outside of Silver Bush after dark and look at its lighted windows. There was a light in the kitchen where Sid was at his lessons ... a light in the parlor where Winnie was practising her music ... a light up in mother's room. A light for a moment flashed in the hall, as somebody went upstairs, bringing out the fan window over the front door.

"Oh, I've got such a *lovely* home," breathed Pat, clasping her hands. "It's such a nice *friendly* house. Nobody ... *nobody* ... has such a lovely home. I'd just like to *hug* it."

Pat had her egg in the kitchen with plenty of butter gravy, and then there was the final ceremony of putting a saucer of milk for the fairies on the well platform. Judy never omitted it.

"There's no knowing what bad luck we might be having if we forgot it. Sure and we know how to trate fairies at Silver Bush."

The fairies came by night and drank it up. This was one of the things Pat was strongly inclined to believe. Hadn't Judy herself seen fairies dancing in a ring one night when she was a girleen in Ould Ireland?

"But Joe says there are no fairies in P. E. Island," she said wistfully.

"The things Joe do be saying make me sometimes think the b'y don't be all there," said Judy indignantly. "Wasn't there folks coming out to P. E. I. from the Ould Country for a hundred years, me jewel? And don't ye be belaving there'd always be a fairy or two, wid a taste for a bit av adventure, wud stow himself away among their belongings and come too, and thim niver a bit the wiser? And isn't the milk always gone be morning, I'm asking ye?"

Yes, it was. You couldn't get away from *that*.

"You're sure the cats don't drink it, Judy?"

"Oh, oh, cats, is it? There don't be much a cat wudn't do if it tuk it into its head, I'm granting ye, but the bouldest that iver lived wudn't be daring to lap up the milk that was left for a fairy. That's the only thing no cat'd ever do . . . be disrespictful to a fairy—and it'd be well for mortal craturs to folly his example."

"Couldn't we stay up some night, Judy, and watch? I'd love to see a fairy."

"Oh, oh, see, is it? Me jewel, ye can't see the fairies unless ye have the seeing eye. Ye'd see nothing at all, only just the milk drying up slow, as it were. Now be off to bed wid ye and mind ye don't forget yer prayers or maybe ye'll wake up and find Something sitting on your bed in the night."

"I niver do forget my prayers," said Pat with dignity.

"All the better for ye. I knew a liddle girl that forgot one night and a banshee got hold av her. Oh, oh, she was niver the same agin."

"What did the banshee do to her, Judy?"

"Do to her, is it? It put a curse on her, that it did. Ivery time she tried to laugh she cried and ivery time she tried to cry she laughed. Oh, oh, 'twas a bitter punishment. Now, what's after plaguing ye? I can tell be the liddle face av ye ye're not aisy."

"Judy, I keep thinking about that baby in the parsley bed. Don't you think . . . they've no baby over at Uncle Tom's. Couldn't you give it to them? Mother could see it as often as she wanted to. We're four of a family now."

"Oh, oh, do ye be thinking four is innything av a family to brag av? Why, yer great-great-grandmother, old Mrs. Nehemiah, had seventeen afore she called it a day. And four av thim died in one night wid the black cholera."

"Oh, Judy, how could she ever bear *that*?"

"Sure and hadn't she thirteen left, me jewel? But they do say as she was niver the same agin. And now it's not telling ye agin to go to bed I'll be doing... oh, no, it's not *telling.*"

3

Pat tiptoed upstairs, past the old grandfather clock on the landing that wouldn't go... hadn't gone for forty years. The "dead clock" she and Sid called it. But Judy always insisted that it told the right time twice a day. Then down the hall to her room, with a wistful glance at the close-shut spareroom door as she passed it... the Poet's room, as it was called, because once a poet who had been a guest at Silver Bush had slept there for a night. Pat had a firm belief that if you could only open the door of any shut room quickly enough you would catch all the furniture in strange situations. The chairs crowded together talking, the table lifting its white muslin skirts to show its pink sateen petticoat, the fire shovel and tongs dancing a fandango by themselves. But then you never could. Some sound always warned them and they were back in their places as demure as you please.

Pat said her prayers... *Now I Lay me*, and the Lord's Prayer, and then her own prayer. This was always the most interesting part because she made it up herself. She could not understand people who didn't like to pray. May Binnie, now. May had told her last Sunday in Sunday School that she never prayed unless she was scared about something. Fancy that!

Pat prayed for everybody in the family and for Judy Plum and Uncle Tom and Aunt Edith and Aunt Barbara... and for Sailor Uncle Horace at sea... and everybody else's sailor uncle at sea... and all the cats and Gentleman Tom and Joe's dog... "little black Snicklefritz with his curly tail," so that God wouldn't get mixed up between Joe's dog and Uncle Tom's dog who was big and black with a straight tail... and any fairies that might be hanging round and any poor ghosts that might be sitting on the tombstones... and for Silver Bush itself... dear Silver Bush.

"Please keep it always the same, dear God," begged Pat, "and don't let any more trees blow down."

Pat rose from her knees and stood there a bit rebelliously. Surely she had prayed for everybody and everything she could really be expected to pray for. Of course on stormy nights she always prayed for people who might be out in the storm. But this was a lovely spring night.

Finally she plumped down on her knees again.

"Please, dear God, if there *is* a baby out there in that parsley bed, keep it warm to-night. Dad says there may be a little frost."

CHAPTER IV

Sunday's Child

1

IT was only a few evenings later that there was a commotion in the house at Silver Bush... pale faces... mysterious comings and goings. Aunt Barbara came over with a new white apron on, as if she were going to work instead of visit. Judy stalked about, muttering to herself. Father, who had been hanging round the house all day rather lazily for him, came down from mother's room and telephoned with the diningroom door shut. Half an hour afterwards Aunt Frances came over from the Bay Shore and whisked Winnie and Joe off on an unlooked-for week-end.

Pat was sitting on Weeping Willy's tombstone. She was on her dignity for she felt that she was being kept out of things somehow and she resented it. There was no resorting to mother who had kept her room all the afternoon. So Pat betook herself to the grave-yard and the society of her family ghosts until Judy Plum came along... a portentously solemn Judy Plum, looking wiser than any mortal woman could possibly be.

"Pat, me jewel, wud ye be liking to spind the night over at yer Uncle Tom's for a bit av a change? Siddy will be going along wid ye."

"Why?" demanded Pat distantly.

"Yer mother do be having a tarrible headache and the house has got to be that still. The doctor's coming..."

"Is mother bad enough to want a doctor?" cried Pat in

quick alarm. Mary May's mother had had the doctor a week before . . . and died!

"Oh, oh, be aisy now, darlint. A doctor's just a handy thing to have round whin a body has oné of thim headaches. I'm ixpecting yer mother to be fine and dandy be the morning if the house is nice and quiet to-night. So just you and Siddy run over to Swallowfield like good children. And since the moon do be at its full at last I'm thinking it's high time for the parsley bed. No telling what ye'll be seeing here tomorrow."

"That baby, I suppose," said Pat, a little contemptuously. "*I* should think, Judy Plum, if mother has such a bad headache it's a poor time to bother her with a new baby."

"She's been waiting for it so long I'm looking for it to iffect a miraculous cure," said Judy. "Innyhow, it's to-night or niver wid that moon. It was be way av being just such a night whin I found *you* in the parsley bed."

Pat looked at the moon disapprovingly. It didn't look like a proper moon . . . so queer and close and red and lanterny. But it was all of a piece with this odd night.

"Come, skip along . . . here's yer liddle nighty in the black satchel."

"I want to wait for Sid."

"Siddy's hunting me turkeys. He'll be over whin he finds thim. Sure, ye're not afraid to go alone? It's only a cat's walk over there and the moon's up."

"You know very well, Judy Plum, that I'm not afraid. But things are . . . queer . . . to-night."

Judy chuckled.

"They do take spells av being that and far be it from me to deny it. Likely the woods are full av witches to-night but they won't be bothering ye if ye mind yer own business. Here's a handful av raisins for ye, same as ye git on Sundays, and niver be bothering yer head wid things ye can't understand."

Pat went over to Swallowfield rather unwillingly, although it was a second home to her . . . the adjoining farm where Uncle Tom and Aunt Edith and Aunt Barbara lived. Judy Plum approved of Aunt Barbara, had an old vendetta with Aunt Edith, and had no opinion of old bachelors. A man should be married. If he wasn't he had cheated some poor woman out of a husband. But Pat was very fond of big, jolly Uncle Tom, with his nice, growly way of speaking, who was the only man in North Glen still wearing a beard...a beautiful, long, crinkly black beard. She liked Aunt Barbara, who was round and rosy and jolly, but she was always a little afraid of Aunt Edith, who was thin and sallow and laughterless, and had a standing feud with Judy Plum.

"Born unmarried, that one," Judy had been heard to mutter spitefully.

Pat went to Swallowfield by the Whispering Lane, which was fringed with birches, also planted by some long-dead bride. The brides of Silver Bush seemed to have made a hobby of planting trees. The path was picked out by big stones which Judy Plum whitewashed as far as the gate; from the gate Aunt Edith did it, because Uncle Tom and Aunt Barbara wouldn't be bothered and she wasn't going to let Judy Plum crow over her. The lane was crossed half way by the gate and beyond it were no birches but dear fence corners full of bracken and lady fern and wild violets and caraway. Pat loved the Whispering Lane. When she was four she had asked Judy Plum if it wasn't the "way of life" the minister talked about in church; and somehow ever since it had seemed to her that some beautiful secret hid behind the birches and whispered in the nodding lace of its caraway blossoms.

She skipped along the lane, light-hearted again, eating her raisins. It was full of dancing, inviting shadows...friendly shadows out for a playmate. Once a shy grey rabbit hopped from bracken clump to bracken clump. Beyond the lane were dim, windy pastures of twilight. The air smelled deliciously. The trees wanted to be friends with her. All the little grass stems swayed towards her in the low breezes. Uncle Tom's barn field was full of woolly-faced lambs at their evening games and three dear wee Jersey calves, with soft, sweet eyes, looked at her over the fence. Pat loved Jersey calves and Uncle Tom was the only man in North Glen who kept Jerseys.

Beyond, in the yard, Uncle Tom's buildings were like a little town by themselves. He had so many of them...pig houses and hen houses and sheep houses and boiler houses and goose houses and turnip houses...even an apple house which Pat thought was a delightful name. North Glen people said that Tom Gardiner put up some kind of a new building every year. Pat thought they all huddled around the big barn like chickens around their mother. Uncle Tom's house was an old one, with two wide, low windows that looked like eyes on either side of a balcony that was like a nose. It was a prim and dignified house but all its primness couldn't resist its own red front door which was just like an impish tongue sticking out of its face. Pat always felt as if the house was chuckling to itself over some joke nobody but itself knew, and she liked the mystery. She wouldn't have liked Silver Bush to be like that: Silver Bush mustn't have secrets from *her*: but it was all right in Swallowfield.

2

If it had not been for mother's headache and the doctor coming and Judy Plum's parsley bed Pat would have thought it romantic and delightful to have spent a night at Swallowfield. She had never been there for a night before... it was too near home. But that was part of its charm... to be so near home and yet not quite home... to look out of the window of the gable room and *see* home... see its roof over the trees and all its windows lighted up. Pat was a bit lonely. Sid was far away at the other end of the house. Uncle Tom had made speeches about doctors and black bags until Aunt Edith had shut him up... or Pat. Perhaps it was Pat.

"If you mean, Uncle Tom," Pat had said proudly, "that Dr. Bentley is bringing us a baby in a black bag you're very much mistaken. *We grow our own babies*. Judy Plum is looking for *ours* in the parsley bed at this very minute."

"Well... I'm... dashed," said Uncle Tom. And he looked as if he *were* dashed. Aunt Edith had given Pat a pin-wheel cookie and hustled her off to bed in a very pretty room where the curtains and chair covers were of creamy chintz with purple violets scattered over it and where the bed had a pink quilt. All very splendid. But it looked big and lonesome.

Aunt Edith turned the bedclothes and saw Pat cuddled down before she left. But she did not kiss her as Aunt Barbara would have done. And there would be no Judy Plum to tiptoe in when she thought you were asleep and whisper, "God bless and kape ye through the night, me jewel." Judy never missed doing that. But to-night she would be hunting through the parsley bed, likely never thinking of her "jewel" at all. Pat's lips trembled. The tears were very near now... and then she thought of Weeping Willy. One disgrace like that was enough in a family. *She* would not be Weeping Pat.

But she could not sleep. She lay watching the chimneys of Silver Bush through the window and wishing Sid's room were only near hers. Suddenly a light flashed from the garret window of Silver Bush ... flashed a second and disappeared. It was as if the house had winked at her ... called to her. In a moment Pat was out of bed and at the window. She curled up in the big flounced and ruffled wing chair. It was no use to try to sleep so she would just cuddle here and watch dear Silver Bush. It was like a beautiful picture ... the milk-white house against its dark wooded hill, framed in an almost perfectly round opening in the boughs of the trees. Besides ... who knew? ... maybe Ellen Price was right after all and the storks did bring the babies. It was a nicer idea than any of the others. Perhaps if she watched she might see a silvery bird, flying from some far land beyond the blue gulf's rim and lighting on the roof of Silver Bush.

The boughs of the old fir tree outside tapped on the house. Dogs seemed to be barking everywhere over North Glen. Now and then a big June-bug thudded against the window. The water in the Field of the Pool glimmered mysteriously. Away up on the hill the moonlight glinting on one of the windows of the Long Lonely House gave it a strange, momentary appearance of being lighted up. Pat had a thrill. A tree-top behind the house looked like a witch crouched on its roof, just alighted from her broomstick. Pat's flesh crawled deliciously. Maybe there really were witches. Maybe they flew on a broomstick over the harbour at nights. What a jolly way of getting about! Maybe they brought the babies. But no, no. They didn't want anything at Silver Bush that witches brought. Better the parsley bed than that. It was a lovely night for a baby to come. Was that a great white bird sailing over the trees? No, only a silvery cloud. Another June-bug ... swoop went the wind around Uncle Tom's apple house ... tap-tap went the fir boughs ... Pat was fast asleep in the big chair and there Sidney found her when he slipped cautiously in at dawn before any one else at Swallowfield was up.

"Oh, Siddy!" Pat threw her arms about him and held him close to her in the chair. "Isn't it funny ... I've been here all night. The bed was so big and lonesome. Oh Sid, do you think Judy has found it yet?"

"Found what?"

"Why ... the baby." Surely it was all right to tell Sid now. It was such a relief not to have a guilty secret from him any longer. "Judy went hunting for it in the parsley bed last night ... for mother, you know."

Sid looked very wise ... or as wise as a boy could look who had two big, round, funny brown eyes under fuzzy golden-brown curls. *He* was a year older than Pat ... *he* had been to school ... *he* knew just what that parsley bed yarn amounted to. But it was just as well for a girl like Pat to believe it.

"Let's go home and see," he suggested.

Pat got quickly into her clothes and they crept noiselessly downstairs and out of doors into a land pale in the morning twilight. The dew-wet earth was faintly fragrant. Pat had no memory of ever having been up before sunrise in her life. How lovely it was to be walking hand in hand with Sid along the Whispering Lane before the day had really begun!

"I hope this new kid will be a girl," said Sid. "Two boys are enough in a family but nobody cares how many girls there are. And I hope it'll be good-looking."

For the first time in her life Pat felt a dreadful stab of jealousy. But she was loyal, too.

"Of course it will. But you won't like it better than me, will you ... oh, *please*, Siddy?"

"Silly! Of course I won't like it better than you. I don't expect to like it at all," said Sid disdainfully.

"Oh, you *must* like it a little, because of mother. And oh, Sid, please promise that you'll never like *any* girl better than me."

"Sure I won't." Sid was very fond of Pat and didn't care who knew it. At the gate he put his chubby arms about her and kissed her.

"You won't every *marry* another girl, Sid?"

"Not much. I'm going to be a bachelor like Uncle Tom. He says he likes a quiet life and I do, too."

"And we'll always live at Silver Bush and I'll keep house for you," said Pat eagerly.

"Sure. Unless I go west; lots of boys do."

"Oh!" A cold wind blew across Pat's happiness. "Oh, you must never go west, Sid ... you *couldn't* leave Silver Bush. You couldn't find any nice place."

"Well, we can't *all* stay here, you know, when we grow up," said Sid reasonably.

"Oh, why can't we?" cried Pat, on the point of tears again. The lovely morning was spoiled for her.

"Oh, well, we'll be here for years yet," said Sid soothingly. "Come along. There's Judy giving Friday and Monday their milk."

"Oh, Judy," gasped Pat, "did you find it?"

"Sure and didn't I that? The prettiest baby ye iver set eyes on and swate beyond iverything. I'm thinking I must be putting on me dress-up dress whin I get the work done be way av cilebrating."

"Oh, I'm so glad it's pretty because it belongs to our family," said Pat. "Can we see it right away?"

"Indade and ye can't, me jewel. It's up in yer mother's room and she's sound aslape and not to be disturbed. She had a wakeful night av it. I was a tarrible long time finding that baby. Me eyesight isn't what it was I'm grieving to say. I'm thinking that's the last baby I'll iver be able to find in the parsley bed."

3

Judy gave Pat and Sid their breakfast in the kitchen. Nobody else was up. It was such fun to have breakfast there with Judy and have the milk poured over their porridge out of her "cream cow"... that little old brown jug in the shape of a cow, with her tail curled up in a most un-cowlike fashion for a handle and her mouth for a spout. Judy had brought the cream cow from Ireland with her and prized it beyond all saying. She had promised to leave it to Pat when she died. Pat hated to hear Judy talk of dying, but, as she had also promised to live a hundred years... *D. V.* ... that was nothing to worry about yet awhile.

The kitchen was a cheery place and was as tidy and spotless as if Silver Bush had not just been passing through a night of suspense and birth. The walls were whitewashed snowily: the stove shone: Judy's blue and white jugs on the scoured dresser sparkled in the rays of the rising sun. Judy's geraniums bloomed in the windows. The space between stove and table was covered by a big, dark-red rug with three black cats hooked in it. The cats had eyes of yellow wool which were still quite bright and catty in spite of the fact that they had been trodden over for many years. Judy's living black cat sat on the bench and thought hard. Two fat kittens were sleeping in a patch of sunlight on the floor. And, as if that were not enough in the cat line, there were three marvellous kittens in a picture on the wall... Judy's picture, likewise brought out from Ireland. Three white kittens with blue eyes, playing with a ball of silk thread gloriously entangled. Cats and kittens might come and go at Silver Bush, but Judy's kittens were eternally young and frisky. This was a comfort to Pat who, when she was *very* young, was afraid they might grow up and change, too. It always broke her heart when some beloved kitten turned overnight into a lanky half-grown cat.

There were other pictures... Queen Victoria at her coronation and King William riding his white horse over the Boyne: a marble cross, poised on a dark rock in a raging ocean, lavishly garlanded with flowers, having a huge open Bible on a purple cushion at its foot: the Burial of the Pet Bird: mottoes worked in wool... *Home, Sweet Home ... Upwards and Onwards*. These had all been judged at successive spring cleanings to be unworthy of the other rooms but Judy wouldn't have them burned. Pat wouldn't have liked them anywhere else but she liked them on the walls of Judy's kitchen. It wouldn't have been quite the same without them.

It was lovely, Pat thought as she ate her toast, that everything was just the same. She had had a secret, dreadful fear that she would find everything changed and different and heart-breaking.

Dad came in just as they finished and Pat flew to him. He looked tired but he caught her up with a smile.

"Has Judy told you that you have a new sister?"

"Yes. I'm glad. I think it will be an improvement," said Pat, gravely and staunchly.

Dad laughed.

"That's right. Some folks have been afraid you mightn't like it... might think your nose was out of joint."

"My nose is all right," said Pat. "Feel it."

"Av course her nose is all right. Don't ye be after putting inny such notions in her head, Long Alec Gardiner," said Judy, who had bossed little Long Alec about when he was a child and continued to do so now that he was big Long Alec with a family of his own. "And ye naden't have been thinking that child wud be jealous... she hasn't a jealous bone in her body, the darlint. Jealous, indade!" Judy's grey-green eyes flashed quite fiercely. Nobody need be thinking the new baby was more important that Pat or that more was going to be made of it.

4

It was well on in the forenoon when they were allowed upstairs. Judy marshalled them up, very imposing in her blue silk dress, of a day when it was a recommendation for silk that it could stand alone. She had had it for fifteen years, having got in in honour of the bride young Long Alec was bringing to Silver Bush, and she put it on only for very special occasions. It had been donned for every new baby and the last time it had been worn was six years ago at Grandmother Gardiner's funeral. Fashions had changed considerably but what cared Judy? A silk dress was a silk dress. She was so splendid in it that the children were half in awe of her. They liked her much better in her old drugget but Judy tasted her day of state.

A nurse in white cap and apron was queening it in mother's room. Mother was lying on her pillows, white and spent after that dreadful headache, with her dark wings of hair around her face and her sweet, dreamy, golden-brown eyes shining with happiness. Aunt Barbara was rocking a quaint old black cradle, brought down from the garret ... a cradle a hundred years old which Great-great-Grandfather Nehemiah had made with his own hands. Every Silver Bush baby had been rocked in it. The nurse did not approve of either cradles or rocking but she was powerless against Aunt Barbara and Judy combined.

"Not have a cradle for it, do ye be saying?" the scandalised Judy had ejaculated. "Ye'll not be intinding to put the swate wee cratur in a basket? Oh, oh, did inny one iver be hearing the like av it? It's niver a baby at Silver Bush that'll be brought up in your baskets, as if it was no better than a kitten, and that I'm telling ye. Here's the cradle that I've polished wid me own hands and into that same cradle she'll be going."

Pat, after a rapturous kiss for mother, tip-toed over to the cradle, trembling with excitement. Judy lifted the baby out and held it so that the children could see it.

"Oh, Judy, isn't she sweet?" whispered Pat in ecstasy. "Can't I hold her for just the tiniest moment?"

"That ye can, darlint,"... and Judy put the baby into Pat's arms before either nurse or Aunt Barbara could prevent her. Oh, oh, that was one in the eye for the nurse!

Pat stood holding the fragrant thing as knackily as if she had been doing it all her life. What tiny, darling legs it had! What dear, wee, crumpled paddies! What little pink nails like perfect shells!

"What color are its eyes, Judy?"

"Blue," said Judy, "big and blue like violets wid dew on them, just like Winnie's. And it's certain I am that she do be having dimples in her chakes. Sure a woman wid a baby like that naden't call the quane her cousin."

> "*The child that is born on the Sabbath day*
> *Will be bonny and blithe and good and gay,*'"

said Aunt Barbara.

"Of course she will," said Pat. "She would, no matter what day she was born on. Isn't she *our* baby?"

"Oh, oh, there's the right spirit for ye," said Judy.

"The baby must really be put back in the cradle now," said the nurse by way of reasserting her authority.

Pat relinquished it reluctantly. Only a few minutes ago she had been thinking of the baby as an interloper, only to be tolerated for mother's sake. But now it was one of the family and it seemed as if it had always been at Silver Bush. No matter how it had come, from stork or black bag or parsley bed, it was *there* and it was *theirs*.

CHAPTER V

"What's in a Name?"

1

THE new baby at Silver Bush did not get its name until three weeks later when mother was able to come down stairs and the nurse had gone home, much to Judy's satisfaction. She approved of Miss Martin as little as Miss Martin approved of her.

"Oh, oh, legs and lipstick!" she would say contemptuously, when Miss Martin doffed her regalia and went out to take the air. Which was unjust to Miss Martin, who had no more legs than other women of the fashion and used her lipstick very discreetly. Judy watched her down the lane with a malevolent eye.

"Oh, oh, but I'd like to be putting a tin ear on that one. Wanting to call the wee treasure Greta! Oh, oh, *Greta*! And her with a grandfather that died and come back to life, that he did!"

"Did he really, Judy Plum?"

"He did that. Old Jimmy Martin was dead as a doornail for two days. The doctors said it. Thin he come back to life . . . just to spite his family I'm telling ye. But, as ye might ixpect, he was niver the same agin. His relations were rale ashamed av him. *Miss* Martin naden't be holding that rid head av hers so high."

"But why, Judy?" asked Sid. "Why were they ashamed of him?"

"Oh, oh, whin ye're dead it's only dacent to *stay* dead," retorted Judy. "Ye'd think she'd remimber that whin she was trying to boss folks who looked after babies afore she was born or thought av, the plum-faced thing! But she's gone now, good riddance, and we won't have her stravaging about the house with a puss on her mouth inny more. Too minny bushels for a small canoe . . . it do be that that's the trouble wid *her*."

"She can't help her grandfather, Judy," said Pat.

"Oh, oh, I'm not saying she could, me jewel. We none of us can hilp our ancistors. Wasn't me own grandmother something av a witch? But it's sure we've all got some and it ought to kape us humble."

Pat was glad Miss Martin was gone, not because she didn't like her but because she knew she would be able to hold the baby oftener now. Pat adored the baby. How in the world had Silver Bush ever got on without her? Silver Bush without the baby was quite unthinkable to Pat now. When Uncle Tom asked her gravely if they had decided yet whether to keep or drown the baby she was horrified and alarmed.

"Sure, me jewel, he was only tazing ye," comforted Judy, with her great, broad, jolly laugh. "'Tis just an ould bachelor's idea av a joke."

They had put off naming the baby until Miss Martin had gone, because nobody really wanted to call the baby Greta but didn't want to hurt her feelings. The very afternoon she left they attended to the matter... or tried to.

But it was no easy thing to pick a name. Mother wanted to call it Doris after her own mother and father wanted Rachel after his mother. Winnie, who was romantic, wanted Elaine, and Joe thought Dulcie would be nice. Pat had secretly called it Miranda for a week and Sidney thought such a blue-eyed baby ought to be named Violet. Aunt Hazel thought Kathleen just the name for it, and Judy, who must have her say with the rest, thought Emmerillus was a rale classy name. The Silver Bush people thought Judy must mean Amaryllis but were never sure of it.

In the end father suggested that each of them plant a named seed in the garden and see whose came up first. That person should have the privilege of naming the baby.

"If we find more than one up at once the winners must plant over again," he said.

This was a sporting chance and the children were excited. The seeds were planted and tagged and watched every day: but it was Pat who thought of getting up early in the morning to keep tabs on the bed. Judy said things came up in the night. There was nothing at dark... and in the morning there you were. And there Pat was on the eighth morning, just as the sun was rising, up before any one but Judy. You would have to get up before you went to bed if you meant to get ahead of Judy.

And Pat's seed was up! For just one moment she exulted. Then she grew sober and her long-lashed amber eyes filled with a troubled wonder. Of course Miranda was a lovely name for a baby. But father wanted Rachel. Mother had named her and Sidney, Uncle Tom had named Joe, Hazel had named Winnie, surely it was father's turn. He hadn't said much... father never said much... but Pat knew somehow that he wanted very badly to name the baby Rachel. In her secret heart Pat had hoped that father's seed would be first.

She looked around her. No living creature in sight except

Gentleman Tom, sitting darkly on the cheese stone. The next moment her seed was yanked out and flung into the burdock patch behind the hen-house. Dad had a chance yet.

But luck seemed against poor dad. Next morning Win's and mother's seeds were up. Pat ruthlessly uprooted them, too. Win didn't count and mother had named two children already. That was plenty for her. Joe's met the same fate next morning. Then up popped Sid's and Judy's. Pat was quite hardened in rascality now and they went. Anyhow, no child ought *ever* to be called Emmerillus.

The next day there was none up and Pat began to be worried. Every one was wondering why none of the seeds were up yet. Judy darkly insinuated that they had been planted the wrong time of the moon. And perhaps father's wouldn't come up at all. Pat prayed very desperately that night that it might be up the next morning.

It was.

Pat looked about her in triumph, quite untroubled as yet by her duplicity. She had won the victory for father. Oh, how lovely everything was! Gossamer clouds of pale gold floated over the Hill of the Mist. The wind had fallen asleep among the silver birches. The tall firs among them quivered with some kind of dark laughter. The fields were all around her like great gracious arms. The popples, as Judy called them, were whispering around the granary. The world was just a big, smiling greenness, with a vast, alluring blueness seawards. There was a clear, pale, silvery sky over her and everything in the garden seemed to have burst into bloom overnight. Judy's big clump of bleeding-heart by the kitchen door was hung with ruby jewels. The country was sprinkled with white houses in the sunrise. A stealthy kitten crept through the orchard. Thursday was licking his sleek little chops on the window sill of his beloved granary. A red squirrel chattered at him from a bough of the maple tree over the well. Judy came out to draw a bucket of water.

"Oh, Judy, father's seed is up," cried Pat. She wouldn't say up *first* because *that* wasn't true.

"Oh, oh!" Judy accepted the "sign" with good grace. "Well, it do be yer dad's turn for a fact, and Rachel is a better name than Greta inny day. Greta! The impidence av it!"

2

Rachel it was in fact and Rachel it became in law one Sunday six weeks later when the baby was baptised at church in a wondrous heirloom christening robe of eyelet embroidery that Grandmother Gardiner had made for her first baby. All the Silver Bush children had been christened in it. Long robes for babies had gone out of fashion but Judy Plum would not have thought the christening lawful if the baby had not been at least five feet long. They tacked Doris on to the name, too, by way of letting mother down easy, but it was dad's day of triumph.

Pat was not sorry for what she had done but her conscience had begun to trouble her a bit and that night when Judy Plum came in to leave her nightly blessing, Pat, who was wide-awake, sat up in bed and flung her arms around Judy's neck.

"Oh, Judy... I did something... I s'spose it was bad. I... I wanted father to name the baby... and I pulled up the seeds as fast as they came up in the mornings. Was it very bad, Judy?"

"Oh, oh, shocking," said Judy, with a contradictory twinkle in her eyes. "If Joe knew he'd put a tin ear on ye. But I'll not be telling. More be token as I wanted yer dad to have his way. He do be put upon be the women in this house and that's a fact."

"His seed was the last one to come up," said Pat, "and Aunt Hazel's never came up at all."

"Oh, oh, didn't it now?" giggled Judy. "It was up the morning afore yer dad's and I pulled it out meself."

CHAPTER VI

What Price Weddings?

1

LATE in August of that summer Pat began to go to school. The first day was very dreadful... almost as dreadful as that day the year before when she had watched Sidney start to school without her. They had never been separated before. She had stood despairingly at the garden gate and watched him out of sight down the lane until she could see him no longer for tears.

"He'll be back in the evening, me jewel. Think av the fun av watching for him to come home," comforted Judy.

"The evening is so far away," sobbed Pat.

It seemed to her the day would never end: but half past four came and Pat went flying down the lane to greet Sid. Really, it was so splendid to have him back that it almost atoned for seeing him go.

Pat didn't want to go to school. To be away from Silver Bush for eight hours five days out of every week was a tragedy to her. Judy put her up a delicious lunch, filled her satchel with her favourite little red apples and kissed her good-bye encouragingly.

"Now, darlint, remember it's goin' to get an eddication ye are. Oh, oh, an eddication is a great thing and it's meself do be after knowing it because I never had one."

"Why, Judy, you know more than anybody else in the world," said Pat wonderingly.

"Oh, oh, to be sure I do, but an eddication isn't just knowing things," said Judy wisely. "Don't ye be worrying a bit. Ye'll get on fine. Ye know yer primer so ye've got a good start. Now run along, girleen, and mind ye're rale mannerly to yer tacher. It's the credit av Silver Bush ye must be kaping up, ye know."

It was this thought that braced Pat sufficiently to enable her to get through the day. It kept the tears back as she turned, at the end of the lane, clinging to Sid's hand, to wave back to Judy who was waving encouragingly from the garden gate. It bore her up under the scrutiny of dozens of strange eyes and her interview with the teacher. It gave her backbone through the long day as she sat alone at her little desk and made pot-hooks . . . or looked through the window down into the school bush which she liked much better. It was an ever-present help in recesses and dinner hour, when Winnie was off with the big girls and Sid and Joe with the boys and she was alone with the first and second primers.

When school came out at last Pat reviewed the day and proudly concluded that she had not disgraced Silver Bush.

And then the glorious home-coming! Judy and mother to welcome her back as if she had been away for a year... the baby smiling and cooing at her... Thursday running to meet her... all the flowers in the garden nodding a greeting.

"I *know* everything's glad to see me back," she cried.

Really, it was enough to make one willing to go away just to have the delight of coming back. And then the fun of telling Judy all that had happened in school!

"I liked all the girls except May Binnie. She said there wasn't any moss in the cracks of *her* garden walk. I said I *liked* moss in the cracks of a garden walk. And she said our house was old-fashioned and needed painting. And she said the wall-paper in our spare-room was stained."

"Oh, oh, and well you know it is," said Judy. "There's that lake be the chimney that Long Alec has niver been able to fix, try as he will. But if ye start out be listening to what a Binnie says ye'll have an earful. What did ye say to me fine Miss May Binnie, darlint?"

"I said Silver Bush didn't need to be painted as often as other people's houses because it wasn't ugly."

Judy chuckled.

"Oh, oh, that was one in the eye for me fine May. The Binnie house is one av the ugliest I've iver seen for all av its yaller paint. And what did she say to *that*."

"Oh, Judy, she said the pink curtains in the Big Parlour were faded and shabby. And that *crushed* me. Because they *are*... and everybody else in North Glen has such nice lace curtains in their parlours."

2

But this was all three weeks ago and already going to school was a commonplace and Pat had even begun to like it. And then one afternoon Judy casually remarked, out of a clear sky so to speak,

"I s'pose ye know that yer Aunt Hazel is going to be married the last wake in September?"

At first Pat wouldn't believe it... simply couldn't. Aunt Hazel *couldn't* be married and go away from Silver Bush. When she had to believe it she cried night after night for a week. Not even Judy could console her... not even the memory of Weeping Willy shame her.

"Sure and it's time yer Aunt Hazel was married if she don't be intinding to be an ould maid."

"Aunt Barbara and Aunt Edith are old maids and they're happy," sobbed Pat.

"Oh, oh, two ould maids is enough for one family. And yer Aunt Hazel is right to be married. Sure and it's a kind av hard world for women at the bist. I'm not saying but what we'll miss her. She's always had a liddle knack av making people happy. But it's time she made her ch'ice. She's niver been man-crazy... oh, oh, her worst inimy couldn't say that av her. But she's been a bit av a flirt in her day and there's been a time or two I was afraid she was going to take up wid a crooked stick. 'Judy,' she wud a'way be saying to me, 'I want to try just a few more beaus afore I settle down.' It's a bit av good luck that she's made up her mind for Robert Madison. He's a rale steady feller. Ye'll like yer new uncle, darlint."

"I won't," said Pat obstinately, determined to hate him forever. "Do *you* like him, Judy?"

"To be sure I do. He's got more in his head than the comb'll iver take out I warrant ye. And a store-kaper he is, which is a bit asier than farming for the wife."

"Do you think he's good-looking enough for Aunt Hazel, Judy?"

"Oh, oh, I've seen worse. Maybe there's a bit too much av him turned up for fate and there's no denying he has flying jibs like all that family. They tuk it from the Callenders. Niver did inny one see such ears as old Hinry Callender had. If ye hadn't been seeing innything but his head ye cudn't have told whether he was a man or a bat. Oh, oh, but it's the lucky thing they've got pared down a bit be the Madison mixture! Robert's got a rale nice face and I'm after telling ye we're all well satisfied wid yer Aunt Hazel's match. We've had our worries I can be telling ye now. There was Gordon Rhodes back a bit... but I niver belaved she'd take a scut like him. Too crooked to lie straight in bed like all the Rhodeses. And Will Owen... to be sure Long Alec liked him but the man had no more to say for himself than a bump on a log. If the Good Man Above had struck him dumb we'd niver av known it. For me own part I like thim a bit more flippant. At one time we did be thinking she'd take Siddy Taylor. But whin she tould him one night that she cudn't abide his taste in neck-ties he went off mad and niver come back. Small blame to him for that. If ye do be wanting a man iver, Pat, don't be after criticising his neck-ties until ye've landed him afore the minister. And yer mother kind av liked Cal Gibson. Sure and he was the ladylike cratur. But he was one av the Summerside Gibsons and I was afraid he'd always look down on yer Aunt Hazel's people. Barring the fact that he was as quare-looking as a cross-eyed cat. . . . But this Robert Madison, he kept a-coming and a-coming, always bobbing up whiniver one of the other lads got the mitten on the wrong hand. Whin the Madisons do be wanting a thing they have the habit av getting it in the long run. Rob's Uncle Jim now. . . didn't I iver tell ye the story av how he pickled his brother in rum and brought him home to be buried?"

"*Pickled* him, Judy?"

"I'm telling ye. Ned Madison died on board Jim's ship back in 1850 whin they were in the middle av the Indian Ocean. Iverybody said he must be buried at say. But Jim Madison swore till all turned blue that Ned shud be tuk home and buried in the fam'ly plot on the Island. So he got the ship's carpenter to make a lead coffin and he clapped young Ned in it and filled it up wid rum. And Ned come home fresh as a daisy. I'm not saying that Jim was iver the same man agin though, mind ye. And that's the Madison for ye. Oh, oh, it's all for the bist as it is and we must have a rale fine widding for the honour av the fam'ly."

Pat found it hard to be reconciled to it. She had always been so fond of Aunt Hazel . . . far fonder than of Aunt Edith or even Aunt Barbara. Aunt Hazel was so jolly and pretty. Her face was as brown as a nut, her eyes and hair were brown, her lips and cheeks scarlet. Aunt Hazel looked her name. Some people didn't. Lily Wheatley was as black as a crow and Ruby Rhodes was pale and washed out.

The rest of the Silver Bush children took it more philosophically. Sidney thought it would be rather exciting to have a wedding in the family. Winnie thought it must be rather good fun to be married.

"I don't see the fun of it," said Pat bitterly.

"Why, everybody has to be married," said Winnie. "You'll be married yourself some day."

Pat rushed to mother in anguish.

"Mother, tell me . . . I don't have to get married ever . . . do I?"

"Not unless you want to," assured mother.

"Oh, that's all right," said relieved Pat. "Because I'll never want to."

"The girls all talk that way," said Judy, winking at Mrs. Gardiner over Pat's head. "There's no jidging the minute I might take the notion meself. Sure and didn't I have the fine proposal the other night. Old Tom Drinkwine shuffled up here and asked me to be his fourth missus, so he did. Sure and I all but dropped the new tay-pot whin he come out wid it. It's the long time I've waited to be axed but me chanct has come at last."

"Oh, Judy, you wouldn't marry him?"

"Oh, oh, and why shudn't I now?"

"And leave us?"

"Oh, oh, there's the rub," remarked Judy, who had sent old Tom off to what she called "the tune the ould cow died on." "'Twud be more than the quarter av inny man that'd tempt me to do that same."

But a *whole* man might tempt Judy some day and Pat was uneasy. Oh, change was terrible! What a pity people had to get married!

3

"The widding's to be the last wake av September, *D. V.*" Judy told her one day.

Pat winced. She knew it must be but to have announced in this indifferent fashion was anguish.

"What does *D. V.* mean, Judy?"

"Oh, oh, it means if the Good Man Above is willing."

"And what if He isn't willing, Judy?"

"Thin it wud niver happen, me jewel."

Pat wondered if she prayed to God *not* to be willing if it would do any good.

"What would happen if you prayed for... for a *wicked* thing, Judy?"

"Oh, oh, you might get it," said Judy so eerily that Pat was terrified and decided that it was wiser to take no risks.

Eventually she became resigned to it. She found herself quite important in school because her aunt was going to be married. And there was a pleasant air of excitement about Silver Bush, which deepened as the days went by. Little was talked of but the wedding preparations. The old barn cat had what Judy called a "clutch" of kittens and nobody was excited over it except Pat. But it was nice to have a bit of a secret. Only she and the barn cat knew where the kittens were. She would not tell until they were too old to drown. Somehow, most of the spring kittens had vanished in some mysterious fashion which Pat never could fathom. Only Tuesday and Thursday were left and Tuesday was promised to Aunt Hazel. So the new kittens were warmly welcomed, but finding names for them had to be left until the wedding was over because Pat couldn't get any one interested in it just now.

The Poet's room was re-papered, much to her joy . . . though she was sorry to see the old paper torn off . . . and when mother brought home new, cobwebby lace curtains for the Big Parlour Pat began to think a wedding had its good points. But she was very rebellious when her room was re-papered, too. She loved the old paper, with its red and green parrots that had been there ever since she could remember. She had never been without a secret hope that they might come alive sometime.

"I don't see why my room has to be papered, even if Aunt Hazel is going to be married," she sobbed.

"Listen to rason now, darlint," argued Judy. "Sure and on the widding day the place'll be full av quality. All yer grand relations from town and Novy Scotia will be here and the Madisons from New Brunswick . . . millionaires, they do be saying. And some av thim will have to be putting their wraps in yer room. Ye wudn't want thim to be seeing old, faded wall-paper, wud ye now?"

No . . . o . . . o, Pat wouldn't want that.

"And I've tould yer mother ye must be allowed to pick the new paper yerself . . . sure and there do be a pattern of blue-bells at the store that you'd love. So cheer up and help me wid the silver polishing. Ivery piece in the house must be rubbed up for the grand ivint. Sure and we haven't had a widding at Silver Bush for twinty years. It do be too much like heaven that, wid nather marrying nor giving in marriage. The last was whin yer Aunt Christine got her man. Sure and I hope yer Aunt Hazel won't have the mischance to her widding veil that poor liddle Chrissy had."

"Why, what happened to it, Judy?"

"Oh, oh, what happened to it, sez she. It had a cap av

rose point that yer great-great-grandmother brought from the Ould Country wid her. Oh, oh, 'twas the illigant thing! And they had it lying in state on the bed in the Poet's room. But whin they wint in to get it, me jewel, ... well, there was a liddle dog here at Silver Bush thin and the liddle spalpane had got into the room unbeknownst and he had chewed and slobbered the veil and the lace cap till ye cudn't tell where one left off and the other begun. Poor liddle Chrissie cried that pitiful ... small blame to her."

"Oh, Judy, what did they do?"

"Do, is it? Sure they cud do nothing and they did it. Poor Chrissy had to be married widout her veil, sobbing all troo the cirrimony. A great scandal it made I'm telling ye. It's meself that will kape the key av the Poet's room this time and if I catch that Snicklefritz prowling about the house it's meself that'll put a tin ear on that dog, if Joe takes a fit over it. And now, whin we've finished this lot av silver, ye'll come out to the ould part and help me pick the damsons. Sure and I'm going to do up a big crock av baked damsons for yer Aunt Hazel. Hasn't she always said there was nobody cud bake damsons like ould Judy Plum ... more be token of me name perhaps."

"Oh, hurry with the silver, Judy."

Pat loved picking damsons with Judy ... and the green gages and the golden gages and the big purple-red egg plums.

"Oh, oh, I'm niver in a hurry, me jewel. There's all the time in the world and after that there's eternity. There's loads and lashins av work if yer Aunt Hazel is to have the proper widding but it'll all be done dacently and in order."

4

Pat couldn't help feeling pleasantly excited when she found that she was to be Aunt Hazel's flower girl. But she felt so sorry for Winnie who was too old to be a flower girl and not old enough to be a bridesmaid, that it almost spoilt her own pleasure. Aunt Hazel was to have two bridesmaids and all were to be dressed in green, much to Judy's horror, who declared green was unlucky for weddings.

"Oh, oh, there was a widding once in the Ould Country

and the bridesmaids wore grane. And the fairies were that mad they put a curse on the house, that they did."

"How did they curse it, Judy?"

"I'm telling ye. There was niver to be inny more laughter in that house... niver agin. Oh, oh, that's a tarrible curse. Think av a house wid no laughter in it."

"And wasn't there ever any, Judy?"

"Niver a bit. Plinty of waping but no laughing. Oh, oh, 'twas a sorryful place!"

Pat felt a little uneasy. What if there never were to be any more laughter at Silver Bush... father's gentle chuckles and Uncle Tom's hearty booms... Winnie's silvery trills... Judy's broad mirth? But her dress was so pretty... a misty, spring-green crepe with smocked yoke and a cluster of dear pink rosebuds on the shoulder. And a shirred green hat with roses on the brim. Pat had to revel in it, curse or no curse. She did not realise... as Judy did... that the green made her pale, tanned little face paler and browner. Pat as yet had no spark of vanity. The dress itself was everything.

The wedding was to be in the afternoon and the "nuptial cemetery," as Winnie, who was a ten-year-old Mrs. Malaprop... called it, was to be in the old grey stone church at South Glen which all the Gardiners had attended from time immemorial. Judy thought this a modern innovation.

"Sure and in the ould days at Silver Bush they used to be married in the avening and dance the night away. But they didn't go stravaging off on these fine honeymoon trips then. Oh, oh, they wint home and settled down to their business. 'Tis the times that have changed and not for the better I do be thinking. It used to be only the Episcopalians was married in church. Sure and it's niver been a Presbytarian custom at all, at all."

"Are you a Presbyterian, Judy?"

Pat was suddenly curious. She had never thought about Judy's religion. Judy went to the South Glen church with them on Sundays but would never sit in the Gardiner pew... always up in the gallery, where she could see everything, Uncle Tom said.

"Oh, oh, I'm Presbytarian as much as an Irish body can be," said Judy cautiously. "Sure and I cud niver be a rale Presbytarian not being Scotch. But innyhow I'm praying that all will go well and that yer Aunt Hazel'll have better luck than yer grand-dad's second cousin had whin she was married."

"What happened to grand-dad's second cousin, Judy?"

"Oh, oh, did ye niver hear av it? Sure and it seems nobody'd iver tell ye yer fam'ly history if ould Judy didn't. She died, poor liddle soul, of the pewmonia, the day before the widding and was buried in her widding dress. 'Twas a sad thing for she'd been long in landing her man... she was thirty if she was a day... and it was hard to be disap'inted at the last moment like that. Now, niver be crying, me jewel, over what happened fifty years ago. She'd likely be dead innyhow be this time and maybe she was spared a lot av trouble, for the groom was a wild felly enough and was only taking her for her bit av money, folks said. Here, give me a spell stirring this cake and don't be picking the plums out av it to ate."

5

During the last week the excitement was tremendous. Pat was allowed to stay home from school, partly because every one wanted her to run errands, partly because she would probably have died if she hadn't been allowed. Judy spent most of her time in the kitchen, concooting and baking, looking rather like an old witch hanging over some unholy brew. Aunt Barbara came over and helped but Aunt Edith did her share of the baking at home because no kitchen was big enough to hold her and Judy Plum. Aunt Hazel made the creams and mother the sparkling red jellies. That was all mother was allowed to do. It was thought she had enough work looking after Cuddles... as the baby was called by every one in spite of all the pother about her name. Mother, so Judy Plum told Pat, had never been quite the same since that bad headache the night Cuddles was found in the parsley bed, and they must be taking care of her.

Pat beat eggs and stirred innumerable cakes, taking turns with Sid in eating the savory scrapings from the bowls. The house was full of delicious smells from morning till night. And everywhere it was "Pat, come here," and "Pat, run there," till she was fairly bewildered.

"Aisy now," remonstrated Judy. "Make yer head save yer heels, darlint. 'Tis a great lesson to learn. Iverything'll sort itsilf out in God's good time. They do be imposing on ye a bit but Judy'll see yer not put upon too much. Sure and I don't see how we'd iver get yer Aunt Hazel married widout ye."

They wouldn't have got the wedding butter without her, that was certain. Judy had kept the blue cow's milk back for a week from the factory and the day before the wedding she started to churn it in the old-fashioned crank churn which she would never surrender for anything more modern. Judy churned and churned until Pat, going down into the cool, cobwebby cellar in mid-afternoon, found her "clane distracted."

"The crame's bewitched," said Judy in despair. "Me arms are fit to drop off at the roots and niver a sign av butter yet."

It was not to be thought of that mother should churn and Aunt Hazel was busy with a hundred things. Dad was sent for from the barn and agreed to have a whirl at it. But after churning briskly for half an hour he gave it up as a bad job.

"You may as well give the cream to the pigs, Judy," he said. "We'll have to buy the butter at the store."

This was absolute disgrace for Judy. To buy the butter from the store and only the Good Man Above knowing who made it! She went to get the dinner, feeling that the green wedding was at the bottom of it.

Pat slipped off the apple barrel where she had been squatted, and began to churn. It was great fun. She had always wanted to churn and Judy would never let her because if the cream were churned too slow or too fast the butter would be too hard or too soft. But now it didn't matter and she could churn to her heart's content. Splash... splash... splash! Flop... flop... flop! Thud... thud... thud! Swish... swish... swish! The business of turning the crank had grown gradually harder and Pat had just decided that for once in her life she had got all the churning she wanted when it suddenly grew lighter and Judy came down to call her to dinner.

"I've churned till I'm all in a sweat, Judy."

Judy was horrified.

"A sweat, is it? Niver be ye using such a word, girleen. Remimber the Binnies may *sweat* but the Gardiners *perspire*. And now I s'pose I'll have to be giving the crame to the pigs. 'Tis a burning shame, that it is... the blue cow's crame and all... and bought butter for a Silver Bush widding! But what wud ye ixpect wid grane dresses? I'm asking ye. Inny one might ave known..."

Judy had lifted the cover from the churn and her eyes nearly popped out of her head.

"If the darlint hasn't brought the butter! Here it is, floating round in the buttermilk, as good butter as was iver churned. And wid her liddle siven-year-old arms, whin nather meself nor Long Alec cud come be it. Oh, oh, just let me be after telling the whole fam'ly av it!"

Probably Pat never had such another moment of triumph in her whole life.

CHAPTER VII

Here Comes the Bride

1

THE wedding day came at last. Pat had been counting dismally towards it for a week. Only four more days to have Aunt Hazel at Silver Bush... only three... only two—only one. Pat had the good fortune to sleep with Judy the night before, because her bedroom was needed for the guests who came from afar. So she wakened with Judy before sunrise and slipped down anxiously to see what kind of a day it was going to be.

"Quane's weather!" said Judy in a tone of satisfaction. "I was a bit afraid last night we'd have rain, bekase there was a ring around the moon and it's ill-luck for the bride the rain falls on, niver to mintion all the mud and dirt tracked in. Now I'll just slip out and tell the sun to come up and thin I'll polish off the heft av the milking afore yer dad gets down. The poor man's worn to the bone wid all the ruckus."

"Wouldn't the sun come up if you didn't tell it, Judy?"

"I'm taking no chances on a widding day, me jewel."

While Judy was out milking Pat prowled about Silver Bush. How queer a house was in the early morning before people were up! Just as if it were watching for something. Of course all the rooms had an unfamiliar look on account of the wedding. The Big Parlour had been filled with a flame of autumn leaves and chrysanthemums. The new curtains were so lovely that Pat felt a fierce regret the Binnies were not to be among the guests at the house. Just fancy May's face if she saw them! The Little Parlour was half full of wedding presents. The table had been laid in the dining-room the night before. How pretty it looked, with its sparkling glass and its silver candlesticks and tall slender candles like moonbeams and the beautiful colours of the jellies.

Pat ran outside. The sun, obedient to Judy's mandate, was just coming up. The air was the amber honey of autumn. Every birch and poplar in the silver bush had become a golden maiden. The garden was tired of growing and had sat down to rest but the gorgeous hollyhocks were flaunting over the old stone dyke. A faint, lovely morning haze hung over the Hill of the Mist and trembled away before the sun. What a lovely world to be alive in!

Then Pat turned and saw a lank, marauding, half-eared cat... an alien to Silver Bush... lapping up the milk in the saucer that had been left for the fairies. So that was how it went! She had always suspected it but to *know* it was bitter. Was there no real magic left in the world?

"Judy,"... Pat was almost tearful when Judy came to the well with her pails of milk... "the fairies *don't* drink the milk. It's a cat... just as Sidney always said."

"Oh, oh, and if the fairies didn't nade it last night why shudn't a poor cat have it, I'm asking. Hasn't he got to live? I niver said they come ivery night. They've other pickings no doubt."

"Judy, did you ever really *see* a fairy drinking the milk? Cross your heart?"

"Oh, oh, what if I didn't? Sure the grandmother of me did. Minny's the time I've heard her tell it. A leprachaun wid the liddle ears av him wriggling as he lapped it up. And she had her leg bruk nixt day, that she had. Ye may be thankful if ye niver see any av the Grane Folk. They don't be liking it and that I'm tellin ye."

2

It was a day curiously compounded of pain and pleasure for Pat. Silver Bush buzzed with excitement, especially when

Snicklefritz got stung on the eyelid by a wasp and had to be shut up in the church barn. And then everybody was getting dressed. Oh, weddings *were* exciting things . . . Sid was right. Mother wore the loveliest new dress, the colour of a golden-brown chrysanthemum, and Pat was so proud of her it hurt.

"It's so nice to have a pretty mother," she exclaimed rapturously.

She was proud of all her family. Of father, who had had a terrible time finding his necktie and who, in his excitement, had put his left boot on his right foot and laced it up before he discovered his mistake, but now looked every inch a Cardiner. Of darling wee Cuddles with her silk stockings rolled down to show her dear, bare, chubby legs. Of Winnie, who in her yellow dress looked like a great golden pansy. Of Sid and Joe in new suits and white collars. Even of Judy Plum who had blossomed out in truly regal state. The dress-up dress had come out of the brown chest, likewise a rather rusty lace shawl and a bonnet of quilted blue satin of the vintage of last century. Judy would have scorned to be seen in public without a bonnet. No giddy hats for her. Also what she called a "paireen" of glossy, patent leather slippers with high heels. Thus fearsomely arrayed Judy minced about, keeping a watchful eye on everything and greeting arriving friends in what she called her "company voice" and the most perfect English pronunciation you ever heard.

Aunt Hazel and her bridesmaids were as yet invisible in the Poet's room. Mother dressed Pat in her pretty green dress and hat. Pat loved it . . . but she ran upstairs to her closet to tell her old blue voile that she still loved it the best. Then the aunts came over, Aunt Barbara very weddingish in a dress and coat of beige lace which Aunt Edith thought far too young for her. Nobody could call Aunt Edith's dress young but it was very handsome and Pat nearly burst with pride in her whole clan.

Uncle Brian from Summerside was going to take the bride and her maids to the church in his new car and it was a wonderful moment when they came floating down the stairs. Pat's eyes smarted a wee bit. Was this mysterious creature in white satin and misty veil, with the great shower bouquet of roses and lilies of the valley, her dear, jolly Aunt Hazel? Pat

felt as if she were already lost to them. But Aunt Hazel
lingered to whisper,

"I've slipped the pansies you picked for me into my
bouquet, darling... they're the 'something blue' the bride
must wear, and thanks ever so much."

And all was well again for a while.

Father took mother and Winnie and Judy and Joe in the
Silver Bush Lizzie but Pat and Sid went in Uncle Tom's
"span." No Lizzie or any other such lady for Uncle Tom. He
drove a great roomy, double-seated "phaeton" drawn by two
satin bay horses with white stars on their foreheads and Pat
liked it far better than any car. But why was Uncle Tom so
slow in coming? "We'll be late. There's a million buggies and
cars gone past already," worried Pat.

"Oh, oh, don't be exaggerating, girleen."

"Well, there was five anyway," cried Pat indignantly.

"There he's coming now," said Judy. "Mind yer manners," she added in a fierce whisper. "No monkey-didoes
whin things get a bit solemn, mind ye that."

Pat and Sid and Aunt Barbara sat in the back seat. Pat
felt tremendously important and bridled notably when May
Binnie looked out enviously from a car that honked past
them. Generally she and Sid walked to church by a short cut
across the fields and along a brook scarfed with farewell
summers. But the road was lovely, too, with the sunny,
golden stubble fields, the glossy black crows sitting on the
fences, the loaded apple boughs dragging on the grass of the
orchards, the pastures spangled with asters, and the sea far
out looking so blue and happy, with great fleets of cloudland
sailing over it.

Then there was the crowded church among its maples
and spruces—the arrangement of the procession—the people
standing up—Aunt Hazel trailing down the aisle on father's
arm—Jean Madison and Sally Gardiner behind her—Pat
bringing up the rear gallantly with her basket of roses in her
brown paws—the sudden hush—the minister's solemn voice—
the prayer—the lovely colours that fell on the people through
the stained glass windows, turning them from prosaic folks
into miracles. At first Pat was too bewildered to analyse her
small sensations. She saw a little quivering ruby of light fall
on Aunt Hazel's white veil... she saw Rob Madison's flying
jibs... she saw Sally Gardiner's night-black hair under her

green hat... she saw the ferns and flowers... and suddenly she heard Aunt Hazel saying, "I will," and saw her looking up at her groom.

A dreadful thing happened to Pat. She turned frantically to Judy Plum who was sitting just behind her at the end of the front pew.

"Judy, lend me your hanky. I'm going to cry," she whispered in a panic.

Judy fairly came out in gooseflesh. She realised that a desperate situation must be handled desperately. Her hanky was a huge white one which would engulf Pat. Moreover the Binnies were at the back of the church. She bent forward.

"If there do be one tear out av ye to disgrace Silver Bush I'll niver fry ye an egg in butter agin as long as I live."

Pat took a brace. Perhaps it was the thought of Silver Bush or the fried egg or both combined. She gave a desperate gulp and swallowed the lump in her throat. Savage winking prevented the fall of a single tear. The ceremony was over... nobody had noticed the little by-play... and everybody thought Pat had behaved beautifully. The Silver Bush people were much relieved. They had all been more or less afraid that Pat would break down at the last, just as Cora Gardiner had done at her sister's wedding, erupting into hysterical howls right in the middle of the prayer and having to be walked out by a humiliated mother.

"Ye carried yerself off well, darlint," whispered Judy proudly.

Pat contrived to get through the reception and the supper but she found she couldn't eat, not even a chicken slice or the lovely "lily salad" mother had made. She was very near crying again when somebody said to Aunt Hazel,

"What is it like to be Hazel Madison? Do you realise that you *are* Hazel Madison now?"

Hazel Gardiner no longer! Oh, it was just too much!

CHAPTER VIII
Aftermath

1

AND then the going away! For the first time in her life Pat found out what it was like to say good-bye to some one who was not coming back. But she could cry then because everybody cried, even Judy, who seldom cried.

"When I feels like crying," Judy was accustomed to say, "I just do be sitting down and having a good laugh."

She would not let Pat stand too long, looking after Aunt Hazel, tranced in her childish tears.

"It's unlucky to watch a parting friend out av sight," she told her.

Pat turned away and wandered dismally through the empty rooms. With everything so upset and disarranged upstairs and down Silver Bush wasn't like home at all. Even the new lace curtains seemed part of the strangeness. The table, that had been so pretty, looked terrible... untidy... crumby... messy ... with Aunt Hazel's chair pushed rakily aside just as she had risen from it. Pat's brown eyes were drowned again.

"Come along wid me, darlint, and help me out a bit," Judy... wise Judy... was saying. "Sure and yer mother has gone to bed, rale played out wid all the ruckus, and small wonder. And Winnie's tying hersilf into kinks wid the stomachache and that's no puzzle ather wid the way she was after stuffing hersilf. So there's nobody but us two to look after things. We'll lave the dining-room as it is till the morning but we'll straighten up the parlours and the bedrooms. Sure and the poor house do be looking tired."

Judy had doffed her silk and high heels and company voice and was in her comfortable old drugget and brogans... and brogue... again. Pat was glad. Judy seemed much more homelike and companionable so.

"Can we put all the furniture back in its right place?" she said eagerly. Somehow it would be a comfort to have the sideboard and the old parlour rocker that had been put out of sight as too shabby, and the vases of pampas grass that had been condemned as old-fashioned, back again where they belonged.

"Oh, oh, we'll do that. And lave off looking as doleful as if yer Aunt Hazel had been buried instid av being married."

"I don't feel much like smiling, Judy."

"There's rason in that. Sure and I've been grinning that much to-day I fale as if I'd been turned into a chessy-cat. But it's been one grand widding, so it has, and the like av it Jen Binnie will never see for all av her city beau. As for the supper, Government House itsilf cudn't bate it. And the cirrimony was that solemn it wud av scared me out av the notion av getting married if I iver had inny."

"I would have cried and spoiled it all if it hadn't been for you, Judy dear," said Pat gratefully.

"Oh, oh, I wasn't blaming ye. I knew a big, handsome bridesmaid onct and she burst out waping right in the middle av the cirrimony. And the things people did be saying . . . such as she was crying bekase she wasn't getting married hersilf, whin it was just her full heart. And that it was better than the bridesmaid that was laughing in the middle av things at Rosella Gardiner's widding. No one iver did be knowing what she laughed at . . . she wud niver tell . . . but the groom thought it was at him, and he niver wud spake to her again. It started a ruckus in the fam'ly that lasted for forty years. Oh, oh, the liddle things that do be having a big inding!"

Pat didn't think that for the bridesmaid to laugh in the middle of the ceremony was a little thing. She was very glad nothing like that had happened to make Aunt Hazel's wedding ridiculous.

"Come now and we'll swape up all this confetti stuff first. The ould days av rice were better I'm thinking. The hins got a good fade innyhow. Oh, oh, this table do be looking like the relics of ould dacency, doesn't it now? I'm seeing one av the good silver crame jugs has got a dint in it. But whin all's said and done it don't be looking much like the table did after yer Great-aunt Margaret's widding over at the Bay Shore farm. Oh, oh, that was a tommyshaw!"

"What happened, Judy?"

"Happened, is it? Ye may well ask. They had a fringed

cloth on the table be way av extry style and whin the groom's cousin... ould Jim Milroy he is now... Jim wid the beard he was called thin... oh, oh, he had the magnificent beard. Sure and 'twas a shame to shave it off just bekase it wint out av fashion... well, where was I at? He wint to get up from the table in a hurry as he always did and didn't one av his buttons catch in the fringe and away wint fringe and cloth and dishes and all. Niver did inny one see such a smash. I was down to the Bay Shore to hilp thim out a bit and me and yer Aunt Frances claned up the mess, her crying and lamenting all the time and small blame to her. All the illigant dishes smashed and the carpet plastered wid the stuff that was spilled, niver to spake av the poor bride's dress as was clane ruined be a great cup av tay tipped over in her lap. Oh, oh, I was a young skellup av a thing thin and I thought it a great joke but the Bay Shore people were niver the same agin. Now, run up to yer room, and put off yer finery and we'll get to work. I belave we're after having a rainy night av it. The wind's rising and it's dark as a squaw's pocket already."

It was such a comfort to put things back in their places. When the job was finished Silver Bush looked like home again. Darkness had fallen and rain was beginning to splash against the windows.

"Let's go into the kitchen now and I'll get ye a tasty liddle bite afore I do be setting the bread. I noticed ye didn't ate innything av their fine spread. I've a pot of hot pay soup I brewed up for mesilf kaping warm on the back av the stove and there's some chicken lift over I'm thinking."

"I don't feel like eating with Aunt Hazel gone," said Pat, rather mistily again. That thought *would* keep coming back.

"Oh, oh, fat sorrow is better than lean sorrow, me jewel. Here now, ain't this snug as two kittens in a basket? We'll shut out the dark. And here's a liddle cat wid an illigant grey suit and a white shirt, be the name av Thursday, wid his small heart breaking for a word after all the neglict av the day."

A fierce yowl sounded outside. Gentleman Tom was demanding entrance.

"Let me let him in, Judy," said Pat eagerly. She did so love to let things in out of the cold. Pat held the door open for a moment. It was a wild night after the lovely day. The rain was streaming down. The wind was thrashing the silver bush mercilessly. Snicklefritz was howling dolefully in the

church barn since Joe was not yet back from the station to
comfort him.

Pat turned away with a shiver. The peace of the old
kitchen was in delightful contrast to the storm outside. The
stove was glowing clear red in the dusk. Thursday was coiled
up under it, thinking this was how things should be. It was so
nice to be in this bright, warm room, supping Judy's hot pea
soup and watching the reflection of the kitchen outside
through the window. Pat loved to do that. It looked so
uncanny and witchlike . . . so real yet so unreal . . . with Judy
apparently calmly setting bread under the thrashing maple by
the well.

2

Pat loved to watch Judy set bread and listen to her
talking to herself as she always did while kneading and
thumping. To-night Judy was reviewing the church wedding.

"Oh, oh, she was dressed very gay outside but I'm
wondering what was undernath. Sure and it's well if it was no
worse than patches . . . Bertha Holms is the pert one. Only
fifteen and she do be making eyes at the b'ys already. I
remimber her at her own aunt's widding whin she was about
the age av Pat here. She was after throwing hersilf on the
floor and kicking and screaming. Oh, oh, wudn't I like to have
had the spanking av her! Simon Gardiner was be way av
being rale groomed up to-day. Sure and whin I saw him, so
starched and proper in his pew, looking as if he was doing the
world a big favour be living, it was hard to belave the last
time I saw him he was so drunk he thought the table was
follying him round, and crying like a baby he was bekase it
wud be sure to catch him, having four legs to his two. It
tickled me ribs, that. Oh, oh, it's liddle folks know what other
folks do be thinking av thim in church. And wud ye listen to
Ould Man Taylor calling his wife sugar-pie and him married
thirty years, the ould softy. Though maybe it's better than
George Harvey and his 'ould woman.' There was ould Elmer
Davidson stumbling in late whin the cirrimony had begun
and sp'iling the solemnity. He'll be late for the resurrection,
that one. Mary Jarvis and her yilping whin they were signing
the papers! Thim that likes can call it singing. Singing,
indade! The Great-aunts av the Bay Shore farm were after

being a bit more stately than common . . . be way of showing
their contimpt for both Gardiners and Madisons I'm thinking.
Sure and it's a wonder they condescend to come at all. Oh,
oh, but the supper wud give thim one in the eye. It's a long
day since they've set down to such a spread I'm thinking. Oh,
oh, but I got square wid Ould Maid Sands. Sez I to her,
sly-like, 'While there's life there's hope.' *She* knew well what
I was maning, so she did."

Judy was shaking with silent laughter as she patted her
bread. Then she grew sober.

"Oh, oh, there was one at the widding that'll be to none
other. Kate MacKenzie has got the sign."

"What sign, Judy?" asked Pat drowsily.

"Oh, oh, I forgot liddle pitchers have the long ears,
darlint. 'Tis the death sign I mint. But it do be life. There's
always the birth and the death and the bridal mixed up
togither. And a nice cheerful widding it was in spite av all."

Pat was almost asleep. The down-trodden black cats
were beginning to trot around the rug under her very eyes.

"Wake up, me jewel, and go to bed properly. Listen at
that wind. There'll be apples to pick up to-morrow."

Pat looked up, yawning and comforted. After all, life at
dear Silver Bush was going on. The world hadn't come to an
end just because Aunt Hazel was gone.

"Judy, tell me again about the man you saw hanged in
Ireland before I go to bed."

"Oh, oh, that do be a tarrible story for bed-time. It wud
make yer hair stand on end."

"I *like* having my hair stand on end. Please, Judy."

Judy picked Pat up on her knee.

"Hug me close, Judy, and tell me."

The harrowing tale was told and Pat, who had heard it a
dozen times before, thrilled just as deliciously as at the first.
There was no doubt about it . . . she enjoyed "tarrible" things.

"Sure and I shudn't be telling ye all these tales av bad
people," said Judy, a bit uncomfortably, looking at Pat's
dilated eyes.

"Of course, Judy, I like to *live* with good people better
than bad, but I like *hearing* about bad people better than
good."

"Well, I do be thinking it wud be a dull world if nobody
iver did anything he oughtn't. What wud we find to talk

about?" asked Judy unanswerably. "Innyway it's to bed ye must be going. And say a prayer for all poor ghosts. If Wild Dick or Waping Willy or ather or both av thim are on the fence to-night 'tis a wet time they'll be having av it."

"Maybe I won't be so lonesome if I say my prayers twice," thought Pat. She said them twice and even contrived to pray for her new uncle. Perhaps as a reward for this she fell asleep instantly. Once in the night she wakened and a flood of desolation poured over her. But in the darkness she heard a melodious purring and felt the beautiful touch of a velvet cat. Pat swallowed hard. The rain was still sobbing around the eaves. Aunt Hazel was gone. But Silver Bush held her in its heart. To lie in this dear house, sheltered from the storm, with Thursday purring under her hand . . . apples to be picked to-morrow . . . oh, life began to beckon once more. Pat fell asleep comforted.

CHAPTER IX
A Day to Spend

1

AGAIN it was September at Silver Bush . . . a whole year since Aunt Hazel was married: and now it seemed to Pat that Aunt Hazel had always been married. She and Uncle Bob often came "home" for a visit and Pat was very fond of Uncle Bob now, and even thought his flying jibs were nice. The last time, too, Aunt Hazel had had a darling, tiny baby, with amber-brown eyes like Pat's own. Cuddles wasn't a baby any longer. She was toddling round on her own chubby legs and was really a sister to be proud of. She had been through all her teething at eleven months. It was beautiful to watch her waking up and beautiful to bend over her while she was asleep. She seemed to know you were there and would smile delightedly. A spirit of her own, too. When she was eight months old she had bitten Uncle Tom when he poked his finger into her mouth to find out if she had any teeth. He found out.

And now had come the invitation for Pat to spend a Saturday at the Bay Shore farm, with Great-aunt Frances Selby and Great-aunt Honor Atkins . . . not to mention "Cousin" Dan Gowdy and a still greater aunt, who was mother's great-aunt. Pat's head was usually dizzy when she got this far and small wonder, as Judy would say.

Pat loved the sound of "a day to spend." It sounded so gloriously lavish to "spend" a whole day, letting its moments slip one by one through your fingers like beads of gold.

But she was not enthusiastic over spending it at the Bay Shore. When she and Sid had been very small they had called the Bay Shore the Don't-touch-it House guiltily, to themselves. Everybody was so old there. Two years ago, when she had been there with mother, she remembered how Aunt Frances frowned because when they were walking in the orchard, she, Pat, had picked a lovely, juicy, red plum from a laden tree. And Aunt Honor, a tall lady with snow-white hair and eyes as black as her dress, had asked her to repeat some Bible verses and had been coldly astonished when Pat made mistakes in them. The great-aunts always asked you to repeat Bible verses . . . so said Winnie and Joe who had been there often . . . and you never could tell what they would give when you got through . . . a dime or a cooky or a tap on the head.

But to go *alone* to the Bay Shore! Sidney had been asked, too, but Sidney had gone to visit Uncle Brian's while his teeth were attended to. Perhaps it was just as well because Sidney was not in high favour at the Bay Shore, having fallen asleep at the supper table and tumbled ingloriously off his chair to the floor, with an heirloom goblet in his hand, the last time he was there.

Pat talked it over with Judy Friday evening, sitting on the sandstone steps at the kitchen door and working her sums to be all ready for Monday. Pat was a year older and an inch taller, by the marks Judy kept on the old pantry door where she measured every child on its birthday. She was well on in subtraction and Judy was helping her. Judy could add and subtract. When her head was clear she could multiply. Division she never attempted.

The kitchen behind them was full of the spicy smell of Judy's kettle of pickles. Gentleman Tom was sitting on the well platform, keeping an eye on Snicklefritz, who was dozing on the cellar door, keeping an eye on Gentleman Tom. In the corner of the yard was a splendid pile of cut hardwood which Pat and Sid had stacked neatly up in the summer evenings after school. Pat gloated over it. It was so prophetic of cosy, cheerful winter evenings when the wind would growl and snarl because it couldn't get into Silver Bush. Pat would have been perfectly happy if it had not been for the morrow's visit.

"The aunts are so . . . so stately," she confided to Judy. She would never have dared criticise them to mother who had been a Selby and was very proud of her people.

"The grandmother av thim was a Chidlaw," said Judy as if that explained everything. "I'm not saying but they're a bit grim but they've had a tarrible lot av funerals at the Bay Shore. Yer Aunt Frances lost her man afore she married him and yer Aunt Honor lost hers after she married him and they've niver settled which got the worst av it. They're a bit near, too, it must be confessed, and thim wid lashings of money. But they do be rale kind at heart and they think a lot av all yer mother's children."

"I don't mind Aunt Frances or Aunt Honor, but I'm a *little* afraid of Great-great-aunt Hannah and Cousin Dan," confessed Pat.

"Oh, oh, ye nadn't be. Maybe ye'll not be seeing the ould leddy at all. She hasn't left her own room for sixteen years and she's ninety-three be the clock, so she is, and there don't be minny seeing her. And ould Danny is harmless. He fell aslape at the top av the stairs and rolled down thim whin he was a lad. He was niver the same agin. But some do be saying he saw the ghost."

"Oh, Judy, is there a ghost at Bay Shore?"

"Not now. But long ago there was. Oh, oh, they were tarrible ashamed av it."

"Why?"

"Ye know they thought it was kind av a disgraceful thing to have a ghost in the house. Some folks do be thinking it an honour but there ye are. I'm not denying the Bay Shore ghost was a troublesome cratur. Sure and he was a nice, frindly, sociable ghost and hadn't any rale dog-sense about the proper time for appearing. He was a bit lonesome it wud seem. He wud sit round on the foot-boards av their beds and look at thim mournful like, as if to say, 'Why the divil won't ye throw a civil word to a felly?' And whin company come and they were all enjying thimselves they'd hear a dape sigh and there me fine ghost was. It was be way av being tarrible monotonous after a while. But the ghost was niver seen agin after yer great-great-uncle died and yer Great-aunt Honor tuk to running things. I'm thinking she was a bit too near, aven for a ghost, that one. So ye nadn't be afraid av seeing him but ye'd better not be looking too close at the vase that makes the faces."

"A vase . . . that makes faces!"

"Sure, me jewel. It's on the parlour mantel and it made a face once at Sarah Jenkins as was hired there whin she was dusting it. She was nather to hold nor bind wid fright."

This was delightful. But after all, Pat thought Judy was a little too contemptuous of the Bay Shore people.

"Their furniture is very grand, Judy."

"Grand, is it?" Judy knew very well she had been snubbed. "Oh, oh, ye can't be telling *me* innything about grandeur. Didn't I work in Castle McDermott whin I was a slip av a girleen? Grandeur, is it? Lace and sating bed-quilts, I'm telling ye. And a white marble staircase wid a golden bannister. Dinner sets av solid gold and gold vases full av champagne. And thirty servants if there was one. Sure and they kipt servants to wait on the other servants there. The ould lord wud pass round plates wid gold sovereigns at the Christmas dinner and hilp yerself. Oh, oh, what's yer Bay Shore farm to that, I'm asking. And now just rin over thim verses ye larnt last Sunday, in case yer Aunt Honor wants ye to say some."

"I can say them without a mistake to you, Judy. But it will be so different with Aunt Honor."

"Sure and ye'd better just shut yer eyes and purtind she's a cabbage-head, darlint. Though old Jed Cattermole didn't be thinking her that whin she put him in his place at the revival meetings."

"What did she do, Judy?"

"Do, is it? I'm telling ye. Old Jed thought he was extry cliver bekase he didn't belave in God. Just be way av showing off one night he wint to one av the revival matings ould Mr. Campbell was having whin he was minister at South Glen. And after all the tistimonies me bould Jed gets up and sez, sez he, 'I'm not belaving there's inny God but if there is He do be a cruel, unrasonable ould tyrant. And now,' sez Jed, swelling up all over wid consate, like an ould tom turkey, 'if there is a God why doesn't he strike me dead for what I've said. I dare Him to do it,' sez ould Jed, feeling bigger than iver. Iverybody was so shocked ye cud have heard a pin fall. And yer Aunt Honor turns round and sez she, cool-like, 'Do you really think ye're av that much importance to God, Jedediah Cattermole?' Iverybody laughed. Did ye iver be seeing one av thim big rid balloons whin ye've stuck a pin in it? Oh, oh, that was me proud Jed. He was niver the same agin. Now yer sums are done and me pickles are done, so we'll just have a bit av fun roasting some crab apples wid cloves stuck in thim for scint."

"I wish Sid was here," sighed Pat. "He does love clove apples so. Will he be back Sunday night, do you think, Judy? I *can't* live another week without him."

"Ye set yer heart too much on Siddy, me jewel. What'll ye be after doing whin ye grow up and have to part?"

"Oh, that'll never be, Judy. Sid and I are never going to part. We'll neither of us marry but just live on here at Silver Bush and take care of everything. We have it all settled."

Judy sighed.

"I wish ye wudn't be so set on him. Why don't ye be after getting yersilf a chum in school like the other liddle girls? Winnie has lashings av thim."

"I don't want anybody but Sid. The girls in school are nice but I don't love any of them. I don't *want* to love any one or anything but my own family and Silver Bush."

2

Since Pat had to go to the Bay Shore farm she was glad it was this particular Saturday because father was going to replace the old board fence around the orchard with a new one. Pat hated to see the old fence torn down. It was covered with such pretty lichens, and vines had grown over its posts and there was a wave of caraway all along it as high as your waist.

Judy had a reason for being glad, too. The ukase had gone forth that the big poplar in the corner of the yard must be cut down because its core was rotten and the next wind might send it crashing down on the hen-house. Judy had plotted with Long Alec to cut it down the day Pat was away for she knew every blow of the axe would go to the darlint's heart.

Joe ran Pat down to the Bay Shore in the car. She bent from it as it whirled out of the lane to wave good-bye to Silver Bush. Cuddles' dear little rompers on the line behind the house were plumped out with wind and looked comically like three small Cuddles swinging from the line. Pat sighed and then resolved to make the best of things. The day was lovely, full of blue, sweet autumn hazes. The road to the Bay Shore was mostly down hill, running for part of the way through spruce "barrens," its banks edged with ferns, sweet-smelling bay bushes, and clusters of scarlet pigeon-berries. There was a blue, waiting sea at the end and an old grey house fronting the sunset, so close to the purring waves that in storms their spray dashed over its very doorstep . . . a wise old house that knew many things, as Pat always felt. Mother's old home and therefore to be loved, whether one could love the people in it or not.

It still made quite a sensation at Bay Shore when any one arrived in a car. The aunts came out and gave a prim welcome and Cousin Dan waved from a near field where he was turning over the sod into beautiful red furrows, so even and smooth. Cousin Dan was very proud of his ploughing.

Joe whirled away, leaving Pat to endure her ordeal of welcome and examination. The great-aunts were as stiff as the starched white petticoats that were still worn at Bay Shore. To tell truth, the great-aunts were really frightfully at a loss what to say to this long-legged, sunburned child whom they thought it a family duty to invite to Bay Shore once in so long. Then Pat was taken up to the Great-great's room for a few minutes. She went reluctantly. Great-great-aunt Hannah was so mysteriously old . . . a tiny, shrunken, wrinkled creature peering at her out of a mound of quilts in a huge, curtained bed.

"So this is Mary's little girl," said a piping voice.

"No. I am Patricia Gardiner," said Pat, who hated to be called anybody's little girl, even mother's.

Great-great-aunt Hannah put a claw-like hand on Pat's arm and drew her close to the bed, peering at her with old, old blue eyes, so old that sight had come back to them.

"Nae beauty . . . nae beauty," she muttered.

"She may grow up better-looking than you expect," said Aunt Frances, as one determinedly looking on the bright side. "She is terribly sunburned now."

Pat's little brown face, with its fine satiny skin, flushed mutinously. She did not care if she were "no beauty" but she disliked being criticised to her face like this. Judy would have said it wasn't manners. And then when they went downstairs Aunt Honor said in a tone of horror,

"There's a rip in your dress, child."

Pat wished they wouldn't call her "child." She would have loved to stick her tongue out at Aunt Honor but that wouldn't be manners either. She stood very stiff while Aunt Honor brought needle and thread and sewed it up.

"Of course Mary can't attend to everything and Judy Plum wouldn't care if they were all in rags," said Aunt Frances condoningly.

"Judy *would* care," cried Pat. "She's *very* particular about our clothes and our manners. That shoulder ripped on the way over. So there."

In spite of this rather unpropitious beginning the day was not so bad. Pat said her verses correctly and Aunt Honor gave her a cooky...and watched her eat it. Pat was in agonies of thirst but was too shy to ask for a glass of water. When dinner time came, however, there was plenty of milk...Judy would have said "skim" milk. But it was served in a lovely old gold-green glass pitcher that made the skimmiest of milk look like Jersey cream. The table was something of the leanest, according to Silver Bush standards. Pat's portion of the viands was none too lavish, but she ate it off a plate with a coloured border of autumn leaves...one of the famous Selby plates, a hundred years old. Pat felt honoured and tried not to feel hungry. For dessert she had three of the tabooed red plums.

After dinner Aunt Frances said she had a headache and was going to lie down. Cousin Dan suggested aspirin but Aunt Frances crushed him with a look.

"It is not God's will that we should take aspirin for relief from the pain He sends," she said loftily, and stalked off, with her red glass, silver-stoppered vinaigrette held to her nose.

Aunt Honor turned Pat loose in the parlour and told her to amuse herself. This Pat proceeded to do. Everything was of interest and now she was alone she could have a good time. She had been wondering how she could live through the afternoon if she had to sit it out with the aunts. Both she and Aunt Honor were mutually relieved to be rid of each other.

3

The parlour furniture *was* grand and splendid. There was a big, polished brass door-handle in which she saw herself reflected with such a funny face. The china door-plate had roses painted on it. The blinds were pulled down and she loved the cool, green light which filled the room ... it made her feel like a mermaid in a shimmering sea-pool. She loved the little procession of six white ivory elephants marching along the black mantel. She loved the big spotted shells on the what-not which murmured of the sea when she held them to her ear. And there was the famous vase, full of peacock feathers, that had made a face at Sarah Jenkins. It was of white glass and had curious markings on its side that did resemble a face. But it did not grimace at Pat though she wished it would. There was a brilliant red-and-yellow china hen sitting on a yellow nest on a corner table that was very wonderful. And there were deep Battenburg lace scallops on the window shades. Surely even Castle McDermott couldn't beat that.

Pat would have liked to see all the hidden things in the h' ıse. Not its furniture or its carpets but the letters in old boxes upstairs and the clothes in old trunks. But this was impossible. She dared not leave the parlour. The aunts would die of horror if they caught her prowling.

When everything in the room had been examined Pat curled herself up on the sofa and spent an absorbed hour looking at the pictures in old albums with faded blue and red plush bindings and in hinged leather frames that opened and shut like a book. What funny old pictures in full skirts and big sleeves and huge hats high up on the head! There was one of Aunt Frances in the eighties, in a flounced dress and a little "sacque" with its sloping shoulders and square scallops ... *and* a frilled parasol. Oh, you could just see how proud she was of that parasol! It seemed funny to think of Aunt Frances as a little girl with a frivolous parasol.

There was a picture of father ... a young man without a moustache. Pat giggled over that. One of mother, too ... a round, plump face, with "bangs" and a big bow of ribbon in her hair. And one of Great-uncle Burton who went away and was "never heard of again." What fascination was in the phrase! Even dead people were heard of again. They had funerals and head-stones.

And here was Aunt Honor as a baby. Looking like Cuddles! Oh, would Cuddles *ever* look like Aunt Honor? It was unthinkable. How terribly people changed! Pat sighed.

CHAPTER X
A Maiden All Forlorn

1

AT dusk there was the question of how Pat was to get home. Aunt Frances, who was the horsewoman of Bay Shore, was to have driven her. But Aunt Frances was still enduring God's will in her bedroom and Aunt Honor hadn't driven a horse for years. As for Cousin Dan, he couldn't be trusted away from home with a team. Aunt Honor finally telephoned to the nearest neighbour.

"Morton MacLeod is going to town. I thought he would, since it is Saturday night. He says he'll take you and drop you off at Silver Bush. You don't mind going as far as the MacLeod place alone, do you? You will be there before dark."

Pat didn't mind anything except the prospect of staying at the Bay Shore overnight. And she was never in the least afraid of the dark. She had often been alone in it. The other children at her age had been afraid of the dark and ran in when it came. But Pat never did. They said at Silver Bush that she was "her father's child" for that. Long Alec always liked to wander around alone at night . . . "enjoying the beauty of the darkness," he said. There was a family legend that Pat at the age of four had slept out in the caraway in the orchard all one night, nobody missing her until Judy, who had been sitting up with a sick neighbour, came home at sunrise and raised a riot. Pat dimly remembered the family rapture when she was found and joy washing like a rosy wave over mother's pale, distracted face.

She said her good-byes politely and made her way to the MacLeod place where bad news met her. Morton's car was "acting up" and he had given up the idea of going to town.

"So you'll have to run back to the Bay Shore," his mother told her kindly.

Pat went slowly down the lane and when she was screened from sight of the house by a spruce grove she stopped to think. She did not want to go back to the Bay Shore. The very thought of spending the night in the big spare room, with its bed that looked far too grand to be slept in, was unbearable. No, she would just walk home. It was only three miles . . . she walked that every day going to school and back.

Pat started off briskly and gaily, feeling very independent and daring and grown-up. How Judy would stare when she sauntered into the kitchen and announced carelessly that she had walked home from the Bay Shore all alone in the dark. "Oh, oh, and ain't ye the bould one?" Judy would say admiringly.

And then . . . the dark chilly night seemed suddenly to be coming to meet her . . . and when the road forked she wasn't sure which fork to take . . . the left one? . . . oh, it must be the left one . . . Pat ran along it with sheer panic creeping into her heart.

It was dark now . . . quite dark. And Pat suddenly discovered that to be alone on a strange road two miles from home in a very dark darkness was an entirely different thing from prowling in the orchard or running along the Whispering Lane or wandering about the Field of the Pool with the homelights of Silver Bush always in sight.

The woods and groves around her, that had seemed so friendly on the golden September day were strangers now. The far, dark spruce hills seemed to draw nearer threateningly. *Was this the right road?* There were no homelights anywhere. Had she taken the wrong turn and was this the "line" road that ran along the back of the farms between the two townships? Would she ever get home? Would she ever see Sid again . . . hear Winnie's laugh and Cuddles' dear little squeals of welcome? Last Sunday in church the choir had sung, *"The night is dark and I am far from home."* She knew what that meant now as she broke into a desperate little run. The white birches along the roadside seemed to be trying to catch her with ghostly hands. The wind wailed through the spruces. At Silver Bush you never quite knew how the wind would come at you . . . from behind the church barn like a cat pouncing . . . down from the Hill of the Mist like a soft bird flying . . . through the orchard like a playmate . . . but it always came as a friend. This wind was no friend. Was that it crying in the spruces? Or was it the Green Harper of Judy's tale who harped people away to Fairyland whether they would or no? All Judy's stories, enjoyed and disbelieved at home, became fearfully true here. Those strange little shadows, dark amid the darkness, under the ferns . . . suppose they *were* fairies. Judy said if you met a fairy you were never the same again. No threat could have been more terrible to Pat. To be changed . . . to be not yourself!

That wild, far-away note . . . was it the Peter Branaghan of another of Judy's tales, out on the hills piping to his ghostly sheep? And still no light . . . she *must* be on the wrong road.

All at once she was wild with terror of the chill night and the eerie wind and the huge, dark pathless world around her. She stopped short and uttered a bitter little cry of desolation.

"Can I help you?" said a voice.

Some one had just come around the turn of the road. A boy . . . not much taller than herself . . . with something queer about his eyes . . . with a little blot of shadow behind him that looked like a dog. That was all Pat could see. But suddenly she felt safe . . . protected. He had such a nice voice.

"I . . . think I'm lost," she gasped. "I'm Pat Gardiner . . . and I took the wrong road."

"You're on the line road," said the boy. "But it turns and goes down past Silver Bush. Only it's a little longer. I'll take you home. I'm Hilary Gordon . . . but everybody calls me Jingle."

Pat knew at once who he was and felt well acquainted. She had heard Judy talk about the Gordons who had bought the old Adams farm that marched with Silver Bush. They had no family of their own but an orphan nephew was living with them and Judy said it was likely he had poor pickings of it. He did not go to the North Glen school for the old Adams place was in the South Glen school district, but they were really next-door neighbours.

2

They walked on. They did not talk much but Pat felt happy now as she trotted along. The moon rose and in its light she looked at him curiously. He had dark-coloured, horn-rimmed glasses... that was what was the matter with his eyes. And he wore trousers of which one leg came to the knee and the other half way between knee and ankle, which Pat thought rather dreadful.

"I belong to Silver Bush, you know," she said.

"I don't belong anywhere," said Jingle forlornly.

Pat wanted to comfort him for something she did not understand. She slipped her little hand into his... he had a warm pleasant hand. They walked home together so. The wind... the night... were friendly again. The dark boughs of the trees, tossing against the silver moonlit sky, were beautiful... the spicy, woodsy smells along the road delightful.

"Where does that road go?" asked Pat once as they passed an inviting path barred by moonlight and shadow.

"I don't know but we'll go and see some day," said Jingle.

They were just like old, old friends.

And then the dear light of Silver Bush shining across the fields... the dear house overflowing with welcoming light. Pat could have cried with joy to see it again. Even if nobody would be very glad to see her back the house would.

"Thank you so much for coming home with me," she said shyly at the gate of the kitchen yard. "I was so frightened."

Then she added boldly... because she had heard Judy say a girl ought always to give a dacent feller a bite when he had seen her home and Pat, for the credit of Silver Bush, wanted to do the proper thing. . . .

"I wish you'd come and have dinner with us Monday. We're going to have chickens because it's Labour Day. Judy says she labours that day just the same as any day but she always celebrates it with a chicken dinner. Please come."

"I'd like to," said Jingle. "And I'm glad McGinty and I happened along when you were scared."

"Is McGinty the name of your dog?" asked Pat, looking at it a little timidly. Snicklefritz and Uncle Tom's old Bruno were all the dogs she was acquainted with.

"Yes. He's the only friend I've got in the world," said Jingle.

"Except me," said Pat.

Jingle suddenly smiled. Even in the moonlight she saw that he had a nice smile.

"Except you," he agreed.

Judy appeared at the open kitchen door, peering out.

"I must run," said Pat hastily. "Monday then. Don't forget. And bring McGinty, too. There'll be some bones."

"Now who was ye colloguing wid out there?" asked Judy curiously. "Sure and ye might av brought yer beau in and let's give him the once-over. Not but that ye're beginning a trifle young."

"That wasn't a beau, Judy," cried Pat, scandalised at the bare idea. "That was just Jingle."

"Hear at her. And who may Jingle be, if it's not asking too much?"

"Hilary Gordon... and I was coming home alone... and I got lost... I was a *little* frightened, Judy... and he's coming to dinner on Monday."

"Oh, oh, it's the fast worker ye are," chuckled Judy, delighted that she had got something to tease Pat about... Pat who had never thought there was any boy in the world but Sidney.

But Pat was too happy to mind. She was home, in the bright kitchen of Silver Bush. The horror of that lonely road had ceased to be... had never been. It was really beautiful to come home at night... to step out of darkness into the light and warmth of home.

"Did ye save a piece of pie for me, Judy?"

"Oh, oh, that I did. Don't I know the skimp males of the Bay Shore? Sure and it's niver cut and come agin there. It's more than a bit av pie I have for ye. What wud ye say now to a sausage and a baked pittaty?"

Over the supper Pat told Judy all about the day and her walk home.

"Think av the pluck av her, starting out alone like that on Shank's mare," said Judy, just as Pat had expected. That was the beauty of Judy. "Though I'm not saying it isn't a good thing that Jingle-lad happened along whin he did. Mind ye ask the cratur over for a liddle bite now and agin. I knew ould Larry Gordon whin he lived on the Taylor farm beyant the store. He's a skim milk man, that he is."

Judy had several classifications of people who were not lavish. You were "saving"... which was commendable. You were "close"... which was on the border line. You were "near"... which was over it. You were "skim milk"... which was beyond the pale. But Judy could not resist giving Pat a sly dig.

"I s'pose me poor kitchen is very tame after the splendours av the Bay Shore farm?"

"Silver Bush kitchen is better than the Bay Shore parlour," declared Pat: but she declared it drowsily. It had been a pretty full and strenuous day for eight years.

"Niver rub yer eyes wid innything but yer elbows, me jewel," cautioned Judy, as she convoyed Pat upstairs.

Mother, who had been singing Cuddles to sleep, slipped in to ask Pat if she had had a good time.

"The Bay Shore farm is such a lovely place," said Pat truthfully. It *was* a lovely *place*. And Pat wouldn't hurt mother's feelings for the world by confessing that her visit to mother's old home had not been altogether pleasant. Mother loved Bay Shore almost as well as she, Pat, loved Silver Bush. Dear Silver Bush! Pat felt as if its arms were around her protectingly as she drifted into dreamland.

CHAPTER XI
Dinner Is Served

1

PAT had a bad Sunday of it. When she found that the old poplar had been cut down she mourned and would not be comforted.

"Look, me jewel, what a pretty bit av scenery ye can see between the hin-house and the church barn," entreated Judy. "That bit av the South river, ye cud niver see it from here afore. Sure and here's yer Sunday raisins for ye. Be ating thim now and stop fretting after an ould tree that wud better av been down tin years ago."

Judy always gave every Silver Bush child a handful of raisins as a special treat for Sundays. Pat ate hers between sobs but it was not until evening that she would admit the newly revealed view was pretty. Then she sat at the round window and watched the silver loop of the river and another far blue hill, so far away that it must be on the very edge of the world. But still she missed the great, friendly, rustling greenness that had always filled that gap.

"I'll never see the kittens chasing each other up that tree again, Judy," she mourned. "They had such fun . . . they'd run out on that big bough and drop to the hen-house roof. Oh, Judy, I didn't think trees *ever* got old."

Monday morning she remembered that she had asked Jingle to dinner. Remembered it rather dubiously. Suppose he came in those awful trousers with part of one leg missing? She dared not, for fear of being teased, ask Judy to put anything extra on the table. But she was glad when she saw Judy putting on the silver knives and forks and the second best silver cream jug.

"Why all this splendour?" demanded Joe.

"Sure and isn't Pat's beau coming to dinner?" said Judy. "We must be after putting our best foot forward for the credit av the fam'ly."

"Judy!" cried Pat furiously. Neither then nor in the years to come could she endure having any one call Jingle her beau. "He isn't my beau! I'm never going to have a beau."

"Niver's a long day," said Judy philosophically. "Ye'd better be shutting Snicklefritz up, Joe, for I understand the young man's bringing his dog and we don't want inny difference av opinion atween thim."

Presently Jingle and McGinty were discerned, hanging about the yard gate, too shy to venture further. Pat ran out to welcome him. To her relief he wore a rather shabby but quite respectable suit, with legs of equal length. He was bare-legged, to be sure, but what of that. All the boys in North Glen went barefooted in summer . . . although not when asked out to dinner, perhaps. Somebody had given his brown hair a terrible cut. His eyes were invisible behind blue glasses, he had a pale face and an over-long mouth. Certainly he was not handsome but Pat still liked him. Also McGinty, who now revealed himself as a very young dog just starting out to see life.

"Doesn't that stuffing smell good?" asked Pat, as she convoyed him into the kitchen. "And Judy's made one of her apple-cakes for dessert. They're delicious. Judy, this is Jingle . . . and McGinty."

The Silver Bush family accepted Jingle calmly . . . Judy had probably warned them all. Dud gravely asked him if he would have white or dark meat and mother asked him if he took cream and sugar. You could always depend on father and mother, Pat felt. Even Winnie was lovely and made him take a second helping of apple-cake. What a family!

As for McGinty, Judy had set a big platter of meat and bones for him on the cellar hatch.

"Go to it, Mister Dog," she told him. "I'll warrant it's a long day since ye saw the like av that at Maria Gordon's."

After dinner Jingle said shyly,

"Listen... I saw some lovely rice lilies in our back field across the brook yesterday. Let's go and get some."

Pat had always longed to explore the brook that ran between Silver Bush and the old Adams place for a field's length and then branched across Adams territory. None of the Silver Bush children had ever been allowed to cross the boundary line. It was well known that old Mr. Adams wouldn't "have young ones stravaging over his fields."

"Do you think your uncle will mind?" asked Pat.

It turned out that neither uncle nor aunt was home. They had gone to spend Labour Day with friends.

"What would you have done for dinner if you hadn't come here?" exclaimed Pat.

"Oh, they left out some bread and molasses for me," said Jingle.

Bread and molasses on a holiday! This was skim milk with a vengeance.

"Mind ye don't poison yerselves wid mushrooms," warned Judy, handing them a bag of cinnamon buns. "I knew a b'y and girl onct as et a lot av toadstools in the woods be mistake."

"And I suppose they were never the same again?" said Joe teasingly.

"They've been dead iver since, if that's what ye mane be niver being the same agin," retorted Judy in a huff.

Once out of sight of the house Jingle's shyness dropped away from him and Pat found him a delightful companion... so delightful that she had a horrible sense of disloyalty to Sid. She could only square matters by reminding herself that she was just terribly sorry for Jingle, who had no friends.

It was Jingle who proposed that they should name the brook Jordan because it "rolled between."

"Between our farm and yours," said Pat delightedly. Here was a pal who liked to name places just as she did.

"And let's build a bridge of stones over it, so that we can cross easy whenever we want to," proposed Jingle, who evidently took it for granted that there would be plenty of crossing.

That was fun; and when the bridge was made... well and solidly, for Jingle would tolerate no jerry-building... they had an afternoon of prowling and rambling. They followed Jordan to its source at the very back of the old Adams place by fields that seemed made of sunshine and silence, over fences guarded by gay companies of golden-rod, through woods dappled with shadows, along little twisted paths that never did what you expected them to do. There was no end of lovely kinks and tiny cascades in the brook and the mosses on its banks were emerald and gold.

McGinty was in raptures. To roam like this was the joy of a little dog's life. He would race madly far ahead of them, then sit on his haunches waiting for them to come up with him, with his little red tongue lolling from his jaws. Pat loved McGinty; she was afraid she loved him better than curly, black Snicklefritz who, when all was said and done, was a one-man dog and a bit snappish with anybody but Joe. McGinty was such a dear little dog... so wistful... so anxious to be loved: with his little white cheeks and his golden-brown back and ears... pointed ears that stuck straight up when he was happy and dropped a bit when he was mournful: and tail all ready to wag whenever any one wanted it to wag.

2

In the end they found a beauty spot... a deep, still, woodland pool out of which the brook flowed, fed by a diamond trickle of water over the stones of a little hill. Around it grew lichened spruces and whispering maples, with little "cradle hills" under them; and just beyond a breezy slope with a few mossy, grass-grown sticks scattered here and there, and a bluebird perched on the point of a picket. It was all so lovely that it hurt. Why, Pat wondered, did lovely things so often hurt?

"This is the prettiest spot I've ever seen," cried Pat... "almost"... remembering the Secret Field.

"Isn't it?" said Jingle happily. "I don't think any one knows of it. Let's keep it a secret."

"Let's," agreed Pat.

"It always makes me think of a piece of poetry I learned at school... *The Haunted Spring*... ever hear it?"

Jingle recited it for her. He must be clever, Pat thought. Even Sid couldn't recite a long piece of poetry off by heart like that. And some of the lines thrilled her like a chord of music... *"gaily in the mountain glen,"*... *"distant bugles faintly ring."* But what did *"wakes the peasants' evening fears,"* mean? What *was* a peasant? Oh, just a farmer... *"wakes the farmer's evening fears..."* no, that was too funny. Better leave it peasant. She and Jingle had one of those chummy laughs that ripen friendship.

They sat on the hill, in the sweet, grass-scented air, and ate their cinnamon buns. Far down over the fields and groves they could see the blue plain of the gulf.

"There's a fairy diamond," cried Pat, pointing... that dazzling point of light sometimes seen for a moment in a distant field where a plough has turned up a bit of broken glass.

Jingle taught her how to suck honey out of clover horns. They found five little yellow flowers like stars by a flat lichened old stone and Jingle gloated over them through his absurd glasses. Pat was glad Jingle like flowers. Hardly any boys did. Joe and Sid thought they were all right... for girls.

McGinty lay with his head on Jingle's legs and his tail across Pat's bare knees. And then Jingle took a bit of birch bark from a fallen tree near them and, with the aid of a few timothy stems, made under her very eyes the most wonderful little house... rooms, porch, windows, chimneys, all complete. It was like magic.

"Oh, how do you do it?" breathed Pat.

"I'm always building houses," said Jingle dreamily, rolling McGinty over and clasping his hands around his sunburned knees. "In my head, I mean. I call them my dreamhouses. Some day when I'm grown up I'm going to build them really. I'll build one for *you*, Pat."

"Oh, will you really, Jingle?"

"Yes. I thought it out last Saturday night after I went to

bed. And I'll think of lots more things about it. It will be the loveliest house you ever saw, Pat, by the time I get it finished."

"It couldn't be lovelier than Silver Bush," cried Pat jealously.

"Silver Bush *is* lovely," admitted Jingle. "It satisfies me when I look at it. Hardly any other house does. When I look at a house I nearly always want to tear it down and build it right. But I wouldn't change Silver Bush a bit."

Canny Jingle! Pat never dreamed of doubting his opinions of houses after that.

McGinty turned over on his back and entreated some one to tickle his stomach.

"I wish Aunt Maria liked McGinty better," said Jingle. "She doesn't like him at all. I was afraid the day he chewed up one of her good table napkins she was going to send him away. But Uncle Lawrence said he could stay. Uncle Lawrence doesn't mind McGinty but he laughs at him and McGinty can't bear to be laughed at."

"Dogs don't," said Pat knowingly, out of her extensive acquaintance of three dogs.

"McGinty has to sleep in the straw shed at nights. He howled so the other night I went out and slept with him. *Mother* would let him sleep indoors and bring his bones in."

Pat's eyes grew big with surprise. Jingle's mother! Judy had called him an orphan. And hadn't he himself said he hadn't a friend in the world except McGinty?

"I thought your mother was . . . dead."

Jingle selected a timothy stalk and began to chew it with an affectation of indifference.

"No, my dad is dead. He died when I was a baby. Mother married again. They live in Honolulu."

"Don't you ever see her?" exclaimed Pat, to whom Honolulu meant simply nothing at all. But something in Jingle's tone made her feel as if it must be very far away.

"Not often," said Jingle, who could not bear to admit that he had no recollection of ever seeing his mother. "You see, her husband's health is bad and he can't stand the Canadian climate. But of course I write to her—every Sunday."

He did not tell Pat that the letters were never sent but kept in a careful bundle in the box under his bed. Perhaps some day he could give them to mother.

"Of course," agreed Pat, who had already accepted the situation with the unquestioning philosophy of eight. "What does she look like?"

"She . . . she's very pretty," said Jingle stoutly. "She . . . she has pale gold hair. . . and big blue, shining eyes . . . eyes as blue as that water out there."

"Like Winnie's," said Pat, understandingly.

"I wish she didn't have to live so far away," said Jingle chokingly. He choked so valiantly that he choked something down. When you were a big boy of ten you simply mustn't cry. . . anyway, not before a girl.

Pat said nothing. She just put her skinny little paw on his and squeezed it. Pat, even at eight, had all the wisdom of the world.

They sat there until the air grew cool and faint blue shadows fell over far-away hills beyond which neither of them had ever been, and little shivers ran over the silver-green water of the Haunted Spring. To other people this might just be Larry Gordon's back field. To Pat and Jingle it was, from that day, forever fairyland.

"Let's name this place, too," said Jingle. "Let's call it Happiness. And let's keep it a secret."

"I love secrets," said Pat. "It's nice to have them. This has been a lovely afternoon."

3

They were late for supper when they got back, but Judy fed them with fried ham and corn-cake in the kitchen. After Jingle and McGinty had gone Judy asked Pat how she and her boy-friend had got on. Boy-friend was not so insulting as beau. Pat, hauling in a big word to impress Judy, condescended to remark haughtily,

"We entertained each other very well."

"Oh, oh, I'm not doubting it. Sure and ye've picked a pretty good one for yer first. Ye can see there's brading behind him."

Judy was always strong on breeding.

"He's dreadful awkward, Judy." Pat thought if she criticised him she might convince Judy there was nothing in this beau business. "Didn't you see how he run into the door when he was coming out of the dining-room and begged its pardon?"

"Oh, oh, that's why I'm saying he's a gintleman. Wud inny one else have begged a dure's pardon?"

"But he was so stupid he thought it was a person he'd run into."

"Oh, oh, he isn't that stupid. No, no, me jewel, he's nobody's fool, that lad. And he's rale mannerly. He et his broth widout trying to swally the spoon and it's meself has niver been able to tache Siddy that yet."

"But he's not a bit nice-looking, Judy... not like Sid."

"Oh, oh, I'm owning thim glasses av his do be giving him a quare look. And a shears-and-basin cut av hair niver improved inny one. But did ye be noticing how nice his ears were set against his head? And handsome is as handsome does. Remimber that, Miss Pat, whin ye be come to picking a man in earnest. He's a bit thin and gangling but thim kind fills out whin they get older. Ye can tell be the look av him that he doesn't be getting half enough to ate. Be sure ye ask him in for a male whiniver ye dacently can. They do be saying his mother neglicts him tarrible, she's so taken up wid her fine new man."

"Did you ever see her, Judy?"

"Niver... and no one else round here. Jim Gordon married her out av Novy Scotia and they lived there. He did be dying just after the baby was born and his lady widow didn't be wearing her weeds long. She married her second whin this Jingle-lad was no more'n two and wint away to foreign parts and left the baby wid his uncle Larry. Jim Gordon was as nice a feller as iver stepped, aven if he did be always trying to make soup in a sieve. I'm thinking he'd turn over in his grave if he knew that Larry had the bringing-up av his b'y. Larry do be taking after his mother. His father was the gay lad wid a flattering tongue. He cudn't spake widout paying ye a compliment. But he was whispered to death."

"*Whispered* to death, Judy?"

"I'm telling ye. He bruk a poor girl's heart and she died. But her voice was always at his ear after that... she whispered him to death for all av his fine new bride. Ye shud av seen him in church wid his head hanging down, hearing something that all the praching and singing cudn't drown. Oh, oh, 'tis an ould story now and better forgotten. There do be few fam'lies that haven't a skiliton in some av their closets. There was

Solomon Gardiner over at South Glen . . . the man who swore at God."

"What happened to him?"

"Nothing."

"Nothing?"

"Just that. Nothing iver happened to him agin. The Good Man Above just left him alone. Oh, oh, but it was hard on the family. Come and hilp me in wid the turkeys now. But what's troubling ye, darlint?"

"I'm afraid, Judy . . . perhaps Jingle has a flattering tongue, too. He said . . . he said . . ."

"Out wid it."

"He said I had the prettiest eyes he ever saw."

Judy chuckled.

"Sure and there's no great flattery in that. And to think av him that shy at dinner ye wud be thinking he cudn't say bo to a goose. There's a bit av Irish in the Gordons be token of their old lady grandmother."

"Do *you* think I have pretty eyes, Judy?" It was the first time Pat had ever thought about her eyes.

"Ye have the Selby eyes and Winnie has the Gardiner eyes and they'll both pass wid a shove. But niver be minding yer eyes for minny a year yet and don't be belaving all the b'ys say to ye, me jewel. Remimber compliments cost thim nothing."

When Judy's fine flock of white turkeys had been shooed off the grave-yard fence and into their house Sid had arrived home in Uncle Brian's car. He had to be told about Jingle and took it quite easily . . . to Pat's relief and something that was not relief. She almost wished he had taken it a little harder. Didn't he *care*?

"He needs a friend so much," she explained. "I've got three brothers now. But of course I'll always love you best, Siddy."

"You'd better, old girl," said Sid. "If you don't I'll like May Binnie better'n you."

"Of course I couldn't love anybody better than my own family," said Pat, still wistfully.

But Sid ran in to coax a snack out of Judy Plum. He was in high spirits for he had just discovered a new wart on his left hand. That meant he was ahead of Sam Binnie at last. They had been ties for quite a time.

Pat crept a bit lonesomely up the back stairs and sat down by the round window. The little pearly pool over in the field was mirroring black spruce trees against a red sunset. For a moment the windows of the Long Lonely House were ablaze... then went sorrowfully out. There was not even a kitten to be seen in the yard. Oh, if Sid had just been a *little* jealous of Jingle! She knew how *she* would feel if he had made a chum of any girl but her. Suppose he should ever like May Binnie better... hateful May Binnie with her bold black eyes. For a moment she almost hated herself for liking Jingle.

Then she thought of Happiness and the water laughing down the stones in that secret place.

"Jingle likes my eyes," thought Pat. "Friends *are* nice."

CHAPTER XII

Black Magic

1

It was in the last week of October that McGinty disappeared. Pat was just as heart-broken as Jingle. It seemed now that Jingle and McGinty had been always part of her life... as if there could never have been a time when they did not come over Jordan every Saturday afternoon or slip into Judy's kitchen in the chill "dims" for an evening of fun and laughter. To Jingle, who had never known a real home, these evenings were wonderful... little glimpses into another world.

The only fly in Pat's ointment was that Sid and Jingle didn't hit it off very well. Not that they disliked each other; they simply did not speak the same language. Had they been older they might have said they bored each other. Sid thought Jingle a queer, moony fellow with his dream houses and his dark glasses and his ragged clothes, and said so. Jingle thought Sid had a bit too high an opinion of himself, even for a Gardiner of Silver Bush, and did not say so. Thus it came about that Pat and Sid played and prowled together after school, but Saturday afternoons, when Sid wanted to be off with Joe at the farm work, she gave to Jingle. For the most they spent them in Happiness and Jingle built no end of houses and had a new idea every week for the house he was going to build for Pat. Pat was interested in it although of course she would never live anywhere but at Silver Bush. They explored woodland and barrens and stream but Pat never took Jingle to the Secret Field. *That* was her and Sid's secret just as Happiness was hers and Jingle's. Pat hugged herself in delight. Secrets were such lovely things. She used to sit in church and pity the people who didn't know anything about the Secret Field and Happiness.

McGinty went everywhere with them and was the happiest little dog in the world. And then... there was no McGinty.

Pat found Jingle in Happiness one afternoon, face downwards amid the frosted ferns, sobbing as if his heart would break. Pat herself had been feeling a good deal like crying. For one thing, that hateful May Binnie had given Sid an apple in school the day before... a wonderful apple with Sid's initials and her own... such cheek!... in pale green on its red side. May had pasted the letters over the apple weeks before and this was the result. Sid was quite tickled over it but Pat would have hurled the apple into the stove if she had dared. Sid put it on the dining-room mantel and she had to look at it during every meal. Then, too, Sid had been cross with her that morning because it had rained the day before.

"You prayed for rain Thursday night... I heard you," he reproached her. "And you *knew* I wanted Friday to be fine."

"No, I didn't, Siddy," wailed Pat. "I heard dad saying the springs were so low... and the one in Hap... the one that Jordan comes from is. That was why I prayed for rain. I'm sorry, Siddy."

"Don't call me Siddy," retorted Sid, who seemed full of grievances just then. "You know I hate it."

"I won't, ever again," promised Pat. "Please don't be mad at me, Siddy... Sid, I mean. I just can't bear it."

"Well, don't be a baby then. You're worse than Cuddles," said Sid. But he gave her a careless hug and Pat was partially comforted. Only partially. She set off for Happiness rather dolefully but the sight of Jingle's distress drove all thoughts of her own troubles from her mind.

"Oh, Jingle, what's the matter?"

"McGinty's gone," said Jingle, sitting up.

"Gone?"

"Gone... or lost. He went with me to the store at Silverbridge last night and he... he disappeared. I couldn't find him anywhere. Oh, Pat!"

Jingle's head went down again. He didn't care who saw him cry. Pat mingled her tears with his but assured him that McGinty would be found... must be found.

Followed a terrible week. No trace of McGinty could be discovered. Judy was of opinion that the dog had been stolen. Jingle put up a notice in the stores offering a reward of twenty-five cents... all he had in the world... for the recovery of McGinty. Pat wanted to make it forty-five cents... she had a dime and was sure she could borrow another from Judy. But Jingle wouldn't let her. Pat prayed every bed-time that McGinty might be found and sat up in the middle of the night to pray again.

"Dear God, please bring McGinty back to Jingle. *Please,* dear God. You know he's all Jingle's got with his mother so far away."

And everything was in vain. There was no trace of McGinty. Jingle went home every night with no little golden-brown comrade running through the yard to meet him. He could not sleep, picturing a little lost dog alone in the world on a bleak autumn night. Where was McGinty? Was he cold and lonely? Maybe he wasn't getting enough... or anything... to eat.

"Judy, can't you do something?" begged Pat desperately. "You've always said there was a bit of a witch in you. You said once your grandmother could turn herself into a cat whenever she wanted to. Can't you find McGinty?"

Judy—who had, however, decided that something must be done before Pat worried herself to death... shook her head.

"I've been trying, me jewel, but I know whin I'm bate. If I had me grandmother's magic book I might manage it. But there it is. My advice to ye is to go and see Mary Ann McClenahan on the Silverbridge road. She's a witch in good standing I belave, though I'm telling the world she do be a bit hefty for a broomstick. If she can't hilp ye I don't know av inny that can."

Pat had been compelled to give up believing in fairies

but she still had an open mind towards witches. They had certainly existed once. The Bible said so. And you couldn't get away from the fact that Judy's grandmother had been one.

"Are you sure Mary Anne McClenahan is a witch, Judy?"

"Oh, oh, she always knows what ye do be thinking av. That shows she's a witch."

Pat ran to tell Jingle. She found him standing on the stone bridge over Jordan, scowling viciously at the sky and shaking his fist at it.

"Jingle . . . you're not . . . praying that way?"

"No, I was just telling God what I thought of the whole business," said Jingle despairingly.

But he agreed to go the next evening to Mary Ann McClenahan's. They asked Sid to go, too . . . the more the safer . . . but Sid was training a young owl he had caught in the silver bush and declined to have any truck with witches. They started off staunchly, although Joe, going off to plough the Mince Pie field, with a delightful jingle of chains about his horses, solemnly warned them to watch out.

"Old Mary Ann signed her name in the devil's book you know. *I'd* jump out of my skin if she looked cross-wise at me."

Pat was not easily frightened and remained in her skin. If God, seemingly, wouldn't pay any attention to your desperate little prayers could you be blamed if you resorted to a witch?

"Mind ye're home afore dark," cautioned Judy. "Sure and 'tis Hollow Eve this blessed night and all the dead folks will be walking. Ye just do be telling Mary Ann yer story straight out and do as she bids ye."

Jingle and Pat went down the lane where the wind blew the shadows of bare birches about and waves of dead leaves lay along under the spruce hedges. The late autumn sunshine flowed goldenly about them. The Hill of the Mist wore a faint purple scarf. Pat had on her new scarlet tam and was pleasantly conscious of it, amid all her anxieties about McGinty. Jingle strode along, his hands in his ragged pockets, and his still raggeder trousers flapping about his bare legs. Pat had never been out on the main road with him in broad daylight before. In Happiness and along the kinks of Jordan it did not matter how he was dressed. But here . . . well, she hoped none of the Binnies would be abroad, that was all.

2

Mrs. McClenahan's little, white-washed house with its bright blue door was a good two miles from Silver Bush, along the Silverbridge road. A huge willow, from which a few forlorn, pale-yellow leaves were fluttering down on the grey roof, overshadowed it, and there was a quaint little dormer window over the door.

"Oh, Pat, look at that window," whispered Jingle, forgetting even McGinty in his momentary ecstasy. "I never saw such a lovely window. I'll put one like that in *your* house."

The window might be all right but the paling was very ragged and the yard it enclosed was a jungle of burdocks. Pat reflected that being a witch didn't seem like a very profitable business after all. She thought shrewdly that if *she* had ever signed her name in the devil's book she would have made a better bargain than that.

Jingle knocked on the blue door. Presently steps sounded inside. A prickly sensation went over Pat. Perhaps after all it was not right to tamper with the powers of darkness. Then the door opened and Mary Ann McClenahan stood on the threshold, looking down at them out of tiny black eyes, surrounded by cushions of fat. Her untidy hair was black too, coal-black, although she must be as old as Judy. Altogether she looked much too plump and jolly for a witch and Pat's terror passed away.

"Now who may ye be and what might ye be wanting wid me," said Mrs. McClenahan with an accent three times as strong as Judy's.

Pat had the Selby trick of never wasting words or breath or time.

"Hilary Gordon here has lost his dog and Judy said if we came to you perhaps you could find it for him. That is, if you really are a witch. Are you?"

Mary Ann McClenahan's look at once grew secretive and mysterious.

"Whisht, child . . . don't be talking av witches in the open daylight like this. Little ye know what might happen. And finding a lost cratur isn't something to be done on a durestep. Come inside . . . and at that ye'd better come up to the loft where I can go on wid me waving. I'm waving a table-

cloth for the fairies up there. All the witches in P. E. Island
promised to do one apiece for thim. The poor liddle shiftless
craturs left all ther tablecloths out in the frost last Tuesday
night and 'twas the ruination av thim."

They went up the narrow stairs to a cluttered loft where
Mrs. McClenahan's loom stood by the window that had
caught Jingle's eye. On the sill a perfectly clean black cat was
licking himself all over to make himself cleaner. His big,
yellow, black-rimmed eyes shone rather uncannily in the
gloom of the loft. In spite of his being a witch's cat Pat liked
the look of him. What she would have felt like had she known
that he was her lost and deplored Sunday, given to Mary Ann
McClenahan by Judy a year before I cannot tell you. Luckily
Sunday had grown out of all recognition.

Mrs. McClenahan pushed a stool and a rickety chair
towards the children and went back to her weaving.

"Sure and I can't be wasting a moment. It's the quane's
own cloth I'm waving and sour enough her Majesty'll look if
it's not finished on time."

Pat knew very well it was only a flannel blanket Mary
Ann was weaving but she was not going to contradict a witch.
Besides... perhaps Mary Ann *did* turn it into a gossamer
web when she had finished it... one of those things of
jewelled mist and loveliness you saw on the grass and on the
fern beds along the woods on a summer morning.

"So ye've come to get me to find the b'y's McGinty," said
Mary Ann. "Oh, I know the name... I'm after knowing all
about it. Yer Aunt Edith's cat was telling mine the whole
story at the last dance we had. Yer Aunt Edith do be too
grand for the likes av us but it's liddle she thinks where her
cat do be going be spells. It's lucky ye come in the right time
av the moon. I cudn't have done a thing for ye nixt wake. But
now there's maybe just a chanct. Why doesn't that fine lady
mother av yours iver be coming to see ye, young Hilary
Gordon?"

Jingle thought witches were rather impertinent. However, if you dealt with them...

"My mother lives too far away to come often," he
explained politely.

Mary Ann McClenahan shrugged her fat shoulders.

"Ye're in the right to make excuses for her, young Hilary,
but I've me own opinion av her and ye nadn't get mad at me

for saying so bekase a witch doesn't have to care who gets mad. And now that I've got that off me chist I'll be thinking av yer dog. It'll take a bit av conniving."

Mrs. McClenahan leaned over and extracted two handfuls of raisins from a paper bag on a shelf.

"Here, stow these away in yer liddle insides whilst I do a bit av thinking."

There was silence for awhile. The children devoted themselves to the business of eating and watching Mrs. McClenahan's shuttle fly back and forth. Pat eyed her wonderingly. Had she really signed her name in the devil's big black book, as Joe said?

Presently Mrs. McClenahan caught her eye and nodded.

"Ye've got a liddle mole on yer neck. Sure and 'tis the witch's mark. Come now, child dear, wudn't ye like to be a witch? Think av the fun av riding on a broomstick."

Pat *had* thought of it. The idea had a charm. Though she would have preferred to fly on a swallow's back, skimming over the steeples and dark spruce woods at night. But...

"Must I sign my name in the devil's book?" she whispered.

Mrs. McClenahan nodded solemnly.

"I'd pick out a rale nice shiny black divil for ye . . . though mind ye, it's the fact that aven divils are not what they used to be."

"I think I'm too young to be a witch, thank you," said Pat decidedly.

Mrs. McClenahan chuckled.

"Sure and it's the young witches that do be having the power, child dear. No sinse in waiting till ye're grey as an owl. Think it over . . . 'tisn't ivery one can be a witch . . . we're that exclusive ye'd niver belave. As for this McGinty cratur. Whin ye lave here folly yer noses up the hill and turn yerselves around t'ree times, north, south, east and west. Then go down the hill to Silverbridge. There's a house just foreninst the bridge wid a rid door like yer Uncle Tom's, only faded like. Turn yerselves about t'ree times again and knock twict on the door. And if inny one comes . . . mind I'm not saying inny one will . . . cross yer fingers and ask, 'Is McGinty here?' Thin, if ye get McGinty . . . mind I'm not saying ye will . . . make a good use av yer legs and ask no questions. That's all I can be doing for ye."

"And what is your charge for the advice?" asked Jingle gravely, producing his quarter.

"Sure and we can't charge folks wid moles innything. It's clane aginst our rules."

"Thank you very much, Mrs. McClenahan," said Pat. "We're very much obliged to you."

"You do be a pair av mannerly children at that," said Mrs. McClenahan. "If you hadn't been it wudn't be Mary Ann McClenahan that wud have hilped ye to a dog. I'm that fed up wid the sass and impidence av most av the fry around here. It was diffrunt whin I was young. Now hurry along . . . sure and wise folks will be indures afore moonrise on Hollow Eve. Don't forget the turning round part or ye may look for yer McGinty till the eyes fall out av yer heads."

Mrs. McClenahan stood on her doorstep and watched them out of sight. Then she said a queer thing for a witch. She said,

"God bless the liddle craturs."

Whereat Mary Ann McClenahan waddled over to Mr. Alexander's across the road and asked if she might use their phone to call up a frind at the bridge, plaze and thank ye.

3

The October day was burning low behind the dark hills when Pat and Jingle left Mrs. McClenahan's. When they reached the top of the hill they turned themselves around three times and bowed gravely to north, south, east and west. When they paused before the red-doored house at Silverbridge they turned three times again. If there were no McGinty at the end of the quest it should be through no failure of theirs to perform Witch McClenahan's ritual scrupulously.

When Jingle knocked twice the door was opened with uncanny suddenness and the doorway filled by a giant of a man in sock feet, with a bushy red head and a week's growth of red whisker. A very strong whiff floated out, reminding Pat of something Judy took out of a black bottle now and again in winter for a cold.

They both crossed their fingers and Jingle said hoarsely, "Is McGinty here?"

The man turned and opened a mean little door at his right. Inside, on a rickety chair, sat McGinty. The look of misery in the poor dog's eyes changed to rapture. With one bound he was in Jingle's arms.

"He come here one night about a wake ago," said the man. "That cold and hungry he was . . . and we tuk him in."

"That was real good of you," said Pat, since Jingle was temporarily bereft of speech.

"Wasn't it that now?" said the man with a grin.

Something about him made Pat remember Witch Mc-Clenahan's advice to make friends of their legs.

"Thank you very much," she said, and pulled the tranced Jingle by the arm.

The red door was shut . . . the red moon was staring at them just over a hill between two tall firs . . . and they had a dog that was nearly dying of happiness in their arms.

What a walk home that was! The whole world was touched with wonder. They went straight over the fields in a cross-country cut, with their long shadows running before them. Jingle walked in a kind of dreamy rapture, hugging McGinty, but Pat had eyes for all the charm of bare, lonely stubble fields, woods where boughs darkled against a sky washed white in moonlight and of a wind that had been only a whisper when they had left home but was now wild, cold, and rustly, sweeping up from the sea. They passed through Happiness where all the little cradle hills were sound asleep and along Jordan. Then down through the silver bush on a path that wound through moonlit birches to the back-yard of home, where Sid had decorated the gateposts with wonderful turnip lanterns and Judy had set her little copper candlestick, saucer-shaped with a curly handle, on the window-sill for welcome, and they had smelt her salt pork frying half way through the bush. Then the warm kitchen, full of delicious smells, and Judy's delight and welcome, and the supper of fried salt pork and potatoes baked in their jackets. Just the three of them. Sidney and Joe were doing the barn chores. Winnie was off with a chum, mother was upstairs with Cuddles, and dad was snoozing on the dining-room lounge.

After supper Pat and Jingle went down into the big, mysterious cellar, spooky with giant shadows, for apples, and then they all sat around the stove that was as good as a fireplace, with its doors that slid so far back, and talked things over. It was lovely to sit there, so cosy and warm, with that eerie wind moaning without . . . full of the voices of ghosts,

Judy said, for this was Hallow E'en. McGinty sprawled out on the black cat rug, his eyes fixed on Jingle, evidently afraid to go to sleep for fear he might waken to find this all a dream. Thursday, who had been missing for a day or two, had turned up, a fat and flourishing prodigal, and Gentleman Tom sat on the bench, thinking. Like Puck of Pook's Hill, Gentleman Tom could have sat a century, just thinking.

"I'm so glad it's got cold enough to have a fire in the evenings," said Pat. "And in winter it'll be even nicer. One can be so *cosy* in winter."

Jingle said nothing. His idea of winter evenings was very different. A cold, dirty kitchen ... a smoking coal oil lamp ... a bed in the unfinished loft. But just now he had his dog back and he was perfectly happy. To sit here and munch apples with Pat while Judy thumped and kneaded her bread was all he asked.

"Oh, oh, she isn't called a witch for nothing, that one," said Judy, when she had heard the whole tale. "I used to be after knowing the McClenahans rale well years ago. Tom McClenahan was a dacent soul although he'd talk the hind-leg off a cat whin he got started. A tarrible talker, I'm telling ye. Onct he got mad whin Mary Ann twitted him wid his good going tongue, and swore he wudn't spake a word for a month. He kept the vow two days but he was niver the same man agin. The strain was too much for him. Mary Ann always belaved it was why he dropped dead in about a year's time. He was a fine fiddler in his day and he had a fiddle that cud make iverybody dance."

"*Make* them dance, Judy?"

"I'm telling ye. Whin folks heard it they *had* to dance. It was an ould fiddle his dad brought out from Ireland. Sure and he tried it on a minister onct, the spalpane."

"Did the minister dance?"

"Didn't he that? It made a tarrible scandal. They had him up afore Presbytery. Tom offered to go and fiddle to the whole lot av thim to prove poor Mr. MacPhee cudn't hilp it, but they wudn't have him. A pity now. Think what a sight it wud av been ... a dozen or more long-tailed ministers all dancing to Tom McClenahan's fiddle. Oh, oh! But they let Mr. MacPhee off and hushed the whole thing up. Is it going ye are, Jingle? Well, say a prayer for all poor ghosts and have as liddle truck wid witches as ye can after this. All very well for onct in a while but not to make a habit av it."

Jingle slipped away, meaning to spend the night in the Gordon hayloft with McGinty, and sleepy Pat went happily to bed.

"Why do you fill those children up with all that nonsense about witches, Judy?" called Long Alec, half laughing, half rebuking, from the dining room. He had been rated that day by Edith for allowing Judy Plum to stuff his children with such lies as she did and felt it was time for one of his spasmodic attempts to regulate her.

Judy chuckled.

"Rest ye aisy, Alec Gardiner. They only half belave it and they do be getting a big kick out av it. I'll warrant Mary Ann had her fun wid them."

"What made you think of sending them to her?"

"Sure now I'd an idea she'd know where McGinty was. She'd in wid that gang at Silverbridge that stole Rob Clark's collie and all Mrs. Taylor's barred rocks wake afore last and thim all ready for market. Mary Ann's be way uv being an aunt be marriage to Tom Cudahy av the rid door. But she's that kind-hearted, the cratur, and rale soft about children and I thought she might hilp. She's got a bit av money saved up and the Cudahys pipe whin she calls the tune. So all's well that inds well and niver be bothering if the children do be having a liddle fun thinking she's a witch. Sure and didn't I bring all of yes up on witches and are ye inny the worse av it? I'm asking ye."

CHAPTER XIII
Company Manners

1

WINTER that year, at least in its early months, was a mild affair, and Pat and Jingle, or Pat and Sid, as the case might be, but seldom the three together, roamed far afield at will, exploring new haunts and re-loving old ones, running through winter birches that wore stars in their hair on early falling dusks, coming in from their frosty rambles with cheeks like "liddle rid apples," to be fed and cossetted and sometimes scolded by Judy. At least, she scolded Sid and Pat when she thought they needed it for their souls' good, but she never scolded Jingle. He wished she would. He thought it would be nice if some one cared enough about you to scold . . . in Judy's way, with sly laughter lurking behind every word and apples and cinnamon buns to bind up your bruised feelings immediately afterwards. Even his aunt did not scold him . . . she merely ignored him as if he had no existence for her at all. Jingle used to go home after one of Judy's tirades feeling very lonely and wondering what it would be like to be important to somebody.

Though snowless, it was cold enough to freeze the Pool solid. Sid taught Pat to skate and Jingle learned for himself, with a pair of old skates Judy dug out of the attic for him. Jingle skating, his long legs clad as usual in ragged trousers, his lanky body encased in an old "yallery-green" sweater whose sleeves his aunt had darned with red, his ill-cut hair sticking out from under an old cap of his uncle's, was rather an odd object.

"Isn't he a sight?" laughed Sid.

"He can't help his looks," said Pat loyally.

"Oh, oh, that b'y will be having the fine figure whin he's filled out a bit and he's got more brains in his liddle finger than ye have in your whole carcase, Sid, me handsome lad," said Judy.

And then unreasonable Pat was furious with Judy for maligning Sid.

"Sure and it's the hard life I have among ye all," sighed Judy. "Be times I'm thinking I'd better have taken ould Tom. Well, they tell me he's single yet."

Whereupon Pat dissolved in tears and begged Judy to forgive her and never, never leave them.

Although once in a while a few delicate white flakes flew against your face in the late afternoons, it was December before the first real snow came, just in time to make a white world for Christmas, much to Judy's relief, since a green Christmas meant a fat grave-yard, she said. Pat sat curled up at her round window and watched gardens and fields and hills grow white under the mysterious veil of the falling snow, and the little empty nests in the maple by the well fill up with it. Every time she looked out the world had grown whiter.

"I love a snowstorm," she said rapturously to Judy.

"Oh, oh, is there innything ye don't love, me jewel?"

"It's nice to love things, Judy."

"If ye don't be loving thim too hard. If ye do... they hurt ye too much in the ind."

"Not Silver Bush. Silver Bush will never hurt me, Judy."

"What about whin ye have to lave it?"

"You know I'm never going to leave Silver Bush, Judy... never. Oh, Judy, see how white the Hill of the Mist is. And how lonesome the Long Lonely House looks. I wish I could go and build a fire in it sometimes and warm it up. It would feel better."

"Oh, oh, ye're not thinking houses raly fale, are ye now?"

"Oh, Judy, I'm *sure* they do. Jingle says so, too. I know Silver Bush does. It's glad when we are and sorry when we are. And if it was left without any one to live in it it would break its heart. I know Silver Bush has always been a little ashamed of me because I could never get up in school Friday afternoons and say a piece like the others. And then last Friday I did. I learned the *Haunted Spring* from Jingle and I got up on the floor... oh, Judy, it was awful. My legs shook so... and May Binnie giggled... and I couldn't get a word out. I was just going to run back to my seat... and I thought of Silver Bush and how could I come home and face it if I was such a coward. And I just up and said my piece right out and Miss Derry said, 'Well done, Patricia,' and the scholars all clapped. And when I came home I'm sure Silver Bush smiled at me."

"Ye're a quare child enough yet," said Judy. "But I'm glad ye didn't let May Binnie triumph over ye. That's a liddle girl I'm not liking much and I don't care who knows it."

"Sid likes her," said Pat, a bit forlornly.

2

Soon Silver Bush became a house full of secrets. Mystery lurked everywhere and Judy went about looking like a bobbed Sphinx. Pat helped her make the pudding and helped Winnie and mother decorate the dining room and wreathe the banisters with greenery from the woods around the Secret Field. And she helped Sid pick his presents in the Silverbridge store for every one but her. She did not feel hurt when he slipped off upstairs in the store to the room where the dishes were kept and she did not ask him what the bulging parcel in his pocket was as they went home. She only wondered a bit dismally whether it was for her or May Binnie.

It was such fun wading home from the mail-box with armfuls of brown parcels that were not to be opened until Christmas morning and then revealed lovely boxes of silver paper tied with gold ribbons. Christmas itself was a wonderful day. Jingle and McGinty came for dinner. They had had a narrow escape from not coming. Pat was so mad because Judy told her to be sure and ask her beau that she wouldn't say a word to Jingle about it until the very "dim" of Christmas Eve. Then she suddenly relented and tore off to the garret to set a candle in the window. There was no telephone at the Gordon place and she and Jingle had agreed that when she wanted him specially she was to set a light in the garret window. Jingle arrived speedily and so got his Christmas invitation by the skin of his teeth.

It was the first time in his life that Jingle had had a real Christmas and McGinty nearly died of the dinner he ate. Everybody got presents . . . even Jingle. Judy gave him a pair of mittens and Pat gave him a little white china dog with blue eyes and a pink china ribbon around its neck . . . the best she could afford after all the family had been remembered out of her small hoard. Nobody knew what earthly use it could be to Jingle but he slept with it under his pillow that night and got more warmth from it than from Judy's mittens. His mother had not sent him anything . . . not even a letter. It took all the comfort Jingle got out of the blue-eyed dog to keep back the tears when he remembered this. He tried to make excuses for her. Perhaps in Honolulu, that land of eternal summer, they didn't have Christmases.

Sidney gave Pat a jug with a golden lining . . . a little fat brown jug that seemed somehow to have grown fat from laughing. Pat loved it but she thought Jingle's present the most wonderful thing she got. A doll's house which he had made himself and which was really a much more wonderful bit of work than Pat had any idea of. Long Alec whistled when he saw it and Uncle Tom said, "By ginger!"

"I hadn't any money to buy you a present," said Jingle, who had spent his solitary, long-saved quarter on a Christmas card for his mother, "so I made this."

"I like something that's made better than something that's bought," said Pat. "Oh, what chimneys . . . and real windows that *open*."

"That's nothing to the house I'll build for you some day, Pat."

Christmas Day was just like all the pleasant Christmases at Silver Bush. The only exciting thing was a terrible fight all over the kitchen between Gentleman Tom and Snooks, the pet owl. Snooks was quite a family pet by now. He endured and was endured by Thursday and Snicklefritz but he and Gentleman Tom had declared war on each other at sight. Gentleman Tom was licked and fled into ignominious retreat under the stove: but there were a good many feathers strewn over the kitchen floor first.

One night the following week Pat excitedly called out to Judy,

"Oh, Judy . . . Judy . . . I've got a growing pain!"

She had never had growing pains and both she and Judy were afraid she wouldn't grow properly. Long Alec talked worriedly of rheumatism but Judy laughed at him and sat up half the night rubbing Pat's legs joyously.

"Ye'll be taking a start this spring and growing like a weed after this," she promised Pat. "Sure and it's a rale relief to me mind, I'm telling ye. I'm not wanting inny sawed-off girls at Silver Bush."

3

After Christmas the snow went away and the January winds whined over cold, hard-frozen pastures and through grey, cold trees. Only the red edges of the furrows in the Mince Pie field had little feathers of white on them and a persistent wreath lay along the north side of the Hill of the Mist.

January evenings were pleasant at Silver Bush. Uncle Tom would come over and he and dad would sit by Judy's

stove and talk, while Pat and Jingle and Sidney listened and
Winnie and Joe studied their lessons in the dining room.
They would talk of politics and pigs and finally drift into
family histories and community tales. The white-washed walls
of the old kitchen re-echoed to their laughter. Sometimes
Uncle Tom got mad and the shadow of his big beard would
quiver with indignation on the wall. But Uncle Tom's rages
never lasted long. One thump of his fist on the table and all
was well again.

Sometimes mother would come in with Cuddles and sit
for awhile just looking beautiful. Mother never talked much.
Perhaps she couldn't get a chance, what with Judy and dad
and Uncle Tom. But sometimes she looked at Pat and Sidney
and little Cuddles with eyes that made a lump come into
Jingle's throat. To have a mother look at you like that!

"Judy," Pat said after one of these evenings, when she
was sleeping with Judy because Winnie had a chum in. "I
don't see how heaven could be any better than this."

"Oh, oh, will ye listen at her?" said the scandalised Judy.
"Sure and do ye be thinking there'll be a biting wind like that
wailing around the windy in heaven?"

"Oh, I like that wind, Judy. It makes it seem cosier . . . to
cuddle here snug and warm and think it can't get at you.
Listen to it tearing down through the silver bush, Judy. Now
please, Judy, tell me a ghost story. It's so long since I've slept
with you . . . please, Judy. Something that'll just make the
flesh creep on my bones."

"Did I iver tell ye about how Janet McGuigan come back
for her widding ring the night after she was buried, her man
having tuk it off her finger afore they coffined her, thinking it
might come in handy for his second? Oh, oh, the McGuigans
do be that far-seeing."

"How did they know she came back for it?"

"I'm telling ye. The ring wasn't in Tom McGuigan's
cash-box the nixt morning. But six years afterwards whin he
tuk a plot in the new grave-yard they tuk up her coffin to shift
it and it bruk open . . . being an economical kind av coffin, ye
see . . . and there on her hand was the ring. Oh, oh, me
saving Tom was niver the same agin."

February and still no snow. Judy began to talk of getting
ready to hook a big crumb-cloth for the dining room, a bigger
one than Aunt Edith's of which she was so proud. "Oh, oh,

I'll be taking the pride av her down a peg or two," vowed Judy. Her dye-pot was always on the stove. She was an expert in home-made dyes. No "bought" dyes for Judy. They faded in a year, she averred. Crottle and lichens and barks... elderberries that gave purple dyes... the inner bark of birch trees for brown... green dye from willow stems... yellow from Lombardy poplars. Judy knew them all and she and the children tramped far afield searching for them.

And then came March, with its mad, galloping winds, and the anniversary of father's and mother's wedding day. The Gardiners always celebrated birthdays and wedding days by a little family gathering of some kind. This year Uncle Brian's family and Aunt Helen Taylor were the guests. They were to come in the afternoon and have dinner at night... an innovation that made Judy's head whirl.

"Oh, oh, this having company isn't what it's cracked up to be," she muttered discontentedly.

Pat was in her element, although she was not looking forward to the party quite as joyously as usual. Uncle Brian was no friend of hers because whenever he came to Silver Bush he was always saying to father, "If I were you I'd make some changes here." And Aunt Helen was coming... rich Aunt Helen, dad's sister but so much older that she seemed more like his aunt than his sister. And Aunt Helen, Judy said, was coming to take either Winnie or Pat back to Summerside for a visit.

Pat hoped and prayed Aunt Helen wouldn't take her. She didn't want to leave Silver Bush... why, she had never slept out of it a night in her life. It would be terrible. But how happy it made her to do little, homely services for the dear house. To dust and polish and bake and run errands. To help get out mother's wedding set of fluted china with the gold pansy on the side of the cups and in the centre of the plates. She and Winnie were allowed to fix up the Poet's Room and make the bed a thing of beauty with a lace spread and cushions like flowers. Judy concocted and baked, and Cuddles tasted everything that came her way, including a frosty latch. After which she tasted no more of anything for a time but lived on malted milk.

When the feast day came Pat was careful to put on her blue georgette dress. She didn't like it as well as her red one but it was its turn and it mustn't be neglected. How she hoped Aunt Helen wouldn't choose her! It took all the fun out of the party for Pat. Suppose she pretended to be sick? No, Judy might give her castor oil, as she had done the last time Pat had a cold.

"Why don't you give me something out of your black bottle, Judy?" Pat had protested. "That smells nicer than castor oil."

"Oh, oh." Judy looked very sly. "'Tis too strong entirely for the likes av ye...."

"*What* is in that bottle, Judy?"

"Oh, oh, 'tis only last wake I was burying a cat that died av curiosity," retorted Judy. "Not another skelp out av ye and swally this tay-spoon at once."

Even Aunt Helen would be better than castor oil. But perhaps she would be sick and not able to come. Would it be wrong, Pat wondered, to pray that somebody might be sick... not very sick... just a little sick... just enough to make them not want to come out on a cold, blustery March day?

Pat wound a blue scarf around her head and she and Jingle climbed up into the hayloft of the church barn where they could watch for the arrivals through the oriel window, while McGinty hunted imaginary rats over the mow or lay before them and pretended to be dead when he thought himself neglected. Every car or buggy that drove up or down the road made Pat squirm with fear that it was Aunt Helen. She *did* come... in Uncle Brian's car and waddled up through the garden.

"She looks just like a jug," said Pat resentfully.

And Uncle Brian's Norma was with them. Pat had hoped Norma wouldn't come either. She didn't like her because Norma was reputed prettier than Winnie.

"*I* don't think she's half as pretty," she said.

"*You* look awful nice in that blue scarf, Pat," said Jingle admiringly.

Which would have been all right if he had stopped there. But he went on and said the thing that spoiled it all.

"Pat... when we grow up... will you be *my* girl?"

Pat, not at all realising that at nine she had just had what was practically her first proposal, went scarlet with anger.

"If you ever say anything like that to me again, Hilary

Gordon, I'll never speak to you as long as I live," she stormed.

"Oh, all right. I didn't mean to make you mad," said Jingle abjectly. "Don't you like me?"

"Of course I like you. But I'm *never* going to be *anybody's* girl."

Jingle looked so woebegone that it made Pat madder still . . . and cruel.

"If I was anybody's girl," she said distinctly, "he'd have to be good-looking."

Jingle took off his spectacles.

"Ain't I better looking now?" he demanded.

He *was*. Pat had never seen his eyes before. They were large and grey and steady with a twinkle somewhere behind their steadiness. But Pat was in no mood to admire.

"Not a great deal. Your hair is all raggedy and your mouth is too wide. Sid says it would take a foot-rule to measure it."

And Pat shook the dust of the hayloft from her feet and departed indignantly.

"Maybe she'll change her mind," said McGinty.

"She'll have to," said Jingle.

4

But the day continued to go criss-cross for Pat. She fell foul of Norma as soon as she went in. Norma was going about, tossing her famous red-gold curls, with her nose cocked up and her greenish-brown eyes full of contempt. "So *this* is Silver Bush," she said. "It's an awful old-fashioned place."

Again Pat crimsoned with wrath.

"Shutters give a house an *air*," she said.

"Oh, I don't mean the shutters. We've got shutters on our house, too . . . ever so much greener than yours. You should just see *our* house. You haven't a verandah . . . or even a garage."

"No. But we've got a grave-yard," said Pat triumphantly.

Norma was a bit floored. She couldn't deny the grave-yard.

"And you haven't got a Poet's room or a round window," went on Pat still more tauntingly. The mention of the window gave Norma an inspiration.

"You haven't *one* bay window," she cried. "Not one. We've got three . . . two in the living room and one in the dining room. A house without any bay window is just *funny*."

To hear Silver Bush called funny! Pat simply couldn't stand it. She slapped Norma's pink-and-white face . . . slapped it hard.

Then there was what Judy called a tommyshaw. Norma screamed and burst into tears. Mother was horrified . . . dad was shocked . . . or pretended to be. Judy came in and frog-marched Pat to the kitchen.

"A nice show ye've made av yerself!"

"I don't care . . . I don't care . . . I *won't* let her make fun of Silver Bush," sobbed Pat. "I'm glad I slapped her. You can scold me all you like. I'm *glad*."

"The timper av her!" said Judy. And then went up to her room and sat on her blue chest and laughed till she cried.

"Oh, oh, didn't me fine Miss Norma get her come-uppance for onct, wid her airs and graces and her slams about the house her father was brought up in!"

Pat was not allowed to have dinner in the dining room. For punishment she must eat in the kitchen. To be punished because she had stood up for Silver Bush. It was too much.

"I'd *rather* eat here with you, Judy, any time," she sobbed. "But it's my *feelings* that are hurt."

There was balm in Gilead. Aunt Helen was so shocked at Pat's behaviour that there was no question of inviting her to Summerside. Winnie went with her. Pat made her peace with the family . . . none of whom cared much for the spoiled Norma . . . and she and Sid and Judy picked the bones of the sacrificial turkeys before they went to bed, while Judy told them all about Norma's grandmother on the mother's side.

"Oh, oh, it's the quare one she was and the foolish things she wud be saying. Her poor husband was long in dying and she did be after grudging him ivery breath he drew. 'If he lives too long I'll niver get another man,' she sez to me, time and time again, mournful like. And nather she did. He hung on till he spiled her chances and it wasn't Judy Plum that was sorry for her, I'm telling ye."

CHAPTER XIV

The Shadow of Fear

1

No sooner had Winnie gone than winter came in a day. Pat's round window was thick furred with snow; the Whispering Lane was filled with huge drifts through which dad and Uncle Tom shovelled a fascinating narrow path until they met at the gate. The piles of stones in the Old Part of the orchard were marble pyramids. The Hill of the Mist shone like silver. The hill field was a dazzling white sheet. Even the stony field was beautiful. Pat remembered that the Secret Field must be lovely, with Wood Queen and Fern Princess standing guard. The grave-yard was filled almost to the level of the paling.

"Sure and aven Wild Dick wud find it hard to get out av that," said Judy, busy providing comforts for cold little creatures . . . cats and dogs and chickens and children.

Pat liked a big storm. Especially did she love to snuggle in warm, fluffy blankets and defy the great, dark, wintry night outside her cosy room, hugging her hot water bottle. A hot water bottle was such a nice thing. You kneaded your toes in it; when your feet were warm as warm could be you held it close in your arms: and finally you put it against the cold spot in your back. And the first thing you knew it was morning and the sun was shining through the drift . . . and the hot water bag was unpleasantly like a clammy dead rat just behind you.

It was rather nice, too, to have one's room all to oneself; still, she missed Winnie terribly . . . the blue laughter of her eyes . . . the silver music of her voice.

"Just two more weeks and Winnie'll be home," she counted exultantly.

It was in school that she heard it. Of course it was May Binnie who told her.

"So your Aunt Helen is going to adopt Winnie."

Pat stared at her.

"She isn't."

May giggled.

"Fancy your not knowing. Of course she is. It's a great thing for Winnie, ma says. And it might have been you if you hadn't slapped Norma's face."

Pat stood staring at May. Something had fallen over her spirit like the cold grey light that swept over the world before a snow squall in November. She was too chilled to resent the fact that Sid must have told May about her slapping Norma. There was no room for any but the one terrible thought. It was only afternoon recess but Pat rushed to the porch, snatched her hat and coat, and started home, stumbling wildly along the deep-rutted, drifted road. Oh, to get home to mother... mother now, not Judy. Judy did for little griefs but for this, only mother... to tell her his ghastly thing was not true... that nobody had ever thought of such a thing as Winnie going to live with Aunt Helen.

"Oh, oh, and what's bringing ye home so early?" cried Judy, as Pat stumbled, half-frozen, into the kitchen. "Ye've niver walked all that way in thim roads... and yer Uncle Tom was going for ye all in his fine new pung."

"Where's mother?" gasped Pat.

"Mother, is it? Sure yer dad and her is gone over to the Bay Shore. They phoned over that yer Aunt Frances was down with pewmony. Whativer is it that's the matter wid the child?"

But for the first time Pat had nothing to say to Judy. The question she had to ask could not be asked of Judy. Judy, rather huffed, let her alone, and Pat ranged the deserted house like a restless ghost. Oh, how empty it was! Nobody there... neither mother nor father nor Cuddles. Nor Winnie! And perhaps Winnie would never be back. Suppose her laugh would never be heard again at Silver Bush!

"Something's been happening in school," reflected Judy uneasily. "I'm hoping she didn't get into a ruckus wid her lady tacher. I niver cud be knowing what the trustees mint be hiring ould Arthur Saint's girl for a tacher, wid her hair the colour av a rid brick."

Pat could eat no supper. Bed-time came and still father and mother were not back. Pat cried herself to sleep. But she

awoke in the night...sat up...remembered sickeningly.
Everything was quiet. The wind had gone down and Silver
Bush was cracking in the frost. Through her window she
could see the faint light of stars over the dark fir trees that
grew along the dyke between the Silver Bush and Swallowfield Pastures. Pat found just then that things always seem
worse in the dark. She felt she could not live another minute
without knowing the truth.

Resolutely she got out of bed and lighted her candle.
Resolutely the small white figure marched down the silent
hall, past Joe's room and the Poet's room to father's and
mother's room. Yes, they were home, sound asleep. A fragrant adorable Cuddles was curled up in her little crib but for
the first time Pat did not gloat over her.

Long Alec and his tired wife, just fallen soundly asleep
after a cold drive over vile roads, were wakened to see a
desperate little face bending over them.

"Child, what's the matter? Are you sick?"

"Oh, dad, Aunt Helen isn't going to adopt Winnie? She
isn't, is she, dad?"

"Look here, Pat." Dad was stern. "Have you come here
and wakened your mother and me just to ask that?"

"Oh, dad, I *had* to know."

Mother understandingly put a slender hand on Pat's
shaking arm.

"Darling, she's not going to adopt her...but she may
keep her for awhile and send her to school. It would really be
a great thing for Winnie."

"Do you mean...Winnie wouldn't come back *here*?"

"It isn't settled yet. Aunt Helen only threw out a hint.
Of course Winnie'll be home *often...*."

2

The following week of dark, tortured days was the hardest
Pat had ever known in her life. She could not eat and the
sight of Winnie's vacant place at meals reduced her to tears.
Her family found it rather hard to make excuses for what they
thought was her unreasonable behaviour.

"Just humour her a liddle," pleaded Judy. "She's that
worked up and miserable she doesn't know which ind of her
is up. A bird cudn't be living on what she ates."

"You spoil her, Judy," said Long Alec severely. He was out of patience with Pat's moping.

"Iverybody do be the better for a bit av sp'iling now and thin," said Judy loyally. But she tried to bring Pat into a more reasonable frame of mind.

"Don't ye want Winnie to get an eddication?"

"She could get an education at home," sobbed Pat.

"Not much av a one. Oh, oh, I'd have ye know the Gardiners don't be like the Binnies. 'We're not going to eddicate Suzanne,' sez me Madam Binnie. 'Soon as she'd get through Quane's she'd marry and the money'd be wasted.' No, no, me jewel, the Gardiners are a differunt brade av cats. Winnie's thirteen. Sure and she'll soon be wanting to study for her intrance and who's ould Arthur Saint's daughter for that I'm asking ye? Ye'll niver convince me she knows a word av the Lating and French."

"English is good enough for anybody," protested Pat.

"Ye'll find it isn't good enough for Quane's," retorted Judy. "Winnie'd be able to go to the Summerside schools and yer Aunt Helen cud do more for her than yer dad iver can, wid his one small farm and the five av ye ating it up. Now, stop fretting, me jewel, and cut rags for me while I do a bit av hooking."

Then came the letter from Aunt Helen for dad. Pat, her hands locked behind her so that no one should see them trembling, stood mutely by while Long Alec deliberately tried on two pairs of spectacles, scrutinised the stamp, remarked that Helen had always been a pretty writer, hunted up a knife to slit the envelope... took out the letter. Outside in the yard somebody was laughing. How dared anybody laugh at such a moment?

"Helen says Brian is bringing Winnie home Saturday," he announced casually. "So I guess she's given up the notion of keeping her. I always thought she would. So that's that."

"Oh, I *must* be flying," thought Pat as she ran to tell Judy. Judy admitted satisfaction.

"It do be just as well I'm thinking. Helen was always a bit of a crank. And I'm not thinking it's a wise-like thing to break up a family inny sooner than nade be."

"Isn't a family one of the loveliest things in the world, Judy?" cried Pat. "And oh, look at Gentleman Tom. Isn't he sitting cute?"

"Oh, oh, it's the different looking girl ye are from the morning. Iverything plazes ye to-night, aven the way a poor cat arranges his hams," chuckled Judy, who was overjoyed to see her darling happy again.

Pat ran out in the twilight to tell the good news to the silver bush and the leafless maples. She looked with eyes of love at the old, snow-rooted house drawing its cloak of trees around it in the still mild winter evening. Even in winter Silver Bush was lovely because of what it sheltered and hoped for.

Then she ran back in and up to the garret to set a light for Jingle. Jingle had been her only comfort during the past dreadful week. Even Sid hadn't seemed to worry much whether Winnie came home or not. He hoped she would, of course, but he didn't lose sleep over it. Jingle had always assured Pat she would. Who, he thought, wouldn't come back to Silver Bush if she could? So now he came to share in Pat's joy. The two of them waded back along Jordan to Happiness; it was buried in snow but the Haunted Spring was still running freshly, hung about with jewels. How lovely the silvery world was . . . how lovely the white hills of snow! They did not get home till nearly eight and Judy scolded.

"I'm not having ye roaming off wid any Jingle if ye can't be home and to bed at the proper time."

"What is the proper time for going to bed, Judy?" laughed Pat. Every word was a laugh with Pat to-night. And oh, how good supper tasted!

"Sure now and ye're asking a question that's niver been answered," chuckled Judy.

Saturday came with more March wind and snow. Oh, it shouldn't storm the day Winnie was coming home. Perhaps Uncle Brian wouldn't bring her if it stormed. But in the late afternoon the sun came out below the storm cloud and made a dazzling fair world. The rooms of Silver Bush were all filled with a golden light from the clearing western sky. All the gardens and yards and orchards were pranked out with the exquisite shadows of leafless trees.

And then they came, right out of the heart of the wild winter sunset. Winnie was very glad Aunt Helen had decided not to keep her.

"She said I laughed too much and it got on her nerves," Winnie told Pat. "Besides, I put pepper in the potatoes instead of salt the day her maid was away... oh, by mistake of course. That settled it. She said I had the makings of a sloppy housekeeper."

"Silver Bush is *glad* to hear you laugh," whispered Pat, hugging her savagely.

The storm came up again in the night. Pat woke up and heard it... remembered that everything was all right and sank happily to sleep again. What difference now how much it stormed? All her dear ones were near her, safe under the same kindly roof. Dad and mother and little Cuddles... Joe and Sidney... Judy in her own eyrie, with her black Gentleman Tom curled up at her feet... Thursday and Snicklefritz behind the kitchen stove. And Winnie was home... home to stay!

CHAPTER XV

Elizabeth Happens

1

"I SMELL spring!" Pat cried rapturously, sniffing the air one day... the day she discovered the first tiny feathery green sprays of caraway along the borders of the Whispering Lane. That same night the frogs had begun to sing in the Field of the Pool. She and Jingle heard them when they were coming home in the "dim" from Happiness.

"I love frogs," said Pat.

Jingle wasn't sure he liked frogs. Their music was so sad and silver and far away it always made him think of his mother.

Never, Pat reflected, looking back over her long life of almost nine years, had there been such a lovely spring. Never had the long, rolling fields around Silver Bush been so green: never had the gay trills of song in the maple by the well been so sweet: never had there been such wonderful evenings full of the scent of lilacs: and never had there been anything so beautiful as the young wild cherry tree in Happiness or the little wild plum that hung over the fence in the Secret Field. She and Sid went back to pay a call on their field one Sunday afternoon, to see how it had got through the winter. It was always spring there before it was spring anywhere else. Their spruces tossed them an airy welcome and the wild plum was another lovely secret to be shared.

Everything was so *clean* in spring, Pat thought. No weeds... no long grass... no fallen leaves. And all over the house the wholesome smell of newly-cleaned rooms. For Judy and mother had been papering and scrubbing and washing and ironing and polishing for weeks. Pat and Winnie helped them in the evenings after school. It was lovely to make Silver Bush as beautiful as it could be made.

"Sure and I do be getting spring fever in me bones," said Judy one night. The next day she was down with flu; it ran through the whole family... lightly, with one exception. Pat had it hard... "as she do be having iverything, the poor darlint," thought Judy... and did not pick up rapidly. Aunt Helen came down unexpectedly one day and decreed that Pat needed a change. In the twinkling of an eye it was decided that Pat was to go to Elmwood for three weeks.

Pat didn't want to go. She had never been away from Silver Bush overnight and three weeks of nights seemed an eternity. But nobody paid any heed to her protestations and the dread morning came when father was to take her to Summerside. Jingle was over and they ate breakfast together, sitting on the sandstone steps, with the sun rising redly over the Hill of the Mist and the cherry trees along the dyke throwing sprays of pearly blossoms against the blue sky....

Pat was more resigned, having begun to thrill a little to the excitement about her. After all, it was nice to be quite important. Sid was blue... or envious... and Jingle was undoubtedly blue. Cuddles was crying because she had got it into her small golden head that something was going to happen to Pat. And Judy was warning her not to forget to write. Forget! Was it likely?

"And you must write me, Judy," said Pat anxiously.

"Oh, oh, I don't be much av a hand at writing letters," said Judy dubiously. The truth being that Judy hadn't written any kind of a letter for over twenty years. "I'm thinking ye'll have to depind on the rest av the folks for letters but sind me a scrape av the pin now and agin for all that."

Pat had put her three favourite dolls to bed in her doll house and got Judy to put it away for her in the blue chest. She had bid tearful farewells to every room in the house and every tree within calling distance and to her own face in the water of the well. Snicklefritz and McGinty and Thursday had been hugged and wept over. Then came the awful ordeal of saying good-bye to everybody. Judy's last glimpse of Pat was a rather tragic little face peering out of the back window of the car.

"Sure and this is going to be the lonesome place till she comes back," sighed Judy.

2

Pat had no sooner arrived at Elmwood than she wrote mother a pitiful letter entreating to be taken home. That first night at Elmwood was a rather dreadful one. The big, old-fashioned bed, with its tent canopy hung with yellowed net, was so huge she felt lost in it. And at home mother or Judy would be standing at the kitchen door calling everybody in out of the dark. "O . . . w!" Pat gave a smothered yelp of anguish at the thought. But . . .

"This is just a visit. I'll soon be home again . . . in just twenty-one days," she reminded herself bravely.

Her next letter to Judy was more cheerful. Pat had discovered that there were some pleasant things about visiting. Uncle Brian's house was quite near and Aunt Helen was surprisingly kind and nice in her own home. It was quite exciting to be taken down town every day and see all the entrancing things in the store windows. Sometimes Norma and Amy took her down Saturday evenings when the windows were lighted up and looked like fairyland, especially the druggist's, where there were such beautiful coloured bottles of blue and ruby and purple.

"Aunt Helen's house is very fine," wrote Pat, beginning also to discover that she liked writing letters. "It is much more splendid than the Bay Shore house. And Uncle Brian's is finer still. But I wouldn't let on to Norma that I thought it fine because she has always bragged so about it. She said to me, 'Isn't it handsomer than Silver Bush?' and I said, 'Yes, much handsomer but not half so lovely.'

"I like Uncle Brian better now. He shook hands with me

just as if I was grown up. Norma is as stuck-up as ever but Amy is nice. Aunt Helen has a plaster Paris dog on the dining-room mantel that looks just like Sam Binnie. Aunt Helen says all Amasa Taylor's apple trees were nawed to death by mice last winter. Oh, Judy, I hope our apple trees will never be nawed by mice. Please tell father not to name the new red calf till I come home. It won't be long now . . . only fourteen more days. Don't forget to give Thursday his milk every night, Judy, and please put a little cream in it. Are the columbines and the bleeding-heart out yet? I hope Cuddles won't grow too much before I get back.

"Aunt Helen gave me a new dress. She says it is a sensible dress. I don't like sensible dresses much. And there are no Sunday raisins here.

"Aunt Helen is a perfect housekeeper. The neighbours say you could eat your porridge off her floor but she never puts enough salt in her porridge so I don't like to eat it anywhere.

"Uncle Brian says Jim Hartley will come to a bad end. Jim lives next door and it is exciting to look at him and wonder what the end will be. Do you think he may be hung, Judy?

"Aunt Helen lets me drink tea. She says it is all nonsense the way they bring up children nowadays not to drink tea.

"Old cousin George Gardiner told me I didn't look much like my mother. He said mother had been a beauty in her day. It made me feel he was disappointed in me. He praised Norma and Amy for their good looks. I don't mind how much he praises their looks but I can't bear to hear their house praised. I think bay windows are *horrid*.

"Oh, Judy, I do hope everything will stay just the same at Silver Bush till I get back."

It was wildly exciting to get letters from home . . . *"Miss Patricia Gardiner, Elmwood, Summerside."* Jingle wrote the nicest letters because he told her things no one else thought of telling her . . . how the Silver Bush folks were pestered with squirrels in the garret and Judy was clean wild . . . how the sheep laurel was out in Happiness . . . what apple trees had the most bloom . . . how Joe had cut off Gentleman Tom's whiskers but Judy said they would grow in all right again . . . how the barn cat had kittens . . . and, most wonderful of all, how the farm with the Long Lonely House had been sold to some strange man who was coming there to live. Pat was thrilled over this: but it was terrible to think of these things happening and she not there to see them.

"Only ten days more," said Pat, looking at the calendar. "Only ten days more and I'll be home."

Judy did not write but she sent messages in everybody's letters. "Tell her the house do be that lonely for her," was the one Pat liked best, and "that skinny beau of yours do be looking as if he was sent for and couldn't go," was the one she liked least.

Pat found Aunt Jessie's afternoon tea, which she was giving for a visiting friend, very tiresome. Norma and Amy were too much taken up with their own doings to bother with her, her head ached with the crowd and the lights and the chatter... "they sound just like Uncle Tom's geese when they all start chattering at once," thought Pat unkindly. She slipped away upstairs to seek a quiet spot where she could sit and dream of Silver Bush and found it in Uncle Brian's snuggery at the end of the hall. But when she pulled aside the curtain to creep into the window seat it was already occupied. A little girl of about her own age was curled up in the corner... a girl who had been crying but who now looked up at Pat with half appealing, half defiant eyes... beautiful eyes... large, dreamy, grey eyes... the loveliest eyes Pat had ever seen, with long lashes quilling darkly around them. And there was something besides beauty in the eyes... Pat could not have told what it was... only it gave her a queer feeling that she had known this girl always. Perhaps the stranger felt something of the same when she looked into Pat's eyes. Or perhaps it was Pat's smile... already "little Pat Gardiner's smile" was, unknown to Pat, becoming a clan tradition. At all events she suddenly shook back her thick brown curls, drew her feet under her, and pointed to the opposite corner of the seat with a welcoming smile on her small, flower-like face. They were good friends before they spoke a word to each other.

Pat hopped in and squirmed down. They heavy blue velvet curtain swung behind her, cutting them off from the world. Outside, the boughs of a pine tree screened the window. They were alone together. They looked at each other and smiled again.

"I'm Patricia Gardiner of Silver Bush," said Pat.

"I'm Elizabeth Wilcox...but they call me Bets," said the girl.

"Why, that's the name of the man who has bought the Long Lonely House Farm at North Glen," cried Pat.

Bets nodded.

"Yes, that's dad. And that's why I've been crying. I...don't want to go away down there...so far from everybody."

"It's not far from me," said Pat eagerly.

Bets seemed to find comfort in this.

"Isn't it...really?"

"Just a cat's walk, as Judy says. Right up a hill from Silver Bush. And it's a lovely old house. I'm so fond of it. I've always wanted to see a light in it. Oh, I'm glad you're coming to it, Bets."

Bets blinked the last tears out of her eyes and thought she might be glad, too. They sat there together and talked until there was a hue and cry through the house for them and Bets was dragged away by the aunt who had brought her to the party. But by this time she and Pat knew all that was worth while knowing about each other's pasts.

3

"Oh, Judy," Pat wrote that night, "I've found the dearest friend. Her name is Bets Wilcox and she is coming to live at the Long Lonely House. It will soon have a light in its windows now. Her full name is Elizabeth Gertrude and she is so pretty, far prettier than Norma, and we've promised each other that we'll always be faithful till death us do part. Just think, Judy, this time yesterday I didn't know there was such a person in the world. Aunt Helen says she is very delicate and that is why her father has sold his farm which is kind of low and marshy and he thinks the Long House farm will be healthier.

"I never thought I could like any one outside my own family as much as I like Bets. It was Norma found us in the window seat and I guess she was jealous because she sniffed and said, 'Birds of a feather, I suppose,' and when I said yes she said to Bets, 'You mustn't cut her out with Hilary Gordon. She's his girl you know.' I said...very dignified, Judy...'I am not his girl. We are just good friends.' I told Bets all about Jingle and she said we ought to try to make his

life happier and she thinks it's awful silly to talk about a boy
being your beau when he is just a friend and she says we can't
think about beaus for at least seven years yet. I said I was
never going to think of them but Bets said they might be nice
to have when you grew up.

"But oh, Judy, I haven't told you the strangest thing.
Bets and I were born on the same day. That makes us a kind
of twins, doesn't it? And we both love poetry *passionately*.
Bets says that Mr. George Palmer, who lives on the farm next
to them, found out his son was writing poetry and whipped
him for it. Bets is going to lend me a fairy story called *The
Honey Stew of the Countess Bertha*. She says there is a lovely
ghost in it.

"Oh, Judy, day after to-morrow I'll be home. It seems
too good to be true."

4

"The best part of a visit is getting home," said Pat.

Uncle Brian drove her down to Silver Bush one evening.
To Uncle Brian it meant a pleasant half-hour's run after a
tiresome day in the office. To Pat it meant a breath-taking
return from exile. It was dark and she could see only the
lights of the North Glen farmsteads but she knew them all.
Mr. French's light and the Floyd light, Jimmy Card's light
and the lights of Silverbridge away off to the right; the
Robinsons' light... the Robinsons had been away for months
but they must be home again. How nice to see their light in
its old place! The dark roads were strange but it was their
own strangeness... a strangeness she knew. And then the
home lane... wasn't that Joe's whistle?... and the friendly
old trees waving their hands at her... and the house with all
its windows alight to welcome her... Gentleman Tom sitting
on the gate-post and all the family to run out and meet
her... except dad who had to go to a political meeting at
Silverbridge. And Cuddles, who was two years old and hadn't
said a word yet, to the secret worry of everybody, suddenly
crowed out, "Pat," clearly and distinctly. Jingle and McGinty
were there, too, and supper in the kitchen with crisp,
golden-brown rolls and fried brook trout Jingle had caught in
Jordan for her. Judy wore a new drugget dress and the
broadest of smiles. Nothing was changed. Pat had been

secretly afraid they might have moved some of the furniture about... that the kittens in the picture might have grown up or King William and his white horse got across the Boyne. It was beautiful to see the moon rising over her own fields. She loved to hear the North Glen dogs barking from farm to farm.

"Did Joe really cut off Gentleman Tom's whiskers, Judy?"

"Sure he did that same, the spalpeen, and a funnier looking baste ye niver saw, but they're growing in agin fine."

"I'll have to get acquainted with everything all over again," said Pat joyfully. "Won't dad be home before I go to bed, Judy?"

"It's not likely," said Judy... who had her own reasons for wanting Pat to get a good night's rest before she saw Long Alec.

Her own dear room... such a quiet pleasant happy little room... and her own dear bed waiting for her. Then the fun of getting up in the morning and seeing everything by daylight. The garden had grown beyond belief but it knew her... oh, it knew her. She flew about and kissed all the trees, even the cross little spruce tree at the gate she had never really liked, it was so grumpy. She flung a kiss to Pat in the well. Life was *too* sweet.

And then she saw father coming from the barn!

They got her comforted after awhile though for a time Judy thought she had them beat. Long Alec had to promise he would let his moustache grow again immediately before she would stop crying.

"Sure and I told ye what a shock it wud be to her," Judy said reproachfully to Long Alec. "Ye know how hard she takes inny change and ye shud av waited until she had her fun out av coming home afore ye shaved it off."

It was a subdued Pat who went along the Whispering Lane to see the folks at Swallowfield and be rejoiced over by an uncle and aunts who had missed her sadly. But still it was lovely to be back home. And thank goodness Uncle Tom hadn't shaved *his* whiskers off!

CHAPTER XVI

The Rescue of Pepper

1

As a matter of fact Long Alec never let his moustache grow again after all. When he asked Pat gravely about it, Pat, having got used to seeing him without it, decided she rather liked the look of him as he was. Besides, as she candidly told Judy, it was nicer for kissing. She had another cry on the day when Winnie's famous golden curls were bobbed at last . . . and a shingle bob at that. And yet, when Winnie had been bobbed for a week, it seemed as if she had been bobbed always.

Judy's disapproval lasted longer.

"Making a b'y out av her," sniffed Judy, as she put the shorn curls tenderly away in her glory box. "Oh, oh, it's not meself that do be knowing what the girls av to-day are coming to. Trying to make thimselves into min and not succading very well at that. Sure and they'll all be bald as nuts be the time they're fifty and that's one comfort."

Worse than the bobbing as far as Pat was concerned was the notion Winnie took one day in Sunday School that she would be a missionary when she grew up and go to India. Pat worried for weeks over it, despite Judy's philosophy.

"Oh, oh, don't borry trouble so far ahead, Patsy dear. She cudn't go for all av tin years yet at the laste and a big lot av water will have run down yer Jordan be that time. So just sit ye down and have a liddle bite av me bishop's bread and niver be minding Winnie's romantic notions av religion."

"I suppose it's very wicked of me not to want her to be a missionary," sighed Pat. "But India is so far away. Do you think, Judy, it would be wrong for me to pray that Winnie will change her mind before she grows up?"

"Oh, oh, I wudn't be meddling much wid that kind of praying," said Judy, looking very wise. "Ye niver can tell how it will be turning out, Patsy dear. I've known minny a quare answer in me time. Just trust to the chanct that Winnie'll change her mind av her own accord. It's a safe bet wid inny girl."

Pat ate her bishop's bread...made from a recipe Judy had brought from Australia and would never give to any one. She had promised to will it to Pat, however.

The latter still had a grievance.

"Mr. James Robinson has gone and cut down the row of spruce trees along the fence in his cow-pasture. I just can't forgive him."

"Listen at her. Sure and hadn't the man a right to do what he liked wid his own? Though ye wudn't catch inny Robinson planting a tree be chanct. Not they. It's aisier to cut down and destroy."

"They weren't his trees half as much as they were mine," said Pat stubbornly. "He didn't love them and I did. I used to watch the red sunrise behind them in the mornings when I woke up. They were so lovely and clear and dark against it. And don't you remember them in the silver thaw last winter, Judy...how they just looked like a row of funny old women that had got caught in a shower without umbrellas walking along one behind the other?"

It was a great day for Pat when the Wilcoxes moved to the Long House farm and for the first time in her recollection a light shone down from its windows that night. It gave Pat such delightful little thrills of comradeship to help Bets get settled. Mr. and Mrs. Wilcox were quiet folks who adored Bets and gave her her own way in everything. This might have spoiled some children but Bets was too sweet and wholesome by nature to be easily spoiled. She was allowed to pick the wall-paper for her own room and Pat went to Silverbridge with her to help choose it. They both liked the same one...a pale green with rose sprays on it. Pat could see it already on the walls of that long room, dim with fir shadows, which had been assigned to Bets.

"Oh, isn't this house glad to have people living in it again," she exulted. "It will always be the Long House but it won't be lonely any more."

Judy was secretly well pleased that Pat had a girl friend of her own age at last. Judy had always felt worried over the fact that Pat had none. Winnie had half a dozen chums, but

Pat, although she got on well enough with the girls at school, had never been closely drawn to any of them.

"Bets is the prettiest girl in school now," she told Judy proudly. "May Binnie can't hold a candle to her. . . and oh, doesn't May hate her! But every one else loves her. I love her *dreadfully*, Judy."

"I wudn't be after loving her too much," warned Judy. "Not too much, Patsy dear."

"As if any one could be loved too much!" scoffed Pat.

But Judy shook her head.

"She'll never comb grey hairs, that one. Sure and that liddle face av hers do be having a bloom that's not av earth," she muttered to herself, thinking of Bets' too brilliant roses and the strange look that went and came in her eyes, as if she had some secret source of happiness no one else knew. Perhaps Bets' charm lay in that look. For charm she had. Every one felt it, old and young.

"Some of the girls in school are jealous because Bets is *my* chum," Pat told Judy. "They've tried and tried to get her away. But Bets and I just hang together. We're twins really, Judy. And every day I find out something new about her. Sometimes we call each other Gertrude and Margaret. We are so sorry for our middle names because they are never used. We think they feel bad about it. But that is one of our secrets. I like *nice* secrets. May Binnie told me a secret last week and it was a horrid one. Oh, Judy, aren't you glad the Wilcoxes have come to the Long House?"

"I am that. It's a trate to have good neighbours. And George Wilcox do be a quiet inoffensive man enough. But his dad, old Geordie, was a terror to snakes in his time. Whin he got in one av his fine rages I've seen him grab the pudding from the pot and throw it out av the door. And that stubborn he was. Whin they voted in church to set for prayers d'ye think me fine Geordie wud do it? Not be a jugful. Stiff as a ram-rod wud he stand up, wid his back to the minister, and his legs a yard apart and glare over the congregation. Oh, oh, he's in heaven now, poor man, and I hope he lets the angels have a bit av their own way."

"What funny things you do remember about people, Judy," giggled Pat.

"Remember, is it? Sure thin and it isn't a funny thing I remember about Geordie's cousin, Matt Wilcox. *He* was be way av having a rat or two in his garret. Thought he was haunted by a divil."

"Haunted by a devil?" Pat had a real thrill.

"I'm telling ye. But his fam'ly didn't be worrying much over until he tuk to liking to hear the cratur's talk. Said its conversation was rale interesting. They tuk him to the asylum thin but sorra a bit did he care, for his divil went wid him. He lived there for years, rale happy and continted as long as they'd just let him sit quiet and listen. Thin one day they found him crying fit to break his heart. 'Sure,' sez he, 'me divil has gone back to his own place and what I'm to do now for a bit av entertainment I don't know.' They tuk him home quite cured but he always said there niver was inny rale flavour in innything folks said to him the rist av his life. He said he missed the tang av...oh, oh, av a place I'll not be mintioning to ye, Patsy dear."

"I suppose you mean hell," said Pat coolly, much to Judy's horror. "I'm sure I hear it often enough. Uncle Tom's man is always telling things to go there. Uncle Tom says he just can't help it."

"Oh, oh, maybe he can't at that. He's ould Andy Taylor's grandson and ould Andy had a great gift av swearing. He was the only man in South Glen that ever did be swearing. Sure and nobody else had the heart to try whin they'd heard what ould Andy cud do. Swearing and laughing he always was, the ould scallywag. 'As long as I can laugh at things I'll get along widout God,' sez he. 'Whin I can't laugh I'll turn to him,' sez he. Whin his own son died he laughed and sez, 'Poor b'y, he's been saved a lot av trouble,' sez he. Whin his wife died he sez, 'There's one mistake corrected,' sez he. But whin ould Soapy John, that he'd hated and quarrelled wid all his life, fell out av his buggy and bruk his neck he sez, 'This is too funny to laugh at,' sez he, 'I'll have to be going to church and getting religion,' sez he. And niver a Sunday he missed from that to the day av his death."

2

Pat had never had such a happy summer. It was lovely to have some one to walk to and from school with. Sid was drifting more and more to the companionship of the other boys, although he and Pat still had their beautiful hours of prowling in the fields or hunting eggs in the barn or looking for strayed turkeys in the dims.

Sometimes Bets would come down to Silver Bush where she and Pat had a playhouse among the birches. Time and again Judy let them have their suppers in it. It was so romantic and adventurous to have meals out of doors, finishing up with a dessert of ruby red currants eaten off a lettuce leaf. Or they sat in the moonlight at the kitchen door and listened to Judy's stories of ghosts and fairies and ancestors and "grey people" that haunted apple orchards in the dusks of eve and morn. No wonder that Pat had to go clear up to the Long House with Bets afterwards. Pat was so pickled in Judy's stories that they only gave her thrills. Bets had the thrills, too, but if her father and mother had known the extent of Judy's repertoire they might not have been so complacent over Bets' visits to Silver Bush.

They helped Judy make her cheeses . . . for the last time. The decree had gone forth that henceforth all the milk must be sent to the factory and the cheese bought there.

"Oh, Judy, I *wish* things didn't have to change."

"But they do, Patsy dear. That do be life. And yer dad nades all the money he can be getting for his milk. But there'll niver be a bit av dacent flavoured cheese at Silver Bush agin. Factory cheese indade!" sniffed Judy rebelliously.

Sometimes Pat would go up to the Long House . . . by a fascinating path up the hill fields . . . a path you always felt happy on, as if the fairies had traced it. She found something new to love every time she traversed it . . . some sunny fern corner or mossy log or baby tree. You went along the Whispering Lane and across the end of Uncle Tom's garden and there was your path. The first outpost of this land of fairy was a big clump of spruce trees where Pat generally lingered to pick a "chew" of gum. Then there was a brook . . . a tiny thread of a brook that ran into Jordan . . . with a lady silver birch hanging over the log bridge. Beyond it a meadow cross-cut enticed you in daisies with an old pine at the top that always seemed to be waiting for something, Pat thought. Then it ran along an upland dyke where you could pick bouquets of long-stemmed strawberries in the crevices and look down far over the lowlands and groves to the sea. Sometimes Bets would come to meet her here . . . or again she would be waving at her from one of her windows as Pat came through the spruces on the hill. Then Silver Bush and the world Pat knew dropped out of sight and before them were the bush-dotted fields of the Long House farm and the shining loops of the Silverbridge river. And it was wonderful just to be alive.

The tragedy of that summer was Thursday's death. Poor Thursday was missing for a couple of days and was found lying stiff and stark on the well platform one morning, having dragged himself home to die.

"Judy, it's dreadful that cats can't live as long as we do," sighed Pat. "You just have time to get so fond of them . . . and they die. Judy, do you think it hurt poor Thursday very much to die?"

Pat took it pretty hard but Thursday had been away a good deal all summer, sometimes for weeks at a time, and Pepper and Salt, two adorable kittens, one smoky grey, one grey and white, with a pansy face, had crept into Pat's heart for her consolation. They had an affecting funeral at which Sid and Jingle were pallbearers and Salt and Pepper reluctant mourners with huge black bows around their necks. Pat and Bets made wreaths of wild flowers for the dead pussy. Pat wanted to bury him in the grave-yard, between Weeping Willy and Wild Dick, because he seemed so much like one of the family. But Judy was horrified at the idea; so they buried Thursday in the little glade among the spruces where the other Silver Bush cats slept the sleep that knows no waking. Clever Bets wrote an epitaph in verse for him and Jingle burnt it on a board. Thursday's funeral was always remembered in Silver Bush annals because Cuddles inadvertently sat down on a Scotch thistle after it and only Pat could comfort her. Cuddles always turned to Pat in her woes.

"At least I suppose I can put flowers on Thursday's grave," said Pat a little defiantly. She found it hard to forgive Judy for refusing Thursday the grave-yard.

3

There was a terrible time one soft, golden end of a rainy day when Pepper fell into the well. Pepper had a knack of getting into trouble. It was only the preceding Sunday night that he had walked up Judy's back and danced on her shoulders when they were all at family prayers in the Little

Parlour. Sid had disgraced himself by laughing out and dad had been very angry.

Pepper was missing one evening when Pat put his saucer of milk on the well platform and when Pat called him lamentable shrieks were heard from somewhere. But from *where*? Pat and Bets hunted everywhere a cat could possibly be but no Pepper. Only those piteous cries that seemed to come now from the sky, now from the silver bush, now from the grave-yard.

"Sure and the cratur's bewitched," cried Judy. "He can't be far off but I'm bate to say where."

Bets finally solved the mystery.

"He's in the well," she cried.

Pat ran to it with a shriek of despair. Nothing could be seen in the dim depths but there was no doubt that Pepper was down there somewhere. As they looked down the shrieks redoubled.

"The water's calm as a clock," said Judy. "Where has the baste got to? Oh, oh, I'm seeing. Look at the eyes av him blazing. He must have fell in the water but me brave Pepper has climbed out on that liddle shelf av rock between the stones and the water. Listen at him. He'll split his throat. And well may he wail for I'm blist if I can be seeing how we're to get him up, what wid yer dad and the b'ys away to the Bay Shore and not likely back till midnight. This do be a tommyshaw."

"We *can't* leave him there all night," cried Pat in agony. She flew to the garret to set the signal light. If only Jingle would see it! Jingle had been spending most of his evenings grubbing young spruces out of a big field Mr. Gordon wanted to clean up, but he saw Pat's light as he tramped home and in a few minutes he and McGinty were in the Silver Bush yard. McGinty, when he found out what was the trouble, sat down and howled antiphonally to Pepper's yells. It was a doleful duet.

"Oh, Jingle, can't *you* save Pepper?" implored Pat.

Jingle was a rather comical knight-errant, to be sure, with his frayed trousers and dark glasses and "raggedy hair," but he came promptly and practically to the help of lady fair. The three of them, aided by Judy, dragged a ladder from the barn and contrived, goodness knew how, to get it down the well. Down went Jingle, while Pat and Bets prevented McGinty from a suicidal leap after him. Terrible moments of suspense.

Up came Jingle, grasping a forlorn, dripping kitten who promptly expressed his gratitude by giving his rescuer a ferocious bite on the wrist.

"Oh, oh," groaned Judy, "but I'm faling as if I'd been pulled through a key-hole. Its been the tarriblo day, what wid Cuddles catching her liddle fingers in the wringer and Snicklefritz ating up one av yer dad's boots and Siddy's owl gone the Good Man Above only knows where. And now," she concluded in a tone of despair, "we'll have to be dragging water up from yer Jordan till we can get the well cleaned. And nobody knowing how minny lizards we'll have to be drinking in that same."

"Lizards!"

"I'm telling ye. Didn't ould Mr Adams' grandfather swally a lizard one day whin he tuk a drink of the brook water? Sure and he was niver the same again... he wud always fale it wriggling about in his insides whin his stomach was impty."

Pat reflected with a grue that she and Jingle had often drunk of Jordan water... though it was generally from the rock spring up in Happiness. She immediately felt something wrong with *her* stomach. But maybe that was only because it was empty. They shut Pepper up in the granary to dry off and went in to a supper of hot meat pie in Judy's kitchen. After so much excitement one really needed a little nourishment....

But that night Pat had a dreadful dream that she had swallowed a frog!

4

Pat found a new delight in life... going up to stay all night with Bets. The first time was in early December when Judy was glad to pack her off to the Long House as soon as she came from school, because Long Alec was killing the pigs and Pat was neither to hold nor bind when they killed the pigs. Not, as Judy sarcastically pointed out to her, that it prevented her later on from enjoying the sausages and fried ham that were among the products of the late lamented.

Pat went up to the Long House over a silver road of new-fallen snow. Every time she turned to look down on home the world was a little whiter. Bets, who had not been in school that day, was waiting for her under the pine. Just above them the Long House, amid its fir trees, was like a little dark island in a sea of snow.

There was something about the long, low-eaved house, with the dormer windows in its roof, that pleased Pat. And Bets' room was a delightful one with two dormers along its side and one at each end. It was very grand, Pat told Judy, with a real "set of furniture" and a long mirror in which the delighted girls could see themselves from top to toe. The west window was covered with vines, leafless now but a green dappled curtain in summer, and the east looked right out into a big apple tree. Pat and Bets sat by the little stove and ate apples until any one might have expected them to burst. Then they crept into bed and cuddled down for one of those talks dear to the hearts of small school-girls from time immemorial.

"It's so much easier to be confidential in the dark," Pat had told Judy. "I can tell Bets *everything* then."

"Oh, oh, I wudn't tell *iverything* to innybody," warned Judy. "Not iverything, me jewel."

"Not to anybody but Bets," agred Pat. "Bets is different."

"Too different," sighed Judy. But she did not let Pat hear it.

To lie there, with the soft swish of the fir trees sounding just outside, and talk "secrets" with Bets . . . lovely secrets, not like May Binnie's . . . was delightful. Bets had recently been to some wedding in the Wilcox clan and Pat had to hear all about it . . . the mysterious pearl-white bride, the bridesmaids' lovely dresses, the flowers, the feast.

"Do you suppose *we* will ever get married?" whispered Bets.

"*I* won't," said Pat. "I couldn't ever go away from Silver Bush."

"But you wouldn't like to be an old maid, would you?" said Bets. "Besides, you could get him to come and live with you at Silver Bush, couldn't you?"

This was a new idea for Pat. It seemed quite attractive. Somehow, when you were with Bets, everything seemed possible. Perhaps that was another part of her charm.

"We were born on the same day," went on Bets, "so if we're ever married we must try to be married the same day."

"And die the same day. Oh, wouldn't that be romantic?" breathed Pat in ecstasy.

Pat woke in the night with just a little pang of homesickness. Was Silver Bush all right? She slipped out of bed and stole across to the nearest dormer window. She breathed on its frosty stars until she had made clear a space to peer through . . . then caught her breath with delight. The snow had ceased and a big moon was shining down on the cold, snowy hills. The powdered fir trees seemed to be covered with flowers spun from moonshine, the apple trees seemed picked out in silver filigree. The open space of the lawn was sparkling with enormous diamonds. How beautiful Silver Bush looked when you gazed down on it on a moonlit winter night! Was darling Cuddles covered up warm? She *did* kick the clothes off so. Was mother's headache better? Away over beyond Silver Bush was the poor, lean, ugly Gordon house which nobody had ever loved. Jingle would be sleeping in his kitchen loft now. All summer he had slept in the hay-mow with McGinty. Poor Jingle, whose mother never wrote to him! How could a mother be like that? Pat almost hated to go back to sleep again and lose so much beauty. It had always seemed a shame to sleep through a moonlit night. Somehow those far hills looked so different in moonlight. A verse she and Bets had learned "off by heart," in school that day came to her mind:

> "Come, for the night is cold,
> And the frosty moonlight fills
> Hollow and rift and fold
> Of the eerie Ardise hills."

She repeated it to herself with a strange, deep exquisite thrill of delight, such as she had never felt before . . . something that went deeper than body or brain and touched some inner sanctum of being of which the child had never been conscious. Perhaps that moment was for Patricia Gardiner the "soul's awakening" of the old picture. All her life she was to look back to it as a sort of milestone . . . that brief, silvery vigil at the dormer window of the Long House.

CHAPTER XVII
Judy Puts Her Foot Down

1

"Just as naked as the day she was born," concluded Aunt Edith . . . and said no more. She felt . . . everybody felt . . . that there was no more to be said.

Mother looked horrified and ashamed. Uncles Tom and Brian looked horrified and amused. Aunt Jessie looked horrified and contemptuous. Norma and Amy looked horrified and smug. Winnie looked horrified and annoyed. Dad and Joe and Sid looked just plain horrified.

Pat stood before this family court, with Aunt Edith's hand on her shoulder, struggling unsuccessfully to keep back her tears. Well might she cry, thought the family; but her tears were not of shame or fear, as they supposed, but of regret over something marvellously beautiful which Aunt Edith had destroyed . . . something which could never be replaced. This was why Pat was crying; the realisation of her enormity hadn't yet come home to her.

For a week Pat had been a lonely soul. Bets was away for a visit. Jingle and Sid were busy with hay-making; and Judy, of all things unthinkable, was away. Judy had never been away from Silver Bush in Pat's recollection. Vacations were unknown in Judy's calendar.

"Sure and I'd niver work if I cud find innything else to do," she would say, "but the puzzle av it is I niver can."

There was trouble at the Bay Shore. Cousin Danny had broken his leg and Aunt Frances was ill, so Bay Shore borrowed Judy from Silver Bush to tide over the emergency. Pat found this especially dreadful. She missed Judy at every turn. The house had never seemed so full of her as when she was away, and even the delight of having mother in the kitchen most of the time and helping her in all household doings did not quite compensate. Besides, Gentleman Tom was gone, too. He had disappeared the very day Judy had been whirled away to Bay Shore; and the back yard and kitchen without Gentleman Tom were lonesome places. And what would Judy say when she came home and found her cat was gone? Perhaps she would think Pat had forgotten to feed him.

Pat consoled herself by working feverishly over the garden, determined that Judy should be satisfied with it on her return. Evening after evening Pat carried pails of water to it. She liked drawing the water up. It was fun to watch the bucket going down. Over that oval of blue sky with her own face framed in it at the bottom of the well. And then, as the bucket struck the water, to see it all blotted out, as if a mirror had been shattered. When the last bucketful had been drawn up Pat hung over the curb and watched the water grow slowly calm again and Pat of the Well coming back, at first very shiveringly, then more clearly, then clear and distinct once more, with just an occasional quiver when a drop of water fell from a fern.

Pat loved watering the garden... giving thirsty things drink after a hot day. First of all she always watered Judy's pets... the row of garden violets under the kitchen window which Judy called "Pink-o'-my-Johns"... such a delightful name!... and a clump of mauve and white "sops-in-wine" by the turkey house and the "pinies" by the gate. Then all the other flowers... and the roses last of all because she liked to linger over them, especially the white roses with the dream of gold in their hearts and the plot of pansies in a far corner that seemed to bloom for her alone.

On this particular evening Pat had been at loose ends. It had rained so heavily the night before that the garden did not need watering and when the "dim" came there was nothing to do and nobody to talk to. But it was a summer evening of glamour and enchantment and mystery and Pat was full of it, as she ran, with her hair streaming behind her, through the silver birches at moonrising, until she came out on the southern side in a little glade misted over with white daisies, lying amid its bracken like a cool pool of frosty moonlight.

She paused there to drink in the loveliness of the scene before her. More and more that summer of her tenth year, Pat had found herself responsive to the beauty of the world around her. It was becoming a passion with her.

The moon was rising over the Hill of the Mist... the moon that Pat had thought, when she was a tiny tot, must be a beautiful world where all was happiness. Little pools of shadow lay here and there all over the farm, among the shorn hayfields. There was one big field of hay that hadn't been touched yet; wind waves went over it in that misty light. Beyond it a field where happy calves were in buttercups to their shoulders... the only living creatures in sight if you were sure those shadows along the edge of the silver bush *were* shadows and not little rabbits dancing.

A warm brooding night... a night that surely belonged to the fairies. For the moment Pat could believe in them wholeheartedly again. Some strange bewitchment entered into her and crept along her veins. She remembered a Judy-story of an enchanted princess who had to dance naked in the moonlight every night of full moon in a woodland glen, and a sudden craving possessed her to dance thus in moonlight, too. Why not? There was nobody to see. It would be beautiful... beautiful.

Pat disrobed. There was not much to do... she was already bare-legged. Her pale-blue cotton frock and two small undies were cast aside and she stood among the shadows, a small, unashamed dryad, quivering with a strange, hitherto unknown ecstasy as the moon's pale fingers touched her through the trees.

She stepped out among the daisies and began the little dance Bets had taught her. A breeze blew on her through the aisles of the shining birches. If she held up her hands to it wouldn't it take hold of them? A faint, delicious perfume arose from the dew-wet ferns she danced on; somewhere far away laughter was drifting across the night... faint, fairy laughter which seemed to come from the Haunted Spring. She felt as light of being as if she were really made of moonlight. On, never had there been such a moment as this! She paused on tip-toe among the daisies and held out her arms to let the cool fire of that dear and lovely moon bathe her slim child-body.

"Pat!" said Aunt Edith, with forty exclamation points in her voice.

Pat came back to earth with a shudder. Her exquisite dream was over. The horror in Aunt Edith's voice enrobed her like a garment of shame. She could not even find a word to say.

"Put on your clothes," said Aunt Edith icily. Not for her to deal with the situation. That was Long Alec's job. Pat dumbly put on her clothes and followed Aunt Edith down through the silver bush and into the Little Parlour where the rest of the Silver Bushites were entertaining the Brianites who had run down for a call. Of course, thought Pat miserably, Norma and Amy, who never misbehaved, would have to be there to see her humiliation.

"How *could* you, Pat?" asked mother reproachfully.

"I . . . I wanted to bathe in the moonlight," sobbed Pat. "I didn't think it was any harm. I didn't think any one would see me."

"I never heard of any decent child wanting to bathe in moonlight," said Aunt Jessie.

And then Uncle Tom laughed uproariously.

2

The punishment of Pat, which the Silver Bush family thought was a very light one, considering the enormity of her offence, was to Pat the most terrible thing they could have devised. She was "sent to Coventry." For a week she was to speak to nobody at Silver Bush and nobody was to speak to her, except when it was absolutely necessary.

Pat lived . . . she could never tell how . . . through three days of it. It seemed like an eternity. To think that *Sid* wouldn't speak to her! Why, Sid had been the most furious of them all. Mother and father seemed sorry for her but firm. As for Winnie . . .

"She looks at me as if I was a stranger," thought poor Pat.

She was not allowed to play with Jingle who came over unsuspectingly the next evening. Jingle was very indignant and Pat snubbed him for it.

"My family have the right to correct me," she told him haughtily.

But she cried herself to sleep every night. On the third night she went to bed sadly, after kissing all her flowers and her two little cats good-night. Below stairs the house was full of light and laughter for Uncle Tom and dad were roaring in the kitchen and Winnie was practising her singing lesson in the Little Parlour and Joe and Sid were playing "grab" in the dining room, and Cuddles was chuckling and gurgling with mother on the front porch. Only she, Pat, had no part or lot with them. She was outcast.

Pat woke up in the darkness . . . and smelled ham frying! She sat up in bed. The Little Parlour clock was striking twelve. Who on earth could be frying ham at midnight in Silver Bush? Nobody but Judy . . . Judy must be home!

Pat slipped noiselessly out of bed, so as not to wake Winnie . . . Winnie who would not even *ask* what she was doing if she did. Sniffing that delectable odour Pat crept down through the silent house. She hoped that Judy would not send her to Coventry; and she thought her heart might stop aching for a little while if she could feel Judy's arms around her.

Softly she opened the kitchen door. Beautiful sight! There was dear old Judy frying herself a snack of ham, her jolly old shadow flying in all directions over the kitchen walls and ceiling as she darted about.

And . . . was it believable? . . . there was Gentleman Tom, sitting inscrutably on the bench, watching her. How peaceful and home-y and comforting it all was!

There had been anything but a peaceful scene in the kitchen two hours before when Judy had arrived home and demanded if all was well with the children. When she was told Pat was in disgrace and why Judy, as she expressed it, tore up the turf. Such a "ruckus" had never been known at Silver Bush. Everybody caught it.

"Suppose she had been *seen*, Judy?" protested mother.

"Oh, oh, but they didn't see her, did they?" demanded Judy scornfully.

"Nobody but Aunt Edith . . ."

"Oh, oh, it is *Aunt* Edith?" sniffed Judy. "And it was me fine *Edith* that dragged her in and blew it all afore Brian and his fine lady wife, ye're telling me? Sure it was like her. It's a pity a liddle thing like that cudn't av been hushed up in the fam'ly. And to punish the tinder-hearted cratur so cruel! Ye ralely ain' wise, Long Alec. A bit av a tongue-lashing might av been all right but to kape on torturing the poor jewel for a wake and her that fond av ye all! It's telling ye to yer face, I am, Long Alec, ye don't deserve such a daughter."

"Well, well," said Long Alec, quite cowed, "I don't think

it's done her much harm. We'll let her off the rest of the week."

"I don't know what possessed the child to do such a thing," said mother.

"Oh, oh, it's a bit av that ould Frinch leddy coming out in her, I warrant ye," suggested Judy.

"Certainly it didn't come from the Quaker side," chuckled Uncle Tom.

"Judy!"

Pat was in Judy's arms, laughing, crying. It was a glorious five minutes. Even Gentleman Tom betrayed a trifle of sympathy.

Finally Judy held Pat off and pretended to look stern.

"I don't want to be hard on ye, Patsy, but what monkey-didoes have ye been cutting up? It's a fine yarn yer dad has been spinning me av ye dancing in the bush widout inny clothes on."

"Oh, Judy, I never saw such a moon... and I was pretending I was a bewitched princess... and Uncle Tom *laughed* at me. That spoiled it worst of all, Judy... and it *was* so beautiful before Aunt Edith came."

There was some wild strain of poetry in Judy that made her understand. She hugged Pat with a fierce tenderness.

"Oh, oh, I've rid the riot act to thim, I'm telling ye. Whin I get me dander up I'm a terror to snakes. There'll be no more visiting in Coventry for ye, me jewel. But ye'd better not be doing any more quare things for awhile."

"The trouble is, *I* don't think the things I do are queer," said Pat gravely. "They seem quite reasonable to me. And Aunt Edith was just... ridiculous."

"Ye niver spoke a truer word. Oh, oh, what a shock it must av been to the poor sowl. She's forgotten she has inny legs, that one. But ye'd better be a bit careful, Patsy, and if ye fale inny more hankering for such bathing just ye tell me and I'll get a pitcherful av moonlight and pour it over ye. And now just sit down and have a liddle bite av ham wid me and tell me all that's happened. Sure and it's good to be home agin."

"Oh, Judy, where did Gentleman Tom come from? He's never been seen here since you went away."

"Are ye telling me? Sure and he was sitting on the durestep when I got out av the Bay Shore rig, looking as if he wasn't knowing where his nixt mouse was coming from. I'm not asking him where he's been. I mightn't be liking the answer. Innyway, here he is and here I am . . . and there's a beautiful pink dress av eyelet embroidery in me grip that yer Aunt Honor sint ye. It'll be one in the eye for Norma whin she sees ye in it."

"I'm going to sleep the rest of the night with you, Judy," said Pat resolutely.

CHAPTER XVIII
Under a Cloud

1

WHEN in mid-September Long Alec suddenly announced to his family that, harvest being over, he meant to take a trip out west to visit a brother who had settled there years ago Pat took it more calmly than they had feared. It was rather dreadful, of course, to think of dad being away for a whole month, but, as he said himself, if he didn't go away he couldn't come back again. There would be his home-coming to expect and plan for, and meanwhile life was very pleasant at Silver Bush. She liked the fall nights because the fires were lighted. Jingle was building an elegant bird-house for her to be put up in the maple by the well when finished; and Mr. Wilcox was going to take Bets and her to the Exhibition in Charlottetown. Pat had never been to one yet. To the small denizens of North Glen a visit to the Exhibition loomed up with as much of excitement and delight as a trip to Europe or "the coast" might to older folks. Socially you were not in the swim unless you had been to the Exhibition. There were the weeks of delightful anticipation . . . the Exhibition itself . . . then weeks of just as delightful reminiscence. All things considered, Pat was quite cheerful about dad's absence. It was Judy who seemed to view it most gloomily . . . Pat couldn't understand why. For the week preceding Long Alec's departure Judy had done an extra deal of talking to and arguing with herself. Disjointed sentences reached Pat's ears every now and again.

"I'm not knowing what gets into the min be times. It do be saming as if they had to have a crazy spell once in so long"..."a bit av Wild Dick coming out in him I'm telling ye"... "'tis the curse av the wandering foot"... "oh, oh, it's too aisy to get about now. Sure and that's what's the matter wid the world."

But when Pat asked what the trouble was Judy's only reply was a curt

"Ax me no questions and I'll be telling ye no lies."

Dad went away one windy, cloudy September morning. Uncle Tom and the aunts came along the Whispering Lane to say good-bye. Everybody was a little sober. The "west" was a long way off... the good-byes a bit tremulous.

"May the Good Man Above give us all good health," muttered Judy, as she dashed back into the kitchen and began to rattle the stove lids fiercely. Pat hopped into the car and went as far as the road with dad. She stood and watched the car out of sight and then turned towards home with a choking sensation. At that moment the sun broke through a black cloud and poured a flood of radiance over Silver Bush. Pat realised afresh how beautiful home was, nestling under its misty blue hill with its background of golden trees.

"Oh, how lovely you are!" she cried, holding out her arms to it. The tears that filled her eyes were not caused by dad's going. She was pierced by the swift exquisite pang which beauty always gave her... always would give her. It was almost anguish while it lasted... but the pain was heavenly.

It was well that Pat had her trip to the Exhibition over before she heard the terrible thing. She did have it... two glorious days with Bets... and, as the gods themselves cannot recall their gifts, she always had it, although for a time it seemed as if she had nothing... would have nothing for evermore... but pain and fear.

Again it was May Binnie who told her... that dad meant to buy a farm out west and settle there!

A strange icy ripple, such as she had never felt before, ran over Pat.

"That isn't true," she cried.

May laughed.

"It is. Everybody knows it. Winnie knows it. I s'pose they were afraid to tell you for fear you'd make a scene."

Pat looked passionately into May's bold black eyes.

"I wouldn't have hated you for telling me this, May Binnie, if you hadn't *liked* telling it. But I am going to *tell God about you to-night*."

May laughed again . . . a little uncomfortably. What she called Pat Gardiner's "rages" always made her uncomfortable. And who knew what Pat might tell God about her?

Pat went home sick and cold with agony to the very depth of her being.

"Mother, it isn't true . . . it isn't . . . say it isn't!"

Mother looked compassionately into Pat's tortured young eyes. They had tried to keep this from Pat, hoping she might never have to be told. Dad might not like the west. But if he did, go they must. When easy-going Long Alec did make up his mind there was no budging it, as everybody at Silver Bush knew.

"We don't know, dear. Father is thinking of it. He had a hankering to go when Allan went, years ago, but he couldn't leave his parents then. Now . . . I don't know. Be brave, Pat, dear. We'll all be together . . . the west is a splendid country . . . more chances for the boys perhaps . . ."

She stopped. Better not say more just now.

"So ye've heard?" was all Judy said, when Pat came, white-faced, into the kitchen.

"Judy, it can't happen . . . it just can't. Judy, God wouldn't let such a thing happen."

Judy shook her head.

"Long Alec will settle that, laving God out av the question, Patsy, me jewel. Oh, oh, it's a man's world, so it is, and we women must just be putting up wid it."

"It will be the end of everything, Judy."

"I'm fearing it will be worse than that," muttered Judy. "I'm fearing it will be the beginning av a lot av new things. Sure, the heart av me will be bruk."

She did not say this aloud. Pat must not know until it became necessary that Judy would not be going west with them. To Judy, the idea of leaving Silver Bush was as dreadful as it was to Pat; but she could not leave the Island. Judy had a secret conviction that if the Gardiners went west she would end her days at the Bay Shore farm, taking Danny's part and waiting on the ould leddy who would live forever...and eating her soul out with longing and loneliness for her own.

"Oh, oh, they do be all I've got," she mourned. "And all I axed was to be let go on working for thim as long as I was on the hoof. To the divil wid Long Alec and his notions and his stubbornness...him that ye wudn't think cud stand up aginst a moonbame. But 'tis in the blood to be set that way whin they think they want innything. His ould Great-uncle Alec was the same but he had a bit av sinse in his pate and whin he onct tuk a notion he wanted to go somewhere he was knowing he shudn't didn't he go and shave his head complate and thin he cudn't go till the hair grew in and be that time the danger was over. Minny's the time I've heard ould Crandfather Cardiner tell av it. 'Twas be way av being a fam'ly joke."

"When will we *know*, Judy?"

"That I can't tell ye, darlint. Long Alec said he'd write as soon as he made up his mind. God hasten the day! There's nothing we can be doing but wait."

Pat shivered. The words were so terrible and so true. How could one wait? To-morrow would be more cruel than to-day.

2

In the weeks that followed Pat felt as if her heart were bleeding drop by drop. She seemed to be alone in her anguish. Sid rather hoped dad wouldn't go west but was not terribly cut up about it. Joe frankly hoped he *would* go. Winnie thought it might be fun. Mother *seemed* quite indifferent to it, in her usual calm, gentle fashion. Even Judy was fiercely silent and would give tongue to neither regrets nor hopes. Bets and Jingle were both in despair but Pat found she could not talk the matter over with them. It went too deep.

She got through the days in school somehow and then wandered about Silver Bush like an unhappy little ghost. She could not read. The books she had loved were no more than printed words. She and Bets had been half way through *The Wind In The Willows*, reading it under the Watching Pine on the hill-top, but now it lay neglected in the bookcase at the Long House. She could not play with Bets or Jingle... she could not bear it when she might soon have to leave them forever. She could not play with Sid because Sid *could* play and showed thereby that he was not feeling as badly as he should be. She could not play with Salt and Pepper because they were too cheerful. McGinty was the only animal that seemed to realise the situation. He and Jingle were a gloomy pair.

Pat slept badly and ate next to nothing.

"That thin she do be getting," worried Judy to Mrs. Gardiner. "Sure there isn't a pick on her bones. It's me belafe that if Long Alec drags that child out west it'll be killing her. She can't live away from Silver Bush. Sure and she do be loving ivery inch av it."

"I wish she didn't love it so much," sighed mother. "But she is young... she will forget. We older ones..." Mother stopped quickly. That was like mother. Mother never showed what she felt. That had been a Bay Shore tradition. The more emotional and expressive Gardiners sometimes thought she had no "feelings."

Pat was having plenty and very dreadful ones they were. Everything she looked at hurt her. It hurt her to be in the house... to think of those dear rooms being cold... perhaps nobody even bothering to light a fire in them. Perhaps there would be no light in the windows at night... in the house that had always overflowed with light: no plumes of homely smoke going up from its chimneys: nobody looking on beauty from the round window. And if there were people in it... she hated that thought, too. Who would be sleeping in her room... who would be ruling in Judy's kitchen?

It was worse outside. The garden would be so lonely. No one there to love or welcome the flowers. The daffodils and the columbines would come up in the sping but she would not be there to see. The bees would hum in the Canterbury bells and she not there to listen. The poplars would whisper but she would not hear them whispering. The tiny, pointed, crimson buds would come on the wild rose-bushes in the lane, not for her gathering. Perhaps the people who would come to Silver Bush would root up the old garden entirely. Pat had heard Uncle Brian say once it was really only an old jungle and Alec should clear it out. They would change and tear up. Oh, she could not bear it!

And yet, somehow, it could never be theirs. In after

years Pat said of this time, "I knew they could never have the soul of Silver Bush. *That* would always be mine."

But she would not be there. There would be no more jolly meals in the old kitchen . . . no more chronicles of Judy on the sandstone steps . . . no more kitten hunts in the old barns . . . no more delightful days and nights at the Long House . . . no more pilgrimages over Jordan . . . no Happiness . . . no Secret Field . . . no Hill of the Mist. There wouldn't be any hills at all on the prairie.

This *must* be a dream. Oh, if she could only wake up!

So many poisonous things were said in school. The girls talked so casually of the Gardiners going west . . . some a little enviously as if they would like to go, too. Jean Robinson said she only wished she could get away from this dull old hole.

And then one day May Binnie said that her father had decided to buy Silver Bush!

"If he does we'll fix it up a bit, I can tell you," she said to Pat. "Pa says he'll cut down that old part of the orchard and plough it up and sow it with beans. We'll build a sunporch of course. And pa says he'll cut down all them birch trees. He says too many trees aren't healthy."

Only sheer malice could have made her say *that*. Pat dragged herself home.

"The Binnies will cut down all our birches, Judy."

"Oh, oh, the Good Man Above may have something to say to *that*," said Judy darkly. But her faithful old heart was heavy. She knew Mac Binnie already looked on Silver Bush as his and was telling everybody about the "improvements" he meant to make.

"Improvements, is it?" Judy had demanded. "Sure he'd better be making some improvements in the manners av himsilf and his daughters, if it's improvements he do be wanting, the ould wind-bag. Mrs. Binnie hersilf cud do wid a few. Fancy her in me kitchen and her looking like a haystack, niver to mention her presiding at the dining room table where a Selby from Bay Shore has been sitting. Oh, oh, 'tis a topsy-turvy world, so it is, and getting no better fast."

"I was so happy just a little while ago, Judy. And now I'll never be happy again."

"Oh, oh, niver's a long day, me jewel."

"I hate May Binnie, Judy . . . I *hate* her!"

"Sure, Patsy dear, hating do be something that's always

bist done yisterday. Life do be too short to waste inny av it hating. Though, if a body *did* have a liddle more time . . . but thim Binnie craturs do be clane benath hating."

"If there was anything we could do to prevent it," sobbed Pat.

Judy shook her head.

"But there isn't . . . not in Canady innyhow. That's the worst av a new land where nather God nor the divil have had time to be getting much av a hold on things. Now, if there was wishing well here like there was in me home in ould Ireland sure and ye cud make it all right in the twinkle av a fairy's eye. All ye'd have to do is go to it at moonrise and ye'd get yer wish."

Pat went to Happiness that night and wished over the Haunted Spring. Who knew?

It was horrible to live with fear . . . and suspense. Dad's first letter came when Pat was in school and Judy told her first thing that there was no news yet. Long Alec thought the west a grand country. Allan had done well. But he hadn't decided yet . . . he was looking about . . . he would be able to tell them next letter.

"So kape up yer pecker, Patsy darlint. There's hope yet."

"I'm afraid to hope, Judy," said Pat drearily. "It *hurts* too much to hope. It would be so much worse when you had to stop hoping."

"Oh, oh, but ye're too young to be larning *that*," muttered Judy. She pounded and thumped and battered her bread, wishing it were Long Alec. Oh, oh, but wudn't she knead some sinse into him! Him wid the good Island farm and a fine growing fam'ly to be draming au pulling up stakes and going to a new country at his age!

3

The next letter came. It was Saturday and Pat had wakened to a grey dawn. The rain against the windows was very dreary. Everybody at Silver Bush expected dad's letter that day though nobody said anything about it, and Pat felt that the rain was a bad omen.

"Oh, oh, cheer up, Patsy darlint," said Judy. "Sure and I remimber a bit av poetry I larned whin I was a girleen . . . 'a

dark and dreary morning often brings a pleasant day.' Often
have I seen it mesilf."

It stopped raining at noon, although the clouds still hung
dark and heavy over the silver bush. Pat was watching from
the garden as the old postman drove up to the mail box. He
was a little bent old man with a fringe of white beard, driving
a crazy buggy behind a lean old sorrel horse. It seemed
incredible that her destiny was in his bag. She went slowly
down the lane, a pale moth of a girl, hardly knowing whether
she wanted to see a letter or not. It would be so terrible to
wait for its opening but at least they would *know.*

The letter was there. Pat took it out and looked at
it . . . *"Mrs. Alex. B. Gardiner, Silver Bush, North Glen, P. E.
Island."* All her life after a letter seemed to Pat a terrible
intriguing, devilish thing. What might . . . or might not . . . be
in it? She remembered that when she had been very small
she had been horribly frightened of a "dead" letter she had
carried home. She had thought it had come from a dead
person. But this was even worse.

She walked back up the lane. Half way up she paused in
a little bay of the fence which was full of the white-gold of the
"life everlasting" that blooms in September. Her knees were
shaking.

"Oh, dear God, please don't let there be any bad news in
this letter," she whispered. And then desperately . . . because
old Alec Gardiner in South Glen had a daughter Patricia,
middle-aged and married, and there must be no
mistake . . . "Dear God, it's Long Alec's Pat of Silver Bush
speaking, not just Alec's Pat."

Somehow everybody was in the kitchen when Pat entered.
Judy sat down on a chair rather suddenly. Bets was just
arriving, having torn breathlessly down the hill when she saw
the postman. Jingle and McGinty were hanging around the
doorstep. McGinty had his ears turned down. Mother, her
eyes very bright and with an unusual little red spot on either
cheek, took the letter and looked around at all the tense,
waiting faces . . . except Pat's. She could not bear to look at
Pat's.

It was a thousand fold worse than when the letter had
come about Winnie.

"We must all be as brave as possible if father says we
must go," she said gently.

She opened the letter steadily and glanced over it. It seemed as if the very trees outside stopped to listen.

"Thank God," she said in a whisper.

"Mother..."

"Father is coming back. He doesn't like the west as well as the Island. He says, 'I'll be very happy to be home again.'"

And at that very moment, as if waiting for the signal, the sun broke out of the clouds above the Silver Bush and the kitchen was flooded with dancing lights and elfin leaf shadows.

"So that's that," said Joe, a bit glumly. He whistled to Snicklefritz and went out.

Pat and Bets were weeping wildly in each other's arms. Judy got up with a grunt.

"Oh, oh, and what's all the tears for, I'm asking ye? I thought ye'd be dancing for joy."

"You're crying yourself, Judy." Pat laughed through her tears.

"Sure and it's the tinder heart av me. I cud niver see inny one crying that I didn't jine in. Haven't I wept the quarts at the funerals av people who didn't be mattering a hoot to me? I'm that uplifted I wudn't call the quane me cousin. Oh, oh, and it's me limon pies that are burned as black as a cinder in me oven. Well, well, I'll just be making another batch. We've had minny a good bite here and plaze the Good Man Above we'll have minny another. It's been a hard wake av it but iverything do be coming to an ind sometime if only ye do be living to see it."

Pat had put on gladness like a garment. She wondered if anybody had ever died of happiness.

"I just couldn't have borne it, Pat, if you went away," sobbed Bets.

Jingle had said nothing. He had sniffed desperately, determined not to let any one see *him* cry. He was at that moment lying face downwards in the mint along Jordan and McGinty could have told you what he was doing. But McGinty wasn't worried. His ears stuck up for he knew somehow that, in spite of shaking shoulders, his chum was happy.

4

Pat came dancing down the hill that night on feet that hardly seemed to touch the earth. She halted under the

Watching Pine to gloat over Silver Bush, all her love for it glowing like a rose in her face. It had never looked so beautiful and beloved. How nice to see the smoke curling up from its chimney! How jolly and comfortable the fat, bursting old barns looked, where hundreds of kittens yet unborn would frisk! The wind was singing everywhere in the trees. Over her was a soft, deep, loving sky. Every field she looked on was a friend. The asters along the path were letters of the poem in her heart. She seemed to move and breathe in a trance of happiness. She was a reed in a moonlit pool... she was a wind in a wild garden... she was the stars and the lights of home... she was... she was Pat Gardiner of Silver Bush!

"Oh, dear God, this is such a lovely world," she whispered.

"A nice hour to be coming in for yer supper," said Judy.

"I was so happy I forgot all about supper. Oh, Judy, I'll always love this day. I'm so happy I'm a little frightened... as if it couldn't be *right* to feel so happy."

"Oh, oh, drink all the happiness ye can, me darlint, whin the cup is held to yer lips," said Judy wisely. "Now be aftor ating yor liddlo bite and thin to bod. I packod yor mothor off whin Cuddles wint. *She* hasn't been slaping much of late ather I'm telling ye, though the Selbys kape their falings to themselves. Oh, oh, and so Madam Binnie won't be bossing things here for a while yet. And what may ye be thinking av that, me Gentleman Tom?"

"I don't know if I'll be able to sleep much even to-night, Judy. It's lovely to be so happy you can't sleep."

But Pat was sound as a bell when Judy crept in to see if the little sisters had the extra blanket for the chill September night.

"Oh, oh, she'll niver be quite that young agin," whispered Judy. "It's such a time as she's had that makes even the liddle craturs old in their sowls. If one cud be after spanking Long Alec now as I did whin he was a b'y!"

CHAPTER XIX

"Am I So Ugly, Judy?"

1

FOR the first time Pat was getting ready to go to a party... a real, evening party which Aunt Hazel was giving for two of her husband's nieces who were visiting her. It was what Uncle Tom called a "double-barrelled party"... girls and boys of Winnie's and Joe's age for Elma Madison and young fry from ten to twelve for Kathleen. Sid pretended to hate the whole thing and vowed he wouldn't go till the last minute when he suddenly changed his mind... perhaps because Winnie twitted him with sulking because May Binnie wasn't invited.

"Sure and ye wudn't be expicting she wud be," said Judy loftily. "Since whin have the Binnies set themselves up for the aquals av the Gardiners... or aven av the Madisons I'm asking ye."

Pat was very glad when Sid decided to go for Bets was laid up with a sore throat and Jingle, though invited, couldn't or wouldn't go because his only decent suit of clothes had become absurdly tight for him. He had hoped that his mother might send him money for a new suit at Christmas but Christmas had passed as usual without present or letter.

"It's lovely to be nearly eleven," Pat was exulting to Judy. "I'm almost one of the big girls now."

"That ye are," said Judy with a sigh.

It was exciting to be dressing for a real party. Winnie had already gone to several and it was one of the dear delights of Pat's life to sit on the bed and watch her getting ready. But to be dressing yourself!

"Yellow's yer colour, me jewel," said Judy, as Pat slipped into her little party frock of primrose voile. "Sure and whin yer mother talked av getting the Nile grane I put me foot down. 'One grane dress is enough in a life-time,' sez I to her. 'Don't ye be remimbering all the bad luck she had in the one ye got her for the widding? Niver once did she put it on but something happened her or it.'"

"That was true, Judy, now that I come to think of it. I had it on when I broke mother's Crown Derby plate . . . and quarrelled with Sid . . . we'd never done that before . . . and found the hole in my stocking leg at church . . . and put too much pepper in the turnips the day Aunt Frances was here to dinner. . . ."

"'And innyhow,' sez I, clinching the matter like, 'grane doesn't be suiting her complexion.' So the yellow it is and ye'll look like a dancing buttercup in it."

"But I won't be dancing, Judy. I'm not old enough. We'll just play games. I do hope they won't play Clap in and Clap out. They do that so often at school and I hate it . . . because . . . because, Judy, none of the boys ever pick me out to sit beside. I'm not pretty, you know."

Pat said it without bitterness. Her lack of beauty had never worried her. But Judy tossed her head.

"They'd better wait till ye come into yer full looks afore they say that, I'm thinking. Now, here's a trifle av scint for yer hanky . . ."

"Put a little bit behind my ears, too . . . please, Judy."

"That I won't. Scint behind the ears is no place for dacency. A drop on yer hanky and maybe a dab on yer frill. Here's yer bit av blue fox for yer neck . . . though I'm not seeing where the blue comes in. But it sets ye. Now hold yer head up wid the best of thim and don't be forgetting ye're a Gardiner. Ye're to recite I'm hearing?"

"Yes. Aunt Hazel asked me to. I've been practising to the little spruce bushes behind the hen-house. Bets was to sing if she hadn't got a bad throat. It's just too mean she's sick. It would have been so wonderful to go to our first party together. I know I'll be lonesome. I don't know many of the Silverbridge girls. And I'll miss Bets so. She's lovely, Judy. They say Kathie Madison is pretty but I'm sure she isn't prettier than Bets."

Joe and Winnie and Sid and Pat all piled into the cutter to drive to Silverbridge through the fine blue crystal of the early winter evening, along roads where slender, lacy trees hung darkly against the rose and gold of the sky. That was fun . . . and at first the party was fun, too. Kathleen Madison *was* pretty. . . the prettiest girl Pat had ever seen in her life. A girl with close-cut curls of dark glossy gold, a skin of milk and roses, a dimpled bud of a mouth, and brilliant bluish-green eyes. Pat heard Chet Taylor of South Glen say she was worth walking three miles to see.

Well and good. It did not bother Pat. The evening went with a swing. The Silverbridge girls were all nice and friendly. They *did* play Clap in and Clap out but Mark Madison asked Pat to sit with him so it did not matter if half a dozen other boys were jealously trying for Kathie. Oh, parties *were* fun!

Then, in an evil moment Pat's hair bow fell off and she ran upstairs to put it on. Kathie Madison was in the room, too, pinning together a rent in the lace of her frock. As Pat stood before the looking-glass Kathie came and stood beside her. There was no particular malice in Kathie. She liked Pat Gardiner, as almost every girl did. But unluckily Mark Madison was the one boy Kathie had wanted for Clap in and Clap out. So she came and stood by Pat.

"It's a lovely party, isn't it?" she said. "Your dress is real pretty. Only . . . do you think yellow goes well with such a brown skin?"

Something happened to Pat, as she looked at herself and Kathie in the mirror. . . something that had never happened before. It was not jealousy. . . it was a sudden, dreadful despair. *She was ugly!* Standing beside this fairy girl she was ugly. Pale hair. . . a brown face . . . a mouth like a straight line and a much too long straight line . . . Pat shuddered.

"What's the matter?" asked Kathie.

"Nothing. I just hit my funny bone," said Pat valiantly. But everything had burst like a bubble. There was no more fun for her that evening. She even hated Mark Madison. He must have asked her to sit with him only out of pity . . . or because Aunt Hazel had ordered him to do it. She could not eat Aunt Hazel's wonderful supper and her recitation fell flat because as Uncle Robert said, she did not put any pep in it. Pep! Pat felt that she would never have pep again. She only wished she could get away home and cry. She did cry, quietly, as they drove home through the sparkling night of windless frost, over shadow-barred moonlit roads, between black velvet trees. All the beauty of the night was wasted on Pat who could see nothing but herself and Kathie side by side in the glass.

When she got home she slipped into the Poet's room to have another look at herself. Yes, there was no doubt about it. She was ugly. One did not mind not being very pretty. When Uncle Brian the last time he had been down, had said to her on leaving, "Try to be better looking when I come back," Pat had laughed with the others . . . all except Judy, who had sent a very black look after Brian.

But to be ugly. The tears welled up in Pat's eyes. She had never thought she was ugly until she had seen herself beside Kathie. Now she *knew*. What a way for a lovely party to end! Talk about green being unlucky! Nothing worse than this could have happened to her in green. It was she who was unlucky. Nobody would ever love her. . . Bets couldn't really care for an ugly friend . . . Jingle must just have been making fun of her when he told her she had a cute nose and lovely eyes. Eyes . . . just between yellow and brown . . . they had looked just like a cat's beside Kathie's enormous blue orbs. And her lashes!

"Even if mine were long I couldn't flicker them like she does," thought Pat disconsolately, forgetting that Kathie had "flickered" them in vain at Mark Madison.

Pat's bed was by the window where she could see the sunrise . . . if she woke early enough. She woke early enough the next morning but the wild red sunrise through the trees and its light falling over the white snow-fields did not thrill her. She had very little to say at breakfast. She told Judy dully that the party had been "very nice." She went to school, blind to the aërial colouring of the opal winter day and the dance of loose snow over the meadows. She kept aloof from all the girls who had also been at the party. They were raving over Kathleen's looks. Pat simply couldn't bear it.

She had never been jealous of a girl's looks before. Bets was pretty and Pat was proud of her. To be sure she had always hated Norma but that was because Norma was said to be prettier than Winnie. She wondered if Jingle thought her *very* ugly. She remembered the coloured chromo of the pretty little girl in the Gordon parlour which she knew Jingle adored. She did not know he adored it because he had heard some one say it looked like his mother. As Pat remembered it it looked like Kathie. Pat writhed.

Did everybody think her ugly? The old man who called around once a week selling fish always addressed her as "Pretty." But then he called everybody pretty. She had never thought she was pretty... she had never thought much about her looks at all. And now she could think of nothing else. She was ugly... nobody would ever like her... Sid and Joe would be ashamed of their ugly sister....

"Patricia, have you finished your composition?"

Patricia hadn't. How could you write compositions when the heart of you was broken?

2

There was company for supper at Silver Bush that night and Judy was too busy to pay any attention to Pat, although she watched her out of the tail of her eye. Pat had to wash the supper dishes. Ordinarily she made a saga of doing it. She liked to wash pretty dishes. Pat loved everything about the house but she loved the dishes particularly. It was such fun to make them clean and shining in the hot soapy water. She always washed her favourites first. The dishes she didn't like had just to wait until she was good and ready for them and it was fun to picture their dumb, glowering wrath as they waited *and* waited and saw the others preferred before them. That hideous old brown plate with the chipped edges... how furious it got! "It's *my* turn now... I'm an old family plate... I won't be treated like this... I've been at Silver Bush for fifty years... that stuck-up thing with the forget-me-nots on the rim has only been here for a year." But it always had to wait until the very last in spite of its howls. To-night Pat washed it first. Poor thing, it couldn't help being ugly.

She was glad of bedtime and crept off in mingled moonlight and twilight, while the purple shadows gathered along the lee of the snowdrifts behind the well and the west wind in the silver bush was twisting the birches mercilessly.

And then Judy, who had been out milking, invaded the room with a resolute air.

"What do be ailing ye, Pat? Sure and if ye're faling the way ye've been looking all day there's something sarious the matter. Wandering around widout a word to throw to a dog and peering into the looking-glass be times as if ye was after seeing if the wrinkles was coming. Make a clane breast av it, darlint."

Pat sat up.

"Oh, Judy, it's such a terrible thing to be ugly, isn't it, Judy? *Am* I so very ugly, Judy?"

"So *that's* it? Oh, oh, and who's been telling ye ye was ugly, if a body may ask?"

"Nobody. But at the party Kathie Madison stood beside me in front of the glass . . . and I saw it for myself."

"Oh, oh, there's not minny girls but wud look a bit plainer than common beside me fine Kathleen. I'm not denying she's handsome. And so was her mother afore her. But she wasn't after getting any more husbands than her homely sister for all av that . . . only one and that one no great shakes I'm telling ye. Wid all her looks she tuk her pigs to a poor market. It isn't the beauties that make the good marriages as a rule, Patsy darlint. There was Cora Davidson now at the Bay Shore. She was that good-looking the min were said to be crazy over her. But it's the fact, Patsy darlint, and her own mother it was that tould me, there niver was but one axed her to marry him. He axed her on Widnesday and on Thursday they took him to a lunatic asylum. Oh, I'm telling ye. And have ye iver heard what happened at her sister Annie's widding supper? They had the cake made in Charlottetown a wake before be way of being more stylish than their neighbours and whin the bride made a jab at it to cut it didn't a bunch av mice rin out and scamper all over the table? Oh, oh, the scraming and jumping! More like a wake than a widding! The Davidsons niver hilt up their heads agin for minny a long day I'm telling you."

It was no use. Pat was not to be side-tracked by any of Judy's tales to-night.

"Oh, Judy, I hate to think I'm so ugly my family will be ashamed of me . . . people will call me 'that plain Gardiner girl.' Last week at the pie social at Silverbridge nobody would buy Minnie Fraser's pie because she was so ugly . . ."

Pat's voice broke on a sob. Judy perceived that skilful handling was required. She sat down on Pat's bed and looked very lovingly at her. The dear liddle thing wid her wide, frindly smile, as if she did be imbracing all the world, and the golden-brown swateness of her eyes! Thinking she was ugly! Setting off in such high cockalorum for her first liddle party and coming home wid her bit av a heart half bruk in two!

"I'm not saying ye're handsome, Patsy, but I *am* saying

it's distinguished looking ye are. Ye haven't come into yer looks yet. Wait ye a few years till ye've outgrown yer arms and legs. Wid yer eyes and a bit av luck ye'll get a finer husband than minny av thim."

"Oh, Judy, it's not husbands I'm thinking of," sobbed Pat impatiently. "And I don't want to be terribly handsome. Bets and I read a story last week about a girl who was so beautiful crowds rushed out to see her and a king died for love of her. I wouldn't want that. I just want to be pretty enough so that people wouldn't mind looking at me."

"And who's been minding looking at ye, I'd like to know," said Judy fiercely. "If that stuck-up puss av a Kathie Madison said innything to hurt yer liddle falings..."

"It wasn't what she said, Judy, so much as the way she said it. 'Such a brown skin'... as if I was an Indian. Oh, Judy, I can't outgrow my skin, can I?"

"There's thim that thinks a brown skin handsomer than all yer Miss Pink-and-whites. She'll freckle in summer, that one."

"And I'm not even clever, Judy. I can only love people... and things."

"Oh, oh, 'tis a great gift that... and it's not ivery one that has it, me jewel. Now, we'll just be seeing where ye are for looks, rale calm and judicial like. Ye've got the fine eyes, as Jingle told ye..."

"And a cute nose, he said, Judy. *Have* I?"

"Ye have that... and the dainty liddle eye-brows... oh, oh, but ye've got no ind av good p'ints... and the nice ears like liddle pink shells. I warrant ye that Kathie one hasn't much to brag av in ears... not if she's a Madison."

"Her hair hid them mostly but I got a glimpse of one.... It *did* stick out," confessed Pat.

"I'm telling ye! Yer mouth may be a bit wide but ye're not seeing the way it curls up at the corners whin ye laugh, darlint. Oh, oh, ye've got a way av laughing, Patsy. And the 'ristocratic ankles av ye! I'll be bound that Kathie one has a bit too much beef on hers."

"Yes, Kathie *has* fat ankles," Pat recalled to her comforting. "But she has such lovely hair. Look at mine... straight as a string and just the colour of ginger."

"Yer hair will be getting darker all the time, me jewel. Sure and the wonder is ye girls have inny skin or hair at all, running round in sun and wind bare-headed as ye do. Yer mother and her leddy sister all wore sunbonnets I'm telling ye."

"Oh, Judy, that would be horrid. I *love* the sun and wind."

"Oh, oh, thin don't be howling bekase yer skin is brown and yer hair all faded. Ye can't ate yer cake and have it, too. I'm guessing it's healthier."

"Winnie has such lovely curls. I don't see why I haven't any."

"Winnie do be Selby and ye do be Gardiner. Yer mother now...oh, oh, but she had the rale permanent, so she had, that yer Aunt Jessie cudn't have if she had her head boiled and baked for a year. But ye've got a flavour av yer own and a tongue as swate as violets whin ye begin blarneying...and whin ye smile yer eyes twinkle like yer Grandmother Gardiner's...and she was the prettiest ould leddy I iver laid me eyes on. And ye've got a way av looking at a body and dropping yer eyes and thin looking agin that's going to play havoc some day. I've seen me lad Jingle's face whin ye looked at him so."

"Judy...have I really?"

"Oh, oh, maybe I shudn't be telling ye av it...not but what ye'd find it out sooner or later. I'm telling ye, Patsy darlint, a look like that is worth all the blue eyes and liddle red mouths in the world. Yer mother had it. Oh, oh, *she* knew all the tricks in her day."

"Father says mother was a great belle when she was a girl, Judy."

"Well may he say it for the hard time he had to get her! Ivery one thought she wud take Fred Taylor. Oh, oh, but he had the silver tongue. He cud wheedle the legs off an iron pot. But whin it came to the last ditch sure and she laped it wid yer dad. Minny was the sore heart at her widding."

"But she was pretty, Judy."

"Her own sister...yer Aunt Doris...wasn't pretty I'm telling ye, and she had more beaus than yer mother aven. Sure and I think it was bekase she always looked so slapy the min wanted to wake her up. She was the lazy one av the Bay Shore girls but ivery one liked her nixt to yer mother. Yer Aunt Evelyn had the prettiest arms and shoulders av the lot...as ye'll have yersilf some day, darlint, whin ye get a liddle more mate on yer bones. Yer Aunt Flora now...*she* was the flirt.

She tried to flirt wid ivery one in sight. Now there's niver no sinse in that, Patsy dear. A few like to kape yer hand in . . . but not ivery one. Remimber that whin yer time comes."

"Kathie told me that Jim Madison climbed to the top of the biggest tree at Silverbridge to see if he could pick a star for her."

"Oh, oh, but did he get the star, darlint? There's inny number av ways av showing off. Now just ye be going to slape wid a good heart. Ye've got a liddle better opinion of yersilf I be thinking?"

"A whole lot better, Judy. I guess I've been pretty silly. But I did look so brown . . ."

"Sure and I'll tell ye an ould beauty secret, Patsy dear. Whin the spring comes just ye run out ivery morning and wash yer face in morning dew. I'm not saying it'll make ye pink and white like Kathleen but it'll make yer skin like satin."

"Really, Judy?"

"Sure and isn't it in me book av Useful Knowledge? I'll be showing it to ye to-morrow."

"Why haven't *you* done that, Judy?"

"Oh, oh, nothing cud make inny diffrunce to me old elephant's hide. Ye've got to begin it young. Georgie Shortreed made a rigular beauty av hersilf that way, so she did, and made a good match in a fam'ly that was as full av ould maids as a pudding av plums. Was I iver telling ye how her sister Kitty lost her one chanct? Sure and didn't she throw a pan av dish-water over her beau one night, accidental like, whin he was standing on the kitchen durestep, trying to get up enough spunk to knock . . . him being a bould young lad av fifty wid a taste for ugly girls and not used to sparking. Away he wint and niver come back, small wonder, for wasn't his bist suit ruint entirely wid grase? The Shortreeds all had that lazy trick av opening the dure and letting the dish-waster fly right and lift widout looking. Was I iver telling ye how their ould dad, Dick Shortreed, quarrelled wid his marching neighbour, Ab Bollinger, over a hin?"

"No." Pat snuggled down on her pillow, happy again and ready to taste Judy's yarns.

"They fought over the hin for three years and wint to law about it . . . to the magistrate innyway . . . and 'twas the joke av the country side. And after they had spint more money than wud buy a hundred hins this same Ab Bollinger's daughter up and married ould Dick Shortreed's son and the ould folks made up their quarrel and killed the hin for the widding supper. 'Twas a tough bite I'm thinking be that time."

After Judy went out Pat slipped out of bed to the window where the moonlight was glittering on the frosted panes. Winnie had not come up yet and the night was very still. Pat could see the fields of crystal snow, the shadows in the Whispering Lane, and the silver fringe of icicles on the church barn. A light was shining in Bets' dormer up at the Long House. She was good friends with the world again. What did it matter if she had no great beauty herself? She had the beauty of shining meadows... of moon secrets in field and grove... of beloved Silver Bush.

Still, it was a comfort as she crept to bed again to remember that Kathie had the Madison ears.

CHAPTER XX

Shores of Romance

1

"SURE and it'll rain afore night," said Judy at noon. "Look how clare ye can see yer Hill av the Mist."

Pat hoped it wouldn't rain. She and Jingle had planned a walk to the shore. This was by way of being a treat to Pat for although you could, from Silver Bush see the great gulf to the north and the shimmering blue curve of the harbour to the east, it was a mile and a half to the shore itself and the Silver Bush children did not often get down. Pat felt that she needed something to cheer her up. Buttons, the dearest kitten that had ever been at Silver Bush... to be sure, every kitten was that... had died that morning without rhyme or reason. All his delights were over... frisking in the "dim"... flying up trees... catching small mice in the jungle of the Old Part... basking on the tombstones. Pat had tearfully buried this little dead thing that only yester-night had been so beautiful.

Besides, she was "out" with Sid over his frog. Pat was always so sorry for imprisoned things and Sid had had that poor frog in a pail in the yard for a week. Every time Pat looked at it it seemed to look at her appealingly. Perhaps it had a father or mother or husband or wife in the pool. Or even just a dear friend to whom it longed to be reunited. So Pat carried it away to the Field of the Pool and Sid hadn't spoken to her for two days.

All the afternoon the heat waves shimmered over the Buttercup Field and the sun "drew water"... as if some far-off Weaver in the west were spinning shining threads of rain between sky and sea. But it was still a lovely evening when Jingle and Pat...and McGinty...started for the shore, although far down on the lowlands was a smudge of fog here and there, with little fir trees sticking spectrally up out of it.

"Don't ye go and get drownded now," warned Judy, as she always did when anybody went to the shore. "And mind ye don't fall over the capes or get caught be the tide or run over by an auty afore ye get to the shore road or..." but they were out of hearing before Judy could think up any more "ors."

Pat loved that long red road that wandered on until it reached the sea, twisting unexpectedly just because it wanted to, among the spruce "barrens," where purple sheep laurel bordered the path and meadow-sweet and blue-eyed grass grew along the fences. "Kiss-me-quicks," Judy called the blue-eyed grasses. Pat liked this name best but you couldn't call it that to a boy. They rambled happily on, sucking honey-filled horns of red clover, a mad, happy little dog tearing along before them with his tongue out. Sometimes they talked and sometimes they didn't. That was what Pat liked about Jingle. You didn't have to talk to him unless you wanted to.

Half way to the shore they had to call at Mr. Hughes', where Jingle had an errand for his uncle. The Hughes house was a rather tumbledown one but it had some funny twinkly windows that Jingle liked. Jingle was always on the lookout for windows. They had a peculiar fascination for him. He averred that the windows of a house made or marred it.

"Will I put windows like that in your house, Pat?"

Pat giggled. Jingle had put all kinds of windows in that imaginary house of hers already.

She would rather have waited outside and looked at the

windows, even if more than one of the panes was broken and stuffed with rags, while Jingle did his errand but he dragged her in. Jingle knew that there were three Hughes girls there and face them alone he would not.

Mr. Hughes was out but they were asked to sit down and wait until he came in. Neither felt at home. The Hughes kitchen was in what Judy would have called a "tarrible kilter" and a black swarm of flies had settled on the dirty dishes of the supper table. Sally and Bess and Cora Hughes sat in a row behind the table and grinned at the callers . . . a malicious grin not in the least likely to put shy or sensitive people at their ease. Pat knew them only slightly but she had heard of them.

"Which of us girls," said Bess to Jingle with an impish, green-eyed smile, "are you going to marry when you grow up?"

Jingle's face turned a dark, uncomfortable red. He shuffled his bare feet but did not answer.

"Oh, ain't you the bashful one?" giggled Sally. "Just look how he's blushing, girls."

"I'm going to get ma's tape and measure his mouth," said Cora, sticking her tongue out at Jingle.

Jingle looked hunted and desperate but still would not speak . . . could not, probably. Pat was furious. These girls were making fun of Jingle. She recalled a word she had heard the minister use in his sermon last Sunday. Pat had no idea what it meant but she liked the sound of it. It was dignified.

"Don't mind them, Jingle. They are nothing but protoplasms," she said scornfully.

For a moment it worked. Then the Hughes temper broke.

"Skinny!" cried Bess.

"Shrimp!" cried Cora.

"Moon-face!" cried Sally.

and,

"*You* needn't get your Scotch up, Pat Gardiner," they all cried together.

"Oh, I'm not angry, if that's what you mean," said Pat icily. "I'm only sorry for you."

This got under the Hughes skins.

"Sorry for us?" Bess laughed nastily. "Better be sorry for your old Witch Judy. She's going straight to the Bad Place when she dies. Witches do."

There was an end to all dignity. Pat tossed her head.

"Judy isn't a witch. I think your father is a cousin of Mary Ann McClenahan's, isn't he?"

There was no denying this. But Sally got even.

"Why doesn't your mother ever come to see you," she asked Jingle.

"I don't think that is any business of yours," said Pat.

"I wasn't addressing you, *Miss* Gardiner," retorted Sally. "Better hang *your* tongue out to cool."

"Now, now, what's all this fuss about?"

Mrs. Hughes waddled into the room with an old felt hat of her husband's atop of her rough hair. She subsided into a mangy old plush chair and looked reproachfully at everybody.

"Who's been slapping your face, Jingle? You girls been teasing him I s'pose. I declare I don't see why you can't try and act as if you'd been *raised*. You mustn't mind their nonsense, Jingle. They're a bit too fond of their fun."

Fun! If it was fun to insult callers! But Mr. Hughes came in at last. Jingle delivered his uncle's message and they got away. McGinty had long since fled and was waiting for them on the shore road.

"Let's forget all about it," said Pat. "We won't spoil our walk by thinking about them."

"It's not *them*," said Jingle, too miserable to care whether he was ungrammatical or not. "It's what they said about... about mother."

2

It was so lovely at the shore that they soon forgot the Hughes episode. They passed by the old, wind-beaten spruces of Tiny Cove and ran down to where the wind and shore were calling each other. Fishing boats went past, wraith-like. Far-off was the thunder of waves on the bar but here the sea crouched and purred. They raced along the shore with the sting of the blowing sand in their faces. They waded in the pools among the rocks. They built "sea-palaces" with shells and driftwood. Finally they sat them down on a red rock in a little curve below the red "capes" and looked far out in the soft fading purple of the long-shore twilight to some magic shore beyond the world's rim.

"Would you like to go away 'way out there, Pat?"

"No." Pat shivered. "It would be too far from home."

"I think *I* would," said Jingle dreamily. "There's so much in the world I want to see . . . the great palaces and cathedrals men have built. I want to learn how to build them, too. But . . ."

Jingle stopped. He knew it was no use to hope for such a thing. He must, as far as he could see, spend his life picking up stones and grubbing out young spruce trees on his uncle's farm.

"Joe used to say he would like to be a sailor like Uncle Horace," said Pat. "He said he hated farming, but he hasn't said anything about it lately. Father wouldn't listen to him."

"School will begin next week," said Jingle. "I hate to go. Miss Chidlaw will want me to join the entrance class . . . and what's the use? I can't get to Queen's . . . ever."

"You want to go, Jingle?"

"Of course I want to go. It's the first step. But . . . I can't."

"Next year they'll want *me* to join the entrance but I'm not going to," said Pat resolutely. "I don't want to go to college. I'm just going to stay at Silver Bush and help Judy. Oh, isn't the salt tang in the air here lovely, Jingle? I wish we could come to the shore oftener."

"The mists down by the harbour look like ghosts, don't they? And look at that little, lonely ship away over there . . . it looks as if it was drifting over the edge of the world. There's a fog coming in from sea. I guess maybe we'd better be going, Pat."

There was only one objection to their going. While they had sat there the tide had come in. It was almost at their feet now. The rocks at the cape points were already under water. They looked at each other with suddenly whitened faces.

"We . . . we can't get around the capes," gasped Pat.

Jingle looked at the rocks above them. Could they climb them? No, not here. They overhung too much.

"Will we . . . be drowned, Jingle?" whispered Pat, clutching him.

Jingle put his arm around her. He must be brave and cool for Pat's sake.

"No, of course not. See that little cave in the cape? We can climb up to it. I'm almost sure the tide never rises as high as that."

"Oh, you can't be sure," said Pat. "Remember Judy's stories of people being caught by the tide and drowned."

"That was in Ireland. I never heard of it happening here. Come... quick."

Jingle caught up McGinty and they raced through the water which was by now almost to their knees. Two rather badly scared children scrambled up into the little cave. As a matter of fact they need not have been scared. The cave was well above high tide mark. But neither of them was quite sure of that. They sat huddled together with McGinty between them. McGinty at least was quite easy in his mind. Indian plains and Lapland snows were all the same to McGinty when the two people he loved were with him.

Pat's panic subsided after a few minutes. She always felt safe with Jingle. And it wasn't likely the tide rose this high. But how long would it be before they could escape? The folks at home would be wild with fright. If they had only remembered Judy's warning!

But, in spite of everything, the romance of it appealed to Pat. Marooned in a cave by the tide was romantic if ever anything was. As for Jingle, if he had been sure that they were quite safe, he would have been perfectly happy. He had Pat all to himself... something that didn't happen very often since Bets had come to the Long House. Not but what he liked Bets. But Pat was the only girl with whom Jingle never felt shy.

"If those horrid Hughes girls could see us now wouldn't they laugh," giggled Pat. "But I'm sorry I let them make me mad. Judy says you must never lower yourself to be mad with *scum.*"

"I wasn't mad," said Jingle, "but what they said about mother hurt. Because... it's *true.*"

Pat squeezed his hand sympathetically.

"I'm sure she'll come some day, Jingle."

"I've given up hoping it," said Jingle bitterly. "She... she never sent me a card last Christmas at all."

"Doesn't she answer your letters, Jingle... ever?"

"I... I never send the letters, Pat," said Jingle miserably. "I've never sent any of them. I write them every Sunday but I just keep them in a box in an old chest. She never answered the first one I sent... so I never sent any more."

Pat just couldn't help it. She felt so sorry for Jingle... writing those letters Sunday after Sunday and never sending them. Impulsively she put her arm around his neck and kissed his cheek.

"There's no one like you in all the world, Pat," said Jingle comforted.

"Hear, hear," said the thuds of McGinty's tail.

Far-away shores were now only dim grey lands. The dark shadows of the oncoming night were all around them.

"Let's pretend things to pass the time," suggested Pat. "Let's pretend the rocks dance..."

"Let's pretend things about that old house up there," said Jingle.

The old house was on the top of the right cape. It was not one of the fish-houses that sprinkled the shore. Two generations ago it had been built by an eccentric Englishman who had brought his family out from England and lived there mysteriously. He seemed to have plenty of money and there were gay doings in the house until his wife died. Then he had left the Island as suddenly as he had come. Nobody would buy a house in such a place and it had sunk into a ruin. Its windows were broken...its chimneys had toppled down. The wind and the mist were the only guests now in rooms that had once echoed to music and laughter and dancing feet. In the gathering shadows the old house had the look of fate which even a commonplace building assumes beneath the falling night...as if it brooded over dark secrets...grim deeds whereof history has no record.

"I wonder if anybody was ever murdered in that house," whispered Pat, with a delicious creepy thrill.

They peopled the old house with the forms of those who had once lived there. They invented the most grewsome things. The Englishman had killed his wife...had thrown her over the cape...had buried her under the house...her ghost walked there on nights like this. On stormy nights the house resounded with weeping and wailing...on moonlit nights if was full of *shadows*...restless, uneasy shadows. They scared themselves nearly to death and McGinty, excited by their tragic voices, howled dismally.

All at once they were too scared to go on pretending. It was dark...too dark to see the gulf although they could hear it. The bar moaned. An occasional bitter splash of rain blew into their cave. The little waves sobbed on the lonely shore. The very wind seemed full of the voices of the ghosts they had created. It was an eerie place... Pat snuggled close to Jingle.

"Oh, I wish somebody would come," she whispered.

Wishes don't often come true on the dot but Pat's did. A dim bobbing light came into sight out on the water... it drew nearer... there was a boat with a grizzled old fisherman in it. Jingle yelled wildly and the boat pulled in to the cape. Andrew Morgan lifted a lantern and peered at them.

"I-golly, if it isn't the Gordon boy and the Gardiner girl! Whatever are ye doing there? Caught by the tide, hey? Well, it's a bit of luck for ye that I took the notion to row down to Tiny Cove for a bag of salt. I heered that dog yelping and thought I'd better see where he was. Climb down now... a bit careful... ay, that's the trick. And where do ye want to go?"

3

Two thankful children were duly landed in the cove and lost no time in scampering home. A lovely clean rain was pelting down but they did not mind it. They burst into Judy's kitchen joyfully... out of the wind and rain and dark into the light of home. Why, the house was holding out its arms to them!

Judy was scandalised.

"Chilled to the bone ye are! Pewmony'll be the last of it."

"No, really, Judy, we kept warm running. Don't scold, Judy. And don't tell any one. Mother would worry so if we ever went to the shore again. I'll slip into a dry dress and Jingle can put on a shirt of Sid's. And you'll give us a snack, won't you, Judy? We're hungry as bears."

"Oh, oh, and ye might have been drowned... or if ould Andy Morgan hadn't come along... sure and for onct in his life the ould ninny was in the right place... ye'd av had to stay there till the tide turned... a nice scandal."

"The Hughes girls would have made one out of it anyway," laughed Pat.

"That tribe!" said Judy contemptuously, when she heard the story. "Sure and that Sally-thing is glib since she got her tongue righted. Charmed be a snake she was whin she was three years ould and cudn't talk plain agin for years."

"Charmed by a snake?"

"I'm telling ye. Curled upon the dure-step me fine snake was and Sally a-staring into its eyes. Her mother fetched it a swipe wid a billet av wood and Sally yelled as if she'd been hit herself. Old Man Hughes told me the tale himsilf so I lave ye to guess how much truth was in it. Maybe they was ashamed av the way she lisped... but there's no being up to snakes and one thing is certain... Sally had the cratur's hiss in her v'ice till she was six. Mary Ann McClenahan was be way av saying she was a changeling. Oh, oh, ye did well to give them a bar about Mary Ann. They ain't proud av the connection I'm telling ye. But... me memory's getting that poor... what was it ye was after calling them now?"

"Protoplasms," said Pat proudly.

"Oh, oh, that sounds exactly like thim, whin I come to think av it," nodded Judy. "Now sit ye down and ate yer liddle bite. I sint yer mother off to bed, niver letting on to her where ye'd gone and don't let me see ye coming home agin wid such didoes to yer credit."

"You know it would be dull if nothing out of the common ever happened, Judy. And if we never have any adventures we'll have nothing to remember when we get old."

"The sinse av her," said Judy admiringly.

CHAPTER XXI

What Would Judy Think of It?

1

WHEN Pat went to Silverbridge in September to spend a few days with Aunt Hazel she went willingly, for a brief exile from Silver Bush was not so terrible as it used to be and Aunt Hazel's home was a jolly place to visit. But when, just as the visit was nearly ended, word came that Cuddles and Sid were down with measles and that Pat must not come home until all danger of catching them was past, it was rather a cat of another colour. However, what with one thing and another,

Pat contrived to enjoy herself tolerably well and consoled herself in her spasms of homesickness by writing letters to everybody.

(The letter to Bets. With a border of dinky little black cats inked in all around it.)

"SWEETHEART ELIZABETH:—

"I think 'sweetheart' is a *tenderer* word than darling, don't you? This is my birthday and your birthday and isn't it a shame we can't spend it together? But even if we couldn't be together I've been thinking of you all day and loving you. Aren't you glad our birthday is in September? I think it is one of the nicest things that ever happened me because September is my favourite month in the year. It's such a friendly month and it seems as if the year had stopped being in a hurry and had time to think about you.

"Bets, just think of it. We're twelve. It seems such a short time since I was a child. And just think, our next birthday we'll be in our teens. Uncle Robert's Maiden Aunt says once you are in your teens the years just whirl by and first thing you know you're old. I can't believe we'll ever be old, Bets... can you?

"I like it pretty well here. Aunt Hazel's place is lovely but everything would be prettier if you could share it with me. The window in my room looks out on the orchard and off to the left is a dear little valley all full of young spruces and shadows. I mean the spruces are young not the shadows. I think shadows are always *old*. They are lovely but I think I am always a little bit afraid of them because they are so very old. Aunt Hazel laughed when I said this and said notions like that were what came of Judy Plum stuffing us all with her yarns about fairies but I don't think that has anything to do with it. It's just that shadows always seem to me to be *alive*, especially when moonlight and twilight are mixing.

"I go over the road to Uncle Robert's brother's house quite often to play with Sylvia Cyrilla Madison. I like that name. It has a nice, ripply, gurgly sound like a brook. She is a nice girl but I can never like any one as well as you, Bets. I *like* Sylvia Cyrilla but I *love* you. Sylvia Cyrilla thinks Sid is very handsome. Somehow I don't like to hear her praise him. When her grown-up sister Mattie said the same thing I was *proud*. But I hated to hear Sylvia Cyrilla say it. Why?

"Sylvia Cyrilla's big brother, Bert, told her I was a cute little skeesicks. But probably he only said it out of politeness.

"Aunt Hazel is teaching me to make fudge and hemstitch. I like doing things like that but Sylvia Cyrilla says it's old-fashioned. She says girls have to have a career now. She is going to have one. But I'm sure I don't want one. Somebody has to make fudge and I notice Sylvia Cyrilla likes to eat it as well as any one.

"Jen Campbell is Sylvia Cyrilla's dearest friend. She is good fun but she doesn't like to be beaten in anything. When I said Sid and Cuddles had the measles she said proudly, 'I had mumps and measles and scarlet fever and middle ear in one year and now I have to get my tonsils out.' It made me feel very inexperienced.

"Jen says she wishes she had been born a boy. I don't, do you? I think it is just lovely to be a girl.

"I am writing this up in Aunt Hazel's garret and it's raining. I love to be in a garret when it's raining, don't you? I love a sweet, rainy darkness like there is outside. The rain seems so friendly when it's gentle. Uncle Rob says I'm a regular garret cat but the reason I like to be up here is because I can see the harbour from one window and Silver Bush from another. From here it just looks like a little white spot against the birch bush. I can't see your house but I can see the Hill of the Mist, only it is north of me now instead of being east. That gives me a queer, Alice-in-the-looking-glass feeling.

"To-night there are windy shadows flying over the harbour under the rain . . . like great long misty wings. It gives me a strange feeling when I look at them . . . it almost hurts me and yet I love them. Oh, Bets, darling, isn't it lovely to be alive and see things like that?

"I am going to tell you a secret. I wouldn't tell it to any one in the world but you. I know you won't laugh and I can't bear to have secrets from *you*.

"I think I fell in love last Sunday night at eight o'clock. Aunt Hazel took me to a sacred concert in Silverbridge given by three blind men. One played the piano and one played the violin and one sang. His singing was just *heavenly*, Bets, and he was so handsome. He had dark hair and a beautiful nose and the loveliest blue eyes although he was blind. When he began to sing I had such a queer sinking feeling at the pit of my stomach. I thought I must be getting religion, as Judy says, and then in a flash I knew what had happened to me because my knees were shaking. I asked Judy once how you could tell when you fell in love and she said, 'Ye'll find yer legs trimbling a bit.'

"Oh, how I wished I could only do some splendid thing to make him notice me, or die for him. I was glad Aunt Hazel had scented my hands with toilet water before I left and that I had on my blue dress and my little blue necklace even if he couldn't see it. It would have been awful to fall in love if you had your old clothes on or if you had a cold in the head like poor Sylvia Cyrilla. She was sniffing and blowing her nose all the evening.

"Oh, I shall never forget it, Bets. But the trouble is it didn't last. It was all over by Monday morning. That seemed terrible because Sunday night I thought it would last to all eternity as it says in books. I don't feel a bit like that about him now, though it makes me a little dizzy just to remember it. Am I fickle? I'd hate to be fickle.

"Won't it be lovely when I can go home and we can be together again? I'm crossing every day off on the calendar and I pray every night that nobody else at Silver Bush will take measles. Please don't read any poetry under the Watching Pine until I get back. I can't bear to think of you being there without me.

"I must go to bed now and get my 'beauty sleep' as Uncle Rob says. I like the words 'beauty sleep.' Just suppose one *could* fall asleep ugly and wake up beautiful. That wouldn't seem so wonderful to you, darling, because you *are* beautiful, but poor me!

"It would be rather nice to have a blind husband because he wouldn't care if you weren't pretty. But I don't suppose I'll ever see him again.

"Think of me every moment you can.

"Your own,

"PATRICIA.

"P. S. Aunt Hazel says I ought to get my hair bobbed. But what would Judy say?"

2

(The letter to mother)

"My Own Sweetest Mother:—

"I'm just making believe you're *here*, mother, and that I'm feeling your arm around me. I'm just starving for you all. There is something pleasant about most of the days here but you seem so far away at night. Do you miss me? And does Silver Bush miss me? Dear Silver Bush. When I came up to the garret to-night and looked to where it was all was dead and dark. Then it just came to life with lights in all its windows and I thought I could see you all there, and Judy and Gentleman Tom, and I guess I cried a little.

"I was so glad to hear Sid and Cuddles were getting on all right. I hope Cuddles won't forget me. I'm glad you baked your letter in the oven so I wouldn't get germs in it, because it would be dreadful if just when I was ready to go home I'd come down with measles here. Mother dearest, I hope you don't have any of your bad headaches while I am away.

"I read my chapter in the Bible every night, mother, and say my prayers. Miss Martha Madison is here for a long visit. Uncle Robert calls her his Maiden Aunt behind her back and you can just see the capitals. Every night she comes in and asks me if I've said my prayers. I don't like strangers meddling with my prayers. It will soon be a year since dad came home from the west but still every night I thank God for it. I just can't thank Him enough. Jen says she has cousins out there and it is a splendid country. Likely it is...but it isn't Silver Bush.

"There's one thing I do like here, mother. The sheepskin rug by my bed. It's so nice to hop out of bed and dig your toes into a sheepskin rug, ever so much nicer than cold oilcloth or even a hooked mat. Can I have a sheepskin rug, mother? That is, if it won't hurt Judy's feelings.

"I had a lovely letter from Bets to-day. Mother, I do love Bets. I'm so glad I have such a beautiful friend. There is something about her voice makes me think of the wind blowing though the Silver Bush. And her eyes are like *yours*, always looking as if she knew something lovely.

"You are just the loveliest mother. I like writing letters because it is easier to write things like that than say them.

"Mother, can my new winter dress be red? I love soft

glowing colours like red. Sylvia Cyrilla says she would like to have a new dress every month but I wouldn't. I like to wear my clothes long enough to get fond of them. I hate to think that my last year's brown has got too small for me. I've had so many good times in that dear old dress. Mind you don't let Judy have any of my old things for hooking until I come home. I know she's got her eye on my yellow middy blouse but you can lengthen the sleeves, can't you, mother?

"There's a lovely moon rising over the harbour to-night although the wind sounds a little sad around the garret. Judy says that when I saw the full moon one night when I was three years old I said, 'Oh, see the man carrying a lantern in the sky.' Did I really?

"The Maiden Aunt says she likes lavender among sheets. When I said we aways put sweet clover between ours she sniffed. Aunt Hazel said yesterday I could make the Brown Betty for dinner but I couldn't do it right with the Maiden Aunt looking on and watching for mistakes. So it wasn't good and I felt *humiliated* but anyhow I think Brown Betty sounds too cannibalish.

"I think Sylvia Cyrilla's mother just worships her parlour. She keeps it locked up and the blind down and only very special visitors ever get into it. I'm glad *we* live all over our house, mother.

"The Maiden Aunt says there will be a frost to-night. Oh, I hope not. I don't want the flowers to be nipped before I get back. But I noticed to-day that the yellow leaves have begun to fall from the poplars so the summer is over.

"I've just thrown a kiss out to the wind to carry to you. And I'm putting lots of kisses in this letter, a kiss for everybody and everything and a special kiss for father and Cuddles. Isn't it lucky love doesn't make a letter weigh any heavier? If it did this letter would be so heavy I couldn't afford the postage.

"Aunt Hazel's new baby is very sweet but not so pretty as Cuddles was. Oh, mother, there really isn't anybody like the Silver Bush people, is there? I think we're *such* a nice family! And you are the nicest person in it.

Your devoted daughter,

"PAT.

"P. S. Aunt Hazel says I ought to have my hair bobbed. Do you think Judy would mind now? Sylvia Cyrilla says her mother cried for a week when she had hers bobbed but she likes it now.

"P. G."

3

(Letter to Sid)

"DEAREST SID:—

"I'm so glad to hear you are getting better and able to eat. The Maiden Aunt says you shouldn't be let eat much when you are getting over measles but I guess Judy knows better than a Maiden Aunt. I hated to think you were sick and me not there to fan your fevered brow or do a single thing for you. But I knew Judy would look after you if mother couldn't spare time from Cuddles.

"I like it here. It is a nice friendly house and Aunt Hazel lets me stay up till half past nine. But I will be glad when I can go home. I hope I won't take the measles but I think it would be real exciting to be sick. They would make such a fuss over me then. When you get well we must go back to our Secret Field and see how our spruces are.

"Sylvia Cyrilla says that Fred Davidson and his sister Muriel used to be devoted to each other just like you and me but they quarrelled and now they never speak. Oh, Sid, don't let us *ever* quarrel. I couldn't bear it.

"Of course they are only Davidsons.

"Sylvia Cyrilla says the South Glen Petersons got a bad scare last week. They thought Myrtle Peterson had eloped. But it turned out she was only drowned. And Sylvia says May Binnie is your girl. She isn't, is she, Sid? You'd never have a Binnie for a girl. They are not in our class.

"I wish you would marry Bets when you grow up. I wouldn't mind *her* coming to Silver Bush. She would love it as much as I do and I'm sure she'd make you a lovely wife. And she wouldn't mind my living with you I know.

"If the grey and white barn-cat has kittens tell Joe to save one for me.

"It will soon be ploughing time. I'll be home in time to help pick the apples. Bert Madison is teaching me how to tie

a sailor's knot and I'll show you but you won't show May
Binnie, will you, Sid?

"Your own dear sister,

"PAT.

"P. S. Aunt Hazel says I ought to have my hair bobbed.
Do you think it would improve me? But what would Judy say?"

4

(Letter to Jingle)

"DEAR JINGLE:—

"It was ripping of you to write me so often. I'm glad you
missed me. Nobody at Silver Bush have *said* they missed me.
I supposed Sid and Cuddles were too sick to, and Winnie and
Joe are so big now I guess I don't matter much to them.

"I'm up in the garret. I like to sit here and watch the
trees in the spruce valley getting black and listen to the wind
moaning round the chimneys. To-night it's the kind that Judy
calls the ghost wind. It makes me think of that piece of poetry
you read the last day we were in Happiness.

> *"The midnight wind came wild and dread*
> *Swelled with the voices of the dead.*

"Those lines always give me a lovely creepy shudder,
Jingle, and I'm glad you feel it, too. Sid thinks it's all bosh. He
laughs at me when I wonder what is the meaning of the things
the trees are always saying and what some of the winds are
always so sorry for. But you never laugh at me, Jingle. Every
night here, before I go to sleep I lie still and think I can hear
the water falling over the mossy rock in dear Happiness.

"How is McGinty? Give him a hug for me. The Maiden
Aunt has a dog but I'm sorry for it. She never lets it out of
her sight and the poor thing has nothing but a rubber rat to
play with. They have several dogs at Sylvia Cyrilla's, Bert's
dog and Myrtle's dog and the family dog, but none of these
are as nice as McGinty. Uncle Rob's father down the road has
a dog but he is not an exciting dog. Uncle Rob says he is
always so tired he has to lean against a fence to bark.
Speaking of dogs, I found such a lovely poem in Aunt Hazel's

scrapbook called *The Little Dog Angel*. I cried when I read it because I thought of you and McGinty. I could just *see* McGinty slipping out of heaven's gates between St. Peter's legs to 'bark a welcome to you in the shivering dark.' Oh, Jingle, I'm sure dear little dogs like McGinty must have souls.

"I wonder what you'd think of Aunt Hazel's house. I think you'd say it was too tall. But it's really very nice inside. Only there are no back steps to sit on and no round window and no dead clock.

"What do you think, Jingle? Old Mr. Peter Morgan from the harbour told me he was a pirate in his young days and buried a treasure worth millions on a West Indies island and never could find the place again. If he had told me that four years ago I would have believed him but he has left it too late. I wish it was as easy to believe things as it used to be.

"The fence back of Uncle Robert's house is the line between Queen's and Prince county. It's perfectly thrilling, Jingle, to think you can go into another county just by climbing over a fence. Somehow you expect everything to be different. I climb over it every day just to get the nice adventure feeling. Aunt Hazel says it doesn't take much to give me a thrill but I think it is lucky. What would live be without a few thrills? And what would life be without Betses and Jingles and Sids and Judys and Silver Bushes?

"CHUM PAT.

"P. S. Aunt Hazel says she thinks I ought to have my hair bobbed. Would you like me bobbed, Jingle?"

5

(Letter to Judy with Judy's comments)

"MY OWN DEAR JUDY:—

"It just seems ages since I left home and I've been so lonesome for you all and the dear old kitchen. Aunt Hazel's kitchen is very up to date but it isn't as cosy as ours, Judy. When I get homesick at nights I go up to the garret and watch the lights of Silver Bush and picture out what every one is doing and I see you setting bread in the kitchen, talking to yourself. (*Fancy that now.*) And Gentleman Tom thinking away on his bench. (*Sure and it's the grand thinker ye are, Tom. I'm after telling the world ye can think more in a day than most folks can in a wake.*) They have no cats here because Uncle Robert's Maiden Aunt visits so often and so long and she doesn't like them. I don't like the Maiden Aunt very well. (*Oh, oh, small blame to ye for that, Patsy.*) She is very homely. I know I'm not much to look at myself but I haven't a nose like hers. Everything, even her hair, seems to be frightened of it and trying to get away from it. (*Sure and there's observation for ye.*) And yet I'm a little sorry for her, Judy, (*oh, oh, the tinder heart av her now*), because she is really lonely. She hasn't anybody or any place to love. That must be dreadful.

"Aunt Hazel has the loveliest blue quilt, quilted in fans, on her spare bed. And she has the rose mat you hooked for her on her living room floor. She is very proud of it and points it out to every one. (*Oh, oh, so I'm getting me name up, it sames.*) She hasn't a parlour or she would have put it there. It isn't fashionable to have parlours now, Sylvia Cyrilla says. I don't know what she'd say if she knew we have *two*. (*Sure and who cares what she'd say? A parlour sounds far grander than a living room inny day.*)

"Mother says I can have a new red dress this winter, Judy. And I hope she'll let me get a little red hat to go with it. (*Oh, oh, but that would be rale chick.*) Jen Davidson says she is going to have two new hats. She says the Davidsons always do. Well, you can't wear more than one hat at a time, can you, Judy? (*The philosophy av her.*) The Maiden Aunt sniffs when I talk of clothes but Aunt Hazel says that is because she can't afford them herself and if Uncle Robert didn't help her out every year she wouldn't have a stitch to her back. (*Sure and folks don't be wanting minny stitches to their backs nowadays, jidging be the fashion books I've been seeing.*)

"Oh, Judy dear, the Maiden Aunt says it isn't right to tell fairy tales, not even that there is a Santa Claus. (*Set her up wid it.*) But I'm going to keep on believing in fairy rings and horseshoes over the door and witches on broomsticks. It makes life so thrilling to believe in things. If you believe in a thing it doesn't matter whether it exists or not. (*Sure and she cud argy a Philadelphy lawyer down, the darlint.*)

"We don't have any eating between meals here, Judy. I guess it's healthier but when bed-time comes I *do* think of your eggs and butter. I think a snack at bed-time *is* healthy. *(Sure and all sinsible people do be thinking the same.)* But Aunt Hazel is a good cook. She can make the loveliest ribbon cake. I wish you would learn to make ribbon cake, Judy. *(Oh, oh, yer ribbon cake, is it? I'm too old a dog to be larning yer new millinery tricks.)* But her cranberry pies aren't as nice as yours, Judy. They're too sweet. *(Oh, oh, the blarney of the cratur! She's after wanting to put me in the good humour.)* Sylvia Cyrilla's mother can make lovely Devonshire cream. *(Devonshire crame, is it? I cud make Devonshire crame afore she was born or thought of. But will ye be telling me where the crame is to come from wid ivery drop of milk sint off to the cheese factory?)* But she isn't a good cook in other ways. Her things *look* all right but something always *tastes* wrong. Not enough salt or too much, or no flavouring or something like that. *(No gumption, me jewel, that's the trouble. No gumption.)*

"Sylvia Cyrilla's father's cousin in Charlottetown tried to cut his throat last week but Sylvia Cyrilla says he didn't succeed and they took him to the hospital and sewed him up. *(Alvin Sutton that wud be. Sure and none av the Suttons iver made a good job av innything they undertook.)*

"Aunt Hazel's father-in-law and mother-in-law live up the road a piece, Mr. and Mrs. James Madison. I often go up on errands. Mr. James has no use for me because I can't eat a plate of porridge. He says it is a dish for a king. But I'm not a king. *(Porridge, is it? Sure and I'm not running down porridge but skinny ould Jim Madison isn't after being much av an advertisement for it.)* They are very proud of their oldest daughter, Mary. She is an M.A. and won some great scholarships and is a teacher in a college. I suppose it is nice to be so clever, Judy. *(Oh, oh, but I'm not hearing av her getting a man, though.)* Mr. James likes to tease his wife. When Sylvia Cyrilla's father asked him if he would get married over again he laughed and said yes, but not to the same woman. Mrs. James didn't laugh though. *(Oh, oh, she was after knowing it might be half fun and whole earnest.)* They say Mr. James was very wild when he was young but he says if he hadn't been there'd have been no stories to tell about him now ... he'd be nothing but a dull old grandfather.

"I've been collecting stories ever since I've been here, Judy, so that I'll have lots to tell when I'm old like you. There is one about a ghost on a farm belonging to Sylvia Cyrilla's uncle who has whiskers. I mean the ghost has whiskers. Isn't that funny? Can you imagine a ghost with whiskers? *(Sure and I knew a ghost in ould Ireland wid a bald head. There's no accounting for the freaks av the craturs.)* And Jen Davidson had a cousin who always cried when he was drunk. I thought it was because he was sorry he was drunk but Jen says it was because he couldn't get drunk oftener. Old Mr. McAllister from the bridge was up to see Mr. James last Monday and said he would have been up Sunday only he was wrestling with Satan all day. Do you suppose he really was, Judy, or was he just speaking poetically. *(Oh, oh, I'm guessing he must av been trying to keep on good terms wid his wife. She'd quarrel wid a feather bed, that one. Sure and he only married her be accident. Whin he proposed to her he was expicting her to say no and whin she said yes poor Johnny McAllister got the surprise av his life.)* His brother was a dreadful man and died shaking his fist at God. *(Ye cudn't be ixpicting a McAllister to have inny manners, aven on his death bed, Patsy darlint.)* The Maltby brothers have made up their quarrel after never speaking for thirty years. I don't think they're half as interesting now. Uncle Rob says they've made up because they've forgotten what they quarrelled about but if anybody could remember it they'd start all over again. And Mr. Gordon Keys at the bridge keeps his wife in order by crocheting lace whenever she won't do as he says. She hates to see him do it and so she gives in.

"The funniest story I've collected so far is this. Several years ago old Sam McKenzie was very sick in Charlottetown and everybody thought he was going to die. He was very rich and prominent, so Mr. Trotter, the undertaker, knew the family would want a fine coffin for him and he imported an extra fine one right off to have it ready because it was a very cold winter and he was afraid the strait might freeze over any day. And then old Sam went and got better and poor Mr. Trotter was left with that expensive coffin on his hands, and nobody likely to buy it. But he kept quiet and one day a few months afterwards old Tom Ramsay, who was rich and prominent, too, dropped dead when nobody expected him to. And Mr. Trotter told the family he had just one coffin on hand that was good enough and they took it and so old Tom Ramsay was buried in Sam McKenzie's coffin. The secret leaked out after awhile and the Ramsays were furious but they couldn't unbury him.

"That is my funniest story but the nicest is about old Mr. George McFadyen who died four years ago and went to heaven. At first he couldn't find any Islanders but after a while he found out there were lots of them, only they had to be kept locked up for fear they would try to get back to the Island. Mr. James Madison told me that but he wouldn't explain how he found out about Mr. McFadyen's experience. Anyway I'm sure I'd feel like that, Judy. If I went to heaven I'd want to get back to Silver Bush.

"I was afraid when it blew so hard last night some of our trees would blow down. If Joe saves a kitten for me be sure you give it some cream, Judy. Jen Davidson has an aunt that has been married four times. *(Oh, oh, the lies she must av been after telling the min, that one!)* Jen seems proud of her but Uncle Rob says she ought to be more economical with husbands when there isn't enough to go round. I think he said that to tease the Maiden Aunt. Madge Davidson is going to marry Crofter Carter. *(Sure and she's a bit shopworn or she wudn't be after looking at him. I've seen the day a Davidson wudn't walk on the same side av the road as a Carter.)* Ross Halliday and Marinda Bailey at Silverbridge are married. They were engaged for fifteen years. I suppose they got tired of it. *(Sure and Marinda Bailey always said she wudn't marry till she got used to the thought av it. She was always a bit soft in the head, that one. But the min same to like that sort I'm telling ye. She niver had inny looks but kissing goes be favour and if Ross is the happy man at last it isn't Judy Plum that'll grudge it to him.)* Mrs. Samuel Carter is dead and the funeral is Friday. They've had a terrible lot of funerals there, Sylvia Cyrilla says, but Mr. Carter says funerals are not as expensive as weddings when all is said and done. *(And that's no drame whin ye have to support yer son-in-laws as Sam Carter has. I'm telling ye.)*

"I hope you won't be tired reading this long letter, Judy. I've written some of it every day for a week and just put down everything that came into my head. I'll soon be home now and we can talk everything over. Don't let anybody change any of the furniture about when I'm away. If this letter is bulgy it's just because I've put so many hugs in it for you.

"Your loving

"PATSY.

"P. S. Aunt Hazel says she thinks my hair would grow darker if it was bobbed. Do you think it would, Judy?

"P."

(Sure and it's the good latter she does be writing. It's the lonesome place around here widout the liddle dancing fate and the dear laugh av her. That way she has av smiling at ye as if there was some nice liddle joke atween ye'll carry her far. But nixt year will be lashings av time to talk av bobbing. Sure and I must be putting this letter in me glory box.)

CHAPTER XXII

Three Daughters of One Race

1

IF the years did not exactly whirl past after you were twelve, as the Maiden Aunt had so dolefully predicted, they really did seem to go faster. Pat and Bets could hardly believe that their thirteenth birthday was so near when mother told Pat that Joan and Dorothy were coming over from St. John for a visit and it would be nice to have a little party for them.

"You can have it on your birthday. That is Bets' birthday, too, and you will kill three birds with one stone," said mother gaily.

Pat was not very keen about parties...not as keen as Judy would have liked her to be. Neither was she especially excited over the visit of Joan and Dorothy Selby, although she was rather curious. She had heard a good deal at one time or another about the beauty of Dorothy. Both Joan and Dorothy had had their pictures in a society paper as "the lovely little daughters of Mr. and Mrs. Albert Selby of Linden Lodge." One would just like to see for oneself if Dorothy were as pretty as family gossip reported.

"I don't believe she's a bit prettier than Winnie."

"Oh, oh, 'tis likely not, if Winnie was dressed up like

her . . . sure and it's sometimes the fine feathers that make the fine birds. But yer Uncle Albert was the fine-looking b'y and they say Dorothy takes after him. He's niver been home much. He got a gay young wife that thought things dull here."

"Joan and Dorothy are being educated at a convent boarding school," said Pat. "I suppose they'll be frightfully clever."

Judy sniffed.

"Oh, oh, cliverness can't be put in wid a spoon aven at yer convints. We do be having *some* brains at Silver Bush. Don't let thim overcrow ye, Pat, wid their fine city ways and convint brading. Howsomiver, I ixpect they're nice liddle girls and seeing as they're yer only cousins on the spindle side I'm hoping ye'll take to thim."

Joan and Dorothy had not been at Silver Bush twenty-four hours before Pat had secretly made up her mind that she was not going to "take" to them. Perhaps, although she would never have owned it, she was a little jealous of Dorothy who certainly lived up to her reputation for beauty. She *was* prettier than Winnie . . . though Pat never could be got to admit that she was prettier than Bets. Her hair was a dark, nutty brown, dipping down prettily over her forehead, and it made Pat's look even more gingery and faded by contrast. She had velvety brown eyes that made Pat's amber-hued ones look almost yellow. She had beautiful hands . . . which she put up to her face very often and which made everybody else's look sunburned and skinny. Joan, who was the brainy one and made no great claims to beauty, was very proud of Dorothy's looks and bragged a little about them.

"Dorothy is the prettiest girl in St. John," she told Pat.

"She *is* very pretty," admitted Pat. "Almost as pretty as Winnie and Bets Wilcox."

"Oh, Winnie!" Joan looked amused. "Winnie *is* quite nice-looking, of course. You would be, too, if your hair wasn't so long and terribly straight. It's so Victorian."

Probably Joan hadn't any very clear idea what Victorian meant but had heard somebody say it and thought it would impress this rather independent country cousin.

"Judy doesn't want me to bob my hair," said Pat coldly.

"Judy? Oh, that quaint old servant of yours. Do you really let her run you like that?"

"Judy isn't a servant," cried Pat hotly.

"Not a servant? What is she then?"

"She's one of the family."

"Don't you pay her wages?"

Pat had really never thought about it.

"I ... I suppose so."

"She *is* a servant then. Of course it's awfully sweet of you to love her as you do but mother says it doesn't do to make too much of servants. It makes them forget their place. Judy isn't very respectful I notice. But of course it's different in the country. Oh, *look* at Dorothy over there by the lilies. Doesn't she look like an angel?"

Pat permitted herself an impertinence.

"I've heard that pretty girls hardly ever make pretty women. Do you think it's true, Joan?"

"Mother was a pretty girl and she is a pretty woman. Mother was a Charlottetown Hilton," said Joan loftily.

Pat knew nothing about Charlottetown Hiltons but she understood Joan was putting on airs, as Judy would say.

This was when they had been several days at Silver Bush. They had been very polite the first day. Silver Bush was such a *charming* spot ... the garden was so "quaint" ... the well was so "quaint" ... the church barn was so "quaint" ... the grave-yard was "priceless." What was the matter? Pat knew in a flash. They were patronising the garden and the well and the barn. And the grave-yard!

"You drink water out of a tap, I suppose," she said scornfully.

"Oh, you are the *funniest* darling," said Dorothy, hugging her.

But after that they did not condescend quite so much. They had all sized each other up and formed opinions that would last for some time. Pat liked Dorothy well enough but Joan was a "blow."

"I wish you could see *our* mums," she said when Pat showed her the garden. "Dad always takes all the prizes at the Horticultural Show with them. Why doesn't Uncle Alec cut that old spruce down? It shades the corner too much."

"That tree is a friend of the family," said Pat.

"I wouldn't have violets in that corner," suggested Dorothy. "I'd have them over at the west side."

"But the violets have always been in that corner," said Pat.

"How this gate creaks!" said Joan with a shudder. "Why don't you oil it?"

"It has *always* creaked," said Pat.

"Your garden is quaint but rather jungly. It ought to be cleared out," said Dorothy as they left it.

Pat had learned a few things since the day she had slapped Norma. For the honour of Silver Bush no guest must be insulted. Otherwise there is no knowing what she might have done to Dorothy.

It was just as bad inside the house. Joan was all for changing the furniture about if it had been *her* house.

"Do you know what I'd do? I'd put the piano in *that* corner. . . ."

"But it *belongs* in this corner," said Pat.

"The room would look so much better, darling, if you just changed it a little," said Joan.

"The room would *hate* you if you changed it," cried Pat.

Joan and Dorothy exchanged amused glances behind her back. And Pat knew they did. But she forgave them because they praised Bets. Bets, they said, was lovely, with such sweet ways.

"Oh, oh, she has the good heart, av course she has the good manners," said Judy.

Pat warmed to Joan when Joan admired the bird-house Jingle had given her. Jingle had a knack of making delightful bird-houses. But when the girls met Jingle Joan lost grace again. Dorothy was sweet to him . . . perhaps a little too sweet . . . but Joan saw only the badly cut hair and the nondescript clothes. And Dorothy enraged Pat by saying afterwards,

"It's awfully sweet of you to be nice to that poor boy."

Patronising! That was the word for it. She had patronised Jingle, too. And yet Jingle liked to hear Dorothy play on the piano. It couldn't be denied she could do it. Winnie's performance was nothing beside hers. Both the Selby girls were musical. . . . Joan practised night and day on her guitar and Dorothy "showed off" her pretty little paws on the piano.

"Ye'd be thinking she mint to tear the kays out be the

roots," muttered Judy, who did not like to see Winnie so eclipsed.

2

So the visit was not a great success although the older folk... all but Judy... thought the girls got on beautifully. Pat found it a bit hard to keep Joan and Dorothy amused... and they had to be amused all the time. They could not hunt their fun for themselves as she and Bets could. Pat showed them the grave-yard and introduced them to all the fields by name, to the Old Part and the Whispering Lane. She even tried not to mind when Sid took Dorothy back and showed her the Secret Field. But it did hurt horribly.

She knew the family thought Sid was "sweet" on Dorothy. Perhaps that was better than being sweet on May Binnie. But Pat did not want Sid to be sweet on anybody.

"You're just jealous of Dorothy because Cuddles has taken such a fancy to her," jeered Sid.

"I'm not... I'm not," cried Pat. "Only... that was *our* secret."

"We're getting too big to have secret fields and all that nonsense," said Sid in a grown-up manner.

"I hate growing up," sobbed Pat. "Oh, Sid, I don't mind you liking Dorothy... I'm glad you like her... but *she* didn't care about that field."

"No, she didn't," admitted Sid. "She said what on earth did we see in it to make a secret of. And what *did* we see, Pat, if it comes to that?"

"Oh!" Pat felt helpless. If Sid couldn't *see* what they had seen he couldn't be made to.

Joan and Dorothy did not care for the play-house in the birch bush; they did not care for hunting kittens in the barn: two fluffy-tailed orange ones left them cold, although Dorothy did distracting things with them when any boys were around. She cuddled them under her lovely chin and even kissed the sunwarm tops of their round, velvety heads... "Just," as Judy muttered to herself, "to be making the b'ys wish they were kittens."

They knew nothing about "pretending adventures." They did not like fishing in Jordan with long fat worms; they could not sit for hours on a fence or boulder or apple-tree bough and talk over the things they saw, as Pat and Bets could. They found nothing delightful in sitting on Weeping Willy's tombstone and looking for the first star. Joe took them driving in the evenings and the party was a bit of excitement. They wore dresses the like of which had never been seen in North Glen before and were remembered for years by the girls who saw them. But they were bored, though they tried politely to hide it.

One thing they did like, however . . . sitting in the kitchen or on the back door-steps in the September twilights, when the sky was all full of a soft brightness of a sun that had dropped behind the dark hills and the birchen boughs in the big bush waved as if tossing kisses to the world, listening to Judy's stories while they ate red, nut-sweet apples. It was the one time when Pat and her cousins really liked each other. Nor . . . though Dorothy thought it so "quaint" to eat in the kitchen . . . did they despise Judy's "liddle bites" after the story telling. Pat caught them exchanging amused glances over Judy's fried eggs and cod-fish cakes but they praised her bishop's bread and doughnuts so warmly that Judy's heart softened to them a bit. Judy felt rather self-reproachful because she did not like these girls better herself after having been so anxious that Pat should like them. Gentleman Tom, who had never noticed any one but Judy, seemed to take a fancy to Joan and followed her about. Pat thought Judy would be jealous but not a bit of it . . . apparently.

"He knows she nades watching, that one," sniffed Judy.

"It is nice here in summer," admitted Joan on one of these evenings, "but it must be frightfully dull in winter."

"It isn't. Winter here is lovely. One can be so cosy in winter," retorted Pat.

"You haven't even a furnace," said Joan. "How in the world do you keep from freezing to death?"

"We've stoves in every room," said Pat proudly. "And heaps of good firewood . . . look at the pile over there. We can *see* our fires . . . we don't have to sit up to a hole in the floor to get warm."

Joan laughed.

"We have steam radiators, silly . . . and open fireplaces. You *are* funny, Pat . . . you're so touchy about Silver Bush. One would think you thought it was the only place in the world."

"It is ... for me," said Pat.

"Joe doesn't think so," said Joan. "I've had talks with Joe when we were out driving. He isn't contented here, Pat."

Pat stared.

"Did Joe tell you that?"

"Oh, not in so many words but I could see. I don't think any of you here really understand Joe. He doesn't like farming ... he wants to be a sailor. Joe is a boy with very deep feelings, Pat, but he doesn't like showing them."

"The idea of her explaining Joe to me," sobbed Pat to Judy, after the girls had gone to their bed in the Poet's room. "I know Joe has some silly ideas about sailing, just as well as she does, but father says he'll soon have more sense. I'm sure Joe would never want to go away from Silver Bush."

"Ye can't all be staying here foriver, darlint," warned Judy.

"But we needn't think of that for years yet, Judy. Joe is only nineteen. And Joan to be putting on airs about 'understanding' him!"

"Oh, oh, that's where the shoe pinches," chuckled Judy.

"And Joan asked me to-day if I didn't think Dorothy had a lovely laugh. She said Dorothy was noted for her laugh. I agreed, just to be polite, Judy ..."

"Oh, oh, if one hadn't to be polite! But thin ... one has."

"But I don't think Dorothy's laugh is half as pretty as Winnie's, Judy."

"Sure and they've both got the Selby laugh and ye can't be telling which av thim is laughing if ye don't see her. But I'm knowing nather ye nor Joan cud be convinced av that. The trouble is, me jewel, that ye and Joan are a bit too much alike in a good minny things iver to be hitting it off very well."

Pat did not tell Judy everything that had stung her. Joan had said,

"After all, that Jingle of yours has a lovely smile."

"He's not *my* Jingle," said Pat shortly. And what difference did it make to Joan whether Jingle had a lovely smile or not? Hadn't she made fun of his hair and his glasses and his frayed trousers? And she had also laughed at Uncle Tom's beard and Judy's book of Useful Knowledge. One was "Victorian" and the other was "outmoded." They condescended to Aunt Edith and Aunt Barbara, too ... they were "such quaint old darlings." Pat had never been so conscious of the leak stain on the dining-room ceiling and the worn places in the Little Parlour carpet until she saw Joan looking at them, and she had not noticed how mossy the shingles of the kitchen roof were growing until Joan said amiably that she rather liked old houses.

"*Our* house is really rather too new. It's of white stucco with a red-tiled roof... a bit glaring. Father says it will mellow with time."

"I never like new houses," said Pat. "They haven't any ghosts."

"Ghosts? But you don't believe in ghosts, do you, Pat?"

"I didn't mean ghosts... exactly."

"What did you mean then?"

"Oh... just that... when a house has been lived in for years and years... *something* of the people who have lived in it *stays* in it."

"You quaint darling!" said Dorothy.

3

Pat exulted in the freedom and silence of home after they had gone. It was altogether delightful to be alone again. The books that had been strewn everywhere were back in their places; the Poet's room was no longer cluttered up with alien dresses and shoes and brushes and necklaces.

"Isn't it nice just to be here by ourselves and no outsiders?" she said to Judy as they sat on the steps. A night of dim silver was brooding over the bush and the pale, perfect gold of the trembling aspen leaves had faded into shadow. The still air was full of far, muted surf thunder. Gentleman Tom had arranged himself beautifully on the well platform and the two orange kittens were blinking their jewel eyes and purring their small hearts out on Pat's lap.

"Mother says she is so sorry I didn't love my cousins. I *do* love them, Judy, but I don't *like* them."

"Oh, oh, but three's a crowd," said Judy. "Two girls can be getting on very well but whin there's three av ye and all high-steppers, some one's bound to get rubbed the wrong way. Often have I been seeing it."

"I liked Joan in spots,... but she made me feel *unimportant*, Judy. She snubbed me."

"Sure and she'd snub the moon, that one. But she's the cliver one for all."

"And she bragged... she *did*."

"The Hiltons always did be liking to make a bit av a splash. And didn't ye do a bit av snubbing and bragging now yersilf, Patsy darlint? Though I'm not saying ye didn't be having the aggravation. There don't be minny families that haven't their own liddle kinks. Even the Selbys now, niver to mintion the Gardiners. Ye have to be making allowances. I'm thinking ye'd av been liking the girls better if it wasn't for yer liddle jealousy, Patsy..."

"I wasn't jealous, Judy!"

"Oh, oh, be honest now, me jewel. Ye was jealous of Joan because Joe liked her and ye was jealous of Dorothy because Sid and Cuddles liked her. Ye have yer liddle faults, Patsy, just as they have."

"I don't tell fibs anyway. They told mother when they went away they had had a perfectly lovely time. They hadn't. That was a lie, Judy."

"Oh, oh... a polite lie maybe... and maybe not all a lie. They had it in spots as ye say, I'm thinking."

"Anyway there's one word I never want to hear again as long as I live, Judy, and that's 'quaint.'"

"Quaint, is it? Sure and whin Joan called Gentleman Tom quaint I'll be swearing the baste winked at me. I cud av been telling Miss Joan her own grandfather was quaint the night he got up to be making a spach at a Tory meeting and his wife, who was born a Tolman and be the same token a Grit, laned over from the sate behind and pulled him down be his coat-tails. Ye cud hear the thud all over the hall. Not a word wud she let him be saying. Oh, oh, quaint!"

"Sometimes, Judy, they made me awful mad... *inside*."

"But ye kept it inside. That shows ye're getting on. It's what we all have to be larning, me jewel, if we want to be living wid folks paceable. Mad inside, is it? Sure and I was mad inside ivry day they was here whin they began showing off in me own kitchen. And that Joan one talking about kaping 'abreast av the times.' Sure, thinks I to mesilf, if chasing around in circles after yer own tail is kaping up wid the times ye're the lady that can be doing it. And thin I wud be thinking that yer Aunts at the Bay Shore were just the same whin they were liddle girls and thinks I, fam'lies must be standing be each other and life will be curing us all av a lot av foolishness. I wudn't wonder if ye'd be mating the girls some time agin whin ye've all got a bit riper and finding ye like thim very well."

Pat received this prediction in sceptical silence. She looked up to the Long House where the light in Bets' window was glowing like a friendly star on a dark hill.

"Anyway I'm glad Bets and I can be alone again. Bets is the only girl I want for a friend."

"What will ye be doing whin she grows up and goes away?"

"Oh, but she never will, Judy. Even if she gets married she will go on living at the Long House because she is the only child. And I'll always be here and we'll always be together. We have it all arranged."

Judy sighed and nudged.

"Don't be after saying thim things out loud, Patsy... not out loud, darlint. Sure and ye niver can tell who might be listening to ye."

CHAPTER XXIII
Mock Sunshine

1

"PAT, can you meet me in Happiness right away?" phoned Jingle.

The Gordons had had a telephone put in at last and Jingle and Pat generally kept the wire from rusting.

Pat knew from Jingle's voice that something exciting had happened... exciting and pleasant. What could it be? Exciting and pleasant things were so rare in Jingle's life, poor fellow. She went to Happiness so speedily that she was there before Jingle, waiting for him in a ferny hollow among the cradle hills. Jingle lingered for a moment behind a screen of young spruces to watch her... her wonderful golden-brown eyes fixed dreamily on the sky... a provoking smile over hidden thoughts lingering around her mouth... just enough of a smile to give it that dear little kissable quirk at the corner that was beginning to make Jingle's heart act queerly whenever he saw it. What was she thinking of? What *did* girls think of? Jingle found himself wishing he knew more about them in general.

Pat looked away from her clouds to see a Jingle she had never seen before with eyes so bright that their radiance shone through even the dark quenching glasses.

"Jingle, you look as if... as if everything had come true."

"It has... for me." Jingle flung himself down on the grass and propped his face on his thin sunburned hands. "Pat... mother's coming... to-morrow!"

Pat gasped.

"Oh, Jingle! At last! How wonderful!"

"The telegram came last night. I phoned right over to Silver Bush but Judy said you were away. Then this morning I had to leave at five to take a load of factory cheese to town. I've just got back... I wanted you to be the first to know."

"Jingle... I'm so glad."

"I am, too... only, Pat... I wish she'd written she was coming instead of wiring it."

"Likely she hadn't time. Where was she?"

"In St. John. Oh, Pat, think of it... I'm fifteen and I've never seen my mother... not to remember her. Not even a picture of her... I haven't the least idea what she really looks like. Long ago... you remember, Pat... the day we found Happiness?... I told you she had blue eyes and golden hair. But I just imagined that because I heard Aunt Maria say once that she was 'fair.' Perhaps she isn't like that at all."

"I'm sure she'll be lovely whatever kind of eyes and hair she has," assured Pat.

"Ever since I saw that Madonna of the Clouds in your little parlour I've been imagining mother looked like that. Of course she must be older... mother is really thirty-five. I couldn't sleep last night for thinking about her coming. I don't see how I can wait till to-morrow. Last night I thought I couldn't wait for *two* morrows."

Jingle's thin, delicately-cut face was dreamy and remote. Pat gazed at him, thrilling with sympathy. She knew what this meant to him.

"I know. Judy says when I was small and promised

anything 'to-morrow' I'd keep plaguing her, 'Where is to-morrow now, Judy?' *Your* to-morrow is somewhere, Jingle . . . right this very minute it must be somewhere. Isn't that nice to think?"

"All day to-day I've just been in a dream, Pat. It didn't seem real. I've taken out and read the telegram a hundred times just to be sure. If it had only been a letter, Pat . . . a letter she had written . . . *touched*."

"You'll have her, herself, to-morrow and that will be better than any letter. How long will she stay?"

"I don't know. She doesn't say anything but that she'll be here. I hope for *weeks*."

"Perhaps . . . perhaps she'll take you away with her, Jingle."

Pat was a little breathless. The idea had gone through her like lightning. It was a very unwelcome one. Jingle gone! Jordan and no Jingle! Happiness and no Jingle! A queer chill seemed to begin somewhere inside of her and spread all over her body.

Jingle shook his head.

"I don't think so . . . some way I . . . I don't think I'd even want to go. But to see her . . . to feel her arms around me just once! To tell her everything. I'm going to give her all the letters, Pat. I got them out of the box last night and read them over. The first ones, when I just had to print the letters, were so funny. But a mother wouldn't think them funny, would she? A mother would like them, don't you think?"

"I'm sure she'll just love them. She couldn't help it."

Jingle gave a sigh of satisfaction.

"You know so much more about a mother than I do, Pat. You've had one all your life."

Pat winked her eyes savagely. It would be absurd to cry. But she was twisted with a sudden fierce pity for Jingle . . . whose mother had never come to see him . . . who had *years* of letters that he had never sent. She was sorry for the mother who had missed them.

But everything would be all right after this.

"You must come over and see mother, Pat."

"Oh, but, Jingle, I don't like to. You'll want to be alone together."

"Most of the time, I suppose. But I want you to see her . . . and I want her to see you. And we'll bring her up here and show her Happiness, won't we, Pat? You won't mind?"

"Of course not. And of course she'll want to see it because it's a place you love."

"I haven't had time to make anything for her. . . ."

"You can get a lovely bouquet ready for her, Jingle. She'll just love that."

"But we haven't any nice flowers at our place."

"Come over early in the morning and get some from our garden. I'll make the bouquet up for you . . . there's some lovely baby's breath out now. You can choose the flowers and I'll arrange them. Judy says I have a knack with flowers. Jingle, what is your mother's name?"

"Mrs. Garrison," said Jingle bitterly. It was a hateful thing to him that his mother's name was not his. "Her first name is Doreen. That is a pretty name, isn't it?"

"So Jim's fine widdy is coming to see her b'y at last?" said Judy when she heard the news. "Well, it's not afore the time. I'm thinking Larry Gordon wrote her a bit av a letter. I've heard him say it was time he knew what her plans for the b'y was if she had inny. The tacher up at South Glen has been at him to take up the branches this year but Larry says what wud the use be. They can't ixpect *him* to foot the bills for Quane's, what wid him being barely able to scrape up his interest ivery year."

"Then . . . you think . . . you don't think Jingle's mother is coming just because she wanted to see him?" said Pat slowly.

"I'm not saying she isn't. But ye do be knowing she's niver wanted to see him for over a dozen years. Howsomiver, maybe she's had a change av heart and let's hope it hard, Patsy, for I'm thinking that poor Jingle-lad is all set up over her coming."

"He is . . . oh, Judy, it just means everything to him. Maybe . . . when she *sees* him. . . ."

"Maybe," agreed Judy dubiously.

2

Jingle was over bright and early to get the bouquet for his mother. He had put on his poor best suit, which was too short for him and had been too short for a year. His aunt had cut his hair and made rather a worse job than usual of it. But his face was flushed with excitement and for the first time it occurred to Pat that Jingle wasn't such a bad-looking boy. If it were not for those awful glasses!

"Jingle, take them off before your mother comes. It couldn't hurt your eyes for a little while."

"Aunt Maria wouldn't like it. She paid for my glasses, you know, and she says I've got to wear them all the time or it would be wasted money. She . . . she knows I hate them, I think . . . and that's really why she gets so cross if I leave them off. When we get mother away by ourselves . . . when we go to Happiness . . . I'll take them off. Pat, think of mother . . . my own mother . . . in Happiness!"

They spent a long time over the bouquet. Jingle was hard to please. Only absolutely perfect flowers must go into it . . . and no delphiniums.

"Delphiniums are so haughty," said Jingle. "And they've no perfume. Just sweet-smelling flowers, Pat. And a bit of southern wood. You know Judy calls it 'lad's love.' So it ought to go in mother's bouquet."

Jingle laughed a bit consciously But he did not mind if Pat thought him sentimental.

"We'll put in some of the leaves of the old sweet-briar . . . they've such a lovely apple scent. I wish there were more roses out. It's too early for them . . . but these little pink buds are darling . . . and those white ones with the pink hearts. There was one lovely copper rose out last night . . . just one on father's new bush. He told me we could have it. But it rained last night and it was all beaten and ruined this morning. I almost cried. But here's one long red bud from Winnie's bush and I'll put it in your coat, Jingle."

"Just two hours more," said Jingle. "Pat, I want you to come over right after dinner, before she comes. Will you?"

"Oh, Jingle . . . wouldn't you want to be alone when you see her first?"

"If I *could* be alone . . . but Uncle Lawrence and Aunt Maria will be there . . . and, somehow . . . I don't know . . . I just feel as if I wanted you there, too, Pat."

In the end Pat went, thrilling from head to foot with excitement . . . and considerable curiosity. She had put her hair in curlers the night before, to look her best before Jingle's mother, but the result was rather bushy and rampant.

"It would look all right if it was bobbed, Judy," she muttered rebelliously.

"Standing out round yer head like a hello," said Judy sarcastically.

Pat braided it in tightly and put on the new blue pull-over Judy had knitted for her, over her cornflower blue skirt. Would Jingle's mother think her just a crude little country girl with a head like a fuzz-bush?

"I don't suppose she'll ever think of me at all," Pat comforted herself. "She'll be so taken up with Jingle."

Jingle was waiting with his bouquet, his lips set tightly to hide their quivering. Larry Gordon's old car clattered in at the gate.

"Here she comes," said Pat... magic, breathless words.

She came. They saw her get out of the car and drift up the stone walk. Jingle had meant to run to meet her. But he found he couldn't move. He stood there stupidly, his breath coming quickly, his bouquet quivering in his hands. Was this his mother... this?

Pat saw her more clearly than Jingle did. Tall, slender, graceful as a flower, in a soft fluttering chiffon dress like blue mist; pale, silvery-golden hair sleeked down all over her head like a cap under a little tilted hat of smooth blue feathers: bluish-green eyes that never seemed to see you, even when they looked at you, under eyebrows as thin as a line drawn in soot; a mouth that spoiled everything, so vividly red and arched was it. She might have stepped off a magazine cover. Beautiful...oh, yes, very beautiful! But not...somehow...like a mother!

"I like a mother who *looks* like a mother," was the thought that whisked through Pat's head. This woman looked... at first... like a girl.

Doreen Garrison came up the walk, looking rather curiously at the two standing by the door. Jingle spoke first.

"Mother!" he said. It was the first time he had ever said it. It sounded like a prayer.

A flash of amazement flickered in Doreen Garrison's restless eyes... a little tinkling laugh rippled over her carmine lips.

"You don't mean to say *you* are my Jingle-baby? Why... why... you're almost grown up, darling."

She stooped and dropped a light kiss, as cold as snow, on his cheek.

She hadn't known him! Pat, looking at Jingle, thought it was dreadful to see happiness wiped out of a human face like that.

"This is for you... mother." Jingle poked the bouquet out to her stiffly. She glanced at it... took it... again the little rippling insincere laugh... that was *not*, Pat thought, laughter... came. Jingle flinched as if she had boxed his ears.

"Angel-boy, what can I do with such an enormous thing? How did you ever get so many flowers into it? It must weigh a ton. Just put it somewhere, honey, and I'll take a bud out of it when I go. I haven't much time... I have to catch the evening boat and I must have a long talk with your Uncle Lawrence. I had no idea how you had grown."

She laid one of her very long, very slender, ivory-white hands, with its tinted, polished nails, on his shoulder and looked him over in a cool appraising manner.

"You're a bit weedy, aren't you, angel? Do you eat enough? But I suppose you're at the weedy age. Take off those terrible glasses. Do you really need them? Have you had your eyes tested lately?"

"No," said Jingle. He did not add "mother" this time. "This is Pat Gardiner," he finished awkwardly.

Mrs. Garrison flicked an eye over Pat, who had an instant conviction that her stockings were on crooked and her hair like a Fiji islander's. Somehow, they all found themselves sitting in the Gordon parlour. Nobody knew what to say, but Mrs. Garrison talked lightly, saying sweet, insincere things in her silvery voice to Mr. and Mrs. Gordon, making such play with her hands that you had to look at them to see how lovely they were. Pat thought of her own mother's hands... a little thin, a little knotted, the palms seamed and hardened a bit with years of work. But hands you liked to have touch you. She couldn't imagine any one liking the touch of Mrs. Garrison's hands.

Jingle stared at the carpet but Pat, her first shyness gone, looked Mrs. Garrison over very coolly. Lovely... very lovely... but what was wrong with her face? In after years Pat found a word for it... a *cheated* face. In after years Pat knew that this woman had worked so hard remaining young and beautiful for a husband whose fancy strayed lightly to every beautiful woman he met that she had spent herself. She was like a shadow... beautiful... elusive... not real. And this was Jingle's mother... who called everybody, even Larry Gordon, "darling" and now and then flung a word to her son as one might throw a bone to a hungry dog. Pat could not fathom the depth of the embarrassment Doreen Garrison was feeling in the presence of this forgotten, unloved boy. But she knew that Jingle's mother would not stay here one moment longer than she had to.

"What an ugly little dog!" laughed Doreen as McGinty dashed in to Jingle. McGinty had been shut up in the stable but had found his way out. He knew he was needed.

"Do you really like dogs, Jingle-baby? I'll send you a nice one."

"McGinty is a nice dog, thank you. I don't want another dog," said Jingle, his face flushing a dark red.

Pat got up and went home. Jingle followed her to the door.

"She... she's pretty, isn't she?" he asked wistfully.

"The prettiest woman I've ever seen," agreed Pat heartily. When she looked at Jingle's face she couldn't help remembering the copper rose, so beautiful in the evening, so broken and battered the next morning. She hated Doreen Garrison... hated her for years... until she had learned to pity her.

"You'll come back as soon as you can, Pat? You know... I want to show her Happiness. And it's as much yours as mine."

Pat promised. She knew that Jingle knew that his mother would not care about seeing Happiness, and she knew he didn't want to be alone with his mother. But Pat learned that day that you may know a great many things you must never put in words.

3

She went back in mid-afternoon to find Doreen Garrison ready to leave.

"But... mother..." Jingle seemed forcing himself to speak the world... "Pat and I want to show you Happiness. It's such a pretty place."

"Happiness? Why in the world do you call it that, you funny darlings?"

"Because it is such a lovely spot we pretend nobody could ever be unhappy there," said Pat.

Amusement flickered into Doreen Garrison's eyes . . . the eyes Jingle had once pretended were as blue as a starlit sky.

"How wonderful to know nothing about life and so be able to imagine everything," she said lightly. "I can't visit your Happiness, Jingle-baby . . . how could heels like these travel over fields and stumps? Besides, I must not risk losing the boat. If I did it would mean missing the steamer at San Francisco. Jingle-baby, you're standing incorrectly . . . so . . . that's better. And you *do* look so much better without those glasses. *Never* put them on again, honey-boy. I've told your uncle to take you to a good oculist and if you really need glasses to have you equipped with proper ones. He's to get you some decent clothes, too, and take you to the barber at Silverbridge . . . there's the car . . . well . . ."

She looked a little uncertainly at Jingle, as if she supposed she ought to kiss him again. But there was something about Jingle just then that did not encourage kissing. Doreen Gardiner felt relieved. It had really been a dreadful day . . . one felt so awkward . . . so ill at ease with this great half-grown hobbledehoy with his preposterous hair and clothes, who couldn't even talk. How had her lovely Jingle-baby ever turned into such a creature? But her duty was done . . . his future was arranged for . . . Lawrence would see to it.

She patted him lightly on the head.

"Bye, honey-boy. So sorry I haven't longer to stay. Don't grow *quite* so much in the next twelve years, please, angel. Good-bye . . . Nora, is it?"

"Good-bye," said Pat haughtily, with the disconcerting conviction that Doreen Garrison did not even notice that she was being haughty.

She flitted down the stone walk like a bird glad to escape its cage, leaving a trace of some exotic perfume behind her. Jingle stood on the step and watched her go . . . this tarnished, discrowned queen who had so long sat on the secret throne of his heart. Would she look back and wave to him? No, she was gone. His bouquet was lying on the hall table. She had not even remembered to take the bud. The southernwood in it was limp and faded.

"Well, how did you like your mother?" asked Aunt Maria.

Jingle winced. His aunt's harsh, disagreeable voice jarred horribly on his sensitive nerves.

"I... I thought she was lovely," he said. It was ghastly to have to lie about your mother.

Aunt Maria shrugged her bony shoulders.

"Well, she's settled things for you anyhow. You're to go in the entrance class next year and after that to college. She says you can be anything you like and she'll foot the bills. As for clothes... she found as much fault with yours as if she'd paid for them. You're to have two new suits... *tailored*. No hand-me-downs for *her* son! Humph!"

Aunt Maria disappeared indignantly into the kitchen.

Jingle looked at Pat with dead lustreless eyes. Something caught at her throat.

"Will you come to Happiness after supper?" he said quietly. "There's something I want you to do for me."

CHAPTER XXIV
Ashes to Ashes

1

JINGLE was lying face downwards among the ferns in Happiness when Pat got there. A little dog with a big heart was sitting beside him, apparently mounting guard over a brown paper parcel on the grass.

Pat squatted down beside him, saying nothing. She was beginning to learn how full of silent little tragedies life is. She wished wildly that she could help Jingle in some way. Judy was fond of telling a story of long long ago when Pat had been four years old and was being trained to say "please." One day she could not remember it. "What is the word that makes things happen, Judy?" she had asked. Oh, for such a magic word now... some word which would make everything right for Jingle.

It was very lovely in Happiness that evening. There was a clear, pale, silvery-blue sky, feathered with tiny, blossom-like clouds, over them. The scent of clover was in the air. A corner of Happiness lay in the shadow of the woods, the rest of it was flooded with wine-red sunset. There was the elfin laugh of the hidden brook and there was the beauty of pale star-flowers along its banks. The only thing in sight that was not beautiful was the huge gash in the woods on the hill where Larry Gordon had got out his winter fuel. It was terrible to see the empty places where the trees had been cut. Trees *had* to be cut... people had to have firewood... but Pat could never see the resultant ugliness without a heartache. Of course time would beautify it again. Great clumps of ferns would grow by the hacked stumps... the crooks of the bracken would unfold along its desecrated paths... slender birches and poplars would spring up as years went by. Perhaps the wounds and scars in human lives would be like that, too.

"I wish," said Jingle suddenly, twisting himself around until his head lay in Pat's lap, "I wish my dream hadn't come true, Pat. It was so much more beautiful when it wasn't true."

"I know," said Pat softly. She patted the rough head with brown hands that were tender and gentle and wise. Their touch unloosed the floods of Jingle's bitterness.

"She... she gave me ten dollars, Pat. It burned my fingers when I took it. And I'm to go to college. But she wasn't interested in my plans. I showed her the house I'd drawn for her... she only laughed."

"Jingle, I think your mother was so... so surprised to find you so big that she felt... she didn't feel... she felt you were a stranger. Next time she comes it may be very different."

"Whose fault is it if I am like a stranger to her? And there will never be a next time... I knew that when she went away. She doesn't love me... she never has loved me. I know that now. I might have known it always if I hadn't been a fool."

Pat couldn't endure the desolation in his tone. She patted his head again.

"*I* love you anyhow, Jingle... almost... *just* as well as I love Sid."

Jingle caught the caressing hand and held it tight against his tear wet cheek.

"Thank you, Pat. And... Pat, will you do me a favour?

Will you call me 'Hilary' after this? I . . . I . . . somehow, Jingle is such a silly nickname for a big boy."

Pat knew his mother had spoiled the name for him. It had been her pet name for him once. Surely she must have loved him then.

"I'll try . . . only you mustn't mind if I call you Jingle sometimes before I get the new habit."

In her heart she was saying, "I'll *call* him Hilary to his face but I'll always think of him as Jingle."

"I told you there was something I wanted you to do for me, Pat," Jingle went on, still with that strange, new bitterness. "I . . . I didn't give her those letters. I'll light a fire over there on that rock . . . and will you burn them for me?"

Pat assented. She knew there was nothing else to be done with those letters now. Jingle built the fire and Pat opened the parcel and fed them to the hungry little flames . . . a burnt offering of a boy's wasted love and faith and hope. Pat hated to burn them. It seemed a terrible thing to do. The tiny scraps of letters written when he was a little boy and paper was hard to come by . . . on a fly-leaf torn from an old school-book or the back of a discarded circular . . . sometimes even on a carefully cut and folded piece of wrapping paper. A mother should have treasured them as jewels. But Doreen Garrison would never read them. The pity of it! Now and then a white line came out for a moment on the quivering black ash . . . Pat couldn't help seeing them . . . *"My own darling mother"* . . . *"perhaps you will come to see me soon, dearest"* . . . *"I was head of my class all the week, mother dearest. Aren't you glad?"* . . . Pat ground her little white teeth in a futile rage against fate.

After the last letter was burned Pat gathered up the little pile of ashes and scattered them in the brook.

"There, that's done." Hilary stood up; he looked older: there was a stern set to his jaw, a new ring in his voice, as of one who had put away childish things. "And now . . . well, I'm going to college . . . and I'm going to be an architect . . . and I'm going to succeed."

They walked back in silence along the ferny windings of Jordan. The moon was rising and the bats were out. An owl was calling eerily from the spruce hill beyond Happiness. A great golden star hung over Silver Bush. They parted on the bridge. Pat lifted her eyes to his.

"Good-night, Jingle dear... I mean Hilary."

"Good-night, Pat. You've been a brick, Pat... your eyes are lovely... lovely."

"Oh, that's just the moonlight," said Pat.

2

Pat helped Judy wash the milk pails and get all the fluffy little golden chicks into their coops while she told her about Doreen Garrison.

"Oh, Judy, she was... she was..."

"Sort of supercilious like," suggested Judy.

"No, no, not that... she was as polite to us as if we were strangers... but... just as if she didn't believe we were there at all. I couldn't have believed there was a mother like that in the world, Judy."

"Oh, oh, ye do be liddle knowing what some mothers are like, more shame to them. And you can't be putting into thim the things the Good Man Above left out, so why be worrying over it? Just be saying a prayer for all poor orphans and be thankful ye've got a mother that has roots."

"Roots?"

"Sure and that's what's the matter wid yer Doreen Garrison. She hasn't a root to her. Nothing to anchor her down and hold aginst the winds. Sure and she may be one av thim things they do be calling a modern mother, I've been hearing av thim."

"I just felt, Judy, as if she had remembered him against her will and would forget him again as soon as he was out of her sight."

"I'm telling ye. Maria Gordon did be saying once that Jim's widdy was the best hand at forgetting things she didn't want to remimber she was iver knowing. I'm rale sorry for yer Jingle. Ye'd better ask him over to dinner to-morrow and give him a liddle bite av blackberry roly-poly. Sure and I'll be making it on purpose for him."

"He wants to be called Hilary after this, Judy. And... it's a funny coincidence... last week Bets and I decided that after this we would call each other Elizabeth and Patricia. But of course," added Pat hastily, "we don't expect other people to call us that."

"Oh, oh, and that same is just as well, me jewel, because ye're Pat to me and niver innything but Pat ye'll be."

"Pat of Silver Bush," said Pat happily. It was beautiful to have home and love and family ties. Bold-and-bad, the kitten of the summer, came flying across the yard to her. Pat picked him up and squeezed some purrs out of him. No matter what dreadful things happened at least there were still cats in the world.

In the moonlight she went along the Whispering Lane and down the field path and up the hill. She had made a tryst with Bets to tell her about Jingle's mother. . . at least as much as Jingle would wish told. Bets must know the state of things so that she would not hurt Jingle's feelings.

Pat reached the Watching Pine first and stood under it, her face against its rough old trunk as she waited. At first the moon was veiled in a misty cloud and Pat thrilled to a dim sense of magic and wonder that came with the glimpse of that cloudy moon through the pine. It was a wonderful night. . . a night when she might see the Little People perhaps. She had believed in them long ago and this was one of the moments she still believed in them. Wasn't that some tiny moonshine creature in a peaked cap with little bells on it sitting on a fence panel? No, only a vibrating strip of dried bark. The soft sweet air blew to her from the secret meadows at the back of the farms. Then the moon came out from her cloud and the little fir trees scattered along the fences were splashes of ink-black shadows in mystic shapes. Below were houses sleeping in moonlit gardens. Far out there was a trail of moonlight on the sea like a lady's silken dress. Pat felt herself a sister to all the loveliness of the world. If only everybody could feel this secret, satisfying rapture! Poor Jingle would be curled up in the hay-loft with McGinty, trying to forget his broken heart. It seemed cruel to be happy when he was miserable but it was no use trying not to be, when the night was full of wonder and Silver Bush with its love was below you, and you could hear Joe's delightful whistle and Snicklefritz's bark even at this distance. And when you were waiting for the dearest friend any girl ever had to join you. There, lilting along the path came Bets, part of the beauty of the night.

"We must love him all the more to make it up to him," said Bets when she had heard the tale. . . all except the burned letters which Pat knew must be a secret always between herself and . . . Hilary.

CHAPTER XXV
His Way Is on the Sea

1

THERE was a family council at Silver Bush when school opened in September. It was decreed that Pat must join the entrance class and prepare herself for the Queen's Academy examinations the next year. Pat protested . . . but father was inexorable. He had let Winnie off, realising that Winnie's golden curls thatched a brain that could never be brought to distinguish between a participle and an infinitive: but Pat's record in school, although never brilliant, had been above the average: so to Queen's she must go and study for a teacher's licence.

"You'll get the North Glen school and board at home," said dad . . . which was the only gleam of hope Pat saw in the whole dismal prospect. She flew to the kitchen and poured out her discontent and rebellion to Judy.

"Oh, oh, and don't ye want to be eddicated, Patsy darling?"

To be educated was all right . . . but to go away from home was all wrong.

"I don't seem to be like other girls, Judy. They all want to go to college and have a career. I don't . . . I just want to stay at Silver Bush and help you and mother. There's work for me here, Judy . . . you know there is. Mother isn't strong. As for being educated . . . I *shall* be well educated . . . love educates, Judy."

"Oh, oh, and ye're not so far out there, girleen. But there's minny a thing to be considered besides. Money doesn't be growing on bushes, darlint."

"What fun if it did!" For a moment Pat was side-tracked

by a vision of little gold dollars hanging from the ends of branches like golden blossoms.

"Yer dad isn't rich . . . and a fam'ly like this is ixpinsive whin they're growing up and nading the pretty clothes. You'll have to get ready to help him out a bit until some av ye are married or gone away."

"I don't want any of us to get married or go away."

"Ye're clane unrasonable, darlint."

Pat was beginning to suspect that she was unreasonable . . . that these things would have to be faced some time. For instance, Winnie had a beau. Not "beaus" . . . she had had beaus for over a year and Pat had grown used to their coming and going and Winnie's resultant chatter about "dates" . . . but "a" beau. Frank Russell of the Bay Shore Russells seemed to have scattered all the others and Winnie was beginning to blush painfully when Judy teased her about him. Pat hated Frank so bitterly that she could hardly be civil to him. Judy got quite out of patience with her.

"Ye ought to be having a liddle bit av sinse, Pat. Young Frank is be way av being a rale good match. The Russells do be all knowing how to make one hand wash the other. An only son and his mother dead and all the Bay Shore girls trying to nab him. Winnie'd just be stepping into that grand ould Russell place at the Bay Shore and be quane, wid niver a mother-in-law to look black at her if she moved a sofy. And that near home and all."

"Winnie's too young to *think* of being married," protested Pat.

"Sure and the darlint is eighteen. There's no question av being married yet awhile . . . she must have her courting time as is proper. But a Russell always means business and young Frank has the glint in his eye. I'm telling ye. He knows where to be coming for a good wife."

"He isn't very intelligent," snapped Pat.

"Will ye listen at her? He ain't much for rading poetry or building fancy houses, like yer Jingle, I'm supposing, but he's got a rale grip on politics, as Long Alec was quick to see, and I'm clane missing me guess if he don't be in Parliamint be the time he's a bit bald. Ye're not nading inny great intilligence for that. Winnie's no rale scholard hersilf, the darlint, but there isn't the like av her for the light biscuit on the Island.

She'll be the grand housekeeper for that fine house. I'm telling ye."

Pat didn't want telling. The thought of Winnie ever leaving home, no matter how long the courting days were, remained intolerable. She continued to hate Frank but she resigned herself to the entrance class and even took up the work with a certain grim determination to do well for the sake of Silver Bush. She knew people thought the Silver Bush family was lacking in ambition. Joe had stubbornly refused to go to school after he was fifteen, Winnie had always been "dumb" when it came to lessons; Sid was determined to know farming and nothing else. So it was up to her to re-establish the Gardiner credit in the halls of learning.

"I'm so thankful Bets is in the entrance class, too, Judy. I was afraid for a long while she couldn't be... her father thought she wasn't strong enough. But Bets coaxed so hard he has given in. If Bets is with me when I go to Queen's it won't be so bad... supposing I ever get there."

"Supposing, is it? Sure and there isn't much doubt but ye'll get there, cliver and all as ye are whin ye give yer mind to it. Whin I watch ye working out them queer *algebra* things it makes me have wheels in me head. As for yer jawmetry stuff, Gintleman Tom himsilf cudn't be seeing through it."

"Geometry is my favourite class, Judy. Bets doesn't like it... but she loves everything else that I love. We have planned to study together each night about all through the winter. We'll study hard for two hours and then we'll talk."

"I belave ye. The liddle tongues av ye do be always clacking."

"Yes, but, Judy, there are times when we don't talk at all. We just sit and think. Sometimes we don't even think... we just *sit*. It's enough just to be together. And oh, Judy, Bets and I..."

"I did be hearing ye was calling each other Elizabeth and Patricia."

Pat laughed.

"We did try to. But it didn't work. Elizabeth and Patricia sounded like strangers... we didn't know ourselves. As I was saying... Bets and I have begun to read the Bible right through. We've not going to skip a single chapter, not even those awful names in Chronicles. You've no idea how interesting the Bible is, Judy, when you read it just as a story."

"Oh, oh, haven't I now? Sure and wasn't I rading me Bible afore ye were born or thought av? But I *did* be skipping the names. There was too minny jaw-breakers among thim for me. I do be wondering if there niver was inny nicknames in thim days. D'ye think now, Patsy dear, that ivery time Jehosaphat's mother called him to his liddle dinner she said the whole name?"

2

The autumn drifted by: maple fires were kindled around the Secret Field: bracken and lady fern turned brown in Happiness: Jordan ran to the sea between borders of purple asters: golden harvest moons looked down over the Hill of the Mist. A gracious September and a mellow October were succeeded by a soft and sad November, when long silken lines of rain slanted across the sere hillsides.

And then one day, without any warning, came the first break in the family at Silver Bush.

They had all, except Joe, been spending Saturday afternoon and evening at the Bay Shore farm . . . where nothing had changed in Pat's remembrance. It was "a world where all things always seemed the same." She was beginning to love the Bay Shore for that very changelessness . . . it seemed the one place you could depend on in a changing world. Aunt Frances and Aunt Honor were just as "stately" as ever, though they had given up asking her to say Bible verses and tapping her on the head when they disapproved of her. They still disapproved of her in many things but Pat liked even the disapproval because anything else would have been change. Cousin Danny still wore his elvish grin. The Great-great was still alive . . . at ninety-eight . . . and not a day older apparently, nor any more complimentary. Every time she saw Pat she said "Nae beauty," in the same peevish tone, as if Pat were entirely to blame for it. The vase that had made the face at Sarah Jenkins still stood on the same bracket and the polished door-knobs still brightly reflected your face. The white ivory elephants had never finished marching across the mantel and the red and yellow china hen had evidently never succeeded in hatching out her eggs.

Bets was with them and this added to the pleasure of the day. It was such fun to show Bets everything. The aunts liked her ... but who could help liking Bets? Even the Great-great peered at her with admiration in her bright old eyes and for once forgot to tell Pat she was no beauty.

When they came back to Silver Bush Pat must walk up the hill with Bets: it had turned colder and the first snow-fall was whitening down over the twilight world when Pat came into the kitchen. At once she saw that something must be wrong ... terribly wrong. Mother was looking as white as if she had been struck ... Winnie was crying ... and Judy, of all people, had been crying. Sid looked as if he were trying not to cry. Father stood by the table holding a letter in his hand. Snicklefritz sat by him, looking up with mute, imploring eyes. Gentleman Tom had an air of not liking things. Even Bold-and-bad, whom ordinarily nothing could subdue, crouched with an apologetic air under the stove.

Pat looked around. Everybody was there ... except ... except ...

"Where's Joe?" she cried.

For a moment nobody spoke. Then Winnie sobbed, "He's gone."

"Gone! Where?"

"To sea. He went to the harbour to-night and sailed in Pierce Morgan's vessel for the West Indies."

"And me niver suspicting it, the gomeril I am," wailed Judy. "Not aven whin he come in, all queer like, and said he wud be taking a run to Silverbridge. Sure and if I'd known what was in his head I'd have hung on to him till after the tide set ..."

"That wouldn't have done any good," said Long Alec, rousing himself from his abstraction. "He was bound to go sooner or later. I've known that for some time. But he was so young ... and to go off like this without a word to one of us ... it was cruel of him. There, there, Mary."

For mother had turned and buried her face on his shoulder with a little, broken cry. Father led her out of the kitchen. Winnie and Cuddles followed. Sid went out and Pat was weeping wildly in Judy's arms.

"Judy, I can't bear it ... I can't bear it! Joe to go ... and like that."

"Sure and it do be cruel, as Long Alec said. The young fry do be cruel be times ... they don't know ... they don't know. Now, don't be breaking yer liddle heart, darlint.

Remimber it's harder for yer mother than for inny av the rest av ye. Joe'll be back some time..."

"But never to *stay*, Judy... never to stay. Oh, I'll always hate this day... always."

"Oh, oh, don't be cynical now," said Judy, who picked up words as the children studied their lessons but not always the exact meaning. "Where's the sinse av hating the poor day? Ye must just be looking this in the face. It's Wild Dick and yer Uncle Horace over again... sure and Joe had always been more like Horace than his own dad. He knew if he tried to say good-bye Long Alec wud be trying to put him off. Now kape up yer pecker, Patsy, for the sake av yer mother. Siddy's here to carry on and it's the smart lad he is. His heart's in the farm as Joe's niver was, and he can aven drive the autymobile which the Good Man Above niver intinded innybody to do. Joe's gone but he hasn't taken Silver Bush wid him. Did ye be after seeing the liddle note he lift on Long Alec's desk... no? There was a missage for ye in it... 'tell Pat to be good to Snicklefritz'... and there was one for me, too, be way av a joke. Joe always had a joke, the darlint. 'Tell Judy to see that those blamed kittens in her picture are grown up be the time I come back.' Sure and wasn't he always laughing at thim same kittens."

But Pat could not laugh again for a long time. She was the last one at Silver Bush to resign herself to the inevitable. Eventually she found herself doing it, with a sense of shame that it could be so. But the raw rainy winter was half over before she ceased to have sleepless nights when it stormed and began looking forward with pleasure to Joe's letters, with bewitching foreign stamps on them which Cuddles proudly collected. They were full of the glamour of strange ports and distant lands, of the lure of adventure and white-winged ships, to which Pat thrilled in spite of herself. Somehow, although she hadn't believed it possible, Silver Bush got on without him. Sid had stepped manfully into his place... in truth Sid was glad of an excuse to leave school... mother began to smile again, Frank Russell consoled Winnie, everybody ceased to listen for the gay whistle that had echoed so often through the twilights around the old barns. Even Snicklefritz stopped wearing a sorrowful cast of countenance and listening mournfully to every footstep on the stone walk.

Change... and worse than change, forgetfulness! It seemed

dreadful to Pat that things could be forgotten. Why, they were just as bad as the family at Silverbridge that had one son in California and one in Australia, one in India and one in Petrograd and didn't seem to mind it at all.

"Oh, oh, how cud we be living if we didn't forget, me jewel?" said Judy.

"But Christmas was so terrible," sighed Pat. "The first time we weren't all here. I couldn't help thinking of something I heard you say once... that once one of a family was away for Christmas it was likely they would never be all together again. I just couldn't eat... and I didn't see how any one else could."

"But do ye be remimbering how ye slipped into the kitchen at bedtime and we had a faste on the bones?" said Judy slyly.

3

Everything passes. Winter was spring before they knew it. Everybody was looking forward with delight to Joe's homecoming. March brought a saddening letter from him. He was not coming home in Pierce Morgan's vessel. He had shipped for a voyage to China. Well, that was a disappointment... but meanwhile March was April, with sap astir and frogs tuning up the field of the Pool, and all the apple boughs that had fallen in winter storms to be gathered up and burned. Sid and Pat did that and they and Bets and Hilary had a glorious bonfire at night: and after it was over Pat couldn't walk home with Bets because Sid did. Pat didn't mind... she was too happy because Sid seemed to be having quite a crush on Bets this spring.

"He'll all out with May Binnie, Judy. Won't it be lovely if he marries Bets some day?"

"Oh, oh, go aisy wid yer match-making," said Judy sarcastically.

Besides, it was nice to sit with Hilary on Weeping Willy's tombstone, in the glow from the smouldering embers in the orchard, and talk about things. Pat had learned to call him Hilary... she was even beginning to think of him as Hilary, though in moments of excitement the old name popped out. Judy never could bring her tongue to call him anything else. To her he would always be Jingle.

"The darlints," she would say to Gentleman Tom, looking out to her kitchen window at them. "I do be wondering what's afore thim in life. And how much longer is it they have to be young and light-hearted."

Gentleman Tom would not tell her.

April was May, with a white fire of wild cherry in Happiness and young daffodils dancing all over the garden and little green cones shooting up in the iris beds. Every day Pat made some new discovery.

"One forgets all through the year how lovely spring really is and so it comes as a surprise every time," she said.

And finally May was June, with a fairy wild plum hanging out in the Whispering Lane and purple waves of lilac breaking along the yard fence and Judy's beds of white pansies all ablow . . . big white, velvety pansies . . . and everywhere all different shades of green in the young spring woods on the hills.

"Spring is nicer at Silver Bush than anywhere else, Judy. Just look what a lovely iris . . . frosty white with a ripple of blue fringing every petal. It's Joe's iris . . . he planted it last spring . . . and now where is he?"

"On the other side av the world belike. Tell me, Patsy dear, do you be understanding how it is they don't fall off down there? I've never been able to get the hang of it into me mind somehow."

Pat tried to explain but Judy still shook her grey bob in a maze of uncertainty.

"Oh, oh, it's me own stupidity I'm knowing."

"No, it's my fault, Judy. I've a headache to-night."

"Sure and it's studying too hard ye are. That al*gebra* now, it's mesilf do be thinking it isn't fit for girls to be larning. Morning, noon and night at it as ye are."

"I *must* study, Judy . . . the Entrance comes in another month and I *must* pass. Father and mother will feel dreadfully if I don't. I'm not afraid of the mathematics; I've always been fond of arithmetic especially. Only . . . do you remember how dreadfully sorry I used to be for poor A and B and C because they had to work so hard. D appeared to have things easier."

"Sure and I do remimber how pitiful ye used to look up and say, 'Doesn't A *iver* have a holiday, Judy?' It's the grand marks ye'll be making in iverything I'm ixpecting."

"No, I'm such a dub in history, Judy. I can't remember dates."

"Dates, is it? And who cares about dates? What difference does it make whin things happened as long as they did happen?"

"The examiners think it makes some difference, Judy. The only two dates I'm positively sure of are that Julius Caesar landed in Britain 55 B.C. and that the battle of Waterloo was fought in 1815. Outside of those everything is in a fog."

"Me own Great-grandfather fell at the battle of Waterloo," said Judy. "And left me Great-grandmother a widdy with nine small children. But what's a widdy more or less in the world now after the Great War? Do ye be remimbering anything av it, Pat?"

"I was five when the armistice was signed. I remember the fireworks at the bridge . . . and, dimly, people talking of it before that. It seems like a dream. *You* never talk of it, Judy."

"Sure and I was ashamed all through it bekase I had none of me own to go . . . and thankful that Siddy and Joe were children. Yer mother and yer Aunt Hazel and mesilf just knit socks for the soldiers and sat tight. It's a time I don't like to be thinking av, wid ivery one ranting at the Kaiser and yer Uncle Tom and yer dad moaning bekase they was too old to go, and us lying awake at night worrying for fear they'd find a loop-hole in spite av the Fam'ly Bible. And yet all av us a bit ashamed in our hearts that we didn't have inny maple leaves in the windies. Not but what there was a bit av fun about it, wid all the girls that proud to be walking wid the boys in khaki and yer Uncle Tom singing a hymn av hate in the back yard at Swallyfield ivery morning afore breakfast. Sure and if I didn't hear him shouting, 'I'd rather die in the trenches than live under German rule,' while I was milking I'd be running over to see if he'd got lumbago. He was that ixcited whin the election for the Union Government was on . . . sure and I did be fearing he'd burst a blood vessel. Whin he found yer Aunt Edith praying that it might go in he was rale indignant. 'Elections ain't won be prayers,' sez he, and he marched her down to vote and her protesting all the way it was unwomanly. Ye niver saw such a tommyshaw. Sandy Taylor at the Bay Shore called his first b'y John Jellico Douglas Haig Lloyd George Bonar Law Kitchener. Ye shud av seen the look av the minister whin he was christened. And after it all the b'ys has just called him Slats all his life, him being so thin. They did be saying that Ralph Morgan married Jane Fisher just to escape inlisting. Sure and I'm no jidge av things matrimonial, Patsy, and niver pretinded to be but it did seem to me that I'd rather be facing the Kaiser and all his angels than marry a Fisher. Maybe Ralph come round to the same way av thinking. Whin we had the memorial service for the boys as had been killed he heaves a big sigh and sez to me, 'Ah, Judy, *they're at peace,*' sez he. Oh, oh, it's all over now and I'm hoping the world will have more sinse that iver to get in a mess like the same agin, more be token that the women can be voting."

"Old Billy Smithson at Silverbridge doesn't agree with you, Judy. He says women are fools and things will soon be in a worse mess than ever."

"Oh, oh, and are ye thinking that possible now?" said Judy sarcastically. "Old Billy shudn't be after jidging all women be his own. Well do I remimber the first time I was iver voting. I wore me blue silk and me high-heeled boots whin I wint to the polls and I was that ixcited I cud niver tell where I put the cross on me ballot. From what I culd ixplain to him yer dad always thought I'd put it in the wrong place. But innyway me man wint in so it was no great matter if I did. I've niver been voting since bekase it always happens I've been canning tomaties or some special job like that whiniver there's an election."

"Uncle Tom says every one ought to exercise her franchise . . . that it's solemn duty."

"Listen at that. Don't it be sounding fine? But wud I be letting me tomaties or me baked damsons spoil bekase I had to traipse off to Silverbridge to be voting? Sure, Patsy dear, governmints may go in and governmints may go out but the jam pots av Silver Bush do have to be filled."

CHAPTER XXVI

Gentleman Tom Sits on the Stairs

1

PAT need not have worried about her history paper. She was not fated to write it that year. The headache she complained of had not disappeared by next morning and it was further complicated by a sore throat. Mother advised her to stay in bed and Pat agreed so meekly that Judy was alarmed. Early next morning she tip-toed anxiously in to see her.

"How's the morning wid ye, me jewel?"

Pat looked at her with burning eyes above a flushed face.

"Tho dead clock out in the hall has begun ticking, Judy. Please stop it. Every tick hurts my head so."

Judy ran out, roused Mrs. Gardiner, and telephoned for Dr. Bentley.

Pat had scarlet fever.

At first nobody was much alarmed. Joe and Winnie had had scarlet fever in childhood and had not been especially ill. But as the days wore on anxiety settled down over Silver Bush like an ever deepening cloud. Dr. Bentley looked grave and talked of "complications." Mother, who had never had scarlet fever herself, was debarred from the sick room and Judy and Winnie waited on Pat. Judy would not hear of a trained nurse. She had never got over Miss Martin and her "Greta." Nobody ever knew when she slept or if she slept at all. All night she sat by Pat's bed in the bandy-legged Queen Anne chair, with its faded red damask seat, which Pat had rescued from the garret because she loved it . . . never dozing or nodding, ready with cooling drink and tender touch. Dr. Bentley afterwards spoke of her as "one of those born nurses who seem to know by instinct what it takes most women years of training to learn."

When Pat became delirious she would do nothing and take nothing for anybody but Judy.

And Pat was very delirious. Delusion after delusion chased each other through her fevered brain. Weeping Willy had carried off the wooden button on the pantry door. *"I'm sure God will think that so funny,"* said Pat, vainly searching for it before God could find out. The cracks in the ceiling wouldn't stay in place but crawled all over. She was on a lonely road, where the dark was waiting to pounce on her, calling to Jingle who was walking away unconcernedly with Emily-and-Lilian's tombstone under his arm. She was at the bottom of the well where Wild Dick had thrown her. She was searching for the Secret Field which Dorothy had taken away. She heard Joe's whistle but could never see Joe. Somebody had changed all the furniture in Silver Bush and Pat was vainly trying to get it back in place. The minister had said in church last Sunday that God held the world in the hollow of his hand. *Suppose He got tired and dropped it, Judy?*

"Sure and that's the one thing He'll niver be doing, Patsy, rest ye aisy."

The wind blew and would never stop . . . *it must be so tired, Judy. Please make it stop.* She was on a road at the head of a long procession of rolling cheeses . . . all the cheeses that had ever been made at Silver Bush . . . she *had* to keep ahead of them. Faces were looking in at the window . . . pressed against the pane . . . or leering in a row along the footboard of the bed like the Bay Shore ghost. Hideous faces, cruel, crafty, terrifying faces. *Please, Judy, drive them away . . . please . . . please.* She had long fierce arguments between Pat and Patricia. Time was running by her like the dark river of the hymn. She couldn't catch up with it. *If we stopped all the clocks couldn't we stop time, Judy? Please!* And who, oh, who would give poor Bold-and-bad his meals?

"Sure and I will, Patsy darlint. Ye nadn't be fretting over Bold-and-bad. He's living up to his name ivery minute of the day, slaping on the Poet's bed and getting rolled up in me shate of fly-paper. Sure and ye niver saw a madder cat. It's Gintleman Tom that's doing the worrying. He do be setting on the landing ivery moment he can spare from his own lawful concerns."

Then came two or three dreadful days when Pat's life hung in the balance. Dr. Bentley shook his head. The family gave her up. But Judy never quailed. She hadn't got the "sign" and as for Gentleman Tom he never budged off the landing, although sometimes he bristled and spat.

"Sure and whativer is after Pat will have the hard time to get past that baste," Judy said confidently.

But the third night, in the wee sma' hours, when Silver Bush was holding its wakeful breath, wondering despairingly what the morrow would bring, Gentleman Tom arose, shook himself, and walked gravely downstairs to his own cushion in the kitchen.

"He was knowing there wasn't inny more nade av sitting there," said Judy at sunrise. "Pat had got the turn. I met him coming down whin I was coming up and he was after giving me a look. Whin I wint in the darlint's room I was ixpecting to see a difference and I did. Look at her there, slaping as paceful as a lamb. Sure and this is a joyful day for Silver Bush. Ye can be watching her, Winnie, the while I brew me a jug av tay. I nade a bit av a stimulant, what wid me knees shaking and me poor head going round in circles."

2

Pat's convalescence was a long one. It was five weeks before she could even sit up in bed and drink her broth out of the dear little yellow bowl with blue roses in it . . . a Bay Shore heirloom . . . which Aunt Honor had sent over for her. She had a little gold cushion that was like a small sun behind her head . . . Aunt Hazel had sent *it* up . . . and wore a lovely jacket of primrose silk which Aunt Edith had brought over for her. Everybody was so good to her. The banished Bets sent her up leaves full of wild strawberries and Hilary brought brook trout for her. When Hilary sprained his ankle so badly that he had to keep the house for a week Judy herself, armed with a can of worms and Sid's hook and line stalked up and down the banks of Jordan to cater to Pat's slowly-reviving appetite. Mother came to the door and looked in with happy eyes. Sometimes Cuddles' darling anxious little face peered through the stair railings, not permitted to come any nearer.

It was seven weeks before Pat was allowed out of bed, despite her pleadings.

"I'm getting so tired of the bed, Judy. I'm sure it wouldn't hurt me to get up for a little and sit in a chair by the window. I want to see *outside* so much. You don't know how tired I am of looking at the blue-bells on the wall-paper. That cluster of them over the wash-stand looks just like a little potbellied elf with a bonnet on and it grins at me. Now, don't look terrified, Judy dear. I'm not out of my head again. You can see it for yourself."

"I'm not denying there's a resimblance. But ye'll not be out av bed for two days more. Thim's the doctor's orders and I'll folly them."

"Well, prop me up on the pillows, Judy, so that I can at least see something out of the window."

That was nice. She could see the slender fir-tops against the blue sky at the bottom of the garden... the cloud-castles that came and went... the swallow-haunted gable end of the barn... the smoke from Uncle Tom's chimney making magic against the hills. Pat lived on this for two days more and then Judy let her sit on a chair by the window for half an hour. Pat managed to walk to the chair although she admitted she felt very like a bowl of jelly that would all fall apart if violently shaken. But her eyes and ears made the most of that half hour. At first it was a shock to see how the summer had gone while she had been sick. But what beautiful colours the world was showing. How wonderful to see again the blue shoulders of the hills across the harbour and the ecstasy of farewell summers in the field of that ilk... the silky wind ripples going over the grass on the lawn and all her own intimate, beloved trees. The breeze whispering from hill to hill and blowing in the scent of flowers to her. The honeysuckle over the grave-yard paling and Judy's ducks squattering around the well. Bold-and-Bad on the window sill of the church barn and a curly black dog, with a white heart on his breast, on the granary steps.

And... could it be?... Bets! A slim lovely girl in a lilac dress, her arms full of peonies, waving to her from the Whispering Lane. Bets had *grown*.

"Judy sent me word I could just look at you from here if I was right on the dot. Oh, Pat, darling, it's just heavenly to see you again. If you knew what I've been through! I wanted to send Hilary word... he's just been frantic... but Judy thought both of us would be too much excitement for you. He'll be here to-morrow."

Every day Pat was allowed to sit up a little longer, until

she could spend the whole afternoon at her window. Hilary and Bets were allowed in the garden now and could shout things up at her, though Judy wouldn't allow her to talk much in return. But it was enough just to be there, looking out on the beautiful moods of the fields, that sometimes twinkled in summer rain and sometimes basked in sunshine. One evening Judy let her stay up after supper. It was lovely to see the "dim" come stealing over the garden again. She recalled the last story she and Bets had read together, of an old enchanted garden in which flowers could talk. Just suppose her own flowers talked at night. That red rose in the corner became a passionate lover and whispered compliments to the white rose. That swaggering tiger lily told tales of incredible adventures. The nodding sleepy poppies gave away all their secrets. But the Madonna lilies only said their prayers.

She hadn't seen the stars for so long. And to watch the moon rise! Bets and she had read a poem once about the moon rising over Hymettus. But it couldn't be more beautiful than the moon rising over the Hill of the Mist with the harbour beyond. The tree shadows were lovely. The tall lilies looked like white saints in the moon-glow.

Judy coming in was quite horrified to find that Pat had not yet returned to bed.

"Ye haven't been slaping, have ye now?" she queried anxiously. "Not slaping in the moonlight, child dear?"

"No. But I'd love to. Why shouldn't I?"

"Listen at her. Don't ye iver go slaping in moonlight. It's liable ye are to go mad. Sure and I knew a man once... he slipt out in the moonlight one night and he was niver the same again."

Pat sighed. She hated to leave that delicious silver bath of moonlight but she *was* tired. It was nice to feel tired again and drift off to sleep so easily.

Ten weeks from the day she took sick Pat came downstairs, feeling a glad freedom. What a day that was! Such a triumphant Judy! All the poppies dancing to do her honour! Comfortably hungry for her dinner once more. Such a delightful meal with everybody exchanging happy looks. Even Gentleman Tom made a fuss over her.

"Sure and the house do be glad to see you round it again," gloated Judy.

It was nice to see everything in the same place. She had

been afraid something would be changed. The garden *had* changed a great deal. And even Bets and Jingle seemed changed . . . older, some way. Jingle had certainly grown taller. Oh, why did things have to change? The old sad question.

"Maybe there's a bit av change in yersilf, darlint," said Judy, a little sadly. Pat *was* changed . . . she looked older in some unmistakeable way.

"Sure and ye can't be going quite so near the gate av death widout it changing ye," whispered Judy to herself. "She isn't the child inny more. She'll never be the same again."

The others thought it was just her pallor and thinness. Uncle Tom told her she had a lovely suit of bones.

"I'll soon fatten up on your cooking, Judy. Life tastes good to-day."

"Sure and life do be having a taste, don't it, Patsy? I'm only a poor ould maid as has worked out all her days for a living and yet I'm declaring life has a taste. Sure and I smack me lips over it."

"Hilary has brought me a jolly book to read . . . Bets is sweeter than ever. On the whole, it's a pretty nice world in spite of change and it's wonderful to be back in it again."

"I'm telling ye. But, Patsy darlint, ye must be going careful. There's to be no running all over for a while yet. Just sit ye still and listen to yer hair growing."

3

Pat found it was more likely she would have to listen to her hair falling out. It began to fall out alarmingly. Judy, assured her that it was only to be expected but even Judy was scared. Everybody was scared. Pat wept and would not be comforted.

"I'm bald, Judy . . . actually bald. I suppose it's a judgment on me for hating my ginger hair. Judy, what if it never comes in again?"

"But av coorse it will," said Judy . . . who was by no means as sure of it as she would have liked to be. She made Pat a cap of lace and silk to wear but there were some bad weeks. Some prophesied dire things. Aunt Edith had known a girl whose hair had come out like that.

"It grew in again *white*," said Aunt Edith.

Then the hair *did* begin to grow in... a dark fuzz at first. Pat was relieved to find it was not white at any rate. Then longer... thicker...

"I do be belaving it's going to be curly," whispered Judy in a kind of awed rapture.

For the first time in weeks Pat wanted a mirror. The hair *was* curly. Not too curly but just lovely natural waves. And *dark*...dark brown. Pat thought she would die of happiness. Her hair was "bobbed" now and at no cost to Judy who was only too glad to see her darling with hair at all.

"So you've made up your mind to be a beauty after all," said Uncle Tom, the first time he saw her without a cap.

"Hardly that," decided Pat, as she scrutinised herself in the mirror that night. "But it *is* an improvement."

"Innyway, ye'll niver be nading a permanent," said Judy, "and that's be way av being a blessing. Sure and Dr. Bentley's wife do be having a permanent, they tell me, and her scalp was burned so bad the hair do be all coming out in patches. I'm thinking she'll be wishing she'd left the Good Man's work alone."

Altogether Pat was well satisfied with her bout of scarlet fever. She had got dark wavy hair out of it and escaped Queen's for another year.

CHAPTER XXVII

Glamour of Youth

1

BETS had passed her entrance but refused to go to Queen's until Pat could go, too. Pat, having missed her exams, must wait until next year.

A nice thing had happened. Hilary had failed to pass his entrance... that was not the nice thing... owing to the fact that the teacher at the South Glen school had been a poor one. Larry Gordon took Hilary away and sent him to the North Glen school. Consequently every morning Hilary and

Bets and Pat walked gaily to school together and found life good. Sid went no longer. He was father's right-hand man now. But Cuddles was going. She started blithely off one September morning and Pat, recalling the day she had "started school," felt very motherly and protective and sentimental as she watched dear Cuddles trotting along before them, hand in hand with another small, gleeful mite from the Robinson family. How little they knew of life, poor wee souls! How very aged and experienced Pat felt herself!

"Can you believe *we* were ever as young as that?" she asked of Bets incredulously.

Bets couldn't and sighed. Yet both of them tripped along the road as if they had been born, like Beatrice, under a dancing star. It was lovely to be old enough to remember childhood with a sigh. It was lovely to have before them a road filled with soft amethyst mist. It was lovely to see dark young fir trees edging harvest meadows. It was lovely to take a short cut through the little wood lane in Herbert Taylor's woods. It was lovely to be together. For it all came back to that. Nothing would have had just the same flavour if it had not been shared with each other.

Joe had never been home. Letters came from him from spicy tropic lands and Arctic wastes and Mediterranean ports, and were great events at Silver Bush. After everybody had read them they were sent over to Swallowfield and from there to the Bay Shore and then back for mother's "glory box," as they called it in imitation of Judy's glory box. Pat had a glory box of her own now in which she kept all kinds of "souvenirs," labelled somewhat systematically... "a flower from Bets' garden"... "new plan for 'my house,' drawn by Hilary Gordon"... "letters from my brother, Joseph A. Gardiner"... "a snap-shop of Bets and me under the Watching Pine"... "a packet of notes from my beloved friend, Elizabeth Gertrude Wilcox"... "the pencil I wrote my first letter to H. H. with."

For "H. H." was Harris J. Hynes... and Pat was over head and ears in love with him! Absolutely sunk, Winnie said. It had happened in church, one dull November day, when the moan of an eerie wind sounded around the tower and Pat was feeling sad for no earthly reason than that it pleased her to feel so. She had not felt sad when she had left Silver Bush for she had on her new scarlet hat under which her amber eyes glowed like jewels. Her skin, which had looked sallow with ginger hair, looked creamy with dark brown. Her lips were as red as her hat.

"Oh, oh, and isn't that chick now!" said Judy admiringly. "I niver saw innything chicker. Oh, oh, Patsy darlint"... Judy sighed... "the beaus will soon be coming."

Pat tossed her head.

"I don't want beaus, Judy."

"Oh, oh, ivery girl shud have a few beaus, Patsy. Sure and it's her right and so I do be telling ould Tillie Taylor last wake whin she was saying she didn't hold wid beaus. 'Ather they manes nothing or they manes too much,' sez she but what she was maning hersilf the Good Man Above only knows and maybe He'd be puzzled."

"Anyway they don't call them beaus now, Judy. That's old fashioned. It's boy-friends now."

"Boy-friends, is it? Oh, oh, Patsy me jewel, some day ye'll be finding the differenct atween a frind and a beau."

Pat and Bets were both pleased to be a bit sorrowful during that walk to church. They confessed they felt old. November was such a dreary month.

"Oh, Bets, the years will just go round like this... and changes will come... you'll marry some one and go away from me. Bets, when I think of it I couldn't suffer any more if I was dying. Bets, I just couldn't bear it."

"I couldn't either," said Bets in a broken voice. Then they both felt better. It was so wonderful to be young and sad together.

2

Pat's mood lasted until the second hymn. Then everything was changed in the twinkling of an eye.

He had come in with some other boys. He was standing just across the aisle from her. He was looking right at her over his hymn book. Looking admiringly. It was the first time Pat had ever noticed a boy looking at her admiringly. She suddenly felt that she was beautiful. And... also for the first time she blushed devastatingly and dropped her eyes. There had never been a boy she couldn't look squarely at before.

She knew what had happened to her... just what had happened years ago at the blind men's concert... and by the same sign. Her legs were trembling.

But *this* was real.

"I wonder if I dare look at him," she thought... and dared.

The hymn was over now. They were all sitting down. He appeared to find his boots interesting. Pat had a good chance to look at him.

He was handsome. Wonderful crinkly golden-brown hair... clear-cut features—all the heroes in stories had clear-cut features... great brown eyes. For he lifted his eyes at that moment and looked at her again. Thousands of electric thrills went over Pat.

She heard not one word of the sermon, not even the text, much to Long Alec's indignation, for it was one of his rules that every one in his family must be able to tell the text at the dinner table on Sundays. But if Pat could not remember the text she would always remember the anthem. *"Joy to the world,"* sang the choir. Could anything be more appropriate? She never glanced his way again but when they left the church she passed him in the porch and again their eyes met. It was quite terrible and Pat was breathless as she went down the steps.

Everything was changed. Even November had its points. The clouds were gone. The wood-path was beaded with pale sunlight. Quiet grey trees on all sides treasured some secret of loveliness.

"Did you see Harris Hynes?" asked Bets.

"Who is Harris Hynes?" asked Pat, knowing quite well, although she had never heard the name before.

"The new boy. His people have bought the Calder place. He sat just across from us."

"Oh, that boy? Yes, I noticed him," said Pat casually. She felt horribly disloyal. It was the first time she had kept anything from Bets.

"He would be rather handsome if it wasn't for his nose," said Bets.

"His nose? I didn't see anything wrong with his nose," said Pat, rather coldly.

"Oh, it's crooked. Of course you only notice it in profile. But he has gorgeous hair. They say he goes with Myra Lockley at Silverbridge."

A dreadful sinking feeling engulfed Pat. Joy to the world, indeed! Where had the sunlight gone? November was a horrid month.

But that look in his eyes.

3

The invitation to Edna Robinson's party came the next day. Would he be there? She thought of nothing else for two days. When Wednesday night came it was an exquisite night of moonlight and frost but because Harris Hynes might be at Edna's dance she was blind to its beauty. It was sweet agony to decide which of two dresses she should wear... the red was the smartest but the blue and silver made her look more grown up... a slender swaying thing of moonshine and twilight. She put it on—she put little dabs of perfume on her hair and throat... she even borrowed a pair of Winnie's milky pearl ear-drops for her ears. It was wonderful to dress for him... to wonder if he would notice what she wore. For the first time she made a little ritual of dressing.

Then she went down to show herself to Judy who was making sausage meat in the kitchen. Judy knew there was something in the wind the moment she sniffed the perfume, but she said only,

"Ye're looking lovely, darlint."

Would *he* think her lovely? That was the question. But she pretended to be interested only in the sausage meat. Judy mustn't forget to put nutmeg in. Father liked nutmeg. Judy shook with laughter when the door closed behind Pat.

"It isn't sausage meat the darlint is thinking av. Oh, oh, I do be knowing the signs."

How dreadful to think he mightn't be there! How thrilling to look at that dark hill against the sunset, just behind which was the old Calder place, now the Hynes place. *He* lived there. If he were at the party and she met him what would she say? Suppose she talked too much... or not enough? Would his people... his mother... like her? She heard not a word that Sid and Bets said. But when May Binnie, seeing the blue and silver dress for the first time in the Robinson guest room, said,

"That's the new shade they call twilight, isn't it? It would be a lovely colour on some people. But don't you think you're too sallow for such a trying blue, Pat?" it worried her. Not that she cared what May Binnie thought... but would *he* think her sallow? She seemed to remember Myra Lockley had a lovely complexion.

She knew the minute he came in...her heart beat suffocatingly when she heard his laugh in the hall. She had never heard it before but there was only one person in the world who could laugh like that. It was wonderful to see him enter the room with the other boys...with them but not of them...set apart...a young Greek god.

Oh, Pat had it very bad.

She was dancing with Paul Robinson when Harris cut in. Then she was dancing with him. It was like a miracle. They hadn't even been introduced. But then they didn't need any introduction. They knew each other...they had known each other for ages. It seemed as if they danced in silence for an eternity. Then...

"Won't you look at me, wonder-girl?" he was saying softly.

Pat lifted her face and looked at him. After that it was all over with her. But she was not Pat Gardiner for nothing. Judy's training stood her in good stead. She made her eyes mocking...challenging. He was not going to know...not just yet. Now that *she* knew what *his* eyes had told. Knowledge *was* power.

"So this is Patricia?" he said. The way he pronounced her name was enchanting. Never, so his tone said, had there been such a beautiful name. "Have you been thinking about me?"

"Now, why in the world should I have been thinking about you?" said Pat airily. Nobody could have dreamed that she had been thinking about nothing else. Nobody would have dreamed how exultant she was at this proof that Sunday had meant to him what it had meant to her.

"Indeed, I don't know why," he agreed with a masterly sigh. "I only know that I want you to be very, very nice to me."

He walked home with her. Sid and Bets faded away into the blue crystal of the night and they were alone. To walk with Harris over the hills, with the dark woods behind and a starry sky above and the cool white birches along the meadow fences, was something never to be forgotten. Pat was afraid everything she said was stupid. But Harris didn't seem to think so. Not that she said a great deal. Harris was the talker. She listened breathlessly while he described his recent trip in an aeroplane. He was going to be a bird-man. No tame career for *him*.

"What a dull old party," yawned Winnie, as she scrambled into bed. Frank had not been there.

And to Pat it had been cataclysmic. She held her pretty dress caressingly to her face before she hung it in her closet. *He* had liked it. She would keep that dress forever. Judy should never have *it* for her hooked rugs. She put the flowery paper serviette *he* had spread over her knee at supper in her glory box, smoothing and folding it with reverent fingers. She lay awake until the pale golden dawn came in, recalling all he had said and saying it over again to herself.

She worried for fear she had been too stiff. Perhaps he wouldn't understand. Judy always said to give them the fun of a chase . . . but Judy was old-fashioned. When she wakened to find the sunshine raining all over her bed she wondered how any one could be unhappy in such a world. She could never feel sad again.

She went about in a dream all day haunted by the ghostly echoes of the violins . . . by *his* voice . . . and by lines of romantic poetry that came and went like beautiful wraiths in her memory. *Read life's meaning in each other's eyes*. Bets had a poem with that line in it in *her* glory box and Pat had once thought it silly. Oh, *this* was life. She knew its meaning now.

"Let me be seeing yer tongue," said Judy anxiously at night. "I'm thinking ye're after catching cold at that dance. Ather that or . . . is it a beau, Patsy darlint? Won't ye be telling ould Judy if it's a beau?"

"Judy, you're too ridiculous."

No matter how hard she tried Pat couldn't hide her secrets from her family. Soon they all knew that Pat "had a crush" on Harris Hynes and got no end of fun out of it. Nobody, to Pat's indignation, took it very seriously . . . except Judy and Bets. She told Bets all about it the first night she spent at the Long House. Every once in so long she and Bets simply *had* to sleep together and talk things over. Bets was quite enthralled to find herself the confidante of a real love affair. She got almost as many thrills out of it as Pat.

CHAPTER XXVIII
Even as You and I

1

FOR life Pat had become a serial of excitement. The curves of the dullest road were intriguing because she might meet Harris J. Hynes around them. The prosiest sermon good old Mr. Paxton might preach became eloquent when her eyes exchanged messages with Harris' across the aisle. She blushed furiously when he entered a room unexpectedly or when he handed her a book from the Sunday School library or held a door open for her to pass through. His manners were so courtly!

She marked a little ring around the date in the calendar in her glory box on which he first called her "dear." He had given her the calendar. . . a calendar in the shape of a pink rose with gilt greetings on its petal months. "To mark your happy days on," he told her. "Frightfully sentimental," jeered Winnie. But Judy was quite enraptured with it.

"I do be kind av liking a sentimental beau, Patsy. They do mostly seem to be too hard-boiled nowadays."

Pat had one of her moments of beauty when he told her he had been watching her window light half the night. (It was really Judy's light but neither Harris nor Pat ever knew that.) It was thrilling to discover that he liked cats and was not in the least annoyed when Bold-and-Bad rubbed against his best trousers and haired them. Really, his temper must be angelic! Pat would not have been surprised to find he had wings under his navy blue coat.

And it was the delight of all delights to go to the movies at Silverbridge with him.

A theatre had been started in the shabby old community hall in Silverbridge and pictures were shown Wednesday and Saturday nights. Judy was persuaded to go once but never again. She said it was too upsetting. Pat was sure she could never forget the first time Harris took her.

"Has any one every told you how lovely you were?" he whispered, as he helped her on with her coat in the Silver Bush kitchen.

"Lots of people," laughed Pat mendaciously, with an impish light in her eyes.

("Oh, oh, that's the way to answer thim," exulted Judy to herself in the pantry. "You won't be finding the Silver Bush girls too aisy, *Mr.* Hynes.")

Pat felt as sparkling as the night. They went to Silverbridge by a short cut up the hill, past the Long House and down over the fields to the river. The white sorcery of winter was all around them and her arm was tucked warmly in the curve of Harris' arm. Just a little ahead were Sid and Bets. Sid was really having quite a case on Bets, much to Pat's delight.

"I couldn't dream of anything more perfect," she told Judy.

"Oh, oh, Bets'll be having a dozen other beaus yet afore she settles down . . . like yerself," retorted Judy. Whereat Pat went off in high dudgeon. Well, old folks couldn't understand.

"I wonder who was the first person to think the new moon beautiful," said Pat dreamily.

"I've no eyes for the moon to-night," said Harris significantly.

Pat felt faintly chilled. The implication of Harris' remark was complimentary . . . but that slim crescent hanging over the snowy spruces that were like silver palms was so exquisite that Pat wanted Harris to share its loveliness with her. Hilary would have. Then she was horrified at such a thought.

She forgot her momentary disloyalty in the theatre. It *was* so wonderful . . . Pat would have worked that word to death that winter if she had not given it an occasional rest by using "marvellous." Crowds were around them but they were alone in the scented darkness. Once Harris took her hand and held it. When she tried to pull it away . . . "say please," whispered Harris. Pat did not say please.

The only fly in her ointment was the beauty of the screen sirens. Did they ever sneeze . . . have cold sores . . . swallow a crumb the wrong way? How could any boy sit and look at them a whole evening and then see *anything* in ordinary, everyday girls? It was almost worse than last Sunday in church when Myra Lockley had been there, the guest of Dell Robinson. Pat couldn't keep her eyes off Myra's dazzling complexion . . . all her own, too. You could tell that. Pat was sure Myra spent the whole service gazing at the navy blue back of Harris Hynes who had taken a notion that day to sit in his family pew up front. She tried to tease Harris a little about Myra the next evening when they were skating on the moonlight pool. Harris had just laughed and said, "There *was* a Myra."

At first Pat was pleased. Then she wondered if the day would ever come when he would say, "There was a Patricia."

2

Her first love letter was another "wonderful" thing. Harris had gone to visit a friend in town and Pat had never expected him to write her. But he did. Pat found the letter behind Judy's clock when she came home from school.

"Sure and I tucked it out of sight so that me bould Siddy shudn't be seeing it," whispered Judy.

Pat was put to it to find a place wherein to read the sacred missive. At that moment there was somebody in every room of the house, even the Poet's room, because Aunt Helen was at Silver Bush for a visit. To read it in the kitchen where Judy was "dressing" a brace of fat hens, was unthinkable.

Pat had an inspiration. She got her snowshoes and was away through the Silver Bush, across the hill field, and through the woods. Soon she found the Secret Field, an untrodden level of spirit-blue snow, where the Wood Queen and the Fern Princess were slender saplings now. The very spot for love-letters. Seated on a grey "longer" under the maples Pat read her letter. *Little Queen* . . . she had always wondered, ever since she and Bets had read Ella Wheeler Wilcox's poems together if any one would ever call *her* "little queen." *I can see you at this very moment, wonderful Patricia . . . I wish I could write you with a rose instead of a pen* . . . and he was *hers unalterably, Harris J. Hynes.*

What *did* the J stand for? He would never tell any one. But he had said,

"I'll tell *you* what it is some day," in a tone implying that it was some beautiful secret that would affect their entire lives.

"Oh, oh, and how minny kisses was there in your billy-doo?" said Judy, when Pat came home, her cheeks crimson from something more than her tramp in the frosty night.

It was no use being angry with Judy.

"They don't call them billets-doux now, Judy," she said, gravely. "They call them mash notes."

"They would that. The uglier the better nowadays. There's something rale romantic in the sound av billy-doo. Now, Patsy darlint, ye'll be writing back to him but don't be forgetting that the written words do be lasting."

Pat had mislaid her fountain pen and the family ink-bottle was dry so she hunted up her very prettiest pencil to answer it, the one Sid had given her on her birthday, all gold and blue, with a big, silk, flame-coloured tassel. Judy need not have worried over what Pat would write back. Her letter was really full of a dainty mockery that made the devoted Harris more "unalterably hers," than ever.

And, having written her letter, she wrapped the pencil in tissue paper and put it away in her glory box, vowing solemnly that it should never be used to write anything else . . . unless another letter to Harris. And she lay awake for hours with Harris' letter under her pillow . . . she did not want to waste this happy night sleeping.

"But what," said Judy very slyly one day, "does Jingle be thinking av all this?"

Pat winced. Hilary's attitude had been a secret thorn in her side all winter. She knew he hated Harris by the fact that he always was dourly silent when Harris was about. One evening when Harris had been bragging a bit what several noted relatives of his had done . . . Judy could have told you all the Hynes bragged . . . Hilary had said quite nastily,

"But what are *you* going to do?"

Harris had been fine. He had just flung up his splendid crest and laughed kindly at Hilary: and when Hilary had turned away Harris had whispered to Pat,

"I'm going to win the most wonderful girl in P. E. Island . . . something no other Hynes has ever done."

Still, Pat hated to feel the little chill of alienation between her and Hilary. They never went to Happiness now. Of course, they hardly ever had gone in winter and Hilary was studying very hard so that he had few foot-loose evenings to spend in Judy's kitchen. Harris, of course, never spent his evenings in the kitchen. He was entertained in the Little

Parlour, where he was supposed to help Pat with her French and Latin. Sometimes Pat thought it would have been much jollier in the kitchen. There were times when, Latin and French being exhausted, she found herself with little to say. Though that didn't matter much. Harris had plenty for both.

But, when the beautiful copper beech at the top of the hill field blew down in a terrific March gale, it was Hilary who understood her grief and comforted her. Harris couldn't understand at all. Why such a fuss over an old tree? He laughed at her kindly as at an unreasonable child.

"Snap out of it, Pat. Aren't there any number of trees left in the world yet?"

"There are any number of people left in the world when some one dies, but that doesn't mend the grief of those who love him," said Hilary.

Harris laughed. He always laughed when Hilary said anything. "The moonstruck house-builder" he called him... though never in Pat's hearing. Just at this moment Pat found herself thinking that Harris' eyes were really *too* brown and glossy. Strange she had never noticed it before. But Hilary understood. Darling Hilary. A wave of affection for him seemed to flood her being. Even when it ebbed it seemed to have swept something away with it that had been there. She went to the picture with Harris that night but it was a little... flat. And Harris was really too possessive. He had his brother's cutter and he was absurdly solicitous about the robes.

"I'm not quite senile yet," said Pat.

Harris laughed.

"So it can scratch."

Why could he never take anything seriously?

When he lifted her out at the gate Pat looked at Silver Bush. It seemed to look back at her reproachfully. It struck her that she had been thinking more about Harris Hynes that winter than of dear Silver Bush. She was suddenly repentant.

"Aren't you ever going to kiss me, Pat?" Harris was whispering.

"Perhaps... when you grow up," said Pat... and laughed too.

Harris had driven angrily away but Pat slept soundly, albeit it was their first tiff. Harris did not show himself at Silver Bush for a week and Sid and Winnie tormented her mercilessly about it. Pat wasn't worried although Judy thought she might be.

"Boys do be like that now and then, Patsy. They take the quare notions. He'll be along some av these long-come-shorts, darlint."

"I haven't a doubt of it," said Pat with a shrug. "Meanwhile, I'll get a little real studying done."

3

Harris came back and everything was as before. Or was it? Where had the glamour gone? Pat felt a little disgusted with herself... and with Harris... and with the world in general. And then Harris went into Mr. Taylor's store in Silverbridge! There was no reason why a clerk in a dry-goods store shouldn't be as romantic as anybody else. But it seemed such a terrible come down after all his bird-man talk! Pat felt as if he were a stranger.

"Mr. H. Jemuel Hynes has taken a position with Mr. Taylor of Silverbridge"... so ran one of the locals in the next paper... perhaps inspired by no friend of Hynes.

"Jemuel! So that is what the J stood for. No wonder he wouldn't tell it," Pat giggled, as Judy read it out to her.

Judy talked to herself as she kneaded her bread that night in a quiet kitchen. For everybody was out except Pat, who was studying in the Little Parlour.

"Sure and the ind's near whin she do be laughing at him. I'm not knowing why he shud be ashamed av a good Bible name. Well, it's been a liddle experience like for her. She'll know better how to handle the nixt one."

There was one final flare-up of romance the night she and Harris walked down the hill from Bets' party. Harris had been very nice that evening; and he really would have been very handsome if his nose hadn't that frightful kink in it. His hair *was* wonderful and he was a wonderful dancer. And it was a wonderful night. After all, there was no use, as Judy said, in expecting too much of any boy. They all had their liddle failings.

"It's cold... hurry," she said impatiently.

If Judy had heard that she would have known that the end was nearer still.

They went through the Whispering Lane and Harris

paused by the garden gate and drew her to him. Pat was looking at the garden, all sparkle and snow in the moonshine. How sweet it was, with its hidden secrets!

"Look, Harris," she said . . . and her voice rippled through a verse she loved.

> "So white with frost my garden lies,
>   So still, so white my garden is,
> Full sure the fields of Paradise
>   Are not more fair than this.
> The streets of pearl, the gates of gold,
>   Are they indeed more peace possessed,
> Than this white pleasaunce pure and cold
>   Against the amber west?"

"Don't let's talk about the weather," Harris was saying. "I want you only to think of me."

The light went out of Pat's face as if some one had blown it out.

"Hilary would have loved that."

She hadn't meant to say it aloud . . . but it seemed to say itself.

Harris laughed. Harris certainly had a frightful knack of laughing at the wrong time.

"That sissy! I suppose he *would* moon over gardens and trees."

Something clicked inside Pat's brain.

"He isn't a sissy," she cried. "The idea of *you* calling him a sissy . . . *you with your curls and your great soft cowey eyes*," she finished, but in thought.

Harris tightened his arm.

"It mustn't be cross," he said fatally.

Pat stepped back and removed his arm.

"I don't want to see you again, Harris Jemuel Hynes," she said clearly and distinctly.

Harris found out eventually that she meant it.

"You're as fickle-minded as a breeze," were his bitter parting words.

Pat was not worried over her fickleness but she was rather worried over the conviction that Harris had always taken a bit too much for granted from the start. He was what horrid May Binnie called horridly, "a fast worker." And she, Pat Gardiner of Silver Bush, had fallen for it.

Judy used a dreadful phrase sometimes of certain girls . . . "a bit too willing."

"Have I been too willing?" Pat asked herself solemnly.

When it became manifest that Pat's case with Harris Hynes was off she was tormented a good deal. Bets was very sweet and understanding and comforting, but Pat did not feel entirely easy until she had talked the matter over with Judy.

"Oh, Judy, it was very exciting while it lasted. But it didn't last."

"Oh, oh, darlint, I niver thought it wud come to innything. Ye're too young for the sarious side. He was just a bit of an excursion like for ye. I wudn't be after criticising him as long as ye'd a liking for him, Pat, but wasn't he a bit too free and aisy now? I do be liking the shy ones better that don't be calling the cows be their first name at the second visit. And he do be standing wid his legs too far apart of real illigance. Now did ye iver notice the way Jingle stands? Like a soldier. He do be such a diffrunt looking b'y since he do be wearing better clo'se and having his hair cut at Silverbridge, niver to mintion his stylish glasses."

It was strange but rather nice just to feel quietly happy again, without thrills and chills and semi-demi-quavers.

"Sid and Hilary are better than all the beaus in the world, Judy. I'm never going to fall in love again."

"Not before the nixt time innyway, Patsy."

"There won't be any next time."

"Oh, oh, it's much more comfortable not to be in love, I'm agreed. And wud ye be wanting that blue dress av yours much longer, darlint? It's all gone under the arms and it do be just the shade for that bit av blue scroll in me mat."

"Oh, you can have it," said Pat indifferently. She burned the letter just as indifferently. Nevertheless, years after, when she came across a little tasselled pencil in an old box in the attic she smiled and sighed.

Hilary came in with his lean brown hands filled with the first mayflowers for her and they went off on a ramble to Happiness.

"Sure and it's the happy b'y that Jingle is this blessed night," chuckled Judy.

"Friendship is much more satisfactory than love," Pat reflected, before she went to sleep.

CHAPTER XXIX
April Magic

1

ONE dim wet evening in early spring, when a shabby old world was trying to wash the winter grime from its face before it must welcome April, there was wild music among the birches and Pat listened to it as she chatted with Judy in the kitchen. Mother was tired and had been packed off to bed early. Somehow, everybody at Silver Bush, without saying anything about it, was becoming very careful of mother.

Cuddles was singing to herself in the Little Parlour... Cuddles had such a sweet voice, Pat reflected lovingly. Judy was mixing her bread with Gentleman Tom on one side of her and Bold-and-Bad on the other. Snicklefritz was curled up by the stove, snoring. Snicklefritz was getting old, as nobody would admit.

And then... there was the sound of footsteps on the stone walk. Dad or Sid coming in from the barn, thought Pat. But Snicklefritz knew better. In an instant he was awake and had hurled himself at the door in a frenzy of barks and scratches.

"Now, whativer's got into the dog?" said Judy. "Sure and it's long wakes since he bothered his liddle old head about inny stranger... and it's the quare dream I had last night... and, hivenly day, am I draming still?"

For the door was open and a bronzed young man was on the step... and Snicklefritz was speechless in ecstasy... and Pat had flown to his arms, wet as he was. Sid and dad were rushing in from the barn... and mother, who had been disobedient and hadn't gone to bed after all, was flying down stairs... and Bold-and-Bad was spitting and bristling at all this fuss over a stranger. And everybody was a little crazy because Joe had come home... Joe so changed and yet the same Joe... hugging mother and the girls and Judy and laughing at the antics of Bold-and-Bad and pretending to be in a fury because the white kittens in Judy's picture hadn't grown up after all.

They had a gay fortnight at Silver Bush. Snicklefritz simply refused to be parted one moment from Joe and insisted on sleeping on his bed at night. And every night Judy crept in to see if Joe was warm and ask the Good Man Above to bless him, as she had done when he was a child.

There were tales to tell of far lands and strange faces and everybody was happy. Pat was *too* happy, Judy thought, with several wise shakes of her head.

"The Ould Ones don't be giving ye a gift like that for nothing, as me grandmother used to say. No, no, you would have to be paying."

And then Joe was gone again. And this time those he left knew that Joe would never belong to Silver Bush again. He would be home for a visit once in a while... with longer intervals between each visit... but his path was on the sea and his way on the great waters. To Pat came bitterly the realisation that Joe was an outsider. The life of Silver Bush closed over his going with hardly a ripple.

"Judy, it seems a little terrible. I was so broken-hearted when Joe went away the first time... I felt sure I couldn't live without him. And now... I love him just as much as ever... and it was queer and lonely without him for a few days... but now it's as if he'd always been away. If... if he had *wanted* to stay home... it doesn't seem as if there was any real place for him. His old place seems to have grown over. And *that* hurts me, Judy."

"It do be life, Patsy darlint. They come and they go. But there do be one liddle heart that can't find comfort. Do ye be looking at the eyes av that poor Snicklefritz. He's too old to be standing such another parting."

Judy was right. The next morning Snicklefritz was found on Joe's bed, with his head on Joe's pillow. And Snicklefritz would waken no more to wail or weep. Pat and Sid and Hilary and Bets and Cuddles buried him in a corner of the old grave-yard. Judy made no objections to this although she would never let a cat be buried there.

"I thought you liked cats better than dogs, Judy," said Cuddles.

"I do that same, but a cat do be having no right in a grave-yard," was all Judy's explanation.

Cuddles prayed that night that Snicklefritz wouldn't be lonesome. Pat knew he wouldn't. He slept with his own. What more could an old dog ask? And perhaps on the nights when Wild Dick sang and Willy wept a jolly little ghost dog would come out of his grave and bark.

2

Pat and Bets were lingering by the little green gate at the top of the hill path, making plans. They were full of plans that spring... plans for the summer... plans for college in the fall... plans for life beyond. They were going to camp out for a week this summer... they were going to room together at Queen's... and in a few years' time they were going to take a trip to Europe. They had been planning imaginary journeys through all their years of comradeship but this one was going to be real... some day.

"Isn't it fun to make plans?" Pat would say happily.

They had spent the afternoon together at the Long House. Pat loved the Long House next to Silver Bush. It was a house that always invited you to enter... a house, Pat often thought, that always said, "So glad you've come." Open doors... geraniums in the windows... wide, shallow, well-trodden steps up to the porch. Inside, to take off the chill of the early spring, glowing fires. They had read poetry, together savouring the wealth of beauty found in linked words; they had discussed their grievances. Bets' mother wouldn't let her wear pyjamas but insisted on nightdresses. And Bets did so crave a lovely pair of yellow ones like Sara Robinson had. So up to date. They did a great deal of laughing, pouncing on their jokes like frolicsome young kittens. And at the end Bets walked to the green gate with Pat and stood there talking for another hour. They just couldn't get talked out. And anyway Pat was going the next day to the Bay Shore for a visit and there were so many last things to say. It was, they agreed, just tragic to be parted so long.

It was the first mild evening of that late, cold spring. Beyond the lowlands the sea was silver grey, save just at the horizon where there was a long line of shining gold. Far, far away a bell was ringing... some bell of lost Atlantis perhaps. A green, mystical twilight was screening all the bare, ugly fields from sight. Faint, enchanted star-fire shone over the spruces behind them. Down below them Uncle Tom was burning brush. Was there anything more fascinating than a fire in the open after night? And somewhere beyond those chilly skies was the real spring of blossom and the summer of roses. They gazed out over the world with all the old hill rapture no dweller in the valley ever knows. Oh, life was sweet together!

"Couldn't we have our tent back in the Secret Field the nights we sleep out?" said Bets. Bets knew about the Secret Field now. Sid had told her and Pat was glad. She couldn't have told herself, after her pact with Sid, but she hated to have Bets shut out of any of her secrets.

"Think of it," she breathed. "Sleeping there... with the woods all around us... and the silver birches in the moonlight... we must arrange for a moon, of course. Bets, can't you *see* it?"

Bets could. Her cherry-blossom face, wrapped in a scarlet scarf, reflected Pat's enthusiasm. That scarf became Bets, Pat reflected. But then everything did. Her clothes always seemed to love her. She could wear the simplest dress like a queen. She was so pretty... and yet you always thought more of the sweetness than the prettiness of her face.

"Sid says we'd be scared to death back there," she said. "But we won't. Not even if the wee green folks of the hills Judy talks about came to our tent door and peeped in."

Suddenly the night laid its finger on their lips. Something uncanny... something fairy-like was abroad. The spruces on the hill against the pale sunset were all at once a company of old crones. They seemed to be listening to something. Then they would shake with scornful laughter. The near-by bushes rustled as if a faun had slipped through them. Pat and Bets instinctively put their arms around each other. At that moment they were elfin-hearted things themselves, akin to the shadows and the silences. They could have knelt down on the dear earth and kissed its clods for very gladness in it.

Did it last for a moment or a century? They could never have told. A light flashing out in the kitchen of Silver Bush recalled Pat to reality.

"I must go. Sid is going to run me over to the Bay Shore when the chores are done."

"Tell them hello for me," said Bets lightly.

"I wish you were going with me. Nothing has the same flavour without you, Bets." Pat leaned over the gate and dropped a kiss on Bets' cool cheek. Life had as yet touched them both so lightly that parting was still "sweet sorrow."

Pat ran lightly down the path, turning her back, although she knew it not, on her years of unshadowed happiness.

A flock of geese flying over in the April night...a grey cat pouncing out from the ferns in the Whispering Lane... lantern shadows in the barn-yard...a girl half-drunk with the sweet, heady wine of spring.

"Oh, Judy, life is so beautiful...and spring is so beautiful. Judy, how can you help dancing?"

"Dancing, is it?" Judy sat down with a grunt. She was tired and she did not like it because it meant that she was growing old. Judy had just one dread in life...that she might grow too old to be of use to Silver Bush. "Whin ye come to my years, Patsy darlint, dancing don't be coming so aisy. But dance while ye can...oh, oh, dance while ye can. And rap a bit av wood."

CHAPTER XXX
One Shall Be Taken

1

PAT was to have stayed two weeks at the Bay Shore farm. She did not mind...much. She had learned how to get along with the aunts and they thought her "much improved." A good bit of Selby in her after all. The Great-great had "passed away" a year ago but nothing else had changed at the Bay Shore. Pat liked this...it gave her a nice sensation of having cheated Time.

But at the end of a week Long Alec came for her one evening. And his face...

"Dad, is anything wrong? Mother..."

No, not mother. Bets. Bets had flu pneumonia.

Pat felt an icy finger touch... just touch... her heart.

"Why wasn't I sent for before?" she said very quietly.

"They didn't think she was in danger until this evening. She asked for you. I think we'll be in time."

Bets "in danger"... "in time,"... the phrases made a meaningless jumble in Pat's head. The drive home was like a nightmare. Nothing was real. It couldn't be real. Things like this simply didn't happen. God wouldn't let them. Of course she would waken soon. Meanwhile... one must keep very quiet. If one said a word too much... one might have to go on dreaming. She had such a queer feeling that her heart was a stone... sinking, sinking, sinking... ever since that finger had touched it.

They drove up to Silver Bush. Pat would go up the hill path. It was quicker so because the lane of the Long House ran to the Silverbridge road. Judy caught Pat in her arms as she stumbled from the car.

"Judy... Bets..." but no, one must be quiet. One mustn't ask questions. One dared not.

"I'll walk up the hill with you, Pat."

It was Hilary... a pale, set-lipped Hilary. Judy... wise Judy... whispered to him,

"No, let her be going alone, Jingle. It'll be... kinder."

"Don't you think there's a little hope, Judy?" asked Hilary huskily.

Judy shook her head.

"I do be getting the sign, Jingle. It's a bit hard to understand. Ivery one loved her so. Sure and hiven must be nading some laughter."

Pat didn't know whether she was alone or not. She ran breathlessly along the Whispering Lane and down the field and up the hill. The Watching Pine watched... *what was it watching for?* A grim red sun with a black bar of cloud across it was setting behind a dark hill as she reached the green gate. She turned for a moment... just a moment before one had to... know. As long as one didn't *know* one could live. The black sea of a cold grey April twilight was far below her. That far-away bell was still ringing. It was only a week since she and Bets had listened to it and made their plans for the summer. A thing like this couldn't come in a week... it would need years and years. How foolish she was to be . . . afraid. One *must* waken soon.

May Binnie was in the Long House kitchen when Pat went in . . . always pushing herself in where she wasn't wanted, Pat reflected detachedly. Then the room where she and Bets had slept and whispered and laughed . . . and Bets lying on the bed, pale and sweet . . . always sweet . . . breathing too quickly. There were others there . . . Mr. and Mrs. Wilcox . . . the nurse . . . but Pat saw only Bets.

"Dearest Pat . . . I'm so glad you've come," Bets whispered.

"Darling . . . how are you?"

"Better, Pat . . . much better . . . only a little tired."

Of course she was better. One had known she must be. Why, then, didn't one waken?

Some one put a chair by the bed for Pat and she sat down. Bets put out a cold hand . . . how very thin it had grown . . . and Pat took it. The nurse came up with a hypodermic. Bets opened her eyes.

"Let Pat do that for me, please. Let Pat do everything for me now."

The nurse hesitated. Then some one else . . . Dr. Bentley . . . came up.

"There is no use in giving any more hypodermics," he said. "She has ceased to react to them. Let her . . . rest."

Pat heard Mrs. Wilcox break into dreadful sobbing and Mr. Wilcox led her from the room. The doctor went, too. The nurse adjusted the shade of the light. Pat sat movelessly. She would not speak . . . no word must disturb Bets' rest. Bets must be better if she were resting. Now and then she felt Bets' fingers give a gentle little pressure against her own. Very gently Pat squeezed back. In a few days she and Bets would be laughing over this . . . next summer when they would be sleeping in their tent in the moonlit Secret Field it would be such a joke to recall . . .

"My breath . . . is getting . . . very short," said Bets.

She did not speak again. At sunrise a little change came over her face . . . such a little terrible change.

"Bets," cried Pat imploringly. Bets had always answered when she called before. Now she did not even lift the heavy white lids of her beautiful eyes. But she was smiling.

"It's . . . over," said the nurse softly.

Pat heard some one . . . Bets' mother . . . give a piteous

moan. She went over to the window and looked out. The sky in the east was splendid. Below in the valley the silver birches seemed afloat in morning mists. Far-off the harbour lighthouse stood up, golden-white against the sunrise. Smoke was curling up from the roofs of Swallowfield and Silver Bush.

Pat wished sickly that she could get back into last year. There were no nightmares there.

The room was so dreadfully still after all the agony. Pat wished some one would make a noise. Why was the nurse tiptoeing about like that? Nothing could disturb Bets now... Bets who was lying there with the dawn of some eternal day on her face.

Pat went over and looked at her quite calmly. Bets looked like some one with a lovely secret. Bets had always looked like that... only now one knew she would never tell it. Pat dimly recalled some text she had heard ages ago... last Sunday in the Bay Shore church. *I am come into deep waters where the floods overflow me*. If one could only wake!

"I think if I could cry my throat wouldn't ache so much," she thought dully.

2

Home... mother's silent hand-clasp of sympathy... Winnie's kind blue eyes... Judy's anxious, "Patsy darlint, ye've had no breakfast. Can't ye be ating a liddle bite? Ye must be kaping up yer strength. Don't grieve, me jewel. Sure and they tell me she died smiling... she's gone on a glad journey."

Pat was not grieving. Death was still incredible. Her family wondered at her calm.

"There's something in her isn't belaving it yet," said Judy shrewdly.

The days were still a dream. There was the funeral. Pat walked calmly up to the Long House by the hill path. She would not have been surprised to see Bets coming dancing through the green gate to meet her. She glanced up at the window that used to frame Bets' laughing face... surely she must be there.

The Long House was full of people. May Binnie was there... May Binnie was crying... May Binnie who had always hated Bets. And her mother was trying to comfort her!

That was *funny*. If only Bets could share in her amusement
over it!

But Bets only lay smiling with that white, sweet peace
on her waxen face and Hilary's cluster of pussywillows from
the tree in Happiness between her fingers. There were
flowers everywhere. The Sunday School had sent a cross with
the motto, *Gone Home,* on it. Pat would have laughed at that,
only she knew she was never going to laugh again. Home!
This was Bets' home . . . the Long House and the garden she
had loved and planned for. Bets was *not* gone home . . . she
had only gone on an uncompanioned journey from which
she must presently return.

May Binnie almost had hysterics when the casket was
closed. Many people thought Pat Gardiner was very unfeel-
ing. Only a discerning few thought that fierce, rebellious
young face more piteous than many tears.

If only she could get away by herself! Somewhere where
people could not look at her. But, if one persisted in dreaming,
one must go to the grave-yard. She went with Uncle Tom,
because Sid and Hilary, who were pall-bearers, had taken the
car. Spring still refused to come and it was a bleak, dull day.
A few snowflakes were falling on the grey fields. The sea
was black and grim. The cold road was hard as iron. And so
they came to the little burying-ground on a western hill
that had been flooded with many hundreds of sunsets,
where there was a heap of red clay and an empty grave.
The boys Bets had played around with carried her to it
over a path heaped with the sodden leaves of a vanished
year; and Pat listened unflinchingly to the most dreadful
sound in the world . . . the sound of the clods falling on the
coffin of the beloved.

"She is in a Better Place, my dear," Mrs. Binnie was
saying to the sobbing May behind her. Pat turned.

"Do you think there is a better place than Silver Bush
and the Long House farm?" she said. "I don't . . . and I don't
think Bets did either!"

"That awful girl," Mrs. Binnie always said when she told
of it. "She talked like a perfect heathen."

Pat wakened from her dream that evening. The sun set.
Then came darkness . . . and the hills and trees drawing
nearer . . . no light in Bets' window.

Pat had never really believed that any one she loved

could die. Now she had learned the bitter lesson that it is possible . . . that is does happen.

"Let me be alone to-night, Winnie," she said; and Winnie sympathetically went away to the Poet's room.

Pat undressed and crept into bed, shivering. The wind at the window was no longer a friend . . . it was a malignant thing. She was so lonely . . . it was impossible to endure such loneliness. If she could only sleep . . . sleep! But then there would be such a dreadful awakening and remembering.

Bets was . . . dead. She, who loved everything beautiful, was now lying in that cold, damp grave on the hill with the long grasses and withered leaves blowing drearily around it. Pat buried her face in her pillow and the long-denied tears came in a flood.

"Darlint . . . darlint . . . don't be mourning like this."

Judy had crept in . . . dear, tender old Judy. She was kneeling by the bed and her arms were about the tortured creature.

"Oh, Judy, I didn't know life could ever hurt like this. I can't bear it, Judy."

"Dear heart, we do all be thinking that at first."

"I can never forgive God for taking her from me," gasped Pat between her racking sobs.

"Child dear, whoiver heard av not forgiving God," said the horrified Judy who did not know her Omar. "But He won't be holding it aginst ye."

"Life has all gone to pieces, Judy. And yet I have to go on living. How can I?"

"Sure and ye've only got to live one day at a time, darlint. One can always be living just one more day."

"She was such a dear, Judy . . . we had so many plans . . . I *can't* go to Queen's without her. Oh, Judy, our friendship was so beautiful. Why didn't God let it go on? Doesn't He like beautiful things?"

"Sure and we can't be telling what He has in mind but we can be belaving it's nothing but good. Maybe He was wanting to *kape* your friendship beautiful, Patsy darlint."

CHAPTER XXXI

Lost Fragrance

WHEN Bets had been dead for a week it seemed to Pat she had been dead for years, so long is pain. The days passed like ghosts. Pat went for long walks over hills and fields in the evenings . . . trying to face her sorrow . . . seeing the loveliness of the crescent spring around her. She only *saw* it . . . she could not *feel* it. *Where was Bets who had walked with her last spring?*

Everything had ended. And everything had to begin anew. That was the worst of it. How was one to begin anew when the heart had gone out of life?

"I wish I could forget her, Judy . . . I wish I could forget her. It hurts so to remember," she cried wildly once. "If I could drink some cup of forgetfulness like that in your old story, Judy . . ."

"But wud ye be after doing it if ye could, darlint? Ye'd forget all the gladness along with the pain . . . all the fun and happiness ye had wid yer liddle chum. Wud ye be wanting *that*?"

No, she would not want that. She hugged her sweet memories to her heart. But how to go on living . . .

"Ye don't be remimbering one day whin ye was a liddle dot av four, Patsy? Ye wint to the door and all the sky was clouded over thick and dark. Ye was frightened to death. Ye did be running to yer mother, crying, 'Oh, mother, where is the blue sky gone to . . . oh, mother!' Ye wudn't be belaving us whin we tould ye it wud come back. But the nixt morning there it was smiling at ye."

Pat still couldn't believe that her blue sky would ever come back . . . couldn't believe that there would come a time when she would be happy again. Why, it would be terrible to be happy without Bets, even if it were possible . . . disloyal to Bets . . . disloyal to love. She despised herself when she had to admit that she felt hungry once more!

Silver Bush was all her comfort now. Her love for it seemed the only solid thing under her feet. Insensibly she drew comfort and strength from its old, patient, familiar acres. Spring passed. The daffodils and spiræa and bleeding heart and columbines bloomed. Bets had loved the columbines so, she should be here to see them. The pansies they had planted together, because, for some mysterious reason, pansies would not grow up on the hill, bloomed at Silver Bush, but no slim girl figure ever came down the hill to pick them in a sunset garden. The big apple tree at the Long House bloomed as it had bloomed for two generations but she and Bets could not sit on the long bough and read poetry. Pat couldn't bear to open the books she had read with Bets . . . to see the lines and paragraphs they had marked. Bets seemed to die afresh every time there was something Pat wanted to share with her and could not.

Summer came. The honeysuckle was thick over the grave-yard paling. To think that the scent of honeysuckles meant nothing to Bets now . . . or the soft stars of evening . . . or the moon on white roses. The little path up the hill field grew over with grass. Nobody ever walked on it now. The Wilcoxes had sold the Long House farm and moved to town. . . . Stranger lights were in it but Bets' room was always dark. Sundays were terrible. She and Bets had always spent the afternoon and evening together. Sid wouldn't talk of Bets . . . Sid in his secret boyish way had been hard hit by her death . . . but Hilary would.

"I could never have lived through this summer if it hadn't been for Hilary," Pat thought.

Yet, undeniably life began to beckon once more. The immortal spirit of beauty again held aloft its torch for her. Pat hated herself because she could enjoy anything with no Bets in the world.

"Judy, I feel as if I oughtn't to be even a little bit happy. And yet, to-day, back in the Secret Field I *was* happy. I forgot Bets for a little while . . . and then . . . oh, Judy . . . I *remembered*. It seemed sad to think I *could* forget her. And the Secret Field was changed somehow . . . more beautiful than ever but still . . . not just the same, Judy."

Judy recalled an old line in a poem she had learned in far-away school days...a poem by a forgotten, outmoded author who yet had the secret of touching the heart.

"*Ye have looked on death since ye saw me last,*" she whispered to herself. But aloud...

"Ye naden't be worrying over being happy, darlint. Bets would be glad av it."

"You know, Judy, at first it hurt me to think of Bets...I couldn't bear it. But now...it's a comfort. I can think of her in all our old haunts. To-night, when the moon came up I thought, 'She is standing in it under the Watching Pine, waiting for me.' And it was sweet...for a little while...just to pretend it. But I'll never have another chum, Judy...and I wouldn't if I could. It hurts too much to lose them."

"Ye're young to have larned that, darlint, but we all have to sooner or later. And as for another...oh, oh, oh, that's all as it's ordered. I've talked to ye as wise as inny av thim, Patsy, about choosing frinds but ye don't be choosing frinds after all. They *come* to ye...or they don't. Just that. Ye get the ones meant for you, be they minny or few, in the time app'inted for their coming."

Summer passed. The old days were once more lovely in remembrance. The root of white perennial phlox Bets had given her bloomed for the first time. The gold and bronze dahlias flamed against the green spruce hedge. The pageant of autumn woods began. Bets had gone "rose-crowned into the darkness"...Joe had forsaken them...but the Hill of the Mist was still amethyst and mysterious on September mornings...the Secret Field held all its old allure...Silver Bush, dear Silver Bush...was still her own, beautiful and beloved. Pat's laughter once more echoed in Judy's kitchen... once more she bandied jokes with Uncle Tom...once more she spent long hours in Happiness with Hilary, talking over college plans. The world *was* sweet again.

> "*Yet in the purple shadow*
> *And in the warm grey rain*
> *What hints of ancient sorrow*
> *And unremembered pain!*"

No, not "unremembered." She would always remember it. She had had Bets for nine wonderful years and nothing could take them from her. Judy had been right as she always was. One would not drink of the cup of forgetfulness if one could.

CHAPTER XXXII
Exile

1

WHEN the pass lists came out in August Hilary led and Pat had a very respectable showing. So it was Queen's in September for both and Pat thought she might like it if she could survive an absence from Silver Bush for two-thirds of the year. She had always had a sneaking sympathy for Lot's wife. Was she really to be blamed so much for lingering to look back at her home? Pat's only comfort was that Hilary would be at Queen's too, and they would be coming home every week-end.

"You wouldn't think a house could be so nice as Silver Bush is in so many different ways, Judy. And the pieces of furniture in it don't seem like furniture. They're *persons*, Judy. That old chair that was Great-grandfather Nehemiah's . . . when I sit in it it just puts its arms around me, Judy. I feel it. And all the chairs just *want* to be sat in."

"Sure and iverything in the house has been loved and took care av and used be so minny human beings, Patsy. It stands to rason they do be more than just furniture."

"I guess I'm hopelessly Victorian, Judy. Norma says I am. I really don't want to do anything in the world but stay on here at Silver Bush and love it and take care of the things in it and plan for it. If I do really get through the licence exams next year and get a school I'm going to shingle the roof with my first quarter's salary. Those new red and green shingles, Judy. Think how lovely they'd look against the silver birches in winter. And we must have a new rug for the Little Parlour. And oh, Judy, don't forget to see that the delphiniums are divided in October, will you? They must be this year . . . and I'm afraid nobody will remember it when I'm not here."

There was some excitement in getting her outfit ready... and secret sorrow, remembering how much fun it would have been to talk things over with Bets. Pat couldn't have a great deal... crops had been poor that year. But the necessary things were managed and Uncle Tom gave her a beautiful coat with a huge fluffy fur collar and Aunt Barbara gave her a smart little hat of brown velvet, tipped over one eye, and the aunts at the Bay Shore gave her an evening dress. Judy knit her two lovely pullovers and Aunt Edith would have given her silk undies if it had not been for the pyjama question. Silver Bush was rocked to its foundation over that. Aunt Edith, who thought even coloured silk nighties immoral, declared pyjamas were immodest and brazen faced. Pat was set on pyjamas. Even Judy favoured them simply because Aunt Edith hated them.

"How," said Aunt Edith solemnly, "would you like to die in your sleep and go before your Maker in pyjamas, Patricia?"

Mother gave the casting vote... as she had a trick of doing—and Pat got her pyjamas.

When the last day came Pat went to the Secret Field to say good-bye and on her return lingered long at the top of the hill field. Autumn was here... the air was full of its muted music. The old farm lay before her in the golden light of the mellow September evening. She knew every kink and curve of it. Every field was an intimate friend. The Pool glimmered mysteriously. The round window winked at her. The trees she had grown up with waved to her. The garden was afoam with starry white cosmos backed by the stately phalanx of the Prince's Feather. Dear Silver Bush! Never had she felt so close to it... so one with it.

Since the Silver Bush treasury was so very lean Pat had to put up with a rather cheap boarding house that always seemed full of stale cooking smells. It was a square, bare house on a treeless lot, on a street that was quiet only for a little while at night... a street where the wind could only creep in a narrow space like a cringing, fettered thing, instead of sweeping grandly over wide fields and great salt wastes of sea. But at least it was not exactly like the other houses on the street. Pat felt that she couldn't have borne to live on a street where the houses were all exactly alike. And it had a little park next to it, with a few trees.

When Pat stood alone in her room that night, with its

mustard coloured ingrain carpet and its dreadful maroon walls and the arrogance of its pert alarm clock, loneliness rolled over her like a wave. Judy had sent her off that morning with "gobs av good luck to ye," but at this moment Pat was sure there was no good luck in the world for her away from Silver Bush.

She ran to the window. Below the street the western train was puffing and chugging. If she could only step on it and go home! Far beyond was cold moonlight on alien hills.

She shut her eyes and imagined she could see Silver Bush. The moon would be shining down on the Secret Field now. The little rabbits would be sitting on the paths among the birches. She heard the gulf wind sighing in the old firs and the maples whispering on the hills of home. She saw the silvery poplar leaves drifting down through the blue "dim." She thought of the old doorstep listening for her footfall . . . of her room missing her. She saw Judy in the kitchen knitting, with Gentleman Tom beside her and Bold-and-Bad in her lap . . . Cuddles perched thoughtfully somewhere about as was her dear habit . . . as *she*, Pat, had perched long years ago.

She was overcome with homesickness . . . submerged in it. She cast herself on her hard little bed and wept.

2

Pat lived through the pangs of homesickness. She was finding out how many things can be lived through. Eventually she was homesick only on rainy evenings when she could imagine the rain splashing on the back doorstones and running down the windows of a kitchen crowded with cats defiant of the weather.

She liked Queen's fairly well. She liked all the professors except the one who always seemed looking with amused tolerance at every one and everything. She imagined him looking just so at Silver Bush. As for studies she contrived to get along with a good average. The only marked talent she had was for loving things very greatly and that did not help you much with Greek verbs and dates. It helped you a bit socially, though. Pat was popular at Queen's, in spite of the fact that the other students always felt she was a little detached and aloof . . . among them but not of them. She was

early elected to membership in the Saturday Satellites and by
New Year's she was a star in the Dramatic Club. She was
voted "not exactly pretty but charming." A bit proud... you
knew her a street off by the way she carried her head. A bit
reserved... she had no chums among the girls. A bit odd... she
would rather sit in that shabby little park by her boarding
house in the evenings than go to a movie.

Pat liked to sit there in the twilight and watch the lights
spring up in the houses along the street and in the valley and
over on the other hill. Commonplace-looking houses, most of
them, but who knew what might be going on inside of them?
Sometimes Hilary sat there with her. Hilary was the only boy
in the world with whom she could be at the same time
taciturn and comfortable. They knew how to be silent together.

Pat took Hilary for granted and did not think about his
looks at all, other than to see that he did not wear weird
neckties. But quite a number of Queen's girls thought Hilary
a charming fellow, although everybody knew that he had eyes
only for Pat Gardiner who did not care a hoot about him.
Hilary was first and foremost a student and cared little for
social doings although he had outgrown all his old awkwardness
and shyness. The week-end trip home with Pat was all the
diversion he sought or desired.

Those week-ends were always delightful. They went on the
train to Silverbridge and then walked home. First along the
road. Up one long, spruce-walled hill... down into a green
valley... another hill... another valley... twists and turns...
"I hate a straight road or a flat one," said Pat. "This is a
road I love... all curves and dips. It's *my* road. Oh, it may
belong nominally to the township but it's *mine*. I love it all,
even that dark little glen Judy calls Suicide Hollow. She used
to tell me the loveliest creepy story about it years ago."

Then they left the road and went straight home over
country... past the eerie misty marsh and across the Secret
Field and through the woods by little paths that had never
been made but just happened. Perhaps there would be
northern lights and a hazy new moon; or perhaps just a soft
blue darkness. Cool running waters... aeolian harps in the
spruces. The very stars were neighbours.

If only Bets could have been with them! Pat never took
that walk home without thinking of Bets... Bets whose grave
on the hillside was covered with a loose drift of autumn leaves.

And then Silver Bush! It came on you so suddenly and beautifully as you stepped over the crest of the hill field. It welcomed you like a friend with all its windows astar... Judy saw to that. Though once they caught her napping when she was late getting in from the barn and mother had gone to bed with a headache. There wasn't a light in Silver Bush and Pat thought she almost loved it best in the dark... so brooding and motherly.

The same dear old creak to the gate... and the happiest dog in the world throwing himself at Hilary. McGinty always came as far as Silver Bush to meet Hilary. Never a Friday night did he miss. Then Judy's kitchen and welcome. Hilary always stayed to supper and Judy invariably had hot pea soup to begin with, just to warm them up a liddle mite after their cold walk. And a juicy bone for McGinty.

The wind snoring round the house... all the news to hear... all the mad, bad, sad deeds Bold-and-Bad had done... three balls of velvet fluff with tiny whiskered faces tumbling about on the floor. Silver Bush was, as Aunt Edith scornfully said, always infested with kittens. As for Bold-and-Bad, he was ceasing to be a cat and was on the way to becoming a family habit.

Judy always gave them a box of cats to take back Monday morning.

"As long as one can get a liddle bite one can kape up," she would say.

Pat wondered how Queen's students who got home only once in a blue moon, survived. But then their homes were not Silver Bush!

CHAPTER XXXIII
Fancy's Fool

1

PAT met him for the first time at the Dramatic Club's exclusive dance in the Queen's auditorium, by which they celebrated the successful presentation of their play *Ladies in Waiting*. Pat had been one of the ladies and had been voted exceptionally good, although in certain vivid scenes she could never look "passionate" enough to satisfy an exacting director.

"*How* can any one look passionate with a cute nose?" she would ask him pathetically. In the end she looked impish and elusive which seemed to take just as well with the audience.

He came up to her and told her that he was going to dance with her. He never asked a girl to dance or drive with him . . . he simply told her that she was going to do it. That, said the Queen's girls, was his "line." It seemed to be a popular one, though the girls he didn't notice talked contemptuously of cave man stuff.

"I've been wondering all the evening who you were," he told her.

"Couldn't you have found out?" asked Pat.

"Perhaps. But I wanted to find out from yourself alone. We are going to the sun-porch presently to see if the moon is rising properly and then we can discover who we are."

Pat discovered that he was Lester Conway and that he was in his third year at Queen's, but had just come back to college after an absence caused by pneumonia. She also discovered that his home was in Summerside.

"I know you're thinking just what I'm thinking," he said gravely. "That we have been living ten miles apart all our lives and have never met till now."

His tone implied that all their lives had been terribly wasted. But then, everything he said seemed to have some special significance. And he had a way of leaning towards you that shut out all the rest of the world.

"What an escape I've had. I was so bored with the whole affair that I was just going to go when . . . you happened. I saw you coming downstairs and ever since that moment I've been afraid to look away for fear you'd disappear."

"Do you say that to every girl half an hour after you've met her?" demanded Pat, hoping that the sound of her voice would keep him from hearing how her heart was thumping.

"I've never said it to any girl before and I think you know that. And I think you've been waiting for me, haven't you?"

Pat was of the opinion that she had but she had enough Silver Bush sense to keep her from saying so. A lovely colour was staining her cheeks. Her French-English-Scotch-Irish-Quaker blood was running like quicksilver through her veins. Yes, *this* was love. No nonsense this time about your knees shaking... no emotional thrills. Just a deep, quiet conviction that you had met your fate... some one you could follow to the world's end... *"beyond its utmost purple rim"* ... *"deep into the dying day"* ...

He told her he was going to drive her home and did, through a night drenched with moonlight. He told her that he was going to see her soon again.

"This wonderful day has come and gone but there will be another to-morrow," he said, dropping his voice and whispering the final word confidentially as he announced this remarkable fact.

Pat thought she was getting very sensible because she slept quite well that night... after she once got to sleep.

It was speedily an item of college gossip that Lester Conway and Pat Gardiner had a terrible "case" on each other. It was a matter of speculation what particular brand of magic she had used, for Lester Conway had never really fallen for any girl before though he had played around with several.

He was a dark lover... Pat felt that she could never bear a fair man again, remembering Harris Jemuel's golden locks. He was not especially good-looking but Pat knew she had got far beyond the stage of admiring movie stars. He was distinguished-looking... with that faint, mysterious scowl. Lester thought he looked more interesting when he was scowling... like *Lara* and those fellows. His psychology was sound. Whenever a girl met him she wondered what he looked like when he smiled... and tried to find out.

He was appallingly clever. There was nothing he couldn't do. He danced and skated and footballed and hockeyed and tennised and sang and acted and played the ukulele and drew. He had designed the last cover the *The Lantern*. Very futuristic, that drawing was. And in the February number he had a poem, *To a Wild Blue Violet*, containing some daring lines in spite of its Victorian title. It was unsigned and speculation was rife as to who had written it and who the wild blue violet was. Pat knew. It speaks volumes for her condition of heart and mind that she didn't see anything comical in being called a blue violet. If she had been sane she would have known that a brown-and-orange marigold was more in her line. She was, in spite of her infatuation, a bit surprised to find that Lester could write poetry. She had faintly and reluctantly suspected that he wouldn't know poetry when he saw it. But A Wild Blue Violet was "free verse." Everything else, Lester told her, was outmoded. The tyranny of rhyme was ended forever. She would never have dared let him know after that that she had bought a second-hand volume called Poems of Passion and underlined half of them. I shall be dust when my heart forgets, she underlined twice.

She was horribly afraid she wasn't half clever enough for him. He completely flabbergasted her one evening by a casual reference to the Einstein theory... looking at her sidewise to see if she were properly impressed. Pat didn't know anything about the Einstein theory. She did not suspect that neither did he and spent much of the night writhing over her ignorance. What must he think of her? She went to the public library and tried to read up about it but it made her head ache and she was unhappy until the next evening when Lester told her she was as wonderful as a new-mooned April evening.

"I'd like to know if you said that because it just came into your head or if you made it up last night," said Pat. Her tongue was always her own, whatever her heart might be. But she was happy again in spite of Einstein. Lester really did not pay many compliments, so one prized it when he did. Not like Harris Hynes whose "line" had evidently been to say something flattering whenever he opened his mouth. Judy had always said he must have kissed the Blarney stone. How wraith-like Harris seemed now, beside Lester's scowls and commands. To think she had ever fancied she cared for him! Mere school-girl infatuation... calf love. He had so little appreciation of the beautiful, poor fellow. She recalled pointing out the Hill of the Mist to him one moonlit winter night and he had said admiringly that it looked like a frosted cake. Poor Harris!

And poor Hilary! He had had to retire into his corner again. No more evenings in the park... no more rambles together. Even the week-end walks did not often come his way now. The car roads held and Lester drove her home in his little red roadster. He was the only boy at Queen's who had his own car. There was no pea soup in Judy's kitchen for him. And Pat almost prayed that he wouldn't notice the terrible crack in the dining-room ceiling.

2

It worried Pat a little that Judy didn't have much of a mind to him. Not that she ever said so. It was what she *didn't* say. And her tone when Pat told her he was one of the Summerside Conways... Lester B. Conway.

"Oh, oh, it do be a noble name. And is it any secret what the B. do be standing for? Not Bartholomew be inny chance?"

"B. stands for Branchley," said Pat shortly. "His mother was one of the Homeburn Branchleys."

"Sure I do be knowing thim all. Conways *and* Branchleys. His mother used to visit here before ould Conway made his pile. She was rale humble thin. Minny's the time I've wiped yer Lester's liddle nose for him whin he was knee high to a toad. Howsomiver," concluded Judy loftily, "it's likely the matter is too high for me. Money makes the mare go and it's the cute one ye are, I'm thinking."

Judy was really impossible. To insinuate that she, Patricia Gardiner, had picked out Lester Conway because he had money.

"She should know me better," thought Pat indignantly.

But she felt the lack of Judy. If darling Bets were only alive! She would have understood. What a comfort it would have been to talk over her problems with Bets. For there *were* problems. For instance, Lester had told her she was to marry him right away as soon as college closed. There was no sense in waiting. He was going right into business with his dad.

This was simply ridiculous. Of course, some day... but she wasn't going to even think of getting married for years yet. She must teach school and help them at home... reshingle and repaint Silver Bush... get a hardwood floor in the dining-room... a brass knocker for the front door... pay for Cuddles' music lessons.

Lester just laughed at this the night of the Saturday Satellites' Easter dance.

"You are too lovely, Pat, to be wasted any longer on a shabby, obscure old farm like Silver Bush," he said.

A little madness came over Pat. The very soul of her was aflame.

"Don't ever speak to me again, Lester Conway," she said, each word falling like a tinkling drop of icy water on a cold stone.

"Why, what have I done?" said Lester in genuine amazement.

That made it worse, if anything could make it worse. He didn't realise at all what he had done. Pat turned her back on him and flew upstairs. To get her wraps was the work of a minute . . . to slip down the back-stairs and through the side-hall, another minute. Then out . . . and back to Linden Avenue. The bite and tang of the cold air seemed to increase her anger. Patricia Gardiner of Silver Bush had never in all her life been so furious.

Lester came down the next evening, looking more Lara-like than ever. He ignored the incident . . . he thought that would be the best policy . . . and told her she was going with him to the Easter Prom.

"Thank you, I'm not," said Pat, "and please don't waste any more of those charming scowls on me. When I tell anybody I'm through with him I'm *through.*"

When Pat said anything in a certain way she was believed.

"Of all the fickle girls," said Lester. Just like Harris. Men were so tiresomely alike.

"I was born in moonlight, they tell me," said Pat coolly. "So I'm naturally changeable. No one can insult Silver Bush in my hearing. And I'm tired . . . very tired . . . of taking orders from you."

The Conway temper . . . Judy could have told you a few things about *it* . . . flared up.

"Oh . . . well . . . if you're going off the deep end about it!" he said nastily. "Anyway, I just began going about with you to put a spoke in Hilary Gordon's wheel."

She was glad he had said that. He had set her free. She had been hating him so bitterly that her hate had made her as much of a prisoner as love had. Now he had simply ceased to exist.

"I've heard Judy use a phrase," said Pat to herself after he had flung away, scowling for once in real earnest, " 'fancy's fool.' Well, I've been fancy's fool. And that is that."

3

It was a good while before she could talk the whole thing over with Judy. *Now* Judy sympathised and understood.

"Oh, oh, Patsy dear, I niver did be liking yer taking up

wid a Conway, not aven if his pockets were lined wid gold.
Gintleman Tom didn't like him ... there was something in
that cat's eye whiniver he saw him. And he was always a bit
too lordly for me taste, Patsy. A man shud be a bit humble
like whin he's courting for if he isn't whin will he be? I'm
asking ye."

"I can never forgive him for making fun of Silver Bush,
Judy."

"Making fun av Silver Bush, was he? Oh, oh, if ye'd seen
the liddle shack his father was raised in, wid the stove-pipe
sticking out av its roof. Sure and the Conways were the
scrapings av the pot in thim days. And the timper av the ould
man. One time he wasn't after liking the colour av a new
petticoat his wife did be buying ... it was grane when he
wanted purple. He did be taking it up to the attic av his
grand house in Summerside and firing it out av the windy. It
caught on the top av a big popple at the back av the house
and there it did be hanging all the rist av the summer. Whin
the wind filled it out 'twas a proper sight now. The folks did
be calling it the Conway flag. Ould Conway cudn't get it
down becase the popple was ralely in Ned Orley's lot and
Ned and him were bad frinds and Ned wudn't be letting inny
one get at the tree. He said he was a better Irishman than
ould Conway and liked a bit av rale Paddy grane in his
landscape."

"Lester admits his father was a self-made man, Judy."

"Oh, oh, that wud be a very pretty story if it was the
true one. Ould Conway didn't be making himsilf. The Good
Man Above attinded to that. And he made his pile out av a
grane and feed store. But I'm saying for him he wasn't skim
milk ... like his brother Jim. *He* was the miser, now. 'Take out
that lamp,' sez he whin he was dying. 'A candle do be good
enough to die by.' Oh, oh there do be some quare people in
the world," conceded Judy. "As for me poor Lester, they tell
me he's rale down-hearted now that his temper fit do be over.
I'm afraid it's ye that do be the deluthering cratur, Patsy. He
did be thinking ye were rale fond av him."

"Of course I admit I was a perfect idiot, Judy. But I'm
cured. I'll never fall in love again ... if I can help it," she
added candidly.

"Oh, oh, why not, me jewel?" laughed Judy. "As yer
Aunt Hazel used to say it's a bit av fun in a dull life. Only

don't be carrying it too far and breaking hearts, aven av the Conways. There do be a big difference atween falling in love and loving, Patsy."

"How do you know all this, Judy? Were *you* ever in love?" said Pat impudently.

Judy chuckled.

"One can be larning a lot be observation," she remarked.

"But, Judy, how can one *tell* the difference between loving and being in love?"

"It do be taking some experience," acknowledged Judy.

Pat burned *Poems of Passion* but when she came across the line... "*spilt water from a broken shard,*" in one of Carman's poems she underlined it. That was all love really was, anyway.

She went to the Easter Prom with Hilary.

"Poor Jingle!" said Judy to Gentleman Tom. "That does be *twicet*. If she gets over the third time..."

CHAPTER XXXIV
"Let's Pretend"

1

"LET us see the handsome houses where the wealthy nobles dwell," quoted Hilary. "In other words let us take a stroll along Abegweit Avenue. There's one of the new houses there I want to show you. I won't tell you which one it is... I want you to guess it. If you're the lass I take you to be, Pat, you'll spot it at sight."

It was a Saturday afternoon in spring with sudden-sweeping April winds. The world seemed so friendly on a day like this, Pat thought. She wore her crimson jersey and tam and knew she looked well in them and that Lester Conway, scowling by in his roadster, knew it, too. But let Lester scowl on. Hilary's quizzical smile was much pleasanter in a companion and Hilary looked brown and wholesome in the spring sunshine. Not much like the ragged little lad who had met her on that dark, lonely road of long ago. But the same at heart. Dear old Hilary! Faithful, dependable Hilary. Such a friend was better than a thousand of Judy's "beaus."

They had not gone home for this week-end, since the Satellites were having a wind-up jamboree that night. Pat could by now survive staying a week-end in town. Yet she felt that she always missed something when she did. To-day, for instance, the wild violets would be out in Happiness ... the white ones ... and they not there to find them.

Abegweit Avenue was the finest residential street in town and at the end it ran out into the country, with a vision of distant emerald hills beyond. It always compelled Pat to admit that there were a few satisfying houses in the world beside Silver Bush. All kinds of houses were built on it—from Victorian monstrosities with towers and cupolas, to the newest thing in bungalows. Pat and Hilary loved to walk along it, talking when they felt like it, holding their tongues when they didn't, discussing and criticising the houses, making changes in most of them, putting in a window here and slicing one off there, lifting or lowering roofs ... "a low roof gives a house a friendly air," said Hilary.

Some houses thrilled them, some charmed them, some annoyed them. Some were attractive, some repellent ... "I'd like to smash a few of your windows," was Pat's reaction to one. Even the doors were fascinating. What went on behind them? Did they let you out ... or in?

Then they had to settle which house they would accept as a gift, supposing they were simply compelled to take one.

"I think I'd take that gentle house on the corner," said Pat. "It has an attic ... I must have an attic. And it looks as if it had been loved for years. I knew *that* the first time I ever saw it. It would like me, too. And that funny little window away off by itself has a joke it wants to tell me."

"I'm choosing one of the new houses this time," said Hilary "I like a new house better than an old one when all is said and done. I would feel that *I* owned a new house. An old house would own *me*."

Pat had kept a keen look-out for Hilary's house. She had thought several of the new ones might be it. But when she saw it she knew it. A little house nestled in a hollow half way up a little hill. Its upper windows looked right out on the top of the hill. Its very chimneys smacked of romance. A tremendous maple tree bent over it. The tree was so enormous and the house so small. It looked like a toy house the big tree had picked up to play with and got fond of it. It had a little garden by its side, with violets in a corner and in the centre a pool with a border of flat stones, edged with daffodils.

"Oh!" Pat drew a long breath. "I'm so glad I didn't miss that. Yes, if they give you that house, Hilary, take it. It's so . . . so *right,* isn't it?"

"That tree in the front should be cut down though," said Hilary thoughtfully. "It breaks the line . . . and spoils the view."

"It doesn't . . . it simply guards it as a treasure. You wouldn't cut that lovely birch down, Hilary."

"I'd cut any tree down if it wasn't in the right place," persisted Hilary stubbornly.

"A tree is always in the right place," said Pat just as stubbornly.

"Well, I won't cut it down yet awhile," conceded Hilary. "But I'll tell you what I am going to do some dark night, Pat. I'm going to sneak up here and carry off that cast-iron deer next door and sink it in the bay fathoms deep."

"Would it be worth while? The whole place is so awful. You couldn't carry off that enormous portico. The house looks like a sanitarium. Did you ever suppose any place could be so hideous?"

"The house next to it isn't hideous . . . exactly. But it has a cruel, secretive look. I don't like it. A house shouldn't be so sly and reserved. And there's a house I'd like to buy and groom it up. It's so out at elbows. The shingles are curling up and the verandah roof is sagging."

"But at least it isn't self-satisfied. The next one *is* . . . positively smug. And *that* one . . . they say it cost a fortune and it's as gloomy as a tomb."

"Shutters on those stark windows would make an amazing difference," said Hilary reflectively. "It's really wonderful, Pat, how much a little thing can do to make or mar a house. But I don't think there's any place for dreaming in that house . . . or for ghosts. There must be a place for dreams and ghosts in every house I'll design."

"There's that unfinished house, Hilary . . . it always makes my heart ache. Why don't they finish it?"

"I've found out why. A man began to build that house just to please his wife and she died when it was only half done. He hadn't the heart to finish it. That white place is a house for the witch of the snow. It's positively dazzling."

"What is the matter with that house in the middle of the block, Hilary? It's very splendid but..."

"It hasn't enough restraint. It bulges like...like..."

"Like a fat woman without corsets," laughed Pat. "Like Mary Ann McClenahan. Poor Mary Ann died last week. Do you remember how we thought she was a witch, Hilary?"

One house was as yet only a hole in the ground, with men setting pipes and running wires in it. Who was waiting for that house? Perhaps a bride-to-be. Or perhaps some tired old body who had never in her life had a house to her liking and meant to have one before she died. There was a house that wanted to be wakened up. And there was one with Dr. Ames coming away from it. He looked grave. Perhaps some one was dying in that house. He wouldn't be looking like that if a baby had come.

"I would like to see all the houses in the world...all the beautiful ones at least," said Hilary. "And I've got a new idea for your house to-day."

He was always getting new ideas for it but nowadays he never told her what they were. Everything was to be a surprise.

They walked back in silence. Hilary was dreaming. All men dream. His dream was of building beautiful homes for love to dwell in...houses to keep people from the biting wind and the fierce sun and the loneliness of dark night. It must be a fascinating thing to build a house...to create beauty that would last for generations and be shelter and protection and friendliness as well as beauty. And some day he *would* build a house for Pat...and she *must* live in it.

Pat was thinking again how nice it was to walk with Hilary. With Harris and Lester she had felt that she must be always bright and witty and sparkling lest they might think her "dumb." Hilary was restful. And he never said embarrassing things. To be sure his looks sometimes said many things his tongue never did. But who could quarrel with looks?

CHAPTER XXXV

Shadow and Sunshine

1

CARE sat visibly on Patricia's brow.

"My vision cannot pierce beyond the darkness of next week, Judy. It is completely bounded by the gloomy shade of licence exams. Judy, what if I don't pass?"

"Oh, oh, but ye will, darlint. Haven't ye been studying all the term like a Trojan? Excipt maybe thim few wakes whin me bould Lester was ordering ye about. So don't be worrying yer head about it. Just take a bit av a walk through the birches and fale thankful that spring do never be forgetting to come. And thin, maybe, ye'll be making Siddy's fav'rite pancakes for supper. It's mesilf can't give thim the turn at the right moment like ye can."

"Judy, you old flatterer! You know nobody can make pancakes like yours."

"Oh, oh, but the pastry now, Patsy. I niver had the light hand wid it that ye do be having. Sure that pie ye was after making last wake-ind . . . it did be looking as if it had just stipped out av the pages av that magazine Winnie takes."

"*Sure and that'll divart her a bit,*" thought Judy. But it didn't.

"I can't help worrying, Judy. It will be dreadful if I don't pass . . . it will hurt mother so. And she *mustn't* be hurt."

For everybody at Silver Bush had become very careful of mother without saying much about it. Nobody ever heard her complain but all winter she had been taking little bitter strychnine tablets for the heart and a "rest" in the afternoons. The shadow had crept towards Silver Bush so stealthily that even yet they hardly realised its grim presence. Father was looking grey and worried. Although none of the children knew it the doctor was advising an operation and Judy and

Aunt Edith were, for the first, last, and only time in their lives of the same opinion about it.

"They'll just cut her up for an experiment," said Aunt Edith wrathfully. "*I* know them."

"Indade and I wudn't put it by thim," agreed Judy bitterly.

Mother herself would not hear of an operation. She felt that it couldn't be afforded: but she didn't tell Long Alec that. She merely said that she was frightened of it. Long Alec rather marvelled at this. He had never associated fear of any kind with his wife. But then neither had he ever associated that strange languor and willingness to lie quietly and let other people do the work. Mother had never hurried through life; she had walked leisurely... Judy was wont to say she had never known any one who made so little noise moving round a house... but she got a surprising amount of work done.

Pat got through the exams eventually and even dared to hope she had done fairly well. She left Queen's with a good deal of regret and grimy Linden Avenue with none at all. Home again to dear Silver Bush, never more to leave it... for the home school was promised her and Pat had already in imagination spent a year's salary on Silver Bush. Several years', in fact... there were so many things she wanted to do for it. How she loved it! The house and everything about it were linked inextricably with her life and thought. There was one verse in the Bible she could never understand. *Forget also thine own people and thy father's house*. It always made her shiver. How could anybody do *that?*

She fell in love with life all over again on those spring evenings when she walked over the hill or by Jordan or in the secret paths of her enchanted birches. Winds... delicate dawns... starry nights... shore fields blurred by a silvery fog... the cool wet greenness of the spring rains... all had a message for her and all made her think of Bets... even yet Pat's voice quivered when she pronounced that name.

Where was Bets?

> *"In what ethereal dances,*
> *By what eternal streams"*

did her footsteps wind?

"I wonder if Bets isn't homesick in heaven for *this*?" Pat pointed to the white lilac over the garden fence. "And she must miss the sunsets. This is just such a night as she loved, Judy. Oh, Judy, last spring she was *here*. All winter at Queen's, where she had never been, it wasn't so hard. But here . . . everything seems to speak of her. To-night, when I smell that white lilac it seems to me that she must be near. She doesn't seem dead any more. She just seems around the corner somewhere, still dear and loving. But oh, I want her so!"

"Pat," came Cuddles' voice, clear and insistent at her elbow, "do you think I have It?"

"We'll be having our hands full wid that same young Cuddles," Judy had confided to Pat that very day. "In a few years that is, whin she grows into her eyes. Yer Uncle Tom sees it. Wasn't it only yesterday he sez to me, 'Ye'll be finding her a handful.' Oh, oh, she'll dance through life, that one."

Pat could not realize that Cuddles was by way of getting to be a big girl. It was only yesterday she had been an adorable baby, with dimpled arms and cheeks, whose very look said "come and love me." And now she was eleven . . . with one teasing, unruly curl hanging down the middle of her forehead and a nose that even at eleven was not the smudge of other elevens. And her eyes! No wonder Cuddles was spoiled. When she looked up sorrowfully and appealingly, she was never punished severely. You couldn't punish a young saint gone astray. Cuddles' eyes were always asking for something and always getting it. Unlike Pat, Cuddles revelled in chums and Silver Bush was over-run with them . . . "chattering like crows," said Judy indulgently. Judy was proud of Cuddles' popularity. As for the opposite sex . . . well, if tributes of sticky candies and moist apples, and stickier and moister dabs of kisses meant anything Cuddles certainly had "It."

"When *I* was eleven," said Pat with the tone of eighty, "I wasn't thinking of such things, Miss Rachel."

"Oh, but I'm a modern child," said Cuddles serenely. "And Trix Binnie says you've got to have It or the boys won't look at you."

Judy shook her grey head solemnly, as if to remark, "If they say these things in the green tree what will they say in the dry?" But Cuddles persisted.

"You might tell me what it is, Pat, and if you think I've

got It. After all"... Cuddles was very serious... "I'd rather get information from my own family than from the Binnies."

"The sinse av her now!" said Judy.

Pat took Cuddles off into the grave-yard and, sitting on Wild Dick's tombstone, tried to give her some "information." She felt that she must fill mother's place with darling Cuddles now. Mother must not be bothered.

2

And then the shadow, which had been creeping nearer and nearer, pounced.

Mother was ill... mother was very, very ill.

Mother was dying.

Nobody said it but everybody knew it. Except Judy who stubbornly refused to believe it. Judy wouldn't give up hope. She hadn't got "the sign."

"And I'll not be belaving it till I do," she said.

Pat wouldn't believe it either.

"Mother can't die," she said desperately, "not *our* mother."

They had always taken mother so for granted. She had always been there... she always would be there. How was it possible to picture anything else?

Pat had not even Hilary to help her through those weeks. Hilary was up west, helping another uncle build a house. The task delighted Hilary. It had an ideal quality for him. Besides, before he could design houses he wanted to know all about building them, from the ground up.

"Bets last year... and now mother," thought Pat.

Then came a torturing hope. The specialist who was called in advised an operation. With it, he conceded, there was a chance. Without it, none.

Judy, when she heard there was to be an operation, gave up hope at once, sign or no sign.

"Oh, oh, it's mesilf shud be dying instid av her," she muttered. "I don't be knowing what the Good Man Above means, so I don't."

Gentleman Tom winked inscrutably.

"Ye can't be doing innything, cat dear. Ye wudn't let what was after Patsy that time get her. But ye can't be guarding Mrs. Long Alec... not if they take her to that hospital to be cut up. And her a Selby av the Bay Shore!"

Pat was up in mother's room. A new Pat...older...graver. But more hopeful. As long as one had a little hope!

Mother had asked to be propped up in bed, so that she might see the green fields she loved. Her hands lay on the counterpane. It was strange to see mother's hands so white and idle.

She was to be taken to the hospital the next day. Mother was very fine and simple and brave about it. But when had mother ever been anything else? Mother had never been excitable like the Gardiners. Her *spirit* was always at rest, so that any one who came into her presence was always conscious of a great calm. Her eyes were still the asking eyes of a girl and yet there was something maternal about her bosom that made you want to lay your head on it if you were tired or troubled.

"The apple blossoms are out. I'm glad I've seen them once more. I was a girl under them once, Pat, like you...and your father..."

Mother's voice trailed off into some hinterland of happy remembrance.

"You'll see the apple blossoms for many more springs, mother darling. You'll come back from the hospital cured and well...and I've ordered a lovely day for you to go on."

Mother smiled.

"I hope so. I've never given myself up yet, Pat. But I'd like to talk to you a little about some things...supposing I don't come back. We must look that in the face, dearest. Winnie will be marrying Frank...and you will have to take my place, you know."

"I...I know," choked Pat. "And I'll never, never marry, mother, I promise that. I'll stay here and keep a home for dad and Sid and Cuddles. Sid won't want to marry ever, when he has me."

Again mother smiled.

"I don't ask you to promise that, dear. I'd like to think you'll marry some day. I want you to be a happy wife and a joyful mother of children. Like I've been. I've been so happy here, Patsy. I was only twenty when I came here. A spoiled child, too...and as for housekeeping, I didn't know the difference between simmering and boiling. Judy taught me...wonderful old Judy. Be good to her, Pat...if I don't come back. But I needn't tell you that. Judy was so good to me. She was even quite fierce about my working...she hated to see my hands spoiled. I *had* pretty hands, Pat. But I didn't mind spoiling them for Silver Bush. I've loved it as you do. Every room in it has always been a friend of mine... had a life of its own for me. How I loved to wake up in the night and feel that my husband and my children were well and safe and warm, sleeping peacefully. Life hasn't anything better to offer a woman than that, Patsy."

Mother didn't say this all at once. There were long pauses when she lay very still...little gasps for breath. Sometimes terrible lances of fear pierced Pat's new armour of hope. When father came in to take her place as watcher Pat went down and out to the dark garden. Every one else was in bed, even Judy. She could not go to bed...she could not sleep. The night was warm and kind. It put its arms around her like a mother. The white iris seemed to shine hopefully in the dark. Bold-and-Bad came padding along the walk and curled up in her lap. There were times when even Bold-and-Bad could behave like a Christian. He knew that Pat needed comfort and he did his best to give it.

Pat sat on the garden bench until dawn came over the Hill of the Mist and Bold-and-bad ran away for a glorious mouse hunt in the grave-yard. The day had begun in a pale windless morning...the day on which mother was to go. *Would she ever return?*

That old hymn she had hated... *"change and decay in all around I see."*

Change was what she had always dreaded.

"Oh, Thou who changest not abide with me."

It was not a hateful hymn after all...it was a hymn to be loved. How wonderful to feel that there *was* something that never changed...a Power under and above and around on which you could depend. Peace seemed to flow into her.

"Child dear, whativer got ye up so early?"

"I wasn't in bed at all. I've been in the garden, Judy...just praying."

"Oh, oh, it's all inny av us can be doing now," said Judy despairingly.

Cuddles had not been allowed to know the worst but she heard it in school that day and Pat had hard work to comfort her that evening.

"And what do you think Trix Binnie said?" she sobbed.

"She said she *envied* me ... it was so exciting to have a death in the house."

"You go down on yer liddle marrow bones this night and thank the Good Man Above he didn't be making ye a Binnie," said Judy solemnly.

Even that day was lived through. At night dad telephoned from town that the operation was successfully over and that mother was coming out of the anesthetic nicely. The Silver Bush folk slept that night; but there was still a long week of suspense to be lived through before they dared really hope. Then dad came home, with a light in his tired eyes that had not shone there for many a day. Mother would live: never very strong perhaps ... never just the woman she had been. But she would live.

"Oh, oh, and didn't I be always telling ye so?" said Judy triumphantly, forgetting all her gloomy dreads of "cutting up." "There' niver was no sign. Gintleman Tom did be knowing it. That cat niver worried himsilf at all, at all."

3

Mother could not come home for six weeks, and during those weeks Pat and Judy ran Silver Bush, for both the aunts at the Bay Shore were ill and Winnie had to go to the rescue. Pat was in the seventh heaven. She loved everything about the house more than ever. The fine hemstitched tablecloths ... Judy's hooked rugs ... the monogrammed sheets ... the cedar chest full of blankets ... the embroidered centerpieces ... the lace doilies ... the dear old blue willowware plates ... Grandmother Selby's silver tea service, the old mirrors that had stolen a bit of loveliness from every fair face that had ever looked into them. All had a new meaning for her. Every window was loved for some special bit of beauty to be seen from it. She loved her own because she could see the Hill of the Mist ... she loved the Poet's window because there was a far-away glimpse of the bay ... she loved the round window because it looked right into the silver bush ... she loved the front hall window because it looked squarely on the garden. As for its attic windows, one saw everything in the world worth seeing from them and sometimes Pat would go up the attic for no earthly reason except to look out of them.

She and Judy didn't make slaves of themselves. Every once in so long Pat would say,

"Now, let's stop thinking housework, Judy, and think wild strawberries,"... or ferns... or June-bells as the case might be, and off they would go for a ramble. And in the "dims" they would sit on the back-door steps as of old and Judy would tell funny tales and Pat would laugh until she took kinks.

"Oh, oh, ye do be knowing how to work, Patsy darlint... stopping for a bit av a laugh once in so long. There's few people do be knowing the sacret. Yer aunts at the Bay Shore... they niver do be laughing and it's the rason they do be taking sick spells so often."

"Uncle Brian and Aunt Jessie are coming for the week-end, Judy. I must cut some iris for the Poet's room. I do love fixing up that room for a guest. And we must have an apple tart with whipped cream. That's Uncle Brian's favourite dessert."

Pat always remembered what a guest liked to eat. And she was, as Judy declared, "a cook be the grace av God." She loved to cook, feeling delightedly that in this one thing at least she was akin to the women of all lands and all ages. Almost all her letters to mother and Hilary and college correspondents began, "I've just put something in the oven." The pantry was never without its box of spicy cookies and the fluffy perfection of her cakes left Judy speechless. As for the fruit cake she proudly concocted and baked one day all on her own, take Judy's word for it, there never had been a fruit cake to match it at Silver Bush.

"I was niver no great hand at fruit cake, darlint," she said sadly. "Yer Aunt Edith always do be saying it takes a born lady to make a rale fruit cake and maybe she is right. But I might av been larning the trick if it hadn't been for a bit av discouragement I was having just after I came to Silver Bush. I thought one day I'd be making a fruit cake and at it I wint, wid more zale than jidgement. Yer Uncle Horace was home thin... and a young imp he was... hanging round to see what he could see and mebbe get a licking av the bowl. 'What do ye be putting in a fruit cake, Judy Plum,' he sez, curious like. 'A liddle bit av iverything,' sez I short like. And whin I turns me back to line the pan what did the young divil do but impty the ink-bottle on the clock shelf into me cake... and me niver knowing it. Sure and yer Aunt Edith do be saying a good fruit cake shud be black. Mine was black enough to plaze her, Patsy darlint."

Pat exulted in finding a new recipe and serving it before anybody else when the Ladies' Aid met at Silver Bush. She loved to pore over the advertisement pictures in the magazines... the lovely cookies and fruits and vegetables... dear little white and red radishes... curly lettuce... crimson beets... golden asparagus with little green tips. She loved going to town to shop. There were certain things in the stores there, *hers*, though she had not yet bought them. She liked to browbeat the butcher and bulldoze the grocer delicately... to resist temptation and yield to it... to save and spend. She loved to think of weary and lonely people coming to Silver Bush for rest and food and love.

And under everything a sense of deep satisfaction in doing the thing she was meant to do. She tasted it to the full in the beautiful silences which occasionally fell over Silver Bush when everyone was quietly busy and the cats basked on the window sills.

And then to prepare for mother's home-coming!

CHAPTER XXXVI
Balm in Gilead

1

"FATHER walks slow to what he used to do," said Winnie with a sigh, as she and Pat shelled peas on the kitchen steps in the sultry August afternoon, with Bold-and-bad sitting between them. An occasional breeze set the leaves of the young aspen by the door shaking wildly. Pat loved that aspen. It had grown up unregarded in a few summers.... Judy always threatening to cut it down... and then over night it had turned from a shrub into a tree. And then dad had declared it must come down but Pat had interceded successfully.

"In a year or two it will shade the steps so nicely. Think of the moonlight falling through it on summer nights, dad."

Dad shrugged and let her have her way. Everybody knew Pat couldn't bear to have a tree cut down. No use having the child cry her golden-brown eyes out.

Over in the field of the Pool Sid was building an oat-stack. Sid, it was said, could build the best oat-stack in P. E. Island.

Pat looked after dad wistfully as he crossed the yard and went over to the field of the Pool. He did walk slower; he was more stooped. Yet how she hated to admit it.

"Is it any wonder? After those dreadful weeks when we didn't know whether mother would live or die. And I don't think he ever really got over Joe's going." Winnie sighed again. Pat looked keenly at her. Winnie had been very remote and dreamy for some days past. Pat suddenly remembered that she had not heard Winnie laughing... since when? Since the last night Frank Russell had been over. And he had not been over for a week.

It had been a suspected thing all through the year that Winnie and Frank would be married in the fall. All through the winter Judy had hooked rugs "like mad." Pat did not warm to the thought but it had to be faced and accepted.

"Winnie, what is the trouble, darling?"

"There's no trouble," said Winnie impatiently. "Don't be silly, Pat."

"I'm not silly. You've been... funny... for a week. Have you quarrelled with your Frank?"

"No," said Winnie slowly. Then her face went white and her eyes filled with tears. She *must* tell somebody and mother mustn't be bothered now. Pat wasn't old enough to understand, of course... Winnie still persisted in thinking of Pat as a mere child... but she was better than nobody at all.

"It's only... he was a little angry when I told him we couldn't be married this fall after all... perhaps not for years."

"But... Winnie... *why?* I thought it was all settled."

"So it was. Before mother took ill. But you know perfectly well, Pat, that everything is changed now. We simply have to look facts in the face. Mother may be spared to us for many years but she'll always be an invalid. You will be teaching and Judy isn't as young as she once was. She can't do all the work that has to be done here, even with your help after school. And it would break her heart to get any one in to help her, even if dad could afford it, which he can't. So I must just give up all thoughts of being married just now. Of course Frank doesn't like it, but he'll just have to reconcile himself to it. If he doesn't... well, there are plenty of other girls ready to keep house for him."

In spite of herself Winnie's voice faltered. The thought of all those willing girls was very bitter. And Frank had been very... difficult. The Russells did not like to be kept waiting. She knew he wouldn't wait for years. And if he did... they would be old and tired and all the first blossom of life would be withered and scentless. Just like poor Sophie Wright. She and Gordon Dodds had waited for fifteen years until her paralysed father died; and Sophie had never seemed like a bride. Just a faded little woman who no longer cared greatly whether she was married or not. Yet Winnie did not falter in her decision. There was good stuff in the Silver Bush girls. They put duty first always, even in a world which was clamouring that the word was outmoded and the thing to do was to grab what you wanted when you wanted it and let everything else go hang.

For just a moment a wild thrill of joy swept over Pat. Winnie wouldn't marry Frank after all. There wouldn't be any more changes at Silver Bush. She and Winnie and Sid would just go on living there, taking care of father and mother, loving Silver Bush and each other, recking nothing of the changing world outside. It would be heavenly.

But Winnie's eyes! They looked like blue violets that somebody had stepped on and bruised horribly.

Pat had never been able to understand how Winnie *could* love Frank as she did. Frank... if you didn't hate him because he was stealing your sister... was a nice enough fellow, with a wholesome pink face and steady grey-blue eyes. But nothing romantic about him... no smart compliments, no Lara-like glooms... nothing to induce such a riot of feeling as Winnie evidently experienced whenever she heard his step at the door.

What did Winnie see in him? Pat gave it up.

All the lawless joy died out of Pat when she saw Winnie's eyes. It was simply ridiculous to think of Winnie's eyes looking so... just ridiculous, that was all. And quite unnecessary. Because she, Pat, had everything nicely planned out already.

"Winnie, do you know you're just talking nonsense? Of course you're going to marry Frank. I am not going to take the school. I decided that as soon as mother came home. I'll be here to help Judy."

"Pat, you can't do that. It wouldn't be fair to ask you to give up your school after you studied so hard at Queen's to get your licence... you *ought* to have your chance..."

Pat laughed.

"My chance! That's just it. I've got my chance... the chance I've been aching for. The chance to stay at Silver Bush and care for it. I've hated the thought of teaching school. Who knows even if I'd get on well in the home school? I might have to go away another year... and *that*... but we needn't go into that. Of course I'd rather have mother well and strong than anything else even if I had to go to the ends of the earth. But since she can't be... well, I have the consolation of knowing I can stay home anyhow."

"What will dad say?"

"Dad knows. Why, Win, he was relieved. He never thought but that you'd be getting married and he didn't know just how things could be managed here. Because he didn't want me disappointed either in having to give up my school. *Disappointed!*" Pat howled again. "Win, parents aren't the selfish creatures so many horrid stories make them out. They *don't* want their children to sacrifice and give up for them. They want them to be happy."

"All but the cranks," said Judy, who had brought her little spinning wheel out to the platform and thought herself at liberty to butt into any conversation. "There do always be a few cranks aven among parents. Oh, oh, but not among the Gardiners."

"I think," said Winnie in a rather unsteady tone, "if you don't mind finishing the peas, Pat... I'll go upstairs for a little while."

Pat grinned. Winnie would go upstairs and write to Frank.

"Likely Winnie will be marrying Frank this fall, Judy," Pat said with a gulp. It seemed to make a thing so irrevocable to *say* it.

"Oh, oh, and why not, the darlint? She can cook and she can sew. She can get along widout things. She do be knowing whin to laugh and whin not to. Oh, oh, she's fit to be

married. It do be eliven years since we had a wedding at
Silver Bush. Sure and that's a liddle bit too much like
heaven, wid nather marrying nor giving in marriage."

"George Nicholson is going to be married to Mary
Baker," announced Cuddles, who had wandered along with a
little spotted barn cat she affected in her arms. "I wish he
would wait till I grow up. I believe he would like me better
than Mary because there is no fun in her. There's a good deal
in me when my conscience doesn't bother me. O . . . h, look
at Bold-and-Bad."

Bold-and-Bad had met his match since Cuddles had
been bringing the barn cat to the house. The barn cat was
scrawny and ugly but she was taking impudence from nobody. Bold-and-Bad was ludicrously afraid of her. It was a
sight of fun to see that whiffet of a cat attack and put to flight
an animal who should have been able to demolish her with a
blow of his paw. Bold-and-Bad fled over the yard and through
the grave-yard and across the Mince Pie field with yowls of
terror.

"Look at Gintleman Tom enjoying av it," chuckled Judy.

"We have nice cats at Silver Bush," said Cuddles
complacently. "Interesting cats. And they have an *air*. They
walk so proud and hold their tails up. Other cats *slink*. Trix
Binnie laughed when I said that and said, 'You're getting just
as crazy as Pat over your old Silver Bush, thinking there's
nothing like it.' 'Well, there isn't,' I told her. And I was right,
wasn't I, Pat?"

"You were," said Pat fervently. "But there comes your
barn cat back and you'd best take her to the barn before dad
sees her. You know he doesn't want the barn cats encouraged
to the house. He says he puts up with Gentleman Tom and
Bold-and-Bad because they're old established customs."

"How old is Gentleman Tom, Judy?"

"Oh, oh, old, is it? The Good Man Above do be knowing
that. All *I* do be knowing is that he come here twelve years
ago, looking as old as he does this blessed minute. Maybe
there isn't inny age about him," concluded Judy mysteriously.
"Ye can't iver be thinking av him as a kitten, can ye now?"

"I'm sure he could tell some queer tales, Judy. It's a pity
cats can't talk."

"Talk is it? Whoiver told ye they cudn't talk, Cuddles
darlint? The grandfather of me heard two cats talking onct

but he niver cud be got to tell what they said. . . . No, no, he didn't want to be getting in wrong wid the tribe. As I was telling Siddy last Sunday whin he was raving mad because Bold-and-Bad had gone to slape on his Sunday pants and they was kivered wid cat hairs, 'Think whativer ye like av a cat, Siddy darlint,' sez I to him, 'but don't be *saying* innything. If the King av the cats heard ye now!"

"And what would have happened if the King of the cats had heard him, Judy?"

"Oh, oh, let's lave that tale for a rale wild stormy winter night, Cuddles, whin ye're slaping wid old Judy snug and cosy. Thin I'll be telling ye what happened to a man in ould Ireland that did be saying things av cats a liddle too loud and careless like. It's no tale for a summer afternoon wid a widding looming up."

2

Winnie was to be married in late September and Silver Bush settled down to six weeks of steady preparation. Judy had a new swing shelf put up in the cellar to fill with rows on rows of ruby jam-pots for Winnie. The wood-work in the Poet's' room was to be painted all over in robin's egg blue and then there was the excitement of choosing paper to harmonise with it. Though Pat hated to tear the old paper off. It had been on so long. And she resented having the chairs in the Big Parlour recovered. There was a sort of harmony about the old room as it was. New things jarred. But Silver Bush must look its best, for Winnie was to have a big wedding.

"The clan do be liking a bit av a show," said Judy delightedly.

"It means a great deal of work," said Aunt Edith rather disapprovingly.

"Work, is it? Ye do be right. It's busy as a hin wid one chick we all are. I do be kaping just one jump ahead. But I'm not liking yer sneaking widdings as if they was ashamed av it. We'll be having one to be proud av, wid ivery relative on both sides and lots av prisents and two bridesmaids and a flower girl. . . . Oh, oh, and Winnie's trosso now! The like av it has niver been seen at Silver Bush. All her liddle undies made be hand. 'An inch av hand-work do be worth a machine mile,' sez I to Mrs. Binnie whin she do be saying her cousin's daughter had two dozen av ivery kind. It do be a comfort to me whin I climb up to me loft at night, faling as if I'd been pulled through a kay-hole."

"Oh, Judy, you and I are getting to be old women," sighed Aunt Barbara.

Judy looked scandalised.

"Yes, yes, but whisht... don't be spaking av it, woman dear," she whispered apprehensively.

Winnie had a dream of a wedding dress... the sort of dress every girl would like to have. Everybody loved it except Aunt Edith, who was horrified at its brevity. Dresses were at their shortest when Winnie was married. Aunt Edith had been praying for years that women's skirts might be longer but apparently in vain.

"It's a condition that can't be affected by prayer," Uncle Tom told her gravely.

Winnie moved through all the bustle of preparation with a glory in her eyes, smiling dreamily over thoughts of her own. Frank haunted Silver Bush to such an extent that Judy was a trifle peeved at him.

"He do be all right in his place but I'm not liking him spread over everything," she grumbled.

"Frank is devoted to Winnie," said Pat rather distantly. "I think it is beautiful." She had finally accepted Frank as one of the family and he had straightway become a person to be defended, even from Judy.

"I wonder how Frank proposed to Winnie," remarked Cuddles, as she helped Pat adorn a cake with pale green slivers of angelica and crimson cherries. "I suppose he would be very romantic. Do you think he went on his knees?"

Sid, in for a drink of water, roared.

"We don't do that nowadays, Cuds. Frank just said to Winnie, 'How about it, kid?' I heard him," Sid salved his conscience by winking at Judy behind Cuddles' back.

"When I grow up and anybody proposes to me he'll have to be a good deal more flowery and eloquent than that. I can tell you, if he wants me to listen to him," she said.

"The frog went a-courting," remarked Judy cryptically.

CHAPTER XXXVII
Winnie's Wedding

1

THE engagement was announced in the papers... a newfangled notion which met with Judy's disapproval.

"Oh, oh, there do be minny a slip 'twixt the cup and the lip," she muttered. "Sure and we'd be in the pretty scrape if innything but good happened Frank in the nixt three wakes. There was Maggie Nicholson now... her beau did be going clane out av his head a wake before the day itsilf and it's in the asylum he's been iver since. Wudn't thim Binnies have the laugh on us if the widding didn't come off after all."

Only three weeks to the wedding day... Winnie's wedding day when she would leave Silver Bush forever. There were moments when Pat felt she couldn't endure it. When Vernon Gardiner said jokingly to Winnie,

"Next time we meet I'll have to call you Mrs. Russell," Pat went upstairs and cried. To think of Winnie being Mrs. Russell. It sounded so terribly changed and different and far away. Her Winnie!

Tears didn't stop the days from flying by. The wedding was to be in the church. Pat wanted Winnie to be married at home under the copper beech on the lawn. Mother couldn't go to the church. But Frank wanted the church. The Russells were Anglicans and had always been married in church. Frank got his way... "of course," as Pat scornfully remarked to the air.

Pat and Judy were up to their eyes in baking and favourite recipes were hunted up... recipes that had not been used for years because they took so many eggs. The traditional Silver Bush bride-cake alone required three dozen.

The Bay Shore aunts and the Swallowfield aunts sent over baskets of delicious confections. Aunt Barbara's basket

was full of different kinds of cookies...orange cookies and
date cookies and vanilla crisps and walnut bars and the Good
Man Above knew how many more.

"Oh, oh, it won't be much like Lorna Binnie's wedding
table," exulted Judy. "Sure and poor Mrs. Binnie thought if
she did be cutting her cookies in a dozen different shapes it
wud be giving thim a different flavour. Now, Patsy darlint,
just ye be kaping an eye on thim chickens while I do be
getting me yard posts whitewashed."

At first dawn Bold-and-Bad was shouting all over Silver
Bush that he had found a mouse and Judy's footsteps sounded
on the kitchen stairs. The morning hush was already broken
by the stir of last-minute preparations. It had rained in the
night but now it was fine and a new, lovely world with its face
washed was blinking its innocent eyes at the sun.

"Sure and the day was ordered," said Judy as she raked
the lawn where robins were pulling out long fat worms.

Pat couldn't eat a mouthful of breakfast. It was a shock to
see Winnie eating so heartily. Pat was sure that if *she* were
going to be married she couldn't eat for a week beforehand.
Of course she wouldn't want Winnie to be like that silly Lena
Taylor, who, it was said, cried for a month before she was
married. But when you were going away from Silver Bush
that day how could you have an appetite?

The forenoon was like a whirlwind. The table had to be
set...*oh, why did families have to be broken up like this?*
Among salads, jellies and cakes Pat moved as to the manor
born. *This time to-morrow Winnie would belong to another
family.* Everybody's place was settled; Pat had a knack of
dovetailing people rather cleverly...*only herself and Siddy
and Cuddles left at Silver Bush*. The rooms bloomed under
her hands. The little alcove Uncle Tom called Cuddle Corner
was a nest of round golden pillows like small suns...*It was
dreadful to find pleasure in these things when Winnie was
going away*.

Flowers must be cut. As a rule Pat didn't like to cut the
flowers. She always felt such a vivid crimson delight in her
splendid blossoms...a feeling that made the thought of
cutting them hurt her. But now she slashed at them savagely.

The table looked beautiful. It would be such a shame to
spoil it...turn it into an after-dinner mess. But, as Judy said,
that was life.

"Anyhow, Silver Bush looks perfectly lovely," thought Pat in a momentary rapture.

In a way it was all like an echo of Aunt Hazel's long-ago wedding day. The same confusion when everybody was dressing. Gentleman Tom was the only calm creature in the house. Judy was distracted because Bold-and-Bad had been seen dashing through the hall with a very large, very dead mouse and the Good Man Above only knew what he had done with it. That vain Cuddles, who had been trying all the mirrors in the house to see which was the most becoming, was in trouble over the hang of her flowered chiffon dress. It had been a bitter pill to Cuddles that she was too old to be Winnie's flower girl. Aunt Hazel's six-year-old Emmy was cast for that part and Cuddles was secretly determined to look prettier than she did.

"What does my nose look like, Pat? Do you think it is too big?"

Cuddles' nose had always worried her. How would it turn out?

"If it is I don't see how you can remedy it," laughed Pat. "Never mind your nose, Cuddles darling. You look very sweet."

"Can't I put a dab of powder on it, Pat? Please. I'm eleven."

"That would only draw attention to it," warned Pat.

Cuddles saw this. She cast a satisfied look at herself in the glass.

"I have decided," she remarked in a matter-of-fact tone, "that I will get married when I am twenty and have three children. Pat, do I have to kiss Frank?"

"*I'm* not going to," said Pat savagely.

Judy, who was set on "witnessing the nuptials," as she expressed it, had again laid aside her drugget dress and her Irish brogue. Out came the dress-up dress and the English pronunciation as good as ever. Only the former was a bit tight. Pat had a terrible time getting Judy hooked into it.

"Sure and I had a waist whin this was made," mourned Judy. "Do you be thinking it's a trifle old-fashioned like, Pat?"

Pat got some lace and did wonders with it. Judy felt real "chick."

Mother was dressed, sitting in state in the Big Parlour with her grey hair and her soft blue eyes. Pat realised with a swift pang that mother had got very grey in the year. But she looked like a picture in her pretty dress of silver-grey and rose, with the necklace dad had given her when she came out of the hospital . . . an amber string like drops of golden dew. Father was not going to the church after all. At the last moment he had decided that he simply could not leave mother alone. Uncle Tom must give the bride away. Winnie was not very well pleased over this. That fierce, immense black beard of his was so old-fashioned. But Winnie was too happy to mind anything much. In her bridal array she was an exquisite, shimmering young thing with face and eyes that were love and rapture incarnate. Pat's throat swelled as she looked at her. Frank Russell suddenly became the man who could make Winnie look like this. She forgave him the offence of becoming her brother-in-law.

The kitchen clock was ten to, the parlour clock was five past, the dining-room clock was striking the hour. Which meant that it was a quarter past and time to go.

2

Sitting in the crowded church, with its decorations of tawny tiger lilies and lemon-hued gladioli . . . the C. G. I. T. girls had done it for Winnie . . . Pat thought busily to keep herself from crying. Winnie had warned her solemnly . . . "Pat, don't you *dare* cry when I'm getting married." She had been so near crying at Aunt Hazel's wedding long ago but this was tenfold worse.

It was odd to see the groom so pale . . . he was always so pink and chubby. But he looked well. She was glad he was nice-looking. If Silver Bush had to have in-laws it should have handsome ones. Uncle Tom's magnificent beard looked purple in the light that fell on it through the stained glass window . . . like some old Assyrian king's. Winnie had said, "I do." How solemn! Just a word uttered or unuttered and a whole life was changed . . . perhaps even the course of history. If Napoleon's mother had said "No," in place of "Yes?" Why, it was over . . . it was over . . . Winnie was Mrs. Frank Russell . . . the bridal party was going into the vestry . . . Uncle Brian's Norma was singing the bridal anthem . . . Pat recalled that long-ago day when she had slapped Norma's face. What was that dreadful old Cousin Sam Gardiner whispering to her over the top of the pew? "I wunner how many husbands and wives in this church would like a change." How many, indeed? Perhaps old Malcolm Madison, who was said to have laughed only three times in his life. Perhaps Gerald Black, whose wife had such a passion for swatting flies that she had bent forward in church one day and swatted one on Jackson Russell's bald head. Or Mrs. Henry Green, whose husband, Pat reflected wildly, looked like his own tombstone. She wondered if the story Judy told of him was true . . . that he had been whipped in school one day because the master caught him writing a love-letter on his slate to Lura Perry who was half gipsy. It couldn't be . . . not with that Scotch-Presbyterian-elder mouth. Old Uncle John Gardiner was improving the wait by snatching a nap. Wasn't there a story about his wooden leg catching fire one day when he dozed by the fire? There was Mrs. James Morgan who had never forgiven her daughter for marrying Carl Porter and had never entered her house. How *could* families act like that?

Mrs. Albert Cody . . . Sarah Malone that was. Judy had a story about her. "Oh, oh, she had one of thim aisy-going fellers . . . wint around wid her for years and years and niver got no forrader. Sarah wint away for a visit to her Aunt in Halifax and writ back great yarns av her beaus and fine times. That scared him and he writ for her to come home and be married. Sure and there hadn't been a word av truth in what Sarah had tould him. Her aunt was that sick and cranky she niver wint out av the house."

Sarah Cody was a Sunday School teacher and looked very meek and devout beside her easy-going Abner. Very likely Judy had made it all up.

(What was that horrid Mrs. Stephen Russell whispering . . . "made the mistake of choosing a prettier bridesmaid than herself." It wasn't true . . . it wasn't . . . Allie Russell wasn't half as pretty as Winnie.) Old Grant Madison, who had told dad once that he had read too many dreadful things in old histories ever to believe in God. How dreadful not to believe in God. How could one live? Mrs. Scott Gardiner had ironed out her wrinkles in some way . . . "beauty tricks," said Judy contemptuously. Why in the world didn't Winnie come back? But there was no Winnie now . . . only a mysterious stranger known as Mrs. Frank Russell. What was darling Cuddles thinking of as she gazed dreamily up at the tinted window, nimbused in its blue and gold. She was really a delightful little thing. Pat recalled in amazement that she hadn't wanted Cuddles to be born.

3

Home again. Hand-shakings and congratulations and kisses. Pat even kissed Frank. But she hugged Winnie fiercely.

"Here's a whole heartful of good wishes for you, dear one," she whispered.

Then she must fly for her ruffled organdy apron. The chilled cocktails must be got out of the ice-house, the creamed chicken put in the patties, the wedding gifts placed with just the right emphasis. Children ran about the grounds like small roses. The house was full. Every Gardiner and half-Gardiner, every Selby, every Russell was there. "This looks like the Day of Judgment," said old Cousin Ralph Russell. He caught Pat by the arm as she flew by him.

"Long Alec's girl. I hear you've got to be a beauty, hey? Let me look at you. No, no, not a beauty... and you've no great brains they tell me... but you've got a way with you. You'll get a man."

How people did harp on getting married! It was disgusting. Even oldish Ellery Madison, who still congratulated himself on escaping traps, called Pat "Ducky" and told her he'd take her if she liked.

"If you wait till we're both grown-up I might think of it," retorted Pat.

"Oh, oh, but that's the way to talk to them," Judy told her as they lighted the candles. "'Twas mesilf that shut him up quick whin he sez to me, sez he, 'It's time *you* were married, Judy.' 'How the min do be hating a woman that's dared to do without thim,' sez I. Sure and I've been snubbing the craturs right and left. They've no more sinse than to be cluttering up me kitchen and ruining the rugs. Ould Jerry Russell sez to me, sez he, 'Miss Plum, do ye be thinking God is God or just a great first cause?' And Mark Russell sez, wid a face as grave as a jidge's, 'What is yer opinion av the governmint bringing on an election this fall, Miss Plum?' Sure and didn't I know they was pulling me leg? I sez to thim, sez I, 'Ye haven't the sinse ye was born wid,' sez I, 'if ye don't know a widding is no place to be talking av God or politics. And I'll thank ye to stop Miss Plumming me,' sez I, and that finished thim. Sure and wasn't the cirrimony grand, Patsy dear? Jake Russell sez to me, 'She's the prettiest bride ye've iver had at Silver Bush,' and I sez to him, sez I, 'For once in yer life ye've said a mouthful.' But that platinum ring now, do ye be thinking it's rale legal? I'm thinking Winnie'd fale a bit safer wid an old-fashioned gold one."

"Judy, how can I *bear* to see Winnie go away?"

"Ye must sind her away wid a smile, Patsy darlint. Whativer comes after, sind her away wid a smile."

CHAPTER XXXVIII
Laughter and Tears

1

It was all over. Winnie had gone.

"Pat darling," she whispered, with her eyes softly full of farewell, "everything was lovely. I've really enjoyed my own wedding. You and Judy were wonderful."

Pat managed to smile as Judy had exhorted, but when Judy found her looking at the deserted festal board she said,

"Judy, isn't it nice to be . . . able to . . . stop smiling? I . . . I hope there won't be another wedding at Silver Bush for a hundred years."

"Why, I wish we could have a wedding every day," said Cuddles. "I suppose the next one here will be your own. And then it will be my turn. That is," she added reflectively, "if I can get any one to have me. I don't want to be an old maid."

"Sure and don't be hurting me falings," said Judy. "I'm an ould maid."

"I always forget that," said Cuddles contritely. "You aren't a bit like an old maid, Judy. You're . . . you're just *Judy.*"

"Mr. Ronald Russell of St. John told me mother was the most beautiful woman he had ever seen," said Pat.

"And ye'll be loving Mr. Ronald Russell foriver bekase av

it. But I'm thinking he's right. Did ye hear him saying to Winnie, 'Are ye going to be making a Prisbytarian av him?'... maning Frank. And Winnie sez, sez she, 'Prisbytarians don't be made, they're born,' sez she. Oh, Oh, wasn't that the answer to me smart gintleman? St. John can't be getting far ahead av Silver Bush I'm thinking. He had his appetite wid him, that one. But I do be liking a man who enj'ys his vittles.'

"He's a member of Parliament," said Pat, "and they say he'll be Premier some day."

"And him ould Short-and-dirty Russell's son! A fat chanct!" said Judy scornfully.

"I hope the pictures will turn out well," said Cuddles. "I was in them all."

"Innyway, Winnie wasn't photygraphed wid her arm round her groom like Jean Madison was. Ondacint I call it. And now, Patsy darlint, will we start claning up or lave it till the morning?"

"Whatever you like, Judy."

"Oh, oh, it's ye are the mistress here now, wid Winnie gone and yer mother niver to be troubled. It's for ye to give orders and for me to obey them."

"Nonsense, Judy. Fancy me giving you orders!"

"I'd rather it that way, Patsy darlint," said Judy firmly.

Pat hesitated. Then quietly accepted the sovereignty of Silver Bush.

"Very well, Judy. We'll leave things just as they are to-night. We're all tired. Do you remember the night after Aunt Hazel's wedding when we did the dining room?"

"It's the darlint ye was, working like a liddle slave to kape from crying."

"And you told me funny stories: Judy, let's have a bit of a fire... there's a chill in the air and the first fire is such a delightful thing. And we'll sit by it and you'll tell stories."

"Ye must av been hearing all me stories a million times over, Patsy. Though I do be thinking whin I saw the Joe Kellers to-day—he did be marrying his wife bekase a liddle girl he was swate on jilted him and she married him bekase Sam Miller av the Bay Shore jilted her. So what wud ye ixpect?"

"That they wouldn't be very happy, Judy."

"Oh, oh, and that's where ye wud be wrong, me jewel.

The marriage was be way av being a big success. That do be life, ye know."

"Life *is* queer, Judy. Winnie and her Frank now... she doesn't seem to have a fear or doubt. *I'd* be frightened... I could never be *sure* I loved any one *enough* to marry him. And then to-day... away down in my heart I was just *sick* over Winnie going... and yet on the surface I was enjoying the excitement, too."

"There do be always something to take the edge off things," said Judy shrewdly. "That do be why nothing is iver as hard as ye think it's going to be."

Hilary came in after having driven some of the guests to the station and joined them. Bold-and-Bad, who had been sulking all day because nobody had admired him, lay down on the rug, gathered his feet and nose and tail into a snug circle, and forgave the world. Old Aunt Louisa, who had seen so much come and go, looked down on them from the wall. The white kittens still gambolled in immortal youth. King William still rode proudly across the Boyne. It was... rather nice to have a feeling of leisure and tranquillity again. And yet Pat was afraid that upstairs there was a dreadful stillness and silence after all the fuss was over that would pounce on her when she went to bed. She kept Hilary as long as she could and was so nice to him that when he said good-night to her on the poplar-patterned doorstep he was bold enough to ask her to kiss him.

"Of course I'll kiss you," said Pat graciously. "I've been kissing so many friends to-day one more or less doesn't matter."

"I don't want a friendly kiss," said Hilary... and went off on that note.

"Oh, oh, and ye might av give him his kiss," said Judy, who was always hearing what she had no business to. "He'll be going away far enough all too soon, poor b'y."

"I...I...was perfectly willing to kiss him," cried Pat chokily. "And don't... *don't* ... talk of his going away. I can't bear it to-night."

2

Pat was very lonely when she went up to bed. The house seemed so strangely empty now that Winnie's laugh had gone out of it. Here was the mirror that had reflected her face. That little vacant chair where she had always sat was very eloquent. Her little discarded slippers that could have danced by themselves the whole night through, so often had Winnie's feet danced in them, comforted each other under the bed. They looked as if her feet had just stepped out of them. Her fragrance still lingered in the room. It was all terrible.

Pat leaned out of the window to drink in the cold, delicious air. The wind sounded eerie in the bushes. A dog was barking over at Swallowfield. Pat had rather thought that when she found herself alone she would cast herself on the bed in an abandonment of anguish. But there was still moonlight in the world . . . still owls in the silver bush. The old loyalties of home were still potent and . . . it *would* be nice to have a room of one's very own.

A house always looks very pathetic and unfriended on a dawn after a festivity. Pat found happiness and comfort in restoring it all from cellar to garret. The presents were packed and sent to the Bay Shore. It *was* fun to read the account of the wedding in the papers.

"*The bride before her marriage was Winifred Alma, daughter of Mr. and Mrs. Alec Gardiner.*" That hurt Pat. Wasn't Winnie *still* their daughter? "*The bridesmaids wore dresses of pink Georgette crêpe with pink mohair hats and bouquets of sweet peas. Little Emmy Madison made a charming flower girl in a smocked frock of pink voile.*" Fancy little Emmy having her name and dress in the papers! *Miss Patricia Gardiner, sister of the bride, was charming in marigold voile.* And oh, oh . . . "*Miss Judy Plum wore blue silk with corsage of roses.*" It must have been that rogue of a Jen Russell who had put that in. Judy was tremendously pleased. Her name right there with all the quality, bracketed with the groom's aunt, the haughty Mrs. Ronald Russell in her black satin with mauve orchids! Though Judy was a bit dubious about "corsage." It sounded . . . well . . . a liddle quare.

Then there were visits to the Bay Shore to help Winnie get settled in her big white house with its background of sapphire water, where there was a colourful, fir-scented garden, full of wind music and bee song, that dipped in terraces to the harbour shore and was always filled with the sound of "perilous seas forlorn." Pat would have been quite happy if she could have forgotten that Hilary was going away.

CHAPTER XXXIX
The Chatelaine of Silver Bush

1

PAT was feeling older than she would probably feel at fifty. Life had all at once grown bare and chilly. Hilary was going to Toronto to take the five-year course in architecture.

His mother had arranged it, he told Pat briefly. Since that bitter day, when Doreen Garrison had finally turned her back on her Jingle-baby Hilary had never spoken of his mother. Pat knew he never heard from her except for some brief note containing a check for his college expenses.

Pat was glad for Hilary's sake. He was on the way to realise all his dreams and ambitions. But on her own account she was very bleak. Nobody to prowl with . . . nobody to tell things to . . . it was always so easy to tell things to Hilary. Nobody to joke with.

"We've always laughed at the same things, Judy."

"Oh, oh, and that's why ye do be such good frinds, Patsy. It's the rale test. It's sorry I am mesilf that Jingle is going. A fine young gintleman he's got to be, that tall and straight standing. And ye tell me he's to be an arkytict. Oh, oh, I'm hoping he won't be like the one I heard of in ould Ireland. He did be buying the plan av a fine house from the Bad Man Below. And the price he had to be paying was his swateheart's soul. 'Twas a grand house I'm telling ye but there was few iver wanted to live in it."

"I don't think Hilary will spend souls buying plans from the devil," said Pat, with a forlorn smile. "He can design plenty himself. But, Judy, it seems to me I just can't bear it. Bets dead . . . Winnie gone . . . and now Hilary."

"It's mesilf that's noticed how things do be going in

threes like that, Patsy. It do be likely nothing but good'll happen to ye for a long time now."

"But life will be so . . . so empty, Judy."

"He'll be coming back some fine day."

Pat shook her head. Talk of Hilary's return was empty and meaningless. She knew he would never come back, unless for a vacation month or two. Their days of happy comradeship were over . . . their hours in Happiness . . . their rambles by field and shore. Childhood was gone. The "first fine rapture" of youth was gone.

"What's to become av McGinty? Oh, oh, there'll be one poor broken-hearted liddle dog."

"Hilary is giving McGinty to me. I know he *will* be broken-hearted. But if love can help him . . ."

Pat choked. She was seeing McGinty's eyes when the morrow brought no Hilary.

"Oh, oh, but I'm glad to hear that. I'm not liking a dogless house. Cats do be int'resting craturs, as Cuddles says, but there's *something* about a dog, now. Sure and there'll be some fun saving bones again."

Pat knew Hilary was waiting for her in Happiness. They had agreed to have their parting tryst there, before Hilary left to catch the night train. Slowly she went to keep it. The air was full of colour; there was just the faintest hint of frost in its sweet mildness; the evening sunshine was exceedingly mellow on grey old barns; as she went over Jordan she noticed the two dark, remote, pointed firs among the golden maples in the corner of the field. Hilary loved those firs. He said they were the twin spires of some mystic cathedral of sunset.

2

Hilary was waiting in Happiness, sitting on an old mossy stone by the spring that the years had never touched. Beside him sat a gay little dog with a hint of wistfulness behind his gaiety. McGinty felt something coming to him . . . something formless and chill. But as long as he was with his dear master what did it matter?

Hilary drew a quick breath: his eyes lit up slowly from within as was their way. She was coming to him over the field . . . a slip of a girl in a gold and orange sweater, the autumnal sunshine burnishing her dark-brown hair and glinting in her amber eyes; her face glowing with warm, ripe, *kissable* tints, her body like a young sapling never to be broken, however it might bend.

"Trusty, dusky, vivid, true,
With eyes of gold and bramble dew."

Why couldn't he have said that instead of Stevenson? It was truer of Pat than it could be of anybody else. Why couldn't he say to her all the burning and eloquent things he thought of in the night but could never utter the next day?

Pat sat down on the stone beside Hilary. They talked only a little and that in rather jerky sentences..

"I'll never come to Happiness again," said Pat.

"Why not? I'd like to think of you sitting here sometimes ... with McGinty."

"Poor little dorglums!" Pat absently caressed McGinty's willing head with one of her slender brown hands ... her *dear* hands, thought Hilary. "No, I couldn't bear to come here without you, Hilary. We've been here so often ... we've been chums for so many years."

"Can't we ... can't we ... some time ... be more than chums, Pat?" blurted Hilary desperately.

Pat instantly became just a little aloof, although her face had flushed to a sudden warm rose. Hilary was such a nice friend ... chum ... brother ... but never a lover. Pat was very positive on that point.

"We've always been wonderful friends, Hilary. Don't spoil it now. Why, we've been chums ever since that night you saved me from heaven knows what on the Line road. Ten years."

"They've been very good years." Hilary seemed to have taken his repulse more philosophically than she had feared. "What will the years to come be, I wonder?"

"They'll be marvellous years for you, Hilary. You'll succeed ... you'll reach the top. And then all your old friends here ... 'specially little old maid Pat of Silver Bush, will brag about having once known you."

"I *will* succeed." Hilary set his teeth together. "With your ... friendship ... I can do anything. I want to tell you ... if I can ... what your friendship and the life I've shared with you at Silver Bush have meant to me. It's kept me from growing up hateful and cynical. You've all been so sure that life is good that I've never been able to disbelieve it... never will be able to. You'll write me often, won't you, Pat? It will be... lonely... at first. I don't know a soul in Toronto."

"Of course I will. And don't forget, Hilary"... Pat laughed teasingly... "you're to build a house for me some day. I'll live in it when Sid gets married and turns me out of Silver Bush. And you'll come to see me in it... I'll be a nice old lady with silver hair... and I'll give you a cup of tea out of Grandmother Selby's pot... and we'll talk over our lives and... and... pretend it's all been a dream... and that we're just Pat and Jingle home once more."

"Wherever *you* are, Pat, will always be home to me."

There he went again. If it were not that they must presently say a long good-bye she would be angry with him. But she couldn't be angry to-night. He would soon forget this nonsense. Hundreds of beautiful clever girls in Toronto. But they would always be friends... the very best of friends... she couldn't imagine *not* being friends with Hilary.

They went back, following the curves of Jordan, talking of old days. It was lovely to remember things together. There were asters along their way. Hilary wanted to pick a rarely dark-blue cluster for her but she would not let him.

"No. Don't pick them because they would fade and that would be my last memory of them. Let's just leave them here and we can always remember them as we saw them together... beautiful and unfaded."

That was the real Pat touch. Hilary remembered that she had never really liked to pick flowers. He never forgot her, as she stood there gloating over them, herself, to him, as beautiful and mysterious as the autumn twilight. Dear... desirable!

The brook was prattling away and crooning to itself. Tall firs, that had been mere saplings when they first explored it, stretched their protecting arms over it: the mosses were green on its banks. In its ripple and murmur the voices of their childhood sounded... all the long-unheard notes were there, blended with the sweet sorrow inseparable from bygones. Hilary at twenty and Pat at eighteen felt themselves to be aged travellers wistfully recalling youth.

They paused on the stone bridge across Jordan. Pat held out her hands. She wanted to cry on his shoulder and knew she must not. If she did . . . he would take her in his arms. That would be nice . . . but . . .

She wanted to tell him that she loved him dearly. She did love him so much . . . better than Joe now . . . almost better than Sidney. She wanted to kiss him . . . but Hilary did not want friendly kisses. Yet they *couldn't* part like this.

"I'm not going to say good-bye half a dozen times before I'm really gone . . . like old Aunty Sarah Gordon," said Hilary, pretending to laugh. "Good-bye, Pat."

But he seemed to have forgotten to let go her hands. This simply couldn't be endured any longer.

"Good-bye, Jingle." The old name came impulsively to her lips. She pulled her hands away from his warm, pleasant grip and ran up the path against the moon.

Hilary stood and looked after her. McGinty huddled shivering against his leg. McGinty knew things were all wrong somehow.

Hilary was thinking of the house he would build for Pat. He could see it . . . he could almost see its lights gleaming through the dusk of some land "beyond the hills and far away." More beautiful than even Silver Bush. For a moment he almost hated Silver Bush. It was the only rival he feared. Then he set his teeth.

"I'll have you yet, Pat."

3

Pat stumbled up the path and across the field blindly and brought up against the garden gate. Then the denied tears came. She simply couldn't bear it. Everything gone! Who *could* bear it?

Rays of the rising moon touched the Hill of the Mist with delicate silver fingers. The night was a blue pearl seaward. The low continual thunder of the gulf tides in the harbour bar filled the air. The dreaming peace of the orchard seemed to beckon. The old barns, that must be alive with the ghosts of all the kittens that had frolicked in them, were huddled together companionably. Silver Bush was full of friendly lights. Pat brushed the tears from her eyes and looked at it.

It was such a loyal old house . . . always faithful to those who loved it. You felt it was your friend as soon as you stepped into it. It was full of dear yesterdays and beautiful

old years. It had been assimilating beauty and loveliness...
which is not quite the same thing...for generations. There
had been so many things in this house and it had not
forgotten one of them. Love and sorrow...tragedies...
comedies. Babies had been born...brides had dreamed...all
sorts of fashions had come and gone before the old mirrors.
Its very walls seemed to hold laughter.

The house remembered her whole life. *It* had always
been the same...*it* had never changed...not really. Only
little surface changes. How she loved it! She loved it in
morning rose and sunset amber, and best of all in the
darkness of night, when it loomed palely through the gloom
and was all her own. This beauty was hers...all hers. Life
could never be empty at Silver Bush. Somebody had pitied
her once..."so out of the world." Pat laughed. Out of the
world? Nay, she was *in* the world here...*her* world. "*I dwell
among my own people.*" Wise Shulamite!

A mysterious content flooded her. This was home.

About the Author

L. M. MONTGOMERY's fascinating accounts of the lives and romances of Anne, Emily, and other well-loved characters have achieved long-lasting popularity the world over. Born in 1874 in Prince Edward Island, Canada, Lucy Maud showed an early flair for storytelling. She soon began to have her writing published in papers and magazines, and when she died in Toronto in 1942 she had written more than twenty novels and a large number of short stories. Most of her books are set in Prince Edward Island, which she loved very much and wrote of most beautifully. *Anne of Green Gables*, her most popular work, has been translated into thirty-six languages, made into a film twice, and has had continuing success as a stage play. Lucy Maud Montgomery's early home in Cavendish, P.E.I., where she is buried, is a much visited historic site.

...ery,

Come to Prince Edward Island for fun and adventure!

Get ready for friendship and romance on magical Prince Edward Island! You'll meet Sara Stanley, the Story Girl, who knows "How Kissing Was Discovered" and the "Tale of the Family Ghost." There's lively Pat Gardiner of Silver Bush and her friend, the mysterious Judy Plum. Jane of Lanternhill dreams of being reunited with her family. And Valancy finds romance in her dreams of The Blue Castle. Join them for the fun!

☐ 21366-0 THE STORY GIRL $2.95

Watch for these other great books by L.M. Montgomery. Collect them all!

☐ 21367-9 THE GOLDEN ROAD $2.95
☐ 28046-5 MAGIC FOR MARIGOLD $2.95
☐ 28047-3 PAT OF SILVER BUSH $2.95
☐ 28048-1 MISTRESS PAT $2.95
☐ 28049-X JANE OF LANTERN HILL $2.95
☐ 28050-3 A TANGLED WEB $2.95
☐ 28051-1 THE BLUE CASTLE $2.95

Prices and availability subject to change without notice.

- -

Bantam Books, Dept. AG5, 414 East Golf Road, Des Plaines, IL 60016

Please send me the books I have checked above. I am enclosing $_____ (please add $2.00 to cover postage and handling). Send check or money order—no cash or C.O.D.s please.

Mr/Ms _____

Address _____

City/State _____ Zip _____

AG5—6/89

Please allow four to six weeks for delivery. This offer expires 12/89.